WESTERN

Rugged men looking for love...

His Unexpected Grandchild
Myra Johnson

His Neighbour's Secret
Lillian Warner

MILLS & BOON

DID YOU PURCHASE THIS BOOK WITHOUT A COVER?
If you did, you should be aware it is **stolen property** as it was reported
'unsold and destroyed' by a retailer.
Neither the author nor the publisher has received any payment
for this book.

HIS UNEXPECTED GRANDCHILD
© 2024 by Myra Johnson
Philippine Copyright 2024
Australian Copyright 2024
New Zealand Copyright 2024

First Published 2024
First Australian Paperback Edition 2024
ISBN 978 1 038 91753 9

HIS NEIGHBOURS SECRET
© 2024 by Lillian Garner
Philippine Copyright 2024
Australian Copyright 2024
New Zealand Copyright 2024

First Published 2024
First Australian Paperback Edition 2024
ISBN 978 1 038 91753 9

® and ™ (apart from those relating to FSC®) are trademarks of Harlequin Enterprises
(Australia) Pty Limited or its corporate affiliates. Trademarks indicated with ® are
registered in Australia, New Zealand and in other countries.
Contact admin_legal@Harlequin.ca for details.

Except for use in any review, the reproduction or utilisation of this work in whole or in
part in any form by any electronic, mechanical or other means, now known or hereafter
invented, including xerography, photocopying and recording, or in any information
storage or retrieval system, is forbidden without the permission of the publisher,
Harlequin Mills & Boon.

This book is sold subject to the condition that it shall not, by way of trade or otherwise,
be lent, resold, hired out or otherwise circulated without the prior consent of the publisher
in any form or binding or cover other than that in which it is published and without a
similar condition including this condition being imposed on the subsequent purchaser.

All rights reserved including the right of reproduction in whole or in part in any form.
This edition is published in arrangement with Harlequin Books S.A..

This is a work of fiction. Names, characters, places, and incidents are either the
product of the author's imagination or are used fictitiously, and any resemblance to
actual persons, living or dead, business establishments, events, or locales is entirely
coincidental.

MIX
Paper | Supporting
responsible forestry
FSC® C001695

Published by
Harlequin Mills & Boon
An imprint of Harlequin Enterprises (Australia) Pty Limited
(ABN 47 001 180 918), a subsidiary of HarperCollins
Publishers Australia Pty Limited
(ABN 36 009 913 517)
Level 19, 201 Elizabeth Street
SYDNEY NSW 2000 AUSTRALIA

Cover art used by arrangement with Harlequin Books S.A.. All rights reserved.

Printed and bound in Australia by McPherson's Printing Group

His Unexpected Grandchild

Myra Johnson

MILLS & BOON

Award-winning author **Myra Johnson** writes emotionally gripping stories about love, life and faith. She is a two-time finalist for the ACFW Carol Award and winner of the 2005 RWA Golden Heart® Award. Married since 1972, Myra and her husband have two married daughters and seven grandchildren. She and her husband reside in Texas, sharing their home with two pampered rescue dogs.

Mercy unto you, and peace, and love,
be multiplied.
—*Jude* 1:2

DEDICATION

For Jacob and Rylee,
I never thought I'd visit Montana except in
summertime, but I wouldn't have missed your
beautiful March wedding by a frozen lake for
anything. Happy first anniversary!

And with gratitude to my friends
from CenTex Christian Writers
for your brainstorming help during
the early stages of this novel. You're the best!

CHAPTER ONE

LANE BROMLEY DIDN'T like surprises. Just under two weeks ago, he'd gotten a big one, and his emotions had run the gamut: Elation. Disappointment. Resentment. Relief. Underlying them all, right down to the soles of his all-weather lace-up boots, was pure panic.

Parked outside the Frasier Veterinary Clinic on the outskirts of Missoula, Montana, he stared through the streaked windshield of his maroon 4x4 truck. He probably should have phoned first to make sure Julia Frasier, DVM, was on duty today. But then he might need to explain why he'd specifically asked for her, and since he hadn't had a pet since he was a kid... Well, that would get a little complicated.

A little? It didn't get much more complicated than having his estranged daughter show up out of the blue with a toddler in tow. Shannon was skinnier than when she'd been a lanky adolescent, and she was so depressed she could barely string three words together.

And the kid. Cute as he was, little Tate arrived looking like Shannon hadn't bathed him or put him in clean clothes for days. Beyond the dirty face, grime under his fingernails and a mild case of diaper rash, he seemed otherwise okay—and surprisingly good-natured despite it all.

I have a grandson!

Lane still hadn't gotten his head around the idea.

Just then, an SUV careened into the space beside his. The driver shoved open his door, smacking the passenger side of Lane's truck.

"Why, you—" Fuming, he got out and stormed around the tailgate to confront the offender. His mud-spattered seven-year-old truck had been through a lot worse, and showed it, but it was the principle of the thing.

"Can you help me? I've hit a dog." The man was red-faced and hyperventilating. He pressed a button on his key fob as he stumbled toward the SUV's liftgate. "I hope I got here in time."

Inside the cargo area lay a massive gray beast, blood seeping from multiple injuries. One hind leg looked mangled. The poor thing whimpered with every breath. At the sight of the suffering animal, Lane was having his own problems drawing oxygen.

He swallowed a couple of times. "I'll go find someone."

Inside, he went straight for the counter and addressed a young guy in green scrubs. "There's a badly injured dog out front. It's huge. You'll need a gurney or something."

The kid—his name badge read Dylan—looked up with a start and then raced down a hallway. Seconds later, he reappeared lugging an orange contraption with carry handles and safety straps. Two more techs followed him.

Lane held the door, pointed toward the SUV and watched from a safe distance while the techs did a quick evaluation before maneuvering the whimpering dog onto the stretcher.

Once they'd taken the animal inside, the driver turned to Lane. "The dog will be okay now, right? Because I can't wait around. I'm already late for an important job interview."

Not my problem, he wanted to say. "I'm sure they'll do what they can. But shouldn't you—"

Before he could finish, the man dived behind the steering wheel and slammed his door. Lane had barely enough presence of mind to memorize the guy's license plate as he sped away. Grumbling, he leaned inside his truck to dig out a pen and scrap of paper from the console.

As he jotted down the plate number, Dylan returned. "Sir, we need to get some information about your dog."

"It's not my dog. And the guy who brought it took off."

The tech's brows quirked. "She's his dog?"

"No, he said he hit it with his car. I have no idea whose dog it is." Lane could barely keep his frustration in check. The morning wasn't going anything like he'd planned. "Look, I just need to speak with Dr. Frasier. Dr. *Julia* Frasier," he emphasized after glancing at the three names stenciled in black and gold on the front door.

"She's taking the dog straight into surgery, so it could be a while. In the meantime, maybe you could tell us what you do know so we can try to locate the dog's owner."

Dragging a hand across his stubbly beard, Lane sighed. "Sure. Whatever."

Good thing his neighbor across the valley had been available to come over and keep an eye on Tate. The Vernons, living off-grid in the Montana mountains even longer than Lane, had raised four kids of their own, so he'd left the tot in good hands.

He hadn't intended to be gone this long, though. On his way into the clinic, he texted to make sure Lila Vernon could stay a little longer. Her thumbs-up reply and quick message to say they were doing fine relieved his mind somewhat.

That still left the problem of why he'd come looking for Julia Frasier. Before he spoke with her, he'd better have a clearer head than he did at the moment.

Behind the counter, Dylan starting typing at his computer terminal. "Your name, sir?"

"Bromley. Lane Bromley." He spelled it out.

"And the man who brought the dog—do you know his name?"

"Never saw him before, and we weren't exactly exchanging pleasantries."

The desk phone buzzed. Dylan picked it up and listened a moment. "Thanks, Amy." He hung up and typed something else into the computer. "The dog isn't microchipped, and she wasn't wearing a collar or tags. Too bad the driver didn't stick around long enough to at least tell us where the accident happened."

"I got his plates." Lane slid the scrap of paper

toward the tech. "But I need that back. He did a number on my truck door."

Dylan copied the information and then returned the paper. "Help yourself to coffee while you wait."

Lane stuffed the scrap into his pocket—like he'd ever really follow through. The hassle wouldn't be worth it. He considered returning to meet Julia Frasier at a better time, but his mountain cabin outside Elk Valley was over an hour's drive northwest from Missoula. For now, at least, the winding roads to his place were clear, but who knew what tomorrow or the next day would bring? This was late August in Montana, when weather at higher elevations could change in the blink of an eye.

Ignoring the curious stares of a couple of clients waiting with their pets, he ambled over to the beverage machine. While a single-serving pod of dark roast brewed, he perused the wall decor. Something about heartworm prevention, another poster touting the value of regular checkups...

Then he came to a portrait of the Frasier family—an older couple, maybe late sixties, and an attractive fortysomething woman, all smiles and wearing white lab coats with stethoscopes looped around their necks.

He leaned in for a closer look at the younger Dr. Frasier. With her heart-shaped face and dark brown hair, there was a definite resemblance to Tate. Looked like he'd found the other half of his grandson's family.

Now the real question was, how would Julia Frasier react to learning her son was a father?

"THAT WAS A close one, Amy." Julia stuffed her surgical gown into the hamper. "She's going to be in a lot of pain when she wakes up, and I don't want that leg getting infected. Keep a close eye on her."

"I will, Dr. J."

The complicated surgery would have been even more touch-and-go without Julia's most qualified tech to assist. The dog should recover, but she'd likely end up with a limp. There'd be some disgruntled patients out front, though, since their appointments had been delayed because of the emergency. Hopefully, Julia's dad had been able to cover for her...for the time being, anyway.

Always in the back of her mind was her parents' impending retirement. They were both in their early seventies now, and over the past few months, Julia had noticed her father's gradually worsening hand tremors. He'd attempted to hide them from both Julia and her mother, but Julia had grown concerned enough that she'd begun monitoring her father's appointment schedule and tactfully stepping in for the more delicate procedures.

Julia's mother, staff veterinarian as well as office manager for over thirty years, had already cut back her hours. On top of her routine appointments, Julia had taken over most of the management responsibilities as well, and the strain was wearing. She desperately needed to hire a new office manager and bring one or two new vets on board—and soon, before she completely burned out. The plan had always been for her son, Steven, to join the practice once he completed veterinary school. But those dreams had died with him.

The phone intercom buzzed. Amy answered, and after listening a few seconds, she glanced back at Julia. "Dylan says that man is still out front waiting to speak to you."

She forced her mind to the present. "And he has no connection with our patient?"

Amy shrugged. "That's what he claims."

"Guess I'd better find out what he wants." Frowning, Julia donned a lab coat over her blue scrubs and adjusted her ponytail.

Slipping up beside Dylan at the front desk, she glanced around. A well-built man in a plaid shirt and jeans stood staring out the front window. The gray in his short, messy hair and scruffy beard gave him a rugged look.

To Dylan, she whispered, "Does our visitor have a name?"

"Lane Bromley."

Didn't ring a bell. She raised her voice. "Excuse me... Mr. Bromley?"

He turned with a start. "Dr. Julia Frasier?"

"Yes. What is it you needed to see me about?"

As he started for the counter, one of the other techs came out to call for the next patient. Julia smiled and nodded as the elderly Mrs. Gardner got up with her feisty black-and-tan min pin. Dad would have his hands full with that little guy, but at least he only needed a routine exam and annual shots.

Mrs. Gardner jerked her head toward Julia's visitor and whispered, "Watch out for him. He's a strange one."

The man's scowl suggested he'd overheard.

He directed his attention to Julia. "We should talk in private."

Frowning, she showed him to her office, where his masculine presence dominated the room.

"I can only spare a moment, Mr. Bromley," she said from behind her desk. "I'm already behind with my patients."

"After what I have to say, you may want to reschedule those appointments."

Her brows shot up. "I'm not sure I care for the tone of this conversation. Maybe you should just come out with it."

"You should sit down."

More than a little unnerved, she could only hope he wasn't about to slap the office with a veterinary malpractice suit. Had her father's tremors caused a problem when she hadn't been on hand to intervene? If only she or Mom could convince Dad to get a checkup.

She lowered herself into her chair, fingers tightening around the armrests. "All right, I'm sitting."

He sat across from her and suddenly didn't look so imposing. Rather, he looked…scared. "Sorry, this isn't easy." He hesitated, his gaze drifting to something behind her on the filing credenza. "Is that your son?"

She didn't have to turn around to know he was looking at one of her last photos of Steven. Her heart squeezed. "Yes," she murmured, lips tight. "He... He passed away two years ago."

"I know."

Her chin shot up. "Who exactly are you, and how do you know my son?"

"I never met your son. I wish I had. Maybe then..." His Adam's apple worked. He looked away.

The suggestion that Bromley's business here had something to do with Steven unsettled her even more. "Would you please get to the point?"

He pulled a cell phone from his shirt pocket. After tapping some icons and scrolling a few times, he slid the phone across the desk. "It's about him."

Her roiling stomach warned her not to touch his phone, much less look at whatever he wanted to show her. Hands still locked on the armrests, she shifted her glance to the phone screen.

Her breath hitched. *Steven?*

She glared at her visitor. "Where did you get a baby picture of my son?"

"That little boy isn't your son. I only snapped this three days ago."

"Then who—" One hand flew to her mouth, as if she could stifle the realization. This couldn't be Steven's child. He would never have kept anything like this from her. They'd always talked about everything. *Everything...*

Really, Julia?

True, they hadn't communicated as often after Steven started college. During his last few months, she'd sensed him holding back about something and had assumed he'd taken the hint that the topic of his rekindled faith in God was off-limits with her.

But a baby? Never in a million years.

Clamping down on a pang of guilt, she swiveled in her chair and gathered the photo of grown-up Steven to her chest. "You'd better start at the beginning."

Bromley gave a weak laugh. "This is almost as new to me as it is to you. I only found out about Tate—that's his name—less than two weeks ago."

Sinking deeper into his chair, he rested his hands on his thighs and looked toward the window. In a quiet voice, he told her how his daughter, Shannon, whom he hadn't seen and had rarely heard from since she left for college five years ago, had shown up unannounced with her nineteen-month-old son. All he could get out of her was that she couldn't cope anymore, that she only wanted to curl up and die—but she couldn't let herself until she knew Tate would be taken care of.

"After she came home," he went on, "I didn't dare leave her alone for a minute for fear she'd harm herself. A friend helped me get her admitted to a mental health facility."

"I'm so sorry." Julia felt for the man, but she had other issues. "You still haven't explained how you determined Tate is…is Steven's."

"I found a marriage certificate among Shannon's things." He produced the document, spread it open in front of her, and indicated the couple's printed names and the signatures beneath them: Shannon Elise Bromley. Steven Edward Halsey.

Julia's heart spasmed. It was unquestionably her son's unique scrawl. "Halsey was my ex-husband's last name," she murmured. Then she read the wedding date. "They were married almost *three years ago*?"

He cast her a thoughtful stare. "You really didn't know."

She briskly shook her head while a thousand different explanations paraded through her mind. Not a single one of them jibed with the person she'd thought her son to be. "Go on," she said stiffly.

"Obviously, I wanted to know who he was and why he'd deserted his wife and child. So I did some digging and learned he'd been a student at Washington State, and that he'd been killed in a motorcycle accident. His obituary made no mention of Shannon, so I assumed it was because his family hadn't approved of their marriage. But seeing your face just now, I realize..." His expression softened. "Doing the math, I figure your son died a few months before Tate was born."

Again, she couldn't speak.

"I get that this is a huge shock for you," the man said. "I know it was for me."

"My son had a wife. A baby!" A sob stole its way into her throat. "Why didn't he tell me?"

"I can't answer that. I still have a lot of questions myself." Bromley fished something else from his pocket. "I did find this among Shannon's things." He extended his closed fist and dropped a ring in the center of her desk.

She immediately recognized the exquisite

antique—the scrolled rose-gold band, the emerald-cut amethyst bearing an intaglio rose of Sharon, a tiny diamond marking its center. Heaving a shaky sigh, she picked up the ring.

"It was passed down from my great-grandmother. When Steven was home on a school break a year or so before he died, he asked to see it. I didn't know he'd kept it."

"I thought it must be an heirloom. I'm guessing it was meant to be Shannon's engagement or wedding ring, but I don't think she'd been wearing it, so if you want it back…"

Pressing the ring to her heart, she pictured her son, how preoccupied he'd seemed in the last year of his life. When he'd stopped coming home as often, she'd wondered if he'd met someone. In fact, she'd cautioned him about not allowing anything to interfere with his studies.

Was that why he'd kept his marriage a secret?

Hurt and bewildered, she placed the ring on Bromley's side of the desk. "Your daughter is my son's widow and the mother of my grandchild. The ring belongs to her."

"That's kind of you. I'll keep it safe until she's better." Pocketing the ring, he stood and roughly cleared his throat. "I know this has taken you by surprise, but after you've had time to process it all, I hope we can come to an understanding about Tate's immediate future."

Her eyes snapped open. "*Understanding?* You show up out of the blue and drop this bombshell on me, and I'm supposed to somehow *process* it so *we* can make decisions about a grandson I never even knew existed?"

"Sorry, guess that sounded a little too…expedient." Releasing a groan, he raked his fingers through his hair. "I wasn't sure how this meeting would go, and I'm still figuring out how to deal with everything."

Julia paused for a bolstering breath. "You're right. We do need to consider the practicalities. But first, I want to meet my grandson and my—" she choked down the lump in her throat "—my son's widow."

He nodded. "They aren't letting Shannon have visitors yet, but you can come out to my place to meet Tate. Under the circumstances, I'm trying to keep things as stable for him as I can."

"Of course." She mentally reviewed her schedule—not that she wouldn't turn the world upside down for this chance. "I could come tomorrow. When would be a good time?"

"Whatever works for you." He retrieved his

phone. "Give me your number and I'll text you directions."

Anticipation building, Julia provided her personal cell phone number. "Is there anything Tate needs? Clothes, toys, other supplies?"

"Shannon didn't bring much, so I've been working through a list. My next priority is a crib and bedding, which I'm planning to pick up while I'm in town today."

"I've kept Steven's crib in storage all these years, hoping someday…" She pressed her trembling lips together.

The man offered an understanding smile. "That would really help, if you're sure you're okay with it."

"Certainly. We can—"

A knock interrupted them, and Amy peeked in. "Excuse me, Dr. J, but…um…your father may need assistance with a patient."

Working closely with Julia's dad, the tech had actually been the first to notice his tremors. Ever since, she'd been helping Julia keep an eye on him.

"I'll be right there." When the door closed again, she turned to Mr. Bromley. "I need to get back to work. We can talk more tomorrow, though. And I'll bring the crib."

"That'd be great, Dr. Frasier. Thanks."

"All things considered, I think we can dispense with formalities. You can call me Julia."

"Julia." He dipped his chin. "In that case, I'm Lane."

"Tomorrow, then… Lane. I'll text when I'm on my way."

Showing him out through the reception area, she fought to corral her scattered emotions. Since long before Steven's death, professional detachment had become her shield. After what she'd just learned about her son on top of everything else weighing her down, she needed that self-control now more than ever.

But once 6:00 p.m. rolled around and she left the clinic behind, she intended to pull out her favorite photos of Steven and indulge in a good, long, purging cry.

SUMMER DAYS IN Montana were long, but once the sun slid behind the mountains, darkness descended quickly. It was after eight thirty by the time Lane finished his errands in town and made it home, so he'd needed his headlights to see the winding gravel road—more to make sure he didn't hit an elk or bear than to show the way. After twenty-plus years living off-grid and turning this remote patch of land into something he could call home, he knew the road's every twist and turn.

He left the engine running while he got out to swing open the wide tubular ranch gate, then closed it again after he'd driven through. Easing past Lila's Jeep, he parked in the carport beneath the cabin. After a quick detour to the barn and chicken house to tend his livestock, he trudged up rough-hewn log steps to the deck and let himself in the front door.

Beneath the yellow-white glow of a reading lamp, Lila looked up from the book in her lap. "You told her?"

"I did." His neighbor knew why he'd made the trip into Missoula. "She's coming out tomorrow to meet him. And bringing a crib— her late son's."

"Oh, that's sweet...and sad." She closed her book and stood. "You must be hungry. I've got some ham-and-bean soup on the stove."

He followed her to the kitchen but wasn't sure he could scrape up an appetite. "Is the baby asleep?"

"Mmm-hmm. That little guy's good as gold. Such a little trouper." She paused to face him, her silver-streaked auburn braid falling across one shoulder. "You've got to make a plan, though, Lane. You know I'll come over to help whenever I can, but with winter right around the corner, we're busier than ever these days."

"I know, I know." Living off the grid meant taking advantage of every warm day to prepare and stock up for next winter. Bleary-eyed, he made his way to the table. Shortly, a steaming bowl of soup appeared in front of him. "Thanks, Lila. You're a good friend. You and Dan both."

"Hah. Ever since we sold you this property, we've been just about your *only* friends. And that's not good, either. You've spent too many years alone in these mountains, Lane. You know good and well it's why Shannon left home in the first place."

He was too tired to argue. Besides, she was right. "It's getting late. You should head home. And watch out for bears."

She harrumphed. "Bears around these parts know better than to mess with me." Shoving her arms into a nubby cardigan, she backed toward the door. "Holler if you need anything. And you might try praying, too."

Pray? Like that would ever happen. "Good night, Lila, and thanks again."

"The train's comin' into the station, so open wide!" Lane made a train-whistle sound as he aimed the spoonful of oatmeal at Tate's mouth.

Balanced on Lane's knee, the little boy spread his lips just enough while eyeing his grandpa as if he'd come from another planet.

He sighed and spooned up another bite. "Sorry, kiddo, my toddler-feeding skills are pretty rusty."

"Mama?" Tate pointed toward the back door.

"Mama's not better yet. I promise we'll visit her as soon as the doctor says it's okay. Now eat your breakfast so you can grow up big and strong."

Across the table, Lane's cell phone chimed. His cabin was barely within range of the nearest cell tower, but with a signal booster, texts usually went through. He handed Tate the spoon. "Here, you try while I see what that's about."

It was a message from Julia Frasier. Just leaving storage unit with crib. Didn't realize you lived so far into the mountains. Should I bring bear spray? Emergency rations? Personal locator beacon?

So the veterinarian had a sense of humor. With Tate dribbling more oatmeal onto Lane's jeans than he managed to swallow, he texted back: Ha. Ha. Gate will be open. Drive on through to the cabin. See you in about an hour, give or take.

More like an hour and a half, considering Julia didn't know the mountain roads like Lane did. He should probably meet her where the Vernons' drive branched off in case she got confused.

Once he got both himself and his grandson cleaned up, he decided he ought to straighten up a bit. While Tate sat on the floor stacking handmade wooden blocks—the same ones Lane had shaped and sanded more than two decades ago for Shannon's enjoyment—he whisked a feather duster over every flat surface, straightened the stack of books by his easy chair, tidied the kitchen and put out clean hand towels in the downstairs bathroom.

Next, he needed to run down and open the gate. With Tate bundled into a lightweight hoodie and pint-size lace-up hiking boots, they began the slow trek down the driveway. Lane was just unlatching the gate when he glimpsed a lime-green Toyota 4Runner rounding the bend. Anyone could see that thing coming a mile away. Recognizing Julia Frasier behind the wheel, he waved and motioned her through.

A short way past him, she pulled to the side and cut the engine. Gaze fixed on Tate, she slowly stepped from the vehicle. She looked much different today in a long-sleeved crimson top and skinny jeans. Her dark brown hair was tucked behind one ear and grazed her shoulders. The overall effect was softer, somehow. More approachable. More real.

"Hi, little guy." Her voice was high-pitched and shaky. "I'm your... I'm..." Taking quick breaths, she seemed unable to finish the statement.

Lane scooped Tate into his arms. "Maybe we should go on to the house."

She nodded, then got back into her vehicle and followed him as he marched ahead. He stood at the base of the steps and pretended not to notice while she sat in the car for a moment to blow her nose.

"Down," Tate insisted, leaning over so far that Lane was afraid he'd fall on his head.

"Easy there." He righted him and gently set him on the ground as Julia emerged from her car.

Kneeling with one hand beckoning Tate, she could no longer hide the tears she obviously hadn't wanted Lane to see.

After a glance up at him, the toddler slowly went to her. He pressed her cheeks between his hands. "No cwy. It be otay."

Now the floodgates opened for real, and Lane's heart twisted to witness Julia's raw emotion as she enfolded their grandson in her arms.

How quickly this little boy must have had to grow up over the past few months if he'd already learned how to comfort a woman in tears.

Shannon, how could you do this to your own son?

CHAPTER TWO

"Go Mama now?" Tate pointed past Julia's shoulder toward her SUV.

Confused, she looked up at Lane, who quietly shook his head. Stroking the little boy's cheek, she said, "No, honey, I'm sorry."

Tate stamped his foot. "Go Mama now!"

"Tate, that's enough." Lane swooped up the little boy and tucked him against his hip. "Let's go inside."

Pulling herself together, Julia followed them upstairs to the deck and entered a rustic but well-appointed living room—paneled walls, wood floors, a woven earth-tone area rug, plush leather sofa and chairs. Across the room, another flight of split-log stairs rose to the second story, probably to the bedrooms. Dying embers glowed behind the glass door of a wood-burning stove, a reminder of how much chillier it could get up here in the mountains, even in

August. Thankfully, the stove had been baby-proofed with a makeshift barrier.

Tate refused to be held a moment longer. "Go Mama!"

Lane had barely set him down when the quick little guy darted past Julia toward the front door.

Picturing him tumbling down the outer stairs, she spun around. "Tate, no!" As he tried to work the door latch, she captured his pudgy fingers. "No, honey, you can't go out there."

Lane caught up and threw a bolt on the upper part of the door. "He won't be able to get it open now."

Fighting to slow her breathing, she stood shakily and swiped at another escaping tear. Her thoughts seesawed between past and present. One moment, she saw this adorable little boy she'd only just met, and the next, her mind was racing back through time to when she'd realized what a mistake she and her then-husband had made letting their ground-level apartment go and moving with fourteen-month-old Steven into a two-story town house.

She felt a tug on her jeans. "It otay now," the boy murmured. "It be otay."

This wasn't right. One hand on her stomach, she cast Lane a troubled frown.

"I know," he murmured. "He kept comforting Shannon like that. She couldn't seem to stop crying."

"It's good you got her into treatment. But what about Tate? Has he seen a doctor yet?"

"It's one more thing on my long and growing to-do list." Grimacing, he sank onto the ottoman in front of an easy chair. "I am so far out of my depth here."

"Clearly." Spying a plush toy on the sofa, Julia used it to distract Tate. "What are you thinking, trying to take care of a toddler up here in the middle of nowhere? This place doesn't even register on my GPS."

"Which is why I gave you explicit directions." Lane glared. "And what gives you the right to start passing judgment on a situation you only walked into five minutes ago?"

"How quickly we forget." It took all her self-control to keep from raising her voice above a whisper-shout. "You *pulled* me into this so-called *situation* when you came to my clinic yesterday. And anyway, when it comes to my grandson, I have as much right as anyone to pass judgment."

"Our."

"What?"

"Tate is *our* grandson."

Momentarily taken aback, she sucked in a breath. "Fine. *Our* grandson needs to be somewhere a lot safer than a remote mountaintop." Chewing her lip, she pondered the options. Now that her mother was semiretired and more available to help, surely Julia could do this. "I think you should let me take him."

"What? No way!" He pushed to his feet, seized her by the elbow and dragged her past the stairs and into the kitchen. "Shannon is Tate's mother and my daughter, so I'll be the one making decisions about his care."

"But didn't you come looking for me so *we* could—I think your exact words were—*come to an understanding* about our grandson's future?"

"Which does *not* mean letting you rip him out of my arms to go live in the wild and dangerous big city." He emphasized the last part of his statement by clawing the air like an angry bear.

She huffed and crossed her arms. "What do you have against the city, anyway, Mr. Mountain Man?"

The wounded look that came into his eyes drove home how very little she knew about Lane Bromley. It also made her wish she could snatch back the last few minutes of this increasingly heated exchange and start over. They were both too emotionally wrecked for anything resembling a rational discussion.

Taking a beat to reassess, she glanced around the kitchen. She was almost surprised to find he had all the modern conveniences—gas range, French-door refrigerator, microwave. Granite countertops, ceramic tile floor, a brass chandelier resembling elk antlers that looked like a smaller version of the one she'd noticed in the living room. For a mountain man, he appeared to live pretty well.

Even so, he was miles from what she considered civilization. Miles from medical help should Tate become ill or fall down the stairs or burn himself on the stove...

Spying a coffeemaker with an almost-full carafe sitting on the warmer, she tipped her head. "Is that fresh?"

Lane blinked as if mentally returning from another time and place. "As of an hour ago."

"May I?"

He gestured toward a cupboard. "Clean mugs are in there. If you want cream, be warned. It's fresh from the source."

So he had a milk cow. Figured. However, she

preferred her dairy products pasteurized. "Black is fine." An almost empty mug embossed with a bison head sat next to the coffeemaker. "This must be yours. Want a refill?"

He glanced toward where they'd left Tate playing in the living room before turning back with a sigh. "Sure. Thanks."

At least they'd returned to polite civility instead of attacking each other. Perhaps now they could make real progress.

After setting his mug on an oblong wood-grain table, she pulled out a padded chair at the opposite end. The set looked custom-made. Waiting for Lane to join her, she took a careful sip and let the coffee's calming warmth seep into her chest.

"This is good," she said. "Dark and full-flavored, the way I like it."

Retrieving his mug, he shifted a chair sideways and sat so he could keep an eye on Tate. His tender devotion to his grandson touched her, but his obstinacy ignited a bonfire of buried resentment. Just like Julia's ex, Lane Bromley needed to face reality and do the right thing for his family.

"Look, I get it. I can't take care of Tate like I should without help. But for reasons I won't get into, I don't care much for the trappings of city life."

His eyes darkened in that haunted expression again. Something traumatic must have triggered his flight to this mountain refuge. Perhaps it had to do with Shannon's conspicuously absent mother? Probably not a good time to bring it up, though.

Instead, she said softly, "I think we both want what's best for Tate. For starters, he should be seen by a pediatrician. Would you trust me to get some recommendations?"

He stared into his coffee mug for so long that she wasn't sure he'd registered the question.

Before she could prompt him to answer her, Tate toddled into the kitchen and raised his arms to Lane.

"Ho' me."

Wordlessly, the man set aside his mug and drew the little boy onto his lap. Julia suppressed a stab of envy—not that she had any right. Tate had spent the last several days getting comfortable with his grandfather. Still, she ached to hold her grandson again.

With Tate nestled under his whiskery chin, Lane glanced toward her and drew a long, slow breath. "Okay, yes, whatever you can find out."

Julia swallowed her emotions along with a quick sip of coffee. "I'll make some calls as soon as I get back to town."

"But Tate stays with me," Lane added with a pointed look. "That's nonnegotiable."

And just when she'd thought they were making headway. *One battle at a time*, she told herself. Eventually, though, she intended to make the obstinate man see things her way.

Did she really believe he hadn't noticed the smug twist of her lips? If the woman thought she could change his mind about keeping Tate, she had another think coming. "You said you brought the crib. Maybe we should get it set up."

Her smugness morphed into barely disguised annoyance. She rose stiffly. "I'll keep an eye on Tate while you bring it in."

"It's close to his mealtime, if you want to feed him. He has a thing for tortillas and hummus with turkey slices. It's all in the fridge. There's apple juice, too."

"Good, I was hoping you knew better than to give him raw cow's milk."

"I'm not totally incompetent." Casting her a withering look, Lane set Tate in the chair he'd just vacated and scooted him up to the table. "Gramps'll be right back, okay? Sit here while this nice lady fixes you some lunch."

"The nice lady has a name, *Gramps*," Julia said with fake levity. "Tate, can you say Grammy?"

"Gammy, Gampy." The little boy pointed to each of them in turn. Then he tapped his own chest. "I Tate."

The kid was a prodigy. Lane couldn't help but grin.

On his way through the living room, his smile faded as he glimpsed a photo collage of Shannon through her childhood years. How had his little girl grown up so fast…and drifted so far away?

Shannon had been around Tate's age when he'd brought her to the mountain to start anew after her mom had been snatched from their lives.

Tessa had been a part-time paralegal at a small downtown law firm where Lane had been an associate. One night, she'd returned to the office after hours to grab a file he'd forgotten. Worried when she'd taken longer than expected, he'd asked a neighbor to watch Shannon while he went looking for her. He'd found the office door ajar and his wife bleeding from a gunshot wound to the chest. By the time an ambulance arrived and rushed her to the hospital, she'd lost too much blood. She died two hours later on the operating table. The police surmised she'd come upon a burglar looking for drug money, but an arrest was never made. For months after, Lane had ping-ponged between helpless rage and unrelenting guilt.

And Julia wondered why he despised the city.

Shaking his head to clear away the memories, he marched out to Julia's SUV. It took three trips to haul in all the crib parts. If any nuts or bolts were missing, he could probably find substitutes in his well-stocked workshop. He'd expanded it over time, right along with his carpentry and mechanical skills—absolute necessities for living off-grid. He also made a modest income from the handcrafted wood furniture he'd developed a knack for creating. He could never thank Dan and Lila Vernon enough for taking him under their wing all those years ago—not to mention how they'd helped him get his bearings as a single father.

After piling crib parts inside the door, he went looking for Julia and Tate. They sat kitty-corner from each other at the kitchen table, and it looked like Julia was wearing most of Tate's lunch.

Using a wet dishcloth to wipe hummus out of her eye, she scowled at Lane. "You could have warned me."

"Why?" He suppressed a snicker. "Seeing you like this is way more fun."

Tate's gleeful cackle wasn't so polite. "Gammy messy!"

"She certainly is, and so are you, little guy." Lane hefted him out of the chair and held him at arm's length. "I'll take him upstairs to clean up. You can use the downstairs bathroom."

After scraping lunch remains off his grandson and dressing him in a fresh pair of dungarees, he figured Julia might appreciate a change of clothes as well. He selected a maroon sweatshirt from his closet, carried it and Tate downstairs, and tapped on the bathroom door. "I'm hanging a clean shirt on the doorknob for you. We'll be in the living room figuring out the crib."

A few minutes later, she appeared wearing the sweatshirt over jeans that showed a few damp areas from spot cleaning. She extended her arms, and the sleeves of his shirt drooped past her fingertips. "It's a little big, but thank you."

Standing there wearing his shirt, her face

washed clean of makeup and her hair swooped into a messy topknot, she looked ten years younger and not nearly so antagonistic. A knot formed in his belly. It wasn't exactly unpleasant, but it was definitely disconcerting.

He cleared his throat and forced his attention back to the crib. "Did you bring directions for this thing?"

She crossed to the chair where she'd set down her purse and returned with a yellowed sheet of paper. "Here you go."

He gave a low whistle. "I'm impressed you still had it after all these years."

"I never throw away anything important. I'm extremely organized."

He might use a slightly different term for that level of efficiency, but he'd keep it to himself. "If I'd had more time, I could have built a bed for Tate."

She stroked the curved back of a wooden rocking chair. "You made this, didn't you? And the table and chairs in the kitchen."

"I did." Woodworking had given him a renewed sense of purpose, something immediate and tangible he could do to ward off the guilt and grief.

Arching a brow, she nodded. "And now I'm duly impressed."

"Aren't we just the mutual admiration society?" He sank back on his boot heels. "So. Are you planning to stand there and supervise, or are you willing to pitch in and help me put this crib together?"

JULIA WASN'T SURE whether he'd meant his remark in jest or as a not-so-subtle criticism. Frowning, she folded her arms. "You should figure out where you're going to put the crib before you get much further."

"Good point. I'm such a sound sleeper that I don't think I'd hear him in Shannon's old room. There's plenty of space in my room, though."

"Where has he been sleeping?"

"In bed with me." Lane snorted. "Which hasn't exactly been conducive to a good night's rest."

Remembering how squirmy Steven was when he used to crawl in bed with her, Julia gave a snicker. "Then let's move it before it gets any more unwieldy. And you should invest in a good baby monitor, too."

"I picked one up while I was in town yesterday."

While Julia kept Tate occupied stacking

wooden blocks, Lane hauled everything up-stairs. Joining him, she found his bedroom to be airy and spacious with a beamed wood ceiling and an expansive view of the forested valley behind the cabin. In truth, *nothing* about this place—other than the rustic-chic decor and the fact that the house was actually made of logs—fit her definition of *cabin*.

With a little help from Julia to hold the various sections in place, Lane soon had the crib assembled. He moved it near a window and, on Julia's advice, shortened the venetian blind cord so Tate couldn't reach it. She'd resigned herself to leaving the little guy with Lane for now, but once she had a better handle on her work and personal life, she'd pressure him into letting her take over their grandson's care.

A peek out the window told her the afternoon was wearing on. And were those snow flurries in the air? "Looks like the weather's changing. I should leave soon."

Together, they stretched a crib pad and fitted sheet over the mattress. In the meantime, Tate had filled his diaper, so she helped Lane change him. Oh, the memories!

Once they'd finished, she decided to get on the road. Downstairs, Lane handed her a canvas shopping bag for the top she'd tried to rinse out in the bathroom sink. "Thanks for bringing the crib. I'm sure Tate and I will both sleep a lot better tonight."

"I didn't save too many of Steven's baby things, but if I come across anything else useful, Tate's welcome to use it." She slid her arm through her purse strap. She hadn't thought to bring a jacket, but Lane's thick sweatshirt should keep her warm until she got home. "I have to be in the clinic all day tomorrow and until noon on Saturday, but if you get desperate for help—"

He scoffed. "Too late for that."

"Just saying." She knelt and held out her arms to Tate. "Got a goodbye hug for Grammy?"

He poked out his lower lip. "Go bye-bye?"

"Yes, but I'll see you again soon." And for keeps, if she had anything to say about it—at least until Shannon recovered. "You take care of Gramps till then. Promise?"

Giving a firm nod, he stepped into her embrace. It was all she could do to tamp down another spate of tears as she gave him a kiss on the cheek. She stood brusquely while she retained any measure of control.

Lane hefted Tate and pulled open the front

door. "Uh–oh. I don't suppose you've switched to snow tires yet?"

Her stomach sank. "It's only August. I hadn't expected to need them already."

"Well, you may be staying the night. It's coming down pretty hard."

She pushed past him to see for herself. He was right. The scattered flurries she'd glimpsed from the upstairs window had thickened into a swirling white curtain. She could barely make out the shape of her vehicle, much less Lane's gate or the road beyond. But this was Montana. Why should she be surprised by a freak August snowstorm?

While her brain raced with all the reasons she absolutely could not get stranded up here, her phone chime signaled an incoming text. Backing away from the door, she fished her phone from her purse.

The message was from Amy: Our hit-and-run patient is running a fever. Leg looks infected. May need more surgery. When will you be back?

One hand to her forehead, she paced to the window. Maybe it wasn't snowing *that* heavily…

"Bad news?" Lane asked.

If anything, the snow was coming down even harder. Julia forced down a swallow. "The dog you brought in yesterday. She's taken a turn for the worse."

"It wasn't me who brought her in, remember?"

"Whatever." She wasn't going to let the poor girl lose a leg if there was any way to save it. "I really have to get out of here."

He set Tate down and heaved an apologetic shrug. "Unless you want to risk sliding off the side of the mountain, I'm afraid you're stuck here."

A long, frustrated groan rumbled in her throat. Each of her patients earned a special place in her heart, but for some reason, it was even more true with this one. It couldn't be because the huge gray dog happened to arrive the same morning Julia learned she was a grandmother.

Her mother's surgical skills weren't as sharp as they used to be, but the thought of her father stepping in if the dog did require another operation... She couldn't take the chance. Maybe she could talk Amy through the procedure, or else have her transport the dog to the veterinary emergency center.

Lane gently took her arm. "You look like you need to sit down."

What she needed was to find a way down this mountain, but apparently, that wasn't happening.

As she sank onto the nearest chair, Tate toddled over and patted her knee. "Gammy sad?"

His tender concern squeezed her heart. "Grammy's worried about a sick doggy."

At the word *doggy*, Tate's eyes lit up. "Gammy have doggies?"

"Yes, I have two little doggies who live with me. Their names are Daisy and Dash." She pulled Tate onto her lap, his sudden interest in dogs a welcome, if temporary, distraction. "Grammy is a doggy doctor. Do you know what a doctor is?"

He gave a firm nod. "Make Mama all better. Go see Mama now?"

Well, she'd opened up that can of worms. She looked to Lane for help.

He knelt next to the little boy and tugged on his shirttail. "Hey, Tater Tot, looks like Grammy's staying for supper. You can help me figure out what to fix, okay?"

While Lane took Tate to the kitchen, Julia considered how to reply to Amy. She hadn't yet told her parents or anyone else about Tate or mentioned where she'd be today. She couldn't, not until she'd confirmed in her own mind that she hadn't dreamed up a grandson or anything else Lane had told her yesterday in her office. A text seemed a cumbersome way to try to convey the gist of the situation, but with barely one bar showing on her phone screen, she didn't have much choice.

Snowed in at a friend's place in the mountains. Phone service horrible. Increase antibiotics & call Dr. Martinez at vet ER if she continues to worsen. Keep me posted.

Amy would understand why she didn't want her father involved. Hopefully, he'd already gone home for the day and wouldn't take it upon himself to intervene. Next, she sent a similarly vague text to her mom and asked her to take care of Daisy and Dash until she could get back to town.

A savory aroma wafting from the kitchen evoked a growl from Julia's stomach. Since she was stranded here, she may as well make herself useful. With a sigh, she pushed to her feet. "Anything I can do to help?"

LANE COULDN'T REMEMBER the last time he'd had an actual dinner guest—much less one who'd be staying overnight. Why hadn't he been paying closer attention to the sky? If he'd taken note of the weather change even an hour earlier, he could have sent Julia on her way and spared himself the awkwardness.

"I hope spaghetti's okay," he said as she joined him in the kitchen. "You could set the table."

"Happy to." Moving toward the cupboard he indicated, she stepped around Tate.

Wielding a wooden spoon, the kid pretended to stir something in a dented metal bowl. He looked up with a mile-wide grin. "I cook."

Hard as it was keeping up with a toddler, the little guy was shining a light into crevices of Lane's heart that had too long persisted in darkness.

Julia carried plates to the table. "That sauce smells delicious."

"It's my special recipe, made from home-grown tomatoes and herbs. Can't claim credit for the pasta, though. My friend Lila makes it from scratch and always sends over a batch."

An arched brow was Julia's only response. He hoped it meant she was revising her opinion of him as an uncouth mountain man.

When the food was ready, Julia filled water glasses while he prepared a small bowl of spaghetti and sauce for Tate.

She frowned as he cut the pasta into spoon-size pieces. "I think you'd better take charge of feeding him tonight—unless you want marinara stains all over the shirt you let me borrow."

He shot her a pointed look. "So he's *my* grandson when you'd rather not get messy?"

"That isn't what I meant." Returning his stare, she set the water glasses at their places and took her seat.

With Tate situated on a chair close enough for Lane to assist as necessary, he scooted up to the table and spread a cloth napkin across his lap. "I'm not religious, but feel free to say grace if you're so inclined."

She fidgeted with her napkin. "I'm not on speaking terms with God, myself."

There was obviously some hidden pain there, not surprising after the death of a son. Lane had lost his faith—what little he'd had—when Tessa died. "Okay, then. Dig in."

An uncomfortable silence descended as they ate, interrupted only when Lane had to stop Tate from slinging spoonfuls of marinara-drenched spaghetti. Afterward, Julia offered to clean up the kitchen while Lane took the boy upstairs for a bath. He wasn't sure who got the worst end of the deal.

With his sweet-scented little grandson wearing footed brushed-flannel jammies, he carried him downstairs and turned him over to Julia in the rocking chair. After stoking the woodstove for the night, he donned jacket and gloves and trudged out to tend his livestock. By the time he returned, Tate had fallen asleep in Julia's arms, and she looked about ready to nod off as well.

Seeing them like that, both looking so peaceful, brought an ache to his chest. All these years, he'd refused to admit how lonely he really was. Now he knew he never wanted to feel that way again.

CHAPTER THREE

LANE AWAKENED THE next morning to the yowls of a hungry toddler. "Out! Me out!" the kid yelled as he shook the crib rails. "Hung'y!"

"All right, I'm coming." Lane stumbled out of bed, surprised he'd slept so soundly. The past several days must be catching up with him. Not to mention for the first night in two weeks, he hadn't been continually hammered by a little boy's nocturnal karate chops.

Beyond the window, morning sun reflected off a fresh layer of snow—close to ten inches, judging from what Lane could see of the fence line. Julia wouldn't be getting out of here any time soon.

Propping the kid on his hip, he tiptoed out. No sound yet from the bedroom across the hall. He went downstairs to get some coffee brewing and to start a batch of scrambled eggs. With one eye on Tate, he stirred the eggs while scrolling through a series of text messages from neighbors asking if he could help clear roads. From early fall through late spring, his truck's snowplow attachment got plenty of use, and normally he wouldn't hesitate. But now he had Tate to consider, and he couldn't be in two places at once.

Although if Julia woke up soon, she'd probably be glad to watch Tate if it meant she could be on her way sooner. The lady vet might be bossy and opinionated, but he'd seen the look in her eyes as she'd read the text about the injured dog. It was like saving the animal's life truly mattered to her.

That was the problem, though. When anything—people, pets, possessions—began to matter too much, things got risky. People died or moved on. Animals, too. Possessions wore out or got stolen. Lane had learned the hard way that the less he cared, the less he got hurt.

Yet here he was setting himself up to be hurt again. He was already getting too attached to the little guy playing bongos on the bottom of an old saucepan.

As he sat sharing a plate of eggs with Tate, Julia wandered in. The coffeemaker drew her like a magnet, and she didn't speak a word until she'd poured herself a mug and taken several tentative sips. Then, as if noticing Lane for the first time, she offered a raspy "Good morning."

"To you, too." He caught himself staring at how unaffectedly pretty she looked with un-combed hair and wearing his raggedy plaid flannel robe over her clothes from yesterday. Clearing his throat, he poked another spoonful of eggs into Tate's mouth. "Soon as this little guy finishes, I'll scramble another batch. I can fry up some sausage, too."

"Coffee's all I need. I don't usually eat break-fast." She plopped down at the opposite end of the table. "When will they get around to plow-ing the roads up here?"

He snorted a laugh. "*They* equates to *me* and a couple of my neighbors. These roads aren't maintained by the county."

"Oh. I didn't think about that." She darted a worried glance toward the window. "But I *have* to be at the clinic this morning."

"Did you hear more about the dog?"

"My senior tech texted a few minutes ago. Last night I had her adjust antibiotics, and she says the swelling is down this morning, so it looks like the leg—" She rolled her eyes. "Sorry, get me talking about my patients and I'll bore you to death."

"It's okay. I can tell you're concerned."

"I am. But not just about the dog." Eyes closed briefly, she gave her head a quick shake. "It's...been a difficult couple of years."

She looked and sounded like a woman who sorely needed to get something off her chest. He wasn't sure he wanted to ask, but he couldn't help himself. "If you feel like venting, you've got a captive audience."

Her dismissive laugh wasn't convincing, especially when the next sound was a choked-off sob. "Steven's death hit me hard." She stood and paced to the window over the sink, as if giving him her back would make it easier to keep talking. "He was smart, gifted, genuine—and so tenderhearted. He would have made a wonderful veterinarian."

Tate had finished eating, and Lane dabbed a smear of egg off the boy's chin. "I didn't realize your son was studying to become a vet."

"He would have joined the family practice after passing his licensing exams. Ever since he first expressed interest as a teenager, I dreamed he'd someday be working alongside me."

Lane knew about broken dreams. "I'm sorry."

Julia refilled her mug and drifted back to the table. "I don't know what I'm going to do now.

My mother has already cut her hours in half, and my dad…" Her jaw clenched. "He won't admit it, but he needs to retire."

"Why? Is something wrong?"

"He's developed a hand tremor. He hides it well, but it's getting worse."

Again, he murmured, "I'm sorry."

"So to keep the practice going, I need to recruit one or two new veterinarians, plus hire an office manager." She looked toward the window. "I had a very promising interview scheduled for ten o'clock this morning, and now I'm going to miss it."

Frowning, Tate patted Lane's wrist. "Gammy sad. Make Gammy all better?"

Giving the kid a gentle hug, he smiled at Julia. "I'm afraid I can't fix all Grammy's problems, but I'll see what I can do about clearing the road."

LESS THAN THREE hours later, Julia was on her way down the mountain. She wouldn't make the interview appointment as scheduled, but the candidate had kindly agreed to come at one o'clock instead.

The hardest part was leaving Tate. Having spent the past twenty-four hours at Lane's place and seeing how conscientiously he cared for the little boy, she had slightly fewer qualms about their grandson's well-being. However, she still believed she was better equipped to be Tate's guardian while his mother underwent treatment. If today's interview went well, she could be that much closer to freeing up the time she'd need.

She made a quick trip home to change clothes—Daisy and Dash would have to stay at Mom's for a few more hours—then hurried to the clinic. The first hour was spent helping to clear the morning's patient backlog. That kept her too busy to answer questions about where she'd gone yesterday and why. There'd be time for explanations later.

Once the waiting room had emptied, she checked on her hit-and-run surgical patient. Amy was in the back tending to another canine patient, and when Julia reached the big girl's kennel, she found a new label on the door.

Head tilted, she turned to the vet tech. "Rowena?"

"It fits, don't you think? I looked it up online, and it can mean 'joy' or 'white mane.'" Amy knelt and scratched the dog's nose through the wire mesh. "She definitely has a white mane, and this pretty girl needs all the joy in life she can get."

"I agree. Bring her out so I can take a closer look at that leg."

The huge dog patiently endured the examination, even licking Julia's chin despite the discomfort she must be suffering. Julia guessed the mostly gray dog to be part Great Dane, part Irish wolfhound, with possibly another large breed or two mixed in. Tipping the scales at nearly 125 pounds, the dog appeared to be between two and four years old.

"Has Dylan had any success tracking down an owner?"

"Nothing," Amy replied. "He did find out where the accident happened, but no one in the neighborhood remembers seeing the dog around there before."

More than likely, someone had fallen in love with her as a puppy, then soon realized they couldn't afford the food bill for a dog that size and turned her out. The mere thought of such irresponsibility made Julia shudder.

"What are we going to do with her, Dr. J?"

"If no one claims her by the time she's ready to be released, I'll ask Maddie if she has space in her kennel, at least for a short-term stay while we find other arrangements." Julia's best friend, Maddie McNeill—Maddie Wittenbauer since her marriage earlier this year—owned and operated Eventide Dog Sanctuary, a loving "forever" home for senior and otherwise un-adoptable dogs.

"Rowena's too sweet to end up at a shelter," Amy said with a pout. "You know how hard it is to find good homes for big dogs like her, which means…"

Julia knew exactly the outcome Amy couldn't bring herself to speak of. "We're not there yet." She gave Rowena a gentle neck massage. "Let's keep asking around, and have Dylan post her photo on our Facebook page."

"She should have a home outside the city with lots of acreage," Amy mused. "A family with kids. She seems like she'd be great with little ones."

Memories evoked a bittersweet smile. After the divorce, Julia and Steven had moved into a house with a big backyard where she still lived. Shortly afterward, they'd adopted Buff, a ninety-pound yellow Lab mix who'd become her son's best pal. Happy little boys and big, tail-wagging dogs…it was a combination that never failed to swell her heart.

Then a new image formed—a giggling Tate clinging to Rowena's shaggy fur as they trotted across the meadow that was Lane's front yard. Oddly, she could picture herself there, too, sharing the moment with Lane…laughing together, holding hands…

She clamped her teeth together. Clearly, she was more emotionally and physically wrung out than she'd realized. After giving Amy further instructions for the dog's care, she escaped to her office. Hopefully, a protein bar and mug of strong coffee would sustain her through the one-o'clock interview.

AFTER FRIDAY'S DISAPPOINTING meeting with a veterinarian who'd blatantly padded his résumé, then an office manager applicant canceling at the last minute on Saturday, Julia felt like she was starting over from square one. Maybe she needed to adjust the job descriptions she'd posted on the employment search websites.

On Monday morning, she drove out to Eventide Dog Sanctuary, where she routinely provided discounted veterinary services to the twenty-plus canines in Maddie's care. Once the dogs were attended to, she asked if Maddie had time to talk.

"Sure. Come to the house and I'll put the kettle on—unless you require the super-caffeinated dark roast you usually drink."

"Actually, a cup of your calming lemon-ginger tea might be in order."

Stepping into the mudroom, Maddie looked back with an arched brow. "This sounds serious."

"Like a heart attack." Julia collapsed into a kitchen chair while her strawberry blonde friend boiled water and set out mugs and tea bags.

A few minutes later, their tea steeping, Maddie sat across from Julia. "All right, what's going on?"

Where to begin? Maybe just blurt it out? "I have a grandson."

"You…*what*?" Her friend looked almost as stunned as she'd been when Lane had first passed the photo of Tate across her desk.

"It's true." Tears formed against her will. "Steven got married without telling me. His son was born a few months after he died." Haltingly, she described her first encounter with Lane, then the trip up the mountain, getting snowed in and the precious hours spent with her little grandson. "Tate looks so much like

Steven that I'm on a continual seesaw between past and present."

"A grandson… I'm speechless." Maddie squeezed her hand. "Do your parents know?"

"I broke the news over the weekend. They're thrilled about having a great-grandchild, of course. But Dad thinks I should hire a lawyer to make sure my rights are protected."

"Is that really necessary at this point?"

Julia dunked her tea bag a few times. "I'd say no, except for the fact that Lane is adamant about being the one to care for Tate. I'm trying to convince him otherwise, but he's this tough off-gridder mountain man, who for unknown reasons has serious issues with anything city-related."

Maddie scoffed. "When Witt first came into my life, I distinctly remember you pestering me about doing a thorough background check."

"Advice you ignored at first."

"Because he'd given me no reason not to trust him. However, in your case, there's a child involved, and while taking legal steps might be premature, you deserve to know a few more details about Tate's other grandparent."

"I don't disagree."

After a thoughtful sip from her mug, Maddie asked, "Is there a Mrs. Bromley?"

"Not as far as I can tell. Lane's place is homey, but I got no sense of a woman's touch anywhere."

"And Tate's mother—you said she's in a mental facility?"

"Lane had her admitted to Mercy Cottage."

"I've heard good things about it. I'll be praying they can help her."

Maddie's faith had grown in leaps and bounds since she'd met Witt. Julia wasn't sure what it would take for her to let God back in. She gulped the last of her tea and stood. "I almost forgot. Do you have space in the kennel for my recovering hit-and-run victim?"

"I wish I could help, but tomorrow I'm taking in two more senior dogs with health problems, so I'm about to be full up again."

"I understand. I'll figure out something." If all else failed, she could keep the dog at her house temporarily—which would mean a huge adjustment for her spoiled-rotten twin dachshunds. "Let me know when your new arrivals are settled, and I'll come check them over."

When Julia returned to the clinic, she recognized Lane's mud-encrusted dark red truck parked out front. Oh, no. Had something happened to Tate?

She drove around to the rear parking area, rushed inside and halted at her open office door. Lane sat facing the opposite wall, one knee jumping nervously.

Heart pounding, she barged in. "Where's Tate? Is he all right?"

He stood abruptly. "He's okay. He's with my neighbor."

"Then what are you doing here?"

"I just came from Mercy Cottage. Shannon had—I forget what the doctor called it—some kind of episode." He collapsed into the chair and pressed his palms against his eyes. "She isn't going to get well any time soon."

"Lane, I'm so sorry." Julia hung her shoulder bag on the rack next to her lab coat, then closed the door and took the chair next to his. "Can I do anything?"

"No," he said, massaging his temples. "I just… I couldn't think straight after leaving there."

He was clearly terrified for his daughter. She lightly touched his shoulder. "At least she's in a safe place and getting care."

The intercom on her desk phone buzzed. Her

mother's voice came over the speaker. "Julia? I thought I heard you come in. Your dad could use some help in exam room two."

Lane stood abruptly and pulled in a noisy breath. "You're busy. Anyway, this isn't your problem. I'll go."

"Lane, wait." She stayed his hand as he reached for the doorknob. "Shannon was my son's wife. She's Tate's mother. I care very much what happens to her."

"I appreciate that, but still… I shouldn't have bothered you. We'll be fine."

"Fine?" The word grated on her. "There's nothing *fine* about this, and certainly not for an innocent little boy whose mother is so depressed she wants to die."

"It was a rhetorical *fine*, okay? Tate's not fine. I'm not fine." Exhaling tiredly, he looked toward the ceiling. "None of us are fine."

His vulnerability threatened to undermine her self-control. Arms folded tightly against her ribs, she murmured, "I do need to get to work, but keep me posted about Shannon. I'll visit Tate again as soon as I can break away. Or you can bring him here. Just let me know."

He replied with a noncommittal grunt and strode out without looking back.

Endearingly unguarded one minute, obstinate and unreadable the next—the man was an enigma. And Julia didn't like puzzles. Life was supposed to make sense.

Hers hadn't since Steven died, no matter how hard she worked at making it so. Especially now, with a grandson who'd quickly stolen her heart, plus the growing urgency to restaff the clinic before her mother fully retired and her father could no longer safely practice.

No, she definitely did not need the added complication of totally unbidden feelings for Lane Bromley.

GOING STRAIGHT TO Julia's office after his visit to Mercy Cottage? What had he been thinking? Lane hated feeling so inadequate. So powerless. So…bereft.

What he *really* hated was this sudden atypical impulse to turn to a relative stranger for help. Let alone a smart, savvy and—yes—beautiful woman like Julia Frasier. He had enough on his plate worrying about his daughter and getting over the shock of becoming a grandfather. Finding himself thinking of Julia in terms of anything other than Tate's other grandparent was both inconvenient and unnerving. Since losing

Tessa, he hadn't so much as considered letting someone new into his life. Hadn't wanted to. Hadn't needed to. And the fact that these feelings were coming out of nowhere *now* threw him even more off-balance than he already was.

Best to keep his focus where it should be—on looking after his grandson and making sure his daughter got better. He could only hope he hadn't made a huge mistake by entrusting Shannon's treatment to the medical system he'd lost all confidence in the day Tessa died.

On the positive side, he was figuring out all over again how to be sole caregiver for a toddler. Dan and Lila's two eldest daughters used to help watch Shannon when she was little, but the Vernon kids were all adults now with families of their own, and he'd already imposed quite a bit on Lila these past several days.

Over the weekend, though, he'd designed and constructed a portable play yard that he could set up near wherever his chores took him. Tate was already getting a kick out of watching his grandpa milk the cow and tend the chickens, and yesterday afternoon, he'd busied himself "planting" with a trowel and pail of garden soil while Lane worked in the greenhouse.

The memory brought a smile to Lane's lips.

It also reminded him he was running low on homogenized milk and a few other food items the picky toddler would eat. Heading home through Elk Valley, he swerved in at the mini mall and parked in front of the grocery mart. The place was never busy. All the same, Lane didn't relish these trips to town, whether it was bustling Missoula or tiny Elk Valley, which was little more than a wide place in the road.

Inside, he grabbed a carry basket and headed straight to the dairy section. He added milk, yogurt and sliced cheese to the basket, then he browsed the breakfast cereal row. Shannon had brought along some sugary brand that couldn't possibly be healthy, but Tate wasn't fond of Lane's hearty steel-cut oatmeal—neither the texture nor the prep time.

As he perused the ingredients list on a box of organic cereal, a woman with a reddish-blond ponytail reached for a box on a nearby shelf. Looking over at him, she smiled. "These labels can be so confusing."

Lane snorted. "Tell me about it. And the picture looks like birdseed. How do I know if my kid will even eat it?"

"How old?"

"Almost twenty months." When the woman's brows lifted ever so slightly, he added, "My grandson. I'm keeping him for a while." He turned away, hoping she'd take the hint.

He could feel her gaze on the back of his neck. Lowering her voice, she said, "Forgive me for making assumptions, but...would he be Julia Frasier's grandchild, too?"

His shoulders tensed. Small towns—go figure. "If you're asking me that, then you already know the answer." He glared over his shoulder. "As I'm sure half of Elk Valley does by now."

Stepping closer, she lowered her voice. "Julia is my best friend, and she confided in me. Naturally, I'm concerned. And, well, you fit her description of a...a..." Color crept up her cheeks.

He faced her squarely. "What? A misanthropic mountain man?"

A guy around Lane's age sauntered up behind the woman. He cast Lane a wary glance before asking, "Everything okay, honey?"

"Just comparing notes on breakfast cereal." With a stiff smile that reminded Lane of his no-nonsense fourth-grade teacher, she offered him the box she'd been holding. "Here, try this one. It's a favorite of ours."

"Th-thanks." Now he was embarrassed for overreacting. He'd descended the mountain more times in the last two weeks than he sometimes did in an entire year, and his people skills showed it.

A soft bark alerted him to the scruffy black-and-tan dog pressed against the man's knee. Taken aback at first, Lane noted the red emotional support animal vest.

"Easy, Ranger," the man said as he offered Lane his hand. "I'm Witt. This is my wife, Maddie. Haven't seen you around before. Are you new in town?"

Apparently, the man wasn't privy to whatever Julia had told his wife. "Not exactly." Lane hesitantly accepted Witt's handshake. "Lane Bromley. I live up the mountain."

"Nice to meet you. And don't mind Ranger. Everyone around here knows we're a package deal, but Maddie thought he should start wearing the vest so we get fewer strange looks." Witt gave the dog a scratch behind the ears. "He's saved my life more than once. Well, him and my amazing wife," he added, tucking the woman under his arm.

Love filled her eyes as she smiled at her husband. It was the same look Lane used to see every time Tessa cast a smile his way. Would he ever stop missing her? "Well, I… I need to get going."

Before he could duck past the couple and their dog, Witt halted him, a knowing look shadowing his deep-set eyes. "Hang on a sec." He took a business card and a pen from his pocket. After jotting something on the back of the card, he handed it to Lane. "This may sound a little weird, but I feel like the Lord's telling me you could use a friend. Here's my cell phone number. Call me anytime."

Lane could only nod as he accepted the card and continued toward the cashier. He didn't doubt he'd been giving off a few too many "disgruntled loner" vibes, but no way was he buying into the idea that God had anything to do with the man's offer.

Either way, it didn't matter. Lane wasn't the type to have heart-to-hearts with guy friends. Bad enough he'd bared his emotions a few too many times already with Julia. What was it about her that brought out his vulnerable side?

Whatever it was, he'd better put a lock on it before this breach in his defenses opened any wider.

CHAPTER FOUR

IT WAS FINALLY the weekend again, and Lane expected Julia any minute. Tied up at the vet clinic all week, she hadn't been able to break away for another trip up the mountain. After Lane had seen her on Monday, she'd texted with a pediatrician recommendation and then followed up often to ask how their grandson was doing. She'd repeatedly asked for photos and videos, but with his spotty cell service, transmitting files that size was next to impossible.

Once she got here, maybe she wouldn't mind watching Tate for a few hours. This time of year, he usually made his last few trips into the forest in search of fallen or standing dead trees to top off his firewood supply for the winter. After three weeks of nearly full-time toddler duty, a solo excursion into the peaceful Lolo National Forest was sounding better all the time.

Mind? Julia would probably shove him out the door and then lock it behind him.

He and Tate had just finished lunch when he glimpsed her lime-green SUV come through the gate.

"Grammy's here." He propped the tot on his hip and strode out to the deck. As last week's snow melted away, the first days of September had turned pleasantly balmy—no need for anything warmer than a flannel shirt over a long-sleeved tee.

"There's my sweet boy!" Julia scurried up the steps and held out her arms for Tate. "I've missed you so much. Have you been good for Gramps?"

Hooking one arm tightly around Lane's neck, the kid gave his head a firm shake. "I want Mama."

Julia's pursed lips betrayed her disappointment.

"I told you, Tater Tot," Lane said. "Mommy's very sick. She'll be home when she's better." He tamped down a twinge of self-satisfaction over the boy's attachment to him. "But Grammy's come all this way to see you, and she looks like she really needs a hug."

After a thoughtful pause, Tate leaned toward

Julia. Snuggling him under her chin, she cast Lane a grateful smile.

A few minutes later, she sat cross-legged on the living room floor and helped Tate stack blocks. Keeping her voice low, she asked, "What's the latest on Shannon? Any improvement?"

"Yesterday, they let me speak with her on the phone for a few minutes." Lane sank onto the ottoman, memories of the call making his stomach knot. "She sounded so...out of it. The doctor said the meds can do that while she adjusts, but I don't like it."

"I'm sure they know what they're doing. Give it time."

The doctors know what they're doing, Mr. Bromley. Yep, he'd heard that before. And then his wife had died in surgery.

He rose abruptly. "Can I leave you two alone for a while? There's stuff I need to do while I've got someone to keep an eye on Tate."

"Please, do whatever you need to. In fact..." Uncurling her legs, she pushed to her feet. "Would you consider letting Tate come home with me for a couple of days? I imagine you have plenty of jobs around here that would be much easier to manage without a toddler underfoot."

He didn't care for her ingratiating smile, but

he couldn't exactly deny the logic of her suggestion. "All his things are here." His reasoning was weak, but it was the best he could come up with.

"So pack him a bag."

"What about his crib?"

"My neighbor has a portable crib I can borrow."

"He can be a picky eater."

"Then make me a list. There's a supermarket just up the road from my place."

Fists jammed against his hips, he forced himself to take a breath. *I need him here*, he wanted to insist. *With me. Where I can be absolutely certain he's safe.*

Except there were no guarantees, were there? He'd tried to keep Shannon safe, and look how she'd ended up.

He exhaled loudly. "Just drop it, okay? We can talk when I get back."

A tug on his pants leg drew his attention. Tate's tiny hand gripped Lane's jeans, while the other clung to the hem of Julia's plaid overshirt. He frowned at each of them in turn. "Gammy, Gampy, no fight. Gammy, Gampy, be nice."

Snickering, Julia shot Lane a wink. "Guess he told us."

Lane stooped to lift the little guy into his arms. "We aren't fighting, Tater Tot." *Not exactly, anyway.* "The thing is, Grammy and Gramps both love you very much, which makes it hard sometimes to agree on what's best for you."

Julia edged close enough to smile at Tate around Lane's shoulder, and a not-exactly-unpleasant ripple snaked up his spine.

"That's right," she said. "But Grammy doesn't live close by, so I'm hoping Gramps will let you come visit me at my house sometimes. Besides, your great-grandparents can't wait to meet you."

Tate drew his caterpillar brows together. "Gate-gamps?"

"Yes!" The brightness in Julia's voice matched her expression. "My mommy and daddy are your great-gramps and great-grammy."

"No need to confuse him." Lane put some space between them, more for his sake than for Tate's.

"What's confusing about letting our grandson know he has extended family?" Julia's smile didn't change, and neither did her tone, but the look in her eyes certainly did. "That he has *lots* of people who love and care about him?"

"Just…never mind. I need to head out." He lowered Tate to the floor, then knelt and tweaked his chin. "Gramps has some stuff to do, so I'm going to leave you with Grammy for a bit. That okay with you?"

Lips skewed, Tate nodded. "Dat otay."

Before Julia Frasier disconcerted him more than she already had, he grabbed his jacket, baseball cap and truck keys, and bolted from the cabin.

With his firewood permit in the glove compartment and his chain saw in the back, he didn't let himself think too much as he chose his route into Lolo National Forest. But when he spied a fallen tree conveniently near the road and prepared to haul out his equipment, the truth hit him like a rockslide: *yeah, you're lonely, but face it, that's no one's fault but yours.*

True, solitary life had become as natural to him as breathing. An only child, he'd been born late in his parents' lives. They'd been private people, too, and both had passed on before he finished law school. As for Tessa's parents, they'd never forgiven him for moving to the mountains with Shannon. They were gone now, as well, which he should be sad about for Shannon's sake—they'd maintained a relationship with their granddaughter as best they could—but he couldn't even imagine the scolding he'd get if they'd lived to see Shannon in her current state.

He deserved a big chunk of the blame, but everything he'd done, every choice he'd made since Tessa died, had all been for his daughter.

Who are you kidding, Bromley? You turned tail and ran—and not just to protect Shannon. Truth is, you couldn't face continuing alone in the life you'd dreamed about and planned with Tessa.

AFTER HER MESSY first experience giving Tate lunch, Julia took precautions this time. Finding cotton dish towels in a kitchen drawer, she used one on Tate as a bib and covered her shirt with another. The toddler really needed a high chair or booster seat, but after Steven had outgrown his, she hadn't kept them. She'd definitely need to invest in some new gear before bringing Tate home to live with her.

Assuming she could convince Lane to part with him. So far, she'd made no progress in that area. One thing was clear—the harder she pushed, the more he dug in his heels. If she looked up *stubborn* in the dictionary, she'd find a picture of Lane Bromley.

No sooner had she cleaned up Tate after lunch than his head started bobbing. She swept him into her arms and started for the stairs. "Time for a nap, little man."

"No. Wock me." He pointed over her shoulder toward the rocking chair.

Within five minutes, the boy had melted against her in sound sleep, his warmth seeping into her shoulder. Memories of rocking Steven just this way brought a lump to her throat. After losing her son so tragically, she'd assumed the joy of holding a grandchild was lost to her forever, which made these moments a pure gift.

It was tempting to cuddle and rock her precious grandson until he awoke from his nap, but when her arm supporting him began to stiffen, she reluctantly carried him upstairs. As she laid him in his crib, he roused only long enough to tuck a flop-eared terry-cloth bunny beneath his arm.

She could stand there all day watching the rise and fall of his tummy and how his lips and eyelids twitched with whatever little boys dreamed about, but at last, she tore herself away. An odd feeling washed over her as she glanced around Lane's room. Though she'd helped him put the crib together in this very room just over a week ago, today it felt as if she were trespassing.

And yet she couldn't suppress her curiosity. Turning slowly, she let her gaze skim the walls and furniture surfaces. The plain decor and casually haphazard array on the bureau definitely said a single guy lived here. A mystery novel and a puzzle book lay on the nightstand, along with books on various aspects of off-grid living—greenhouse gardening, canning and preserving produce, solar power maintenance, emergency first aid...

Tucked behind the bedside lamp, as if he'd wanted to keep it near at hand but not *too* near, sat a framed photo of an attractive fair-haired woman. Seated behind a desk, she appeared to be laughing at the photographer—and not merely with amusement, but with genuine love in her eyes. The old-style bulky computer monitor on her left confirmed the photo wasn't recent.

Shannon's mother?

Lane's wife?

Swamped at the clinic all week, she'd put off delving into the man's background. Maybe it was time she followed up.

After another peek at Tate, she slipped downstairs and pulled out her cell phone. Attempts to use the internet browser quickly proved futile, so she texted Maddie and asked if she had time to search for anything connected with Lane Bromley. Moments later, Maddie replied with a thumbs-up, and then Julia paced from window to window while she waited. Hopefully, whatever Lane had gone off to do this afternoon would keep him busy for a while.

Almost half an hour went by before Maddie replied. As a part-time English tutor, she had access to newspaper archives and had come across an obituary for Tessa Bromley, survived by her husband and their infant daughter. More research had turned up a report about the law office robbery and the shooting that had ended Tessa's life.

Knuckles pressed to her lips, Julia squeezed her eyes shut. She could begin to understand now why the man had fled to this mountaintop refuge. He'd needed to grieve and to heal. Even more importantly, to create a sheltered place where his little girl could grow up in safety.

What he'd failed to account for was the cost of prioritizing Shannon's physical safety over her mental and emotional well-being. Had he fully realized it yet, or, if given the chance, would he repeat those mistakes with his grandson?

Julia absolutely could not let that happen.

AFTER TATE'S NAP and a snack of dried apple slices, Julia laced up the boy's tiny hiking boots and zipped him into a hoodie. The shadows were already lengthening, but there was still a broad sunny patch in Lane's front yard. Once again, Julia imagined the little guy toddling through the grass alongside Rowena. She really must talk to Lane about bringing the dog up here, if only to foster until a good home could be found.

"Go see cow." Tate pulled her toward the barn.

"Um, I don't know about that, sweetie." Large-animal medicine had been a facet of Julia's veterinary school curriculum, and she occasionally treated Maddie's horses for their most basic needs. Cows, on the other hand? Not her cup of java.

After another surprisingly strong tug on her arm from such a little boy, she reluctantly followed. Before they reached the barn, the sound of tires on gravel drew her attention to the road, where Lane's truck had stopped on the other side of the gate. Getting out to open it, he saw Julia and waved.

"Gampy back!" Tate would have run straight toward the truck if Julia hadn't had firm hold of his hand.

At least she'd been spared a visit with the cow. "Let's wait here for Gramps, okay?"

As Lane drove past, she glimpsed a load of logs in the truck bed. He pulled up beside a long, open-sided firewood shed that looked nearly full. Dropping the tailgate, he called, "Are you okay watching Tate while I unload this wood?"

"I think I can manage." What did the man think she'd been doing all afternoon?

Tate pointed. "Help Gampy?"

"No, honey, we'd just be in the way." Certainly Lane didn't need more evidence of the folly of attempting to raise a toddler under such demanding circumstances. Keeping a safe distance, she asked nonchalantly, "How old was Shannon when you moved up here?"

Muscles bulging as he hefted a log, he glanced from her to their grandson. "A little younger than Tate, I guess." He swung around and dropped the log onto the growing pile next to

the woodshed. "And I know what you're thinking. I managed then, I'll manage now."

Not without a lot of help, she wanted to say, but
bit her tongue.

She was soon entranced by Lane's rhythmic
workflow as he emptied the truck bed. Each
log had to weigh between seventy and a hundred pounds, yet he maneuvered them with
practiced ease. Barely breathing hard, he paused
only now and then to press his damp forehead
against his shirtsleeve.

Realizing her heart was beating faster, she
inhaled a deep breath of her own. No matter how strong or good-looking he may be,
no matter how tragic the loss of his wife had
been, no matter how tenderhearted he seemed
toward his daughter and grandson, she must *not*
let Lane Bromley get under her skin. Tate's future depended on it.

HE COULD FEEL her watching him. Judging him.
Plotting how she'd convince him to let her take
Tate.

He slung the last log onto the pile and latched
the tailgate. Tucking his leather gloves into a
pocket, he discreetly rolled his aching shoulders. This particular job got harder every year,

but his only backup heat source was propane, and if he ran low, delivery could get dicey once the winter snows set in.

Julia cast a pointed glance at his store of logs. "Cutting all that wood must take a huge chunk of your time."

Her implication was clear. "I team up with Dan Vernon and another neighbor or two to fill all our sheds." With a point of his own to drive home, he continued, "I'd even venture to say that all my daily chores combined don't take near as much time as what you put in at your thriving vet clinic."

Her tight frown said he'd hit the intended nerve.

"If you're done here, I should probably be going."

"Wait." Feeling bad about needling her, he narrowed the space between them. Besides, for Tate's sake if nothing else, they needed to find a way to get along. "As late as it is, you might as well stay for supper." He scooped Tate into his arms. "How does grilled elk steaks and baked potatoes sound?"

She slacked her jaw. "I... I don't know if that's such a good idea."

"What? The steaks or the potatoes?"

"No, I meant—"

Tate giggled and stretched to touch the toe of his boot. "Tate toes!"

That elicited a laugh from Julia, and the tension between them dissipated.

"So." Lane hiked a brow. "Will you join us?"

She returned his smile with a thoughtful one of her own. "I suppose it would be okay. Now that I've been here a couple of times, I'm not as worried about getting lost going home."

Just then, the slanting sun lit a spark in her brown eyes, and Lane worried he was in danger of getting lost. He drew a quick breath. "Guess I should get cooking."

An hour later, he served up two perfectly grilled elk steaks along with bacon-seasoned green beans and tender baked potatoes topped with home-churned butter. Elk would be a little tough for Tate's tiny teeth, so Lane substituted strips of grilled chicken breast for him.

"This is all delicious," Julia said after a few bites. "Did you grow the vegetables yourself?"

"The beans are from this summer's crop. I grow potatoes in the greenhouse year-round."

She contemplated a morsel of steak. "And the elk… I suppose you're a hunter."

He glanced up. "Does that bother you?"

"I get that it's a food source, and hunting is necessary for population control." She laid her fork aside to take a sip of water. "I just couldn't do it myself."

"I didn't grow up in a hunting family. It was something I had to learn and get used to. Same as…" He cleared his throat meaningfully while pointing at the chicken on Tate's plate.

Her eyes widened. "You mean—"

"Where do you think your store-bought chicken comes from? I can assure you, my methods are a lot more humane."

"Yes, I… I'm sure the chicken had a very happy life, right up until…" Stabbing a green bean, she muttered, "I knew I should have become a vegetarian."

He stifled a chuckle. "If you can't finish your steak, I'm happy to help."

"That's okay." She sawed off another forkful of meat. "I shall somehow force myself to enjoy every last bite."

Which she did, to Lane's great amusement. While he cleaned up the kitchen, Julia took Tate upstairs for a bath and a bedtime story. When he heard her returning footsteps, he poured two mugs of fresh decaf and met her at the bottom of the steps.

Accepting the mug, she inhaled the aroma and released a blissful sigh. "You've discovered my greatest weakness."

Oddly, that pleased him. He motioned toward the sofa and then took the easy chair across from her and propped one foot on the ottoman. "Did the little guy go to sleep okay?"

"One story and he was out like a light." She sipped her coffee. "Actually, now that we have a chance to talk, I've been meaning to run an idea by you."

More pressure to let her take Tate? He wouldn't make it easy for her. Back stiffening, he set aside his mug and silently waited.

Looking a little less sure of herself, she sat forward and placed her mug on the coffee table. "You remember the injured dog that arrived at the clinic the same time as you?"

Not the direction he'd expected the conversation to take. "Hard to forget."

"Well, as quickly as she's healing, she'll be ready to leave the clinic soon."

"That's good…isn't it?" Where was she going with this?

"Yes, but we still haven't tracked down her owner, and she's too sweet to end up at a shelter. So I thought…" Her gaze became imploring. "You have such a great place here, and lots of room for a big dog to run—"

"Hold on." He lowered his boot to the floor. "You want *me* to take the dog? After you've been not-so-subtly hinting at how I've already got too much on my plate to take care of my grandson?"

"Our."

How like her to throw the word back in his face. He met her saccharine smile with a glare. "Yes, *our* grandson. Which is another reason I can't believe you're suggesting this. That dog's the size of a pony. She could hurt— Oh, wait. I get it now. You want to trade the dog for Tate."

"No!" Eyes closed, she inhaled slowly through her nose. When she lifted her gaze again, whatever subterfuge he'd imagined had vanished, replaced by a wistful melancholy. "It's just that I remember how much Steven loved the dog he grew up with. They were such great pals, and I…" The slightest tremor entered her tone. "I'd love for Tate to have that kind of special companionship."

An unexpected rush of sympathy—the only feeling he'd admit to—propelled him to the sofa. Easing down beside her, he slid his arm around her to pat her shoulder. "It's okay, Julia. It'll be okay."

She cocked her head, a quirky grin skewing one side of her mouth. "Learn that from Tate?"

He snickered. "Sometimes I think that kid is smarter than both of us put together."

"You'll get no argument from me."

"At last," he said, rolling his eyes, "one thing we can agree on."

"In addition to what's best for Tate." She shifted to face him, and his arm fell away. "So how about if I bring her tomorrow for a trial visit? We can see how the two of them get along."

"I don't know…" He already missed the brush of her silky dark hair across the back of his hand. "I was thinking I'd call Mercy Cottage tomorrow and ask if Shannon's doctor would okay an in-person visit."

"Perfect. If they won't let you bring Tate yet, you can leave him with me. Afterward, I'll follow you home with Rowena."

He narrowed one eye. "Rowena?"

"My tech gave her the name. Pretentious, I know, but it fits her regal stature."

Was he really letting her talk him into this? He stood before she weakened his resolve any further. "Okay, but just so you understand, I'm not committing to anything."

She seemed satisfied with that—*seemed* being the operative word. After finishing her decaf, she thanked him for supper and said her good-byes.

Closing the gate behind her as she drove away, he realized he'd been so distracted by her presence that he'd neglected his evening barn chores. After checking on Tate with the baby monitor receiver he carried in his pocket, he trekked to the barn.

He most certainly didn't need another animal to feed and clean up after. He'd let Julia bring the dog for the afternoon if she must, but no way was he letting it stay.

CHAPTER FIVE

BABYSITTING TATE ON Sunday morning gave Julia the opportunity to introduce him to her parents. They came straight over as soon as their church service ended, and to Julia's great relief, the excitement of meeting Tate effectively sidetracked them from their usual subtle hints about getting her back to church.

Once Tate understood these were the great-grandparents Julia had told him about, he ran to them for a hug. "Gate-gamps! Gate-gammy!"

Eyes filling with tears, Mom glanced up at Julia. "He looks so much like…"

"I know." Julia sniffed back a tear of her own.

Her father settled into a chair and pulled Tate onto his lap. "When you first told us Steven had a son, I had my doubts. I don't anymore."

All too soon, Lane returned from seeing Shannon. He was polite enough but seemed on edge as Julia introduced him to her parents.

Her father didn't make it any easier. "Julia says you live off-grid up in the mountains. That can't be the safest environment for a toddler."

Lane stiffened. "We're managing just fine."

"You should see Lane's place," Julia said brightly. "He's made it into a very comfortable home."

He looked surprised that she'd defended him. She'd surprised herself as well.

"Gampy." Tate grabbed Lane's hand and tugged. "See doggies."

At his questioning glance, Julia murmured, "My dachshunds. He's been playing with them in the backyard."

The little boy wasn't to be deterred, so they all filed outside. Observing Tate's fun with the frisky twins boded well for when he'd meet Rowena later. Julia only hoped the big dog's size wouldn't be too overwhelming.

More worrisome was the fact that Julia's two little dogs seemed to so thoroughly intimidate Lane. He gave them each a nervous pat, then straightened and crossed his arms. "We need to be going soon, Tater Tot."

Already? She'd find it a lot harder to let them leave if they hadn't already confirmed plans for her to come up to the cabin today…unless Lane had changed his mind. "We're still on for this afternoon, right?"

"Give me an hour or so. I need some time."

For what, she couldn't imagine, unless he'd had a difficult visit with Shannon. Later, she'd ask him how it went.

As soon as Lane drove away, Julia's mother cornered her in the entryway. "Honey, that little boy is as precious as he can be, and I understand why you want him here with you until his mother gets well. But how do you propose to manage the clinic *and* raise a child? Not that I won't help as much as I can, but—" Glancing into the den to where Julia's father had tuned to a football game on TV, she lowered her voice. "I know you've been covering for your dad's tremors. Once he admits it's time to retire, I'm afraid I'll have more than I can handle just taking care of him."

It was the truth, though not what Julia wanted to hear. "I know, Mom. I'll figure out something. In the meantime, Tate's doing okay with Lane, and I'm going up to check on them as often as I can."

"And the interviews?" Her mother worried her lower lip. "Julia, we have to make some decisions soon."

"I spoke with a couple of promising candidates last week." She grimaced. "But Dad insists on having the final say, and he's been digging in his heels."

Mom squeezed Julia's hand. "You pick the people *you* want to work with. Let me deal with your dad."

"Thanks, Mom." She gave her mother a hug. "I know this isn't easy for you, either. I promise I'll do everything possible to make sure Frasier Veterinary Clinic continues to thrive."

It was just after two thirty that afternoon when Julia parked in front of Lane's cabin. She made sure she had her cell phone ready to video Tate's reaction when he met Rowena for the first time.

"Gammy back!" Tate called as Lane walked him down from the deck.

She smiled and waved. "Yes, and Grammy's got a big surprise for you, sweetie."

Leaning into the back seat, she clipped a leash on Rowena's collar and guided the dog to the ground. Fresh from the bath and toenail clip Dylan had given her yesterday, the gray canine with white mane looked every bit as regal as her name implied. The blue cast on her hind leg would remain for another month or so, but the dog had adapted well. Her superficial injuries had almost fully healed.

Camera at the ready, Julia moved to the side so Tate could get his first glimpse of Rowena. His wide-eyed gasp of delight didn't disappoint.

"Gampy!" he shouted, bouncing on his toes. "Dat my pony?"

"No, Tater Tot," Lane said, his expression skeptical, "that's just a great big hairy dog."

Julia walked the dog closer. "She's a lot bigger than Daisy and Dash, but she's very friendly. Her name's Rowena. Want to pet her?"

"Hey, careful." Lane positioned himself between Tate and the dog.

But Tate had a mind of his own. "Moo, Gampy." He shoved at Lane's knee. "I pet Weena."

"Slowly, though," Julia cautioned. "Remember how I showed you how to say hi to Daisy and Dash the first time?" She knelt and stretched out her arm, palm down, fist lightly closed. "Hold your hand like this and let her sniff it."

Rewarded with a wet tongue across his knuckles, Tate pulled back with a giggle and then tentatively extended his hand again. This time, Rowena nosed his pudgy fingers open and offered her head for a pat.

Tate's look of exquisite joy swelled Julia's heart. Her thoughts flashed back to Steven's first encounter with Buff as a squirming puppy, and for a moment, she couldn't breathe.

"Here, let me," Lane said softly, taking her phone. "I'll get some shots of all three of you."

"Oh. Thanks." She'd almost forgotten the video camera was running. There'd probably be several shaky frames of sky and earth.

Dabbing her damp cheeks with her sweater sleeve, she laughed with Tate as Rowena patiently accepted his clumsy pats and unintentionally vigorous tugs on her fur. Soon, he asked for the leash so he could walk Rowena himself. When he took over like a pro, and the dog obediently followed, Julia thought her heart would burst.

Giving a loud sniffle, she stood. "What did I tell you? They're going to be besties forever."

He snorted and returned her phone. "I don't even know how to take care of a dog."

"What? You never had one growing up?" She noticed the video was still recording and pushed the stop button.

"My mother had a froufrou lapdog that had

to go to the groomer once a month. She came home with hair ribbons and painted toenails and smelling like a cross between roses and flea dip. The critter never did like me, and I still have scars to prove it."

"Oh, Lane." Julia stifled a chuckle, now understanding his discomfort around the dachshunds. On impulse, she snapped a photo of his grumpy expression.

"Hey, delete that." He grabbed for her phone.

"No way." She danced out of reach. "That shot needs to go in Tate's baby book."

His brow furrowed. "I don't even know if he has one."

"Shannon didn't start one for him?"

"If she did, it wasn't with her stuff."

Considering what the young mother had gone through, losing her husband, raising their baby alone, Julia suspected Shannon hadn't had the emotional energy to even think about a baby book. In that case, Julia would take on the project, both to capture Tate's childhood years and as a tribute to Steven.

The thought brought a resurgence of her own grief. She clamped down hard to keep her chin from trembling. *I miss you so much, Steven. I wish you could see this little boy of yours.*

Tate was walking Rowena in a small circle in front of them. When he stumbled, Lane caught his arm and steadied him.

"I otay." The little boy shrugged off Lane's hold and shot him a withering stare.

Smile returning, Julia snapped another picture. She'd make Tate's the best baby book ever.

"All right, enough." Lane rolled his eyes. "Or at least let me take some incriminating photos of you."

"You'll get your chance, I'm sure." She wiped away another escaping tear.

Lane studied her. "Are you okay?"

"Just...so many memories." Willing a semblance of composure, she motioned toward her vehicle. "I brought bedding and food bowls for Rowena. There's a big sack of dog food, too. Want to give me a hand?"

"Wait—you're leaving her here? I thought this was only a get-acquainted visit."

"You can have the rest of today, tonight and all day tomorrow to get even better acquainted. As soon as I get off work tomorrow, I'll drive up to see how it's going and check Rowena's leg."

"And then you'll take her back with you?"

She replied with a vague lift of her brow. "As I said, we'll see how it's going."

WHEN IT CAME to dogs, Lane's little grandson seemed to be a natural. He must take after the Frasier branch of his family tree in that regard, because the boy sure didn't get it from the Bromleys.

With Tate happily walking Rowena around the yard, Julia had taken a seat on the bottom step. Lane rested an elbow on the banister. "They make quite a pair, I have to admit."

"Don't they, though?" Julia scooted over. "Join me? I can fill you in about Rowena's routine."

Gritting his teeth against a resigned sigh, Lane sank down next to her. When his shoulder brushed hers, a tingle ran down his arm. He scrubbed it roughly with his other hand.

Julia offered a concerned frown. "Did you get into some poison ivy in the woods yesterday?"

"No." He locked his hands between his knees. "You were saying?"

She spent a few minutes outlining the dog's daily care, how much to feed her, how often to let her out for potty breaks. "And you should put her bed in your room at night so she'll feel safe."

"She's the size of a full-grown timber wolf. What's she got to be afraid of?"

The bossy veterinarian's narrow-eyed stare could have singed his eyebrows. "How would *you* feel if you'd been abandoned, hit by a car and put through major surgery to save your shattered leg?"

He grimaced. "Point taken."

Her expression softened. "Just give her lots of affection and TLC, and you'll have a friend for life."

"Gammy! Gampy!" Tugging on the leash, Tate led Rowena to the foot of the steps. One arm wrapped around the big dog's neck, he beamed a mile-wide grin. "Dis my doggy now?"

Lane glared at Julia. "This was your plan all along, wasn't it?"

She merely snickered.

He let out a long, slow breath. "Well, Tater Tot, if you promise to help me take care of this walking shag carpet, I guess we can let her stay. For now, anyway," he added with a sharp glance at Julia.

"Yay! Yay! Yay!" The kid bounced on his toes. "I wuv Weena!"

"I'm so glad, honey," Julia said as she pushed up from the step. "But Rowena's still getting better from her accident, so maybe we should take her inside and let her rest for a bit."

Tate stooped to inspect the dog's blue cast, then gave her a kiss on the ear. "Weena has owie. Poor Weena."

While Julia helped Tate guide the limping dog up to the deck, Lane grabbed the sack of food and other dog paraphernalia from Julia's SUV. No way could he say no to the dog now. He hadn't seen Tate smile that big in the whole three weeks he'd been here. And not once since Lane had picked him up at Julia's earlier had the kid asked about his mom.

Julia met him in the living room and took the dog bowls from him. "Shall I put her dishes by the pantry door?"

"Sure, why not? It'll be convenient for when I need to haul out this two-ton sack of food."

"Oh, stop bellyaching." She rolled her eyes and started for the kitchen. "Set her bed in front of the woodstove for now. The warmth will be good for her."

"Yes, your majesty." He didn't think she'd heard the murmured remark until she lasered him with another piercing stare.

No sooner had he placed the giant-size foam bed near the stove than Rowena stepped onto it, circled a couple of times and stretched out on her side with a contented sigh.

"Aw, Weena sweepy." Tate knelt beside her and gently rested his cheek against her shoulder, one hand stroking her neck.

Lane edged closer, ready to rescue his grandson at the first hint of a growl or snap. But Rowena merely lifted her head to lick Tate's nose and then lay back down. With a giggle, the boy snuggled beneath her foreleg and closed his eyes.

Coming up beside Lane, Julia smiled. "Looks like they're both ready for a nap."

"You're absolutely sure he's safe with her?"

She already had her phone out to snap a photo. "I'd certainly keep an eye on them for now, but from the looks of things, you have nothing to worry about."

Arms crossed, he swiveled to face her. "So if I let the dog stay, does it mean you'll quit bugging me about taking Tate to live with you?"

"Well, I…" Lips tight, she tucked her phone away. "I do still have some details to work out."

"That's what I thought."

"But so do you." Heaving a groan, she trudged to the sofa and slumped against the cushions. "The fact is neither of us is currently in the best position to parent a toddler. And it isn't fair to Tate."

He marched over and faced her across the coffee table. "I still think I'm better equipped than you are. For one thing, I'm not tied up with a full-time job. I'm right here pretty much 24/7."

"But can you really keep him safe while you're splitting logs or working in your wood-shop or hunting elk or…or…whatever other potentially dangerous chores living off the grid requires?"

"I managed with Shannon, didn't I?"

"Not without a lot of help from your neighbors, as I recall. And that was twenty-plus years ago. I'm guessing you're around fifty now, and you're not getting any younger."

"Neither are you," he blurted, and immediately regretted it. Rugged mountain living had definitely taken a toll on his appearance, whereas city girl Julia Frasier hardly looked a day over thirty-five. Even those deepening worry lines around her eyes couldn't detract from her striking dark-haired good looks.

You need to nip this line of thinking in the bud right now, Bromley. Stay focused on the goal—keeping your grandson right where he belongs.

With a glance at the little boy, now sound asleep next to Rowena and looking as peaceful as he'd ever seen him, Lane sank onto the ottoman. "Look, Julia, I'm tired of going back and forth with you about this. For now, can't we let things be? Tate's happy here—even more so now that you've foisted this dog on us. Besides, you know I'd never let anything happen to him."

She opened her mouth as if to continue the argument but then snapped it shut and looked away. "Fine. I'll drop it for now, but only until I get things under control at the clinic. You'll never convince me Tate wouldn't be better off in town with me."

"Then maybe I'll have to do something about that."

Studying him, she asked slowly, "Like what?"

He'd surprised himself with the flippant remark, so now he needed to stall while he figured out exactly what it would take to put an end to this toddler tug-of-war.

"Well, for one thing," he began, an idea clicking into place, "I could file for custody."

"You wouldn't." Her reply came out in a menacing growl.

"Why not? Considering Shannon entrusted him with me while she's hospitalized, I doubt

I'd have any trouble convincing a judge to make it official."

Julia stood abruptly. "You'd really do that? Just to keep me away from my grandson?"

"Not to keep you away, no." He hadn't meant his words to come across as a threat...or had he? His gaze drifted to the sleeping Tate. "The truth is, I should have applied for temporary guardianship as soon as Shannon was admitted."

"I can get a lawyer, too, you know. And I'd have just as much right."

Palms upraised, Lane stepped around the coffee table. "Please, I don't want to fight with you in court or out. Legal guardianship would be strictly for Tate's protection while Shannon is unable to take care of him."

"And obviously you'd have a double advantage—as Shannon's father and as a former attorney yourself."

He flinched. "How did you—"

"Yes, I looked into your background. Why shouldn't I know something about Tate's other grandparent?"

A bitter taste rose in his throat. He wanted to be angry at her for snooping, but he couldn't deny her point. "Great. What else did you learn about me?"

"I… I know about your wife." She closed her eyes briefly, her expression softening. "Lane, I'm sorry, truly. I can understand why you'd want to turn your back on that part of your life, why you brought your daughter up here where you thought she'd be safe."

He heard the *but* in her tone. "Go on, say it. If I hadn't been so overprotective with Shannon, she might not be where she is now. And you're afraid I'll do the same with Tate."

"No, I think you're smarter than that. And that's why I believe you'll think with your head instead of your heart this time."

"Because that's worked so well for you, right?" He scoffed. "This from the woman who had no idea her own son was married with a baby on the way. I have to wonder why he never got around to telling you."

Chin quivering, she snatched up her purse. "I think I should go."

"Julia, wait." He caught up with her as she fumbled with the door latch. "I was out of line. I'm the last person who should blame any parent for lack of communication with their kid."

"But you're not wrong." She pressed her forehead against the closed door. "I've asked myself a million times why Steven didn't think he could talk to me about any of this. It kills me to realize I may never get answers now."

The pain in her voice ripped through Lane's chest. A part of him wanted to take her in his arms and tell her it'd be okay, just like little Tate had an uncanny knack for doing. But reassuring words weren't going to fix things. Neither would telling himself all the choices he'd made had been for Shannon's sake. What else could either of them do now except deal with the present and hope to do better for their grandson?

"Please," he said. "Don't go yet. Not like this, anyway. Besides, don't you want to be here when Tate wakes from his nap? He'll miss you if you're gone already."

"He'll be fine, and I've obviously overstayed my welcome." Straightening, she opened the door and stepped through without looking back. "I'll check with you tomorrow to see how Rowena's doing."

Watching her drive away, he berated himself for ruining the afternoon. If only he weren't so stubborn. If only he'd learn to bend a little…

CHAPTER SIX

"JULIA, TAKE A BREAK." Her mother, in for the afternoon to take care of some office work, snagged Julia's elbow as she rushed from one exam room to another.

"I can't, Mom. Did you see the waiting room? That emergency bowel obstruction put us behind by a good two hours."

"And you won't be of use to anyone if you don't take care of yourself." With a glance over her shoulder, she continued in a whisper, "I know you stepped in to assist with two of your dad's appointments. Then you skipped lunch for another interview."

"Yes, so you and Dad can both eventually retire with peace of mind." She forced a smile and eased her arm free. "Excuse me, but I really need to get to my next patient."

Before Julia could reach for the chart, her mother grabbed it and perused the details. "This is a routine checkup and annual vaccines. I'll handle it. And you, my dear, will get something to eat and put your feet up for fifteen minutes."

"Mom—"

Her mother breezed through the exam room door and closed it firmly behind her, leaving Julia gaping in the corridor. She debated between following her mother's orders or heading up front to call the next patient.

Her growling stomach and a glance at her watch—*it's 3:17 already?*—made the decision for her. After a detour to the break room for a container of blueberry yogurt and a coffee refill, she ensconced herself behind her desk and kicked off her shoes. After the day she'd had, it did feel good to finally draw a full breath.

Today's lunchtime interview held promise, anyway. Currently living and working in Billings, Dr. Gene Kruger had twelve years' experience and excellent references. He needed to relocate to Missoula for family reasons, but he'd promised one month's notice before leaving his current position. Julia only hoped she could hold out that long—and in the meantime hire a reliable office manager and possibly one more vet.

As she swallowed the last spoonful of yogurt, her thoughts drifted to the big gray wolf-hound…and to yesterday's disastrous end to the afternoon with Lane. Could they have been any more hurtful to each other? How was it that discussing the fate of one precious little boy could so easily bring out the worst in them?

As much as she preferred to avoid risking another argument, she did have a responsibility to the dog, and she'd told Lane she'd follow up today. Her only consolation was that weak cell service on the mountain meant she didn't have to actually speak with him.

Taking out her phone, she composed a text: Checking on Rowena. I'll come for her if necessary, but it will be much later. Busy day at the clinic.

The text showed *delivered*, and then she watched those three little dots come and go, suggesting he was composing a reply.

We're good, came the response. Leg looks okay, plenty of food. I'll text if any problems. Otherwise, check back in a few days.

A few days? Yesterday, he'd been apprehensive about keeping the dog for a single night. Guess he was equally averse to another clash of grandparent egos.

Or maybe he was already following through

with his threat to gain custody of Tate. Right. Keep Grammy Frasier at arm's length until he had all the official paperwork in place. Maybe he needed another reminder that he'd sought her out so they could collaborate on how best to care for the grandson they shared.

Nothing she could do about it at the moment, and she had plenty more patients to see before closing time.

Before she could drag herself from the chair, the intercom buzzed, followed by Dylan's voice. "Call on line two, Dr. J. It's a doctor from Mercy Cottage."

Wasn't that where Lane had admitted Shannon? But why would they be calling here?

She picked up the receiver. "This is Julia Frasier."

The caller identified herself as Dr. Irene Yoshida. "Shannon Halsey is my patient, and I understand she was married to your son, Steven."

"Yes, that's correct. I've never met Shannon, though." Then she blurted, "Actually, I never even knew about the marriage until three weeks ago."

"So I was told," the doctor said softly. "Shannon has recently expressed a desire to connect with her late husband's family, and I believe it would be helpful in her recovery if you could join us for one of our sessions. Would you be willing to do that?"

"I… I suppose so." She touched a hand to her throat. "When did you have in mind?"

"Possibly Thursday morning? I'd like to prepare Shannon for the meeting. And I'm sure you may need to prepare yourself." Tenderness laced the woman's tone. "I expect this will be very emotional for both of you."

No doubt about that. Julia opened the appointment calendar on her computer. Thursday morning looked fairly routine, and Mom probably wouldn't mind covering for her. "What time should I be there?"

"How does ten fifteen sound?"

"I'll make it work."

"That's wonderful. Thank you." Dr. Yoshida explained how to check in with reception and briefly what to expect during the session.

With her pulse thrumming, Julia couldn't guarantee she'd remember everything, but she attempted to respond appropriately. Hanging up, she wondered if Lane knew about his daughter's request. Not that he'd have any reason to object. Shannon had every right to want to meet her mother-in-law. And Julia certainly wanted to get to know the woman her son had loved and married and fathered a child with.

Fist knotted, she swiveled toward the credenza, her gaze drawn to Steven's photo. "Why?" she murmured. "Why did you think you couldn't tell me?"

AFTER RESPONDING TO the text from Julia, Lane buckled Tate into his car seat and drove partway down the mountain. For a conversation with his attorney, he needed reliable cell service.

"So what do you think, Harry? Is it doable?"

Harry Rowe, his former colleague at Clarkson, Glass and Howitt, hemmed and hawed for a moment. "Do I think you have a case? Possibly. But are you sure you want to go for full custody?"

"Shannon's doctor doesn't think she'll be getting out of the hospital any time soon, so I need to ensure my rights to make any and all decisions regarding my grandson." He glanced over his shoulder at Tate, who was paging through a storybook. He hoped the kid wasn't picking up on the gist of this conversation.

"There's a better likelihood of gaining temporary guardianship," Harry said. "It could be granted for up to six months, after which time it can be reassessed and extended if necessary." He paused. "As for your daughter, have you considered some level of conservatorship? It would strictly be for her protection."

Lane's legal career had focused on tax law and estate planning, so he wasn't up on the finer points of family law. "I hadn't thought of that. Can you get the ball rolling for me…on both counts?"

"I strongly advise you attempt to get your daughter's agreement first. Because if she resists, standing against her in court could have unpleasant ramifications."

"I hear you." Lane massaged his temple. Somehow, he'd have to make Shannon understand this was all for the best—both for her sake and for her son's.

"Gampy," Tate demanded from the rear seat. "Go home see Weena."

"In a minute, Tater Tot." He hadn't meant to sound so snappish. To Harry, he said, "Just… draw up a plan and get back to me, okay? The sooner, the better."

Over the next few days, life fell into a surprisingly comfortable rhythm. Lane hadn't thought having a dog around would turn out so well, but with Rowena helping to keep Tate entertained, it was proving easier to handle daily chores plus get some work done in his woodshop.

Should he be concerned that Julia hadn't been in touch since Monday? Either she'd stayed too busy at the clinic or she was outright avoiding him. Not that he could blame her after last Sunday. They definitely knew how to ruffle each other's feathers.

Like it or not, Bromley, you miss her.

More than he wanted to admit.

Late Wednesday afternoon, Harry texted to say he'd drawn up preliminary paperwork for Lane to look over and asked if he could make it into town first thing Thursday. Lane enlisted Lila Vernon to watch Tate, but once she grasped the purpose of Lane's trip into Missoula, she didn't hold back her opinions. "You're playing with fire, you know. No matter how good your intentions."

"It's only temporary, just until Shannon's better. She'll understand." *He hoped.*

He scooped up Tate for a goodbye hug. Warm and snuggly in his footed jammies, the little boy still smelled of the lavender baby lotion Lane had applied after his bath last night.

Tate patted Lane's whiskery cheek. "I go see Mama?"

"Not today, kiddo. Maybe soon." He set him down. "Be good for Aunt Lila, and take care of Rowena, okay?"

"I be good, Gampy." One eye narrowed, Tate jabbed a pudgy finger in his direction. "Gampy be good, too."

Lila chuckled. "That'll be the day." She reached for Tate's hand. "Let's go get you some breakfast, little man."

By eight twenty, Lane was sitting at a conference table with Harry Rowe while the attorney explained the documents he'd drafted and what the process would involve. Lane wasn't so far removed from practicing law that the details were over his head, but he was glad for Harry's expertise.

Forty-five minutes later, he sat back with a sharp exhalation. "How long to set all this in motion?"

Harry toyed with a pen. "I take it you haven't discussed any of this with your daughter yet."

"As soon as we finish here, I'll head over to Mercy Cottage. I'm hoping Shannon's doctor will help me convince her."

"Good. With Shannon's cooperation, I know a judge who might be willing to move things along quickly, especially considering you're already acting as your grandson's caregiver."

"Okay, then. I'll call you once I get everything squared away."

Lane's reply held more confidence than he felt. His stomach heaved just thinking about how Shannon might react. He had to remind himself that at her lowest point, she'd chosen to come home to him. That had to count for something, despite their years-long estrangement.

Even so, as he signed the Mercy Cottage visitors' log a few minutes before ten, his hands were so slick with perspiration that he could barely grip the pen.

The receptionist consulted her computer screen and then smiled up at Lane. "Dr. Yoshida is in session with Shannon right now. It may be another hour or so, but if you don't mind waiting, I'll inform the doctor you're here."

With Lila available to watch Tate all morning, waiting made more sense than arranging a time to come back later. Besides, he needed to get this guardianship thing moving forward. He nodded and took a seat.

Too jumpy to sit for long, he was soon pacing in front of the windows. When he glimpsed a familiar lime-green SUV pull into the parking area, his heart lifted briefly before questions and doubts kicked in. What was Julia doing here? Had she been here before? Was she already conspiring with Shannon to gain custody of Tate?

As she strode toward the entrance, she slowed near his truck and then halted abruptly. After giving it a thoughtful stare, she swung her head around until her piercing brown gaze collided with Lane's through the window glass.

He waited stiffly while the receptionist buzzed Julia in. She barely glanced his way as she approached the front desk.

"You're a few minutes early, Dr. Frasier," the receptionist said. "Make yourself comfortable, and Dr. Yoshida will call you back shortly."

Giving a nod, Julia turned toward the waiting area. She cast Lane an uneasy smile. "I didn't realize you'd be here."

He tipped his head toward the front desk. "I gather you were expected?"

She looked away briefly and adjusted the shoulder strap of her purse. "Shannon asked to meet me. Her doctor called me a few days ago to set this up."

Which meant she *hadn't* been plotting against him. Now he felt ridiculously paranoid.

Julia folded her arms. "Do you have a problem with my being here?"

"No." Actually, he had all kinds of feelings about her being here, but those could be a little hard to explain. "It's just—"

The inner door opened. An attendant in a white shirt and khaki slacks, obviously the staff uniform of the day, peeked out. "Julia Frasier? Dr. Yoshida is ready for you."

Drawing a shaky breath, she squared her shoulders and marched through. When the door whispered shut behind her, Lane was left feeling snubbed and resentful. He dropped down hard onto the nearest chair. What was wrong with him, anyway, that he'd begrudge his own daughter the chance to meet her late husband's mother?

As he hauled in several steadying breaths, his gaze lifted to a plaque he hadn't noticed before. Centered over the inner doors, it read, "Mercy unto you, and peace, and love, be multiplied.— Jude 2."

That stopped him cold. Moments of genuine peace had been few and far between these past few weeks—the last twenty-plus years, if he were honest. As for his current intentions, he couldn't be sure whether they were loving or merely selfish.

And mercy? For too long, it had been just a word to him. Abstract, intangible, mysterious.

Not for the first time, he pondered the fact that if he'd gone to the office for that forgotten file instead of sending Tessa, she'd still be alive. Even if he'd been shot and killed instead, their daughter wouldn't have grown up without a mother.

Can you ever forgive me, Tessa? Can our daughter?

He recalled his initial conversation with Dr. Yoshida the day he'd admitted Shannon. The first thing the slender, raven-haired doctor had suggested was that they pray together. Still too numb with shock to explain he put no stock in prayer, he'd nodded distractedly, ready to get the whole process over with. Now the closing words of Dr. Yoshida's prayer filled his thoughts: *Holy Lord, Your love is everlasting, and Your peace is beyond comprehension. In mercy may You surround, heal and uphold this family, today and always.*

Whether it was merely the words themselves or something—*Someone?*—more, he sensed the tiniest measure of that longed-for peace.

He didn't deserve it, didn't understand it, but maybe he didn't have to. Maybe that was the truest meaning of mercy.

JULIA HAD BOTH longed for and dreaded this meeting. The one thought tormenting her more than all others was that Shannon knew more about the last years of Steven's life—his hopes, his plans, his loves, his losses—than Julia might ever learn.

A dark-haired woman wearing tortoiseshell glasses greeted her in the corridor. "Hello, I'm Irene Yoshida. Thank you for coming." She offered her hand. "May I call you Julia?"

"Please." Accepting the polite handshake, she glanced past the doctor into an empty sunlit office.

"I'll have Shannon join us shortly," the doctor said as if reading the question in Julia's eyes. "First, I'd like to chat with you for a few minutes."

Dr. Yoshida showed Julia to a cozy sitting area at one end of the spacious room. When the doctor offered coffee, Julia accepted out of habit and then wished she hadn't. A jolt of caffeine wouldn't do her jangling nerves any favors. Sipping sparingly, she tried to smile as she replied to casual but clearly intentional questions about her work at the clinic, how long she'd lived in the Missoula area, how she'd managed as a single mom. Shannon must have mentioned the fact that Steven's parents were divorced.

"It wasn't easy," Julia replied, "but I had a lot of help from my mom and dad."

"I'm sure." The doctor's smile warmed. "Tell me more about your son."

"He— He was—" Her throat closed. She snatched a tissue from the box on an end table and pressed it beneath her eyes. "Sorry."

Leaning closer, Dr. Yoshida touched Julia's knee. "Never apologize for grief."

"I thought after two years it wouldn't hurt so much. But now…"

"Now you have a daughter-in-law you've never met and a grandson you never expected."

"Exactly." Voice breaking, she murmured, "It makes me wonder if I ever knew my son at all."

"Of course you knew him. But every child must eventually find his or her own way in the world. And if we look closely," the doctor continued with a thoughtful tilt of her head, "we will see our own reflections mirrored in the lives they have forged."

Julia was beginning to feel like *she* was the one in therapy. "So I'm the reason my son kept his marriage from me? It's my fault he couldn't tell me he was about to become a father?"

"Those are troubling questions, to be sure, and I'm sorry I can't offer answers." The doctor stood and moved toward the door. "I think it's time for you to meet Shannon. I sense God has a plan for you to find strength in each other on this path toward healing."

God? A plan? Right. Then where had He been all these years?

Julia barely had time to process the absurd thought before Dr. Yoshida reappeared, her arm around the shoulders of a pale, slender blonde. "Shannon, this is Steven's mother."

Julia stood, her heart suddenly so full she could hardly breathe. This was her son's wife, the mother of her grandson. *My daughter-in-law.*

"Hi," she said, her voice a mere tremor. "I'm Julia."

As if in slow motion, the girl stumbled toward her and threw her arms around her neck. "I miss him. I miss him so much!"

She returned Shannon's embrace, their tears mingling. "I know, I know. I do, too."

"He'd be so mad at me right now."

Julia tipped her head back to peer into Shannon's eyes. "Oh, honey, why would you think such a thing?"

"Because I can't take care of our son. I can't even take care of myself."

She pressed Shannon close. "Steven would

understand how hard it's been, everything you've had to face without him. He—" she choked back a sob "—he was the most forgiving, caring person I ever knew."

Shannon's head jerked up and down in fierce agreement. "That's why I need him, why I can't go on without him."

"Honey, you have to." She gave the girl's shoulder a reassuring rub. "That's why your dad brought you here, so you can get well and get back to being Tate's mom."

The girl shifted, tilting her tear-streaked face to look up at Julia. A smile lifted the corners of her mouth. "I get it now. You're the answer to my prayer."

"What?" She glanced across the room to where Dr. Yoshida observed from a distance. The woman's brows lifted, whether in concern or curiosity, Julia couldn't tell.

Gripping Julia's hands, Shannon tugged her over to a settee. "I only came home to my dad's because I was sick and desperate and didn't know where else to go. But now I'm in here, and Tate's up there on the mountain with him—"

"If you're worried about Tate, I promise you, he's doing fine."

"You don't understand." Shannon's voice rose. "I don't know how long I'm going to be here, and I can't bear the thought of my little boy so...so *alone* up there." Her fingers tightened around Julia's. "But you could take him. You could keep him until I'm well. Please—"

Dr. Yoshida strode over. "Shannon, remember how you've been practicing to stay calm."

Trembling, the girl nodded. Hand to her chest, she inhaled through her nose, then blew out slowly through pursed lips. "Sorry. I just— I just—"

"It's okay," Julia soothed. She didn't dare say aloud how much she'd been hoping for the very thing Shannon was asking of her. "I know it's hard being away from your son, but it's obvious your dad loves him very, very much. I visit them every chance I get." Remembering the photos she'd taken of Tate last Sunday, she tugged her phone from her purse. "Look, Tate has a new friend. This is Rowena."

Shannon's eyes brightened even as fresh tears fell. "My baby boy has a dog." A tiny laugh bubbled up as she touched the image of Tate hugging Rowena's neck. "She's so big."

"But gentle as can be." Julia's throat tightened. "Steven always loved big dogs, too."

It was the wrong thing to say. Doubling over, Shannon hugged her knees and burst into uncontrollable sobs. Dr. Yoshida stepped into the corridor briefly, and moments later, two attendants gently escorted Shannon from the room.

Julia stood on shaky legs. "I'm so sorry."

"Not your fault. Such breakdowns are all part of the healing process." The doctor glanced at her watch. "I've been informed Shannon's father has come to visit her but wants to discuss something with me first. It would be of value to Shannon's plan of care if I could speak with you and Mr. Bromley together. Would you mind?"

"I suppose not." What else could she say?

A few moments later, Lane lowered himself into the chair next to hers. Jaw muscles bunching beneath his whiskers, he shot Julia a quick glance before addressing Dr. Yoshida. "I'd prefer to talk with you privately concerning a, uh, personal matter I need to handle with Shannon."

The back of Julia's neck tingled. "If this involves Tate, I think I'd better hear it, too."

Before the doctor could comment, an attendant called her to the door. Turning to Lane and Julia, she apologized that she had a "patient situation" to deal with and would have to postpone their conversation until a better time.

Julia only hoped the patient involved wasn't Shannon. She'd never witnessed such brokenness in another human being. After Steven's death, she'd denied herself the consolation of a full-blown meltdown—not in front of her parents, and most certainly not with the church-sponsored grief support group they'd dragged her to. One meeting, and she was out of there.

Lane's touch to her arm pulled her out of the memories. "Julia? You okay?"

"Yes, I'm fine." Squaring her shoulders, she faced him. "I fervently hope this 'personal matter' you referred to isn't what you brought up last Sunday. Because it would be a huge mistake."

CHAPTER SEVEN

LANE'S FRAGMENTARY PEACE was long gone. He met Julia's glare with one of his own. "How is it a mistake to want to protect my daughter and her son?"

"Of course you want to protect them. So do I." Looking toward the door, she shuddered. "But if you could just for a moment grasp a mother's fierce love, the all-consuming drive to ensure your child's future, to protect him from everything you couldn't control about your own life…"

He suspected she wasn't merely talking about Shannon. Even so, he got the message loud and clear, and it hurt. "She told you she doesn't want me keeping Tate."

Her eyes fell shut. "Yes."

He strode to the window. It was a bright morning, sunlight glinting off the windshields in the parking lot, a breeze stirring leaves just beginning to turn. How could the world appear so calm out there when here in this room he felt like his insides were being ripped apart?

How much more damage can you do to the daughter you profess to love?

He reached into the inside pocket of his jacket and removed the thick brown envelope containing the documents Harry had prepared. Without a word, he handed it to Julia.

She cast him a dubious frown. "What's this?"

"Exactly what you think. Almost, anyway." Sinking into his chair, he palmed his eye sockets. "I'm only trying to look out for my daughter and grandson. *Our* grandson."

Papers rustling told him Julia had opened the envelope. He kept his head down as she perused the contents.

Just when he couldn't bear the silence any longer, she murmured, "I hate to say it, but this makes sense."

He swung around to face her. "You mean it?"

"Yes, I do." Acquiescence softened her tone. "Someone does need to manage Shannon's affairs while she's hospitalized. And someone needs the legal authority to make care decisions for Tate."

"But apparently, Shannon doesn't want that

someone to be me." Lane sank deeper into the chair. "And if I push her on this, she'll hate me more than she already does."

"She doesn't hate you, Lane."

"How do you know?"

"Because when she hit rock bottom, you're the one she came to." Julia touched his arm. "You're her dad. You'll always be her dad."

"The dad who failed her. We've already established I'm to blame for driving her away in the first place."

"Stop right there." She gave his arm a shake. "Dwelling on whatever mistakes you made in the past isn't helping Shannon or you, and especially not Tate. All that matters is doing the right thing now."

"Which is…what? Because where my daughter's concerned, I'm not exactly batting a thousand."

The legal documents rested on her lap. She tapped the stack with her index finger. "This, right here. But with one small change, if you're willing."

He studied her. "I'm listening."

"Include me as co-guardian."

The suggestion threw him for a moment. "How would that work, exactly? I mean—"

sarcasm entered his tone "—considering how you and I are always so much in agreement."

Wincing, she glanced away. "I know I can be opinionated and somewhat controlling—"

"You mean bossy?" He couldn't stifle a chuckle. When she glared at him, he swiveled to gently seize her wrists. "Hey, I need 'bossy' sometimes to counteract my own stubbornness."

That brought a smile from her. "At least you finally admitted it."

"So we've both got our faults." Suddenly conscious of their physical closeness, he released his hold on her and sat back. "If joint guardianship is even a legal option, we'll have to do a better job of communicating."

"I promise to try if you will."

The door eased open, and Dr. Yoshida stepped in. "Oh, you're both still here."

"Sorry, we got to talking," Julia said as she and Lane stood. "We'll get out of your way."

"If you can stay a little longer, I have time now for our conversation." When all were seated again, she went on, "I just came from Shannon's room. She's much calmer now, but she's had an emotionally exhausting morning.

I'm sorry, Mr. Bromley, but it might be better to visit her another time."

"Of course. Whatever's best for my daughter."

Dr. Yoshida adjusted her glasses. "I believe you had something specific in mind when you asked to see me."

"I did, but…" He glanced over at Julia.

"Before you returned," she supplied, "we were discussing temporary guardianship for Tate. Also, Lane has consulted an attorney about establishing a conservatorship for Shannon while she's in treatment." She passed the document across to the doctor.

After taking a few moments to look it over, Dr. Yoshida nodded. "Many of our patients have such arrangements with family members. I can certainly talk about this with Shannon and help her understand the implications."

"It's only until she gets well," Lane stated. "Please assure her I'm not trying to take over her life. And same with Tate's guardianship." He explained he and Julia would be looking into a shared arrangement.

"I'm sure that would be a relief for Shannon. I hope you can work out the details." The doctor stood. "I'll be in touch about this soon. I'd also like to arrange for you to bring Tate one day next week. By then, I believe Shannon will be emotionally ready for some time with her little boy."

"That'd be great," Lane said as the doctor held the door for them. "Tate's really been missing his mom."

At the threshold, Julia paused. "What about Tate's feelings? What will it do to him to have a short visit with his mother and then have to be separated from her again?"

Lane gnawed his lip. "Julia's right. It took nearly three weeks before he stopped asking for his mom several times a day—and then only after the dog came to live with us."

"Dog?" Curiosity lit Dr. Yoshida's expression.

"A stray I treated at my clinic." Julia briefly explained about Rowena and how the dog had become a companion for Tate.

"I had serious doubts at first," Lane added, "but those two are inseparable now." He shared a warm look with Julia and then had trouble tearing his gaze away.

The doctor nodded thoughtfully. "Then bring the dog with you for the visit. She'll serve both as a conversation focus and comfort for Tate when it's time to return home."

"Okay, we'll give it a try."

JULIA WAS HAPPILY surprised at the way her trip to Mercy Cottage had concluded. Could she and Lane have finally reached the point of declaring a truce? His heart was in the right place. She'd never doubted that. And she was slowly becoming resigned to the fact that Tate should stay at Lane's for the time being. However, if this shared guardianship thing worked out, at least she'd have a say in whatever decisions needed to be made.

On their way out to the parking area, Lane said he'd contact his attorney friend to discuss revising the petition. "Or…maybe you'd like to go along? I can call him right now and see if he's available. We could even get some lunch somewhere on the way."

His hopeful tone, not to mention the boyish glint in those smoky green eyes, stirred something deep in Julia's chest.

Admit it, he's burrowing a little deeper under your skin every time you're around him.

But she needed to be sensible. There was no room in her life to entertain anything resembling romantic interest, whether with Lane Bromley or anyone else on her radar.

Except there was no one else. She hadn't allowed anyone this close since Steven's dad had thoroughly let her down—let them *both* down.

Lane scuffed his boot heel on the sidewalk. "Forget it. I know you're busy."

Wincing, she glanced away. "My mom's been covering for me at the clinic, and I really need to get back."

"And I should head home to relieve Lila. I hadn't expected to be gone this long."

"Well, there you have it. Two busy people with things to do and places to be." Her light-hearted lilt was the only defense against the part of her that wanted to throw obligation to the wind and find out what, if anything, could come of this reluctant friendship.

"Okay, well…have a good day." He cringed the instant the words left his mouth. "Wow. How corny did *that* sound?"

Corny actually looked pretty cute on the guy. Hiding her smile, Julia moved toward her SUV. "You have a good day, too. Give Tate a hug from Grammy, and tell him I'll come see him in a couple of days."

"I'll do that. And… Julia?"

She met his gaze over her open car door. "Yes?"

"The guest room's yours anytime you want to stay for the weekend."

"And risk getting snowed in again?" She shivered just thinking about it—and *not* because of feeling cold. Nope, it was forced proximity with an all-too-attractive mountain man. "Not sure I want to chance it."

He shrugged. "Just offering."

Hard to believe the man used to be a lawyer. Weren't they supposed to have poker faces? Lane Bromley wore his emotions too close to the surface, and right now, disappointment was written all over his face.

Great. The obvious signs were getting harder to ignore. She could tell he was starting to like her, too. Could this relationship get any more complicated?

Sliding behind the wheel, she called, "Keep me posted about the guardianship plan. I'll be in touch about visiting Tate this weekend."

She glimpsed his half-hearted wave as she backed out of her parking spot, and then his wide-mouthed stare an instant before a car horn blared. She slammed on the brakes in time to miss crashing into a minivan. Hands shaking, she watched in the rearview mirror for the van to go on by.

A tap on her side window startled her. It was Lane. "You okay?"

She lowered the window. "Other than slightly embarrassed? A few too many things on my mind, apparently."

"Just be careful." A half smile turned up one corner of his mouth. "Tate needs both his grandparents around."

Returning his smile, she began to relax. They could do this. Whatever differences lay between them, wherever this inconvenient—and apparently mutual—attraction might lead, they could handle anything for the sake of their precious grandson.

JULIA'S PHONE VIBRATED as she moved between patient rooms on Friday afternoon. She snatched it from her lab coat pocket and read the incoming text from Lane: Update from my attorney. We need to talk. Coming up tomorrow?

Could he be any more cryptic? Since yesterday, she'd done her best to put both Lane and the co-guardianship idea out of her mind. It was exhausting enough managing her patient load while also reviewing résumés and discreetly keeping an eye on her dad. Now Lane had her worried that their idea had hit a snag.

Dylan passed her in the hallway and then backtracked. He glanced in both directions before facing her. "I was in an exam room with your dad a few minutes ago, and…he's not looking so good."

She stiffened. "What do you mean?"

"Several of us have noticed his hands shaking," Dylan whispered. "Amy said you've been keeping it on the down-low, and we want to respect his privacy. But for a moment just now, his speech seemed a little slurred. He laughed it off and recovered quickly, but you should get him to see a doctor."

"Yes, I know." Her stomach twisted. How much longer could she count on the staff's discretion?

How much longer before something went disastrously wrong and they were caught up in a costly malpractice suit? Even worse, what if these minor episodes her father seemed determined to ignore proved to be signs of a far more serious health condition?

She touched Dylan's arm. "Thank you for coming to me. Please assure the staff that my mother and I are keeping a close eye on the situation. If anyone ever feels at all uneasy about my father's ability to treat a patient, don't hesitate to ask me or my mother to step in."

"I understand. If there's anything any of us

can do to help, just ask." He started to go, then turned back to say, "It'll all work out, Dr. J. We're praying for your dad. And for you."

"Th-thanks," she murmured, realizing only after Dylan had walked away that she meant it.

Usually, when anyone mentioned they'd be praying for her, a sour taste rose in her mouth. Those were just empty words and false comfort. But since yesterday, she hadn't been able to stop thinking about Dr. Yoshida's remark that God had a plan for her and Shannon. And then Shannon's unexpected words, *You're the answer to my prayer...*

How could she be *anyone's* answered prayer when she could barely manage her own hectic life?

The exam room door in front of her cracked open, and Amy peeked out. "Lucy's ready for you, Dr. J. It looks like an eye infection."

"Be right in. I, uh, just need to...um..." She looked down at the hand clutching her cell phone. It was shaking harder than she'd ever observed her father's tremble. She thrust both hands into her pockets. "Excuse me," she muttered, and fled to her office. Slamming the door, she collapsed against it.

What is wrong with me? She never used to get

this rattled. She was always the one people came to when they needed clear thinking and an orderly plan of action.

Someone tapped on the door. "Dr. J, it's Amy. Sorry, but Lucy's howling up a storm, and Mrs. Springer is getting impatient."

She swiped at her damp cheeks. "I need a minute, please."

A pause. "Can I get you anything?"

"No, thanks," she said with forced brightness. "I'll be right there."

Straightening her shoulders, she checked her appearance in the mirror behind the door. She hadn't shed enough tears to ruin her makeup, but the face staring back at her looked anything but calm and in control.

A pained laugh escaped. "Nothing a week or two at a secluded beach resort wouldn't cure."

Who are you kidding?

It would take a lot more than a tropical vacation to fix everything wrong in her life. There was no escaping her father's failing abilities or the pressure to keep the clinic up and running. She certainly couldn't duck out on her grandson. And she could never in a million years outrun her grief over losing her son.

Yet she kept trying, didn't she? She kept attempting to control everything, even her emotions. Wasn't that just another form of escapism?

On the other hand...what if all this tumult was the cosmos—*God?*—telling her it was time to try a different approach? Did she have the courage to drop the reins, to admit she didn't always have the answers, to lean on someone else instead of thinking she had to do it all?

She turned away from the woman in the mirror and reached for the doorknob. She only needed to hold it together for two more hours. Then later, alone with her thoughts and those two needy but lovable dachshunds she shared her home with, she'd figure all this out.

Or not.

IN HIS WORKSHOP Saturday morning, Lane looked up from the bookcase he was staining and grinned at the sight of Tate playing ball with Rowena. The kid had scooted into one corner of the portable play yard and was rolling the ball across to the dog in the opposite corner. She'd gotten the hang of corralling it between her front paws and then nudging it back to him with her nose. Each time, he'd clap his hands and release one of his high-pitched giggles.

Too bad Julia had to miss this. The thought

reminded him she'd never responded to his text yesterday afternoon. She wasn't going to like Harry's answer regarding co-guardianship, so Lane had decided it'd be better to explain in person. He'd assumed she'd drive up today after the clinic closed at noon, but now he was beginning to wonder. She did have a life beyond her career and her grandson…although he couldn't claim to have seen any evidence of that.

Nope, Julia Frasier was as doggedly single-minded as he was.

He snorted at his own pun. Since Rowena had joined the family, he'd discovered he was more of a dog person than he would have believed.

After finishing with the bookcase, he washed up at the work sink, collected Tate and Rowena, and headed to the cabin. While the two of them trotted ahead, he checked his phone to make sure he hadn't missed a reply from Julia.

Still nothing. He paused at the foot of the deck stairs and debated whether to text her again.

Then a motion caught his eye. He jerked his head up to see Tate already halfway up the steps and tumbling backward. The phone fell to the ground as Lane dived to catch his grandson—

except Rowena beat him to it, blocking Tate's fall with her big furry body. Whether going upstairs or down, how did the dog always seem to know that she should position herself a couple of steps below Tate?

Heart thudding, and even more grateful for Rowena's presence, he leaned past her to snatch up Tate. After giving the kid a quick once-over, he clutched him against his chest. "How many times have I told you to wait for Gramps before going up the steps?"

"I sorry, Gampy." Tate freed one of his hands to pat Lane's cheek. "No be mad, otay?"

"I'm not mad, Tater Tot." He should be angry with himself for not paying closer attention. "You scared me, is all. You could have been hurt really bad."

"I not hurt. Weena save me."

"She did indeed." He made a conscious effort to slow his racing pulse and made a mental note to give the dog a big hunk of the elk steak he'd set out to thaw for tonight's supper.

Which reminded him he'd been about to try Julia again before Tate's stumble. He glanced around for his phone and found it near his boot, the screen a spiderweb of cracks. Groaning, he stooped to retrieve it.

Tate poked out his lower lip. "Uh-oh. Gampy phone have owie."

"Yep, looks like it's a goner." So much for checking in with Julia. Or anyone else, for that matter. "How about some lunch? You hungry?"

They sat down to Tate's favorite, tortillas and sliced turkey with hummus. The mixture of flavors was starting to grow on Lane, although he liked his with a dash of Tabasco. After lunch, he propped Tate on his lap in the rocking chair and read him a story before taking him upstairs for a nap. As usual, Rowena curled up on the fuzzy dog blanket he'd spread near Tate's crib. Her loyalty to the boy continued to amaze him.

Next, he puttered around the cabin, sweeping the floor, wiping kitchen counters and dabbing water spots off the bathroom faucets. Then, just in case Julia decided to stay over—if she even made the drive up this afternoon—he freshened the spare room.

With no sign of her by midafternoon, he grew more than a little concerned. The Julia Frasier he'd come to know was prompt and organized, not to mention tenacious about ensuring Tate's well-being.

He poked at his cell phone again, confirming the thing was hopelessly dead. His communications backup was shortwave radio, not that he expected to reach Julia that way, but he could ask the Vernons to relay a text message.

Upstairs, he peeked in on Tate and Rowena, both still fast asleep, then continued down the hall to his study. As he pulled up a chair in front of the radio, his ears picked up the metallic squeal of his front gate. He darted back downstairs and out to the deck, his heart lifting at the sight of Julia's lime-green SUV turning in.

He waited at the bottom of the steps while she parked and then strode over. "I wasn't sure—"

She threw open her door and practically jumped from the vehicle. "I've been texting you since noon. Is everything okay?"

"Yeah, yeah, it's fine." Steadying her with a gentle grip on her forearms, he offered an embarrassed frown. "I had a little accident with my cell phone." Better all around if he spared her the details.

Face contorting in a mixture of relief and annoyance, she jerked her arms free. "Don't scare me like that ever again!"

"What was I supposed to do? Drive all the way into town and tell you in person just so you wouldn't worry?" Bad enough how he'd worried about *her*.

"Well, you could have— I don't know—" She turned away, her shoulders rising and falling in a long, purposeful breath. When she faced him again, a semblance of calm had returned. A forced calm, if he was any judge, as was her tight smile. "Sorry for overreacting. Accidents happen."

He set his hands on his hips. "What's going on with you, Julia?"

"Nothing." After another deep breath and an exaggerated eye roll, she muttered, "What you've just witnessed is my attempt—and obvious failure—to stop being such a control freak."

A laugh exploded from deep in his chest. At her hurt expression, he immediately silenced it. "Tate should be waking up from his nap soon. How about we go inside and put on a pot of coffee?" Arching a brow, he added, "I'm thinking decaf."

This time, a genuine smile lifted the corners of her mouth. "That's probably wise."

Following her up the steps, he couldn't deny there was something different about her today. For one thing, she'd passed up a perfect opportunity to rake him over the coals about his broken phone and the dangers of being so isolated up here on the mountain.

But how long would her attitude adjustment last once he told her that Harry Rowe had nixed the co-guardianship idea?

CHAPTER EIGHT

"No possibility of co-guardianship? That's just great." Julia shoved up from the kitchen table and paced to the counter. Good thing they were drinking decaf, or she'd be slamming cupboard doors right now.

"Don't shoot the messenger." Lane lifted both hands. "I'm only relaying what my lawyer told me."

"And I suppose the thing about possession being nine-tenths of the law means I have zero rights where my grandson is concerned."

"Once again, Tate is and always will be *our* grandson. Anyway, that old saying has no real legal basis."

She huffed. "It's still pretty much true in this case, isn't it?"

"Julia, would you—"

"Gampy!" Tate's shrill voice echoed from upstairs. "I wake!"

Directing an exasperated frown her way, Lane excused himself.

The interruption gave Julia time to bridle her runaway temper. So far, her resolve to be less controlling wasn't going very well. Why did it always come down to a choice between commanding the situation or getting her needs and wants trampled by everyone else? There had to be middle ground, didn't there?

Hearing a trio of footsteps, she pasted on a cheerful smile for her grandson. Rowena appeared first. She stopped at the bottom of the staircase, tail wagging, and licked Tate's cheek as he hopped off the last step. Warmth flooded Julia's chest at the picture those two made. Later, she'd give the dog a quick once-over and check the cast leg.

She knelt as Tate toddled into the kitchen. "There's my sweetie pie!"

"Gammy!" He tumbled into her outstretched arms. "Miss you, Gammy."

"I missed you, too." She kissed his forehead, gripped his tiny shoulders, and looked him up and down. "Wow, I think you've grown an inch since I saw you last Sunday."

Lane made a show of massaging his lower back. "I'm pretty sure he's gained a couple of pounds."

"I big now." Tate puffed out his chest and gave it a boastful pat, eliciting laughter from both his grandparents.

While Lane made a snack for Tate, Julia returned to her chair and pulled the little boy onto her lap. "Have you had a fun week with Rowena?"

He nodded fiercely. "We p'ay ball. An' Weena save me."

"She did?" Julia knit her brow.

"Here you go, Tater Tot." Lane set a saucer of banana slices on the table, then scooped him off Julia's lap and plopped him into a chair. "And don't feed Rowena your banana. I'll get her a treat from the pantry."

"Otay, Gampy."

When Lane returned with a handful of dog treats, Julia whispered, "Rowena saved him? What's he talking about?"

"Nothing. She always keeps a close eye on him." Lane offered the treats to Rowena before sitting down and taking a swig of coffee.

Mumbling over a mouthful of banana, Tate said, "I fall an' Gampy phone got owie."

Julia gaped at Lane. "He *fell*?"

"I told you, it was nothing. You can see he's perfectly fine."

"There's clearly more to it than you're saying. How exactly did Rowena *save* him?"

Lane grimaced. Avoiding her icy stare, he described how he was distracted checking his phone, and how Tate stumbled on the steps with Rowena right behind him. "It only happened because I was worried about *you*," he said, a defiant twist to his mouth. "You never answered my text yesterday."

Julia cycled through indignation, amazement, gratitude and finally chagrin. "Yesterday wasn't one of my better days." Slanting him a look, she added, "And that's in large part thanks to you."

"Me?"

"On top of everything I was dealing with at the clinic, your cryptic message threw me for a loop. Which reminds me." She cast a wary glance at Tate, who was methodically nibbling around the edges of a banana slice. "We haven't finished our discussion."

Lane pulled a hand down his face. "I wanted the co-guardianship thing to work as much as you did. As I was about to explain before Tate woke up, for a judge to even consider it, we'd have to be married or, at the very least, living together as a couple."

"Well, *that's* never happening." She slapped the table.

Startled, Tate gaped at her. "Gammy mad?"

"No, honey." She immediately regretted the outburst. "Grammy's just feeling a little cranky."

Lane went to the sink and came back with a wet cloth to wipe Tate's mouth and fingers. "I've got even more reason to be cranky," he muttered. "I thought we'd found a solution that would placate Shannon. She'll never grant me sole guardianship, even temporarily."

Julia stifled the momentary burst of satisfaction. Her chances of having Tate live with her may have just shot up, but gloating would serve no purpose. Besides, she had yet to work herself into a position to keep him full-time, especially after what Dylan had mentioned yesterday about her father.

The reminder made her stomach knot. She and Mom couldn't keep putting off the hard conversation they needed to have with Dad. Being forced to confront his failing ability to serve their patients would break his heart, but the clinic's reputation was at stake, and Dad, more than all of them, would want its success to continue.

"So I was hoping you'd help me convince

her." Lane brought over the coffee pot and topped off her mug.

She glanced up. "Sorry, what were you saying?"

"Shannon. The guardianship thing. Since she apparently trusts you more than she does me, maybe you could smooth things over about me keeping Tate until she's better."

Tate climbed down from his chair and tugged on Lane's jeans. "Go see Mama?"

"In a few more days, kiddo." Lane tousled the boy's mop of dark hair. "Hey, why don't you take Rowena to the living room? You can sit on the rug and roll the ball."

"Otay!" Tate patted the dog's side. "C'mon, Weena."

Cradling her mug, Julia rose and leaned in the archway. A wistful smile formed as she watched the boy and dog begin their game. "They are so sweet together."

"They are indeed."

Her thoughts returned to Lane's request, and she shifted to face him. "I only just met Shannon. I don't know what I could say to help your cause."

Jaw clenched, he crossed his arms. "Why? Because you'll be pushing her to grant *you* temporary guardianship?"

A week ago, even a day ago, the answer would have been a resounding yes. But now… "It pains me to admit it," she said over the growing lump in her throat, "but you've been right all along. I am presently in no position to—to take on—" Her voice broke, and she pressed a fist to her mouth.

"Hey, now." Lane stood and relieved her of the coffee mug, setting it on the table. He slid his arm around her shoulders.

She couldn't stop herself from leaning into him, and the warmth of his solid chest comforted her in a way she hadn't experienced in too long to recall.

Then awkwardness set in. Unable to look at him, she cleared her throat and stood erect. "I may have mentioned I've been a bit stressed lately."

He backed off only a small step, but to her, ridiculously, the distance felt like a chasm. He stuffed his hands into his jeans pockets. "How do we continually go off the rails with each other?"

"Good question." She dared a smile. The real question, one she couldn't ask aloud, was, what exactly was she beginning to feel for this man?

Propping himself across from her in the archway, he released a noisy breath. "We keep saying we're on the same side and both want what's best for our grandson, so let's start right there."

She cast him a pensive frown. "I'm listening."

"As I see it, even if co-guardianship isn't a legal option, it doesn't mean we can't make this work. I know you've had doubts about my ability to keep Tate safe up here on the mountain—"

"Which were only reinforced after you told me he nearly fell down the steps today."

Lane dipped his chin. "I *will* be more careful, you have my word. But since you're not able to take him right now anyway, it looks like you're going to have to trust me."

Tate's high-pitched giggle drew her attention back to the living room. He was vigorously rubbing Rowena's belly while she squirmed with pure delight and pawed the air.

Chuckling, Lane said, "That's one of their favorite games."

She sniffed to hold back a sudden spate of tears. "Moments like these…that's what makes it all so hard."

"What? Why?"

"Because of everything I'm missing out on." Now the tears fell in earnest. "Even if I were to take him, I'd have to leave him with a sitter five or six days a week. I still wouldn't be there for all the special moments." Her heart lurched. "Just like I was never there for Steven."

Closing the space between them, Lane pressed her face between his strong but gentle hands. "I don't believe that." His gaze grew tender as he thumbed away the wetness beneath her eyes. "Not for a single minute."

"But it's true. After the divorce, I started working longer and longer hours. I was a desperate single mom just trying to make ends meet and—"

"You don't have to justify yourself to me." He drew her into his arms. "Your son knew you loved him, and based on everything I've gleaned from you and Shannon, you raised him to be a kind and caring young man."

"I miss him so much!" She nestled deeper into the softness of Lane's fleece vest. He smelled of soap and woodsmoke, masculine scents that made her feel protected, secure. Before today, she'd vehemently resisted such signs of weakness—the competent, controlled, independent Julia Frasier had no need of a man to comfort her.

Yet right now, right here in Lane Bromley's arms…it was the only place she wanted to be.

How MANY TIMES lately had he let his thoughts wander to visions of holding Julia exactly like this?

Well, not *quite* like this. Not with her so vulnerable, immersed in grief and regret. No, he'd pictured something a little more along the lines of two people who acknowledged their attraction to each other and were willing to chance a relationship in spite of their differences.

He grazed his lips across her forehead and felt her shiver. "Maybe we should…"

"I, um… Sorry." Sniffling, she edged away and brushed at her cheeks.

Lightly touching her elbow, he said, "We'll figure this out, Julia. Together. I don't know how exactly, but we will, because Tate needs you, and I… I need you, too."

She glanced back, brows pinched into sideways question marks.

"Well, I do." He tried to laugh off the remark, because otherwise she might read between the lines and make things *really* awkward. "I need you to hold me accountable—for both Tate and that silly dog you saddled me with."

"Oh, don't worry. I will." A glimmer of the snarky Julia he'd unexpectedly grown to care for shone through. "Which reminds me, I want to take a look at Rowena's leg before I go."

"You're not leaving any time soon, I hope. I'm grilling elk steaks for supper again."

"No arm twisting required." Smile returning, she shifted her gaze toward Tate and Rowena. "Besides, we've been so busy talking—"

He squeezed one eye shut. "Don't you mean arguing?"

"Okay, *arguing*—which I hope we can dispense with once and for all. What I was going to say is, I haven't spent enough time with that little guy today."

"Then have at it. I've got barn chores and a few other things to tend to before I start grilling. You guys can play as long as you want."

As he brushed past her, she caught his sleeve. "Lane?"

"Yeah?"

"Thank you."

Her unguarded smile made him long to kiss her—*really* kiss her this time. He swallowed hard before asking, "For what?"

"For being a friend when I needed one."

He could only nod. Then he berated himself all the way out to the barn for letting himself even think of wanting more from her. When

he'd explained that co-guardianship would require them to be a committed couple, her emphatic veto had stung. He wanted to believe the
swift reply had been pure reflex. He wanted to
believe she'd also felt something as he'd held
her.

He wanted to believe there was a reason Julia
Frasier had come into his life when she did.
For Tate's sake, certainly, but also because for
too many years he'd desperately needed someone like Julia. Someone spirited and determined
enough to drag him off this mountain—figuratively, if not literally—and back into the real
world again.

Filling the cow's feed pan, he snorted. His
cracked cell phone was one more reason he'd
be making the trek into Missoula. Until a few
weeks ago, he'd considered the phone a necessary nuisance. But finding himself suddenly cut
off today had been unnerving. If Julia hadn't
shown up when she did… He'd been minutes
away from loading Tate and the dog into the
truck and hightailing it into town to find her.

With evening chores attended to, he started
back to the cabin. No doubt about it, things
went much faster when he didn't have to set up
Tate in the portable play yard and then try to

keep one eye on him while he worked. He'd had a similar arrangement when Shannon was a toddler and managed fine—but that was twenty-plus years ago. Not that fifty qualified him as *old*, but a glance in the mirror confirmed the years were creeping up.

Years he could never get back. Mistakes he could never undo. Dreams that would forever go unfulfilled.

Tessa.

With a jolt, he realized she'd crept into his thoughts less often lately. Was it merely because he'd been preoccupied with the needs of their daughter and grandson...or because he'd begun to contemplate the future rather than regretting the unchangeable past while stagnating in the all-too-predictable present?

At the foot of the outer stairs, he glanced up to the window and saw Julia framed by the yellow-orange glow of lamplight. When she smiled and wiggled her fingers in a wave, his heart gave a tiny leap. The fatigue that had slowed his trek from the barn evaporated, and he jogged upstairs with the energy of his youth. They might be a long way from anything more than friendship, but he'd let it be enough—for now, anyway.

She met him at the door. "Thought you'd never finish out there. I'm getting hungry for that steak you promised."

"I'll fire up the grill right now."

Soon, they sat down to dinner, and by the time they finished, Tate was beginning to nod. Julia offered to get him ready for bed while Lane did the dishes. He'd just started the coffeemaker when she returned to the kitchen.

"Tate and his faithful companion are all tucked in." She rubbed her hands together. "Mmm, I smell fresh coffee."

Setting out two mugs, he grinned over his shoulder. "I can also break out my secret stash of dark chocolate, if you're interested."

Her brows shot up. "You have chocolate and this is the first I'm hearing of it? You are *so* in trouble, Lane Bromley."

As he went to the pantry, all kinds of hopeful feelings washed over him. Julia had seemed much more relaxed over dinner, their conversation flowing easily without so much as a hint of dissension. She'd opened up about herself—her failed marriage, Steven's childhood, her love for animals and her dedication to the family veterinary practice.

In turn, he'd shared about how he'd met

Tessa and their joy over Shannon's birth. He couldn't bring himself to talk much about Tessa's death, but he alluded to the pain and shock of suddenly finding himself a widower with a baby girl to raise.

There'd been moments of silence then, as if they'd each taken time to ponder their common experiences as single parents. As he reached for the canister where he kept his chocolate, he decided maybe he and Julia weren't that much different. They'd each coped as best they could with the hand God had dealt them.

The thought drew him up short. *So you're blaming God for your problems?*

Maybe before, yes. But if God really was in control, didn't He deserve gratitude for the good things, too?

The words on the plaque in the Mercy Cottage lobby flashed across his mind's eye: *Mercy unto you, and peace, and love, be multiplied.*

Truth be told, there'd been plenty of good in Lane's life. The peace he'd known on this mountain. Countless kindnesses from his friends the Vernons. The love of that little boy sleeping upstairs. His heart was opening up again, no denying it. If this was God's doing, he'd try a little harder to show his gratitude.

Julia's voice sounded behind him. "Did you get lost in there?"

Garnering his thoughts, he grabbed a chocolate bar and backed out of the pantry. "Just making sure my stash hadn't been raided."

"If I'd known it was there, it would already be long gone." She snatched the bar from his hand and studied the label. "Fair-trade eighty percent dark. Yum. You weren't kidding around."

"Dark chocolate has many health benefits." He tried to reclaim the bar, but she skittered out of reach.

"Uh-huh, I'm sure that's the only reason you buy it."

"It's an indulgence, but I'm disciplined about it. One square a day's my limit."

"Wow." She cast him a sheepish look. "I've already admitted my weakness for strong coffee. You can add dark chocolate to the list now, too. Here." She reluctantly handed over the chocolate bar. "You'd better take charge of this before I abscond with it."

Chuckling, he peeled back the foil wrapper, broke off an entire row of four squares and offered it to her. "Enjoy."

"Really? Thank you!" As she savored her first

bite, her eyes darkened with pleasure. "This. Is. So. Good."

"It tastes even better with coffee." He snapped one square off the next row for himself, then a second, just because. He quickly rewrapped the bar so he wouldn't be tempted to take more. Grabbing a couple of napkins along with his mug of decaf, he motioned toward the living room. "Shall we?"

He took a chance and joined her on the sofa—not so close as to intrude on her space, but near enough that if he stretched his arm across the back cushion, he might feel the silky sweep of her hair across his hand. The flickering firelight from the woodstove behind them created a cozy ambience…and maybe one that was also a tiny bit romantic? It hadn't been his intention, but now he felt inclined to go with it.

Grinning, he watched her finish the last bite of chocolate. After a sip of decaf, she sighed appreciatively. "You're right, coffee and dark chocolate are the perfect pairing. I'll have to… um…" Her voice trailed off as their gazes met.

He let his fingers creep along the back of the sofa. "Have to…what?"

"I forgot what I was going to say." A nervous laugh escaped. She set down her mug and stood abruptly. "I didn't realize how late it's gotten. I should go."

"Do you have to?" He followed her across the room as she scooped up her jacket and purse. "I mean, we're actually talking for a change. It's been nice, and I was hoping you'd stay awhile."

Turning, she frowned. "A lonely mountain man makes me dinner and tops it off with chocolate and pleasant conversation in a firelit room. Where, exactly, did you assume all this was leading?"

"Whoa. Totally wrong idea." Hands raised, he took a giant step backward. "I just thought if you wanted to talk a little longer, the spare room's still made up and—"

The chime of her cell phone interrupted him. Tugging it from her purse, she gave her head a quick shake. "Sorry, I shouldn't have jumped to conclusions. It's just…it's been a long time since…" She glanced at her phone screen and went suddenly pale. "Oh, no."

He moved closer. "What's wrong? One of your patients?"

"No. My dad. He—he's in the hospital." Her breath came in shallow gasps. She fumbled with her things, nearly dropping her phone as she reached for the doorknob.

"Julia, slow down." Stepping between her and

the door, he gripped her shoulders. "You're too upset to get behind the wheel. Let me drive you."

She hesitated. "But Tate—"

"I'll bundle him up. He sleeps fine in his car seat." With a firm stare, he added, "Promise me you'll wait right here while I get him."

When she gave a weak nod, he dashed upstairs. Jostling the boy as little as possible, he got him into his hooded jacket and wrapped a blanket around him. Rowena followed them downstairs and bolted out the front door ahead of them. She seemed determined not to let Tate out of her sight, and nothing Lane said or did could coax her back in the house.

"All right, girl, if you're gonna be that way, it looks like you're riding along." He didn't know how he'd manage with the dog at the hospital, but he'd figure it out later.

All he knew was that Julia needed him, maybe for the first time since they'd met, and he had no intention of letting her down.

CHAPTER NINE

LETTING LANE DRIVE her to the hospital seemed a wise decision. Julia tucked her icy fingertips beneath her crossed arms and tried to focus on breathing in and out as Lane sped down I-90 into Missoula.

As soon as they reached better cellular coverage, she phoned her mother for more details. Her mom told her they'd been making supper, and her dad had gone to the pantry to put away the olive oil. The bottle had slipped from his hand and cracked, sending oil across the tiles. The next thing they knew, her dad's feet had gone out from under him. He fell against the refrigerator, banging up his hip and shoulder pretty badly, but the doctor's most pressing concern was the possibility of a concussion and brain bleed.

It was nearing nine o'clock when Lane pulled to a stop at the emergency room entrance. "I'd go in with you, but…" He tipped his head toward the back seat, where Tate snoozed. Rowena, curled up on the seat next to him, rested her chin on his leg.

"Thanks, but I'll be okay." She shrugged and quirked a smile. "Maybe the silver lining in all this is that my father will finally have to face his limitations."

He nodded. "Text or call me when you know more. We'll be waiting in the parking lot."

She'd expected to be dropped off and for Lane to head back to the cabin. "Really, you don't have to stay." Although the fact that he'd offered warmed a tender spot in her heart. "You should get Tate home and back in his own bed."

Eyes darkening, he reached across the console to touch her arm. "I'm more worried about you."

Now she couldn't speak at all. When she found her voice, she murmured, "Then at least go over to my place. You can put Tate to bed in the portable crib." She handed him her keys. "And would you let my dogs out and put a scoop of food in their bowls? Rowena can have some, too. The canister is in the pantry."

"Sure. Don't worry about anything but looking after your dad."

Making herself open the door and get out of the truck was a thousand times harder than she'd imagined. Today, something had shifted in her relationship with Lane, and it both thrilled and terrified her. How long had it been since she'd allowed herself to be this open with anyone? To reveal her emotions with such honesty?

How long had it been since *not* being in control actually felt freeing?

She watched from beneath the portico as Lane drove away. When his taillights disappeared around the corner, she turned with a sobering breath and marched into the ER. The desk nurse buzzed her through the inner doors, and she found her mother alone in a curtained cubicle.

She gave her mother a hug. "Where's Dad?"

"More tests." Looking drained, Mom drew her toward two beige plastic chairs, and they both sat. "After I described what happened— and *why*—the doctor read your dad the riot act for not seeing our primary care physician about his symptoms long before now." She sniffed and blew her nose. "I blame myself, too. I should have been more insistent."

Julia scoffed. "How long have you been married to that guy now? Dad wrote the book on masculine mulishness." They shared a teary-eyed laugh. Serious again, Julia squeezed her mother's hand. "Has the doctor said anything yet about what could be going on with Dad?"

Mom shook her head. "That's what he's hoping the tests will reveal."

They both looked up as a nurse entered. "Just letting you know your husband is being admitted, Mrs. Frasier. They'll be taking him to his room in another half hour or so." She handed Julia's mother a slip of paper. "Here's the room number if you want to wait for him there."

"Thank you." Julia helped her mother to her feet. When Mom wavered, Julia gave her a hard look. "Did you even get to eat supper?"

"No, I guess not."

"Then let's go to the cafeteria first."

"But I couldn't—"

"You can, and you will. No matter what they find with Dad, you need to keep up your own strength."

On their way out to the corridor, Mom looped her arm through Julia's and patted her hand. "What would I do without you? You've always been the strongest one in the family."

If you only knew it's all a front! Especially tonight, when she only wanted to go home, change into her coziest robe and slipper socks, and find herself safely in the arms of the first man to burrow into her heart since those early years with her ex-husband.

The thought almost made her stumble. Her mother noticed. "Honey, are you sure *you're* all right?"

"A little tired, that's all." She gave herself a mental shake.

Because she could not—absolutely *could not*—be falling for Lane Bromley...could she?

LANE COULD HARDLY believe he was holding Julia in his arms, kissing her, being kissed in return, again and again and—

He sputtered awake to find two dachshunds prancing on his chest, their tongues going a mile a minute across his face. Next to his right ear, Rowena's hot, panting breath sounded like a locomotive.

"Hey! Knock it off, you guys." He jerked upright, sending Daisy and Dash scrambling to the other end of the sofa. Best he could recall, he'd nodded off shortly after Julia had called with an update around eleven fifteen last night.

Noticing daylight creeping through the blinds, he gave his messy hair a brisk rub. He heard Tate's whimpers coming from down the hall, the early morning, not-quite-awake kind that would soon give way to loud and forceful demands for breakfast.

No wonder the dogs had been trying to rouse him. Too bad he couldn't have lingered a little longer in that oh-so-sweet dream world.

As he brought Tate to the kitchen to scrounge up something to feed him, a knock sounded on the back door. He peeked through the curtain to see a disheveled Julia on the other side. He twisted the lock and yanked open the door.

She smiled wanly and patted Tate's cheek as she trudged inside. "Sorry if I woke everybody up. I gave you my keys."

"No problem. We were just getting breakfast." Still a bit groggy, Lane opened the fridge and then turned abruptly. "Wait. How'd you get here?"

"My mom dropped me off. She's on her way home to rest for a bit."

He studied her, concern in his eyes. "Looks like you should do the same."

"I will. But first…" She cast him a raised-brow stare. "I hope you aren't planning to give Tate *that* for breakfast."

Taking a closer look at the jar of pasta sauce

he'd grabbed from the fridge, he winced and tried to cover with an excuse. "Of course not. I was just moving it out of the way."

"Mmm-hmm."

"Gampy." Tate jabbed Lane's kneecap. "I hung'y wight now!"

Julia snorted. "Gramps, why don't you let me handle breakfast? Smells like you-know-who could use a diaper change."

By the time Lane returned with a freshly diapered and even *hangrier* little boy, all three dogs had their muzzles buried in their kibble bowls, and Julia had scrambled eggs and toast on the table. The aroma of hazelnut-flavored dark roast wafted from the coffeemaker.

As he settled Tate into his booster seat, he noticed Julia's cup held an herbal tea bag. "What? You're passing on your usual morning java?"

"When we're done here, I plan to take a good, long nap. I'll get my caffeine hit after I wake up."

After filling a mug for himself, Lane joined them at the table. Spooning eggs into Tate's bowl and then onto his own plate, he asked, "How's your dad this morning?"

"He's recovering okay from the fall—no concussion, just some bruises—but the neurologist they called in is pretty sure Dad has Parkinson's."

"Oh, wow. How's he taking it?"

"Not well. I think we're all in shock."

"Julia, I'm so sorry." Lane reached toward her across the table. "But at least you have answers, and he can be treated…right?"

"Meds can mitigate the symptoms, but there's no cure." She bit her lip. "If only I'd found the courage to confront him weeks ago. If only he'd seen a doctor sooner—"

"You can't let yourself go down that road. You…you have to trust…" Lane surprised himself with what he was about to say, but against all logic, he knew it to be true. He came around the table and knelt at her side. "You have to trust that God will take care of him. That God *is* taking care of him right this very minute and has been all along."

Brow furrowed, she frowned at him. "You really believe that? But I thought…"

"And you'd have been right." He tucked a loose strand of hair behind her ear. "I'm not real sure what's happening with me in the faith department. All I do know is that years of denying God did nothing but turn me into an embittered loner. So I guess I'm ready to give Him the benefit of the doubt, and I think it might be time you should, too."

"I don't know if I can." Looking away, she shook her head. "Honestly, I'm not sure I even remember how to pray."

Tate laid down his spoon with a clatter and folded his hands. "I pway, Gammy."

Lane and Julia both gaped at the boy.

He squeezed his eyes shut and tucked his chin. "God bwess Mama and Gammy and Gampy and Gate-Gammy and Gate-Gampy and Weena and Daisy and Dash and me." Looking up with a grin, he ended with a joyful "Amen."

"Amen," Lane and Julia whispered in unison.

He looked back at her to find tears cascading down her cheeks. Moisture filled his eyes as well, and he blinked rapidly to keep the wetness from spilling over. Rising to hand her a napkin, he asked, "You okay?"

She replied with something between a nod and a shrug. Mopping her face, she glanced at Tate, who'd returned to polishing off his eggs and toast.

"Guess I shouldn't be surprised our grandson knows how to pray. His mother obviously taught him well," she murmured.

"I'm ashamed to say Shannon didn't learn it

from me." He turned to fetch a handful of tissues from the box on the counter. Sharing most of them with Julia, he used one to blot his eyes and blow his nose. Back in his chair, he asked, "Was Steven a believer?"

"We stopped going to church when he was pretty young, but in college, he connected with a campus ministry." Her eyes welled again. "He tried countless times to share his faith with me, but I didn't want to hear it."

"I'm pretty sure faith doesn't come with an expiration date."

"Maybe not, but I—" A cavernous yawn interrupted her. "I'm too tired to think straight—about faith or anything else."

"I get it. I should be heading home anyway."

She gave a tiny gasp. "Oh, Lane, your livestock."

"I used your iPad to text Dan Vernon last night. Hope that was okay. He's looking after things at my place." He stood and brushed a brief kiss across her forehead. "Go on, get some rest. I'm going to stop somewhere and pick up a new phone, so you can text me later with any news about your dad. And don't worry, I'll figure out how to get your car to you."

She gave a weak nod and a smile of thanks.

Before he made it out the door with Tate and Rowena, she'd traipsed down the hall to her room.

Later, with a new cell phone in his pocket, he drove past the Elk Valley mini mall and recalled the day in the grocery mart when those friends of Julia's had introduced themselves. He now regretted how aloof he'd been in response.

He still had the business card around somewhere. Maybe the Wittenbauers wouldn't mind helping him get Julia's car back to her.

Then he remembered what the man had told him that day: *I feel like the Lord's telling me you could use a friend.*

Even more so, Lane desperately needed someone he could trust with a deep conversation about God and faith.

Yes, he just might give Witt Wittenbauer a call.

"JULIA FRASIER!" MADDIE WITTENBAUER sounded well past peeved. "Why did I have to hear secondhand that your father is in the hospital?"

"It all happened so fast, and then I came home and slept for six hours." Phone on speaker in her lap, Julia absently stroked Daisy and Dash, who were stretched full-length on either side of her in the recliner. "Wait. How *did* you hear about my dad?"

"From Witt, who learned it from your mountain man. He called to ask if Witt could ride up the mountain with him and bring your car back."

"Lane called Witt?" Julia shifted abruptly, causing the dogs to squirm into more comfortable positions. "I didn't know they were acquainted."

After a moment of silence, Maddie described how she and Witt had run into Lane at the grocery mart a couple of weeks ago. "Witt had a strong sense that Lane could use a friend, so he gave him his number. He gets those feelings sometimes, you know, like a nudge from God."

A lump rose in Julia's throat. How many times in the past few months had she caught Witt looking at her with those deep-set, discerning eyes, as if he and Maddie knew a secret she didn't? A secret they'd give anything to be able to share with her if only she'd lower her guard?

Steven had acted the same way the last several times he'd been home. Maybe they all knew something she didn't. Maybe they all had a faith she could never grasp.

I'm pretty sure faith doesn't come with an expiration date, Lane had said. She was counting on that.

"Anyway," Maddie continued, "during the drive up to Lane's, he said he needed some spiritual advice. He followed Witt to our house, and they just left to meet with Pastor Peters at the church."

If Julia had any sense—and if she didn't have a million things she should be doing in preparation for running the clinic without her dad—she'd have Maddie take her straight to the church to join them. God knew only too well how much help Julia would need to get her relationship with Him back on track.

In the meantime, maybe a long conversation with her best friend was in order. "Maddie, can you come over now?"

"I'll hop in your car and be right there. Witt can pick me up when their meeting's over."

Half an hour later, they sat at the kitchen table, Julia with a mug of coffee strong enough to kick her sluggish brain cells into gear, and Maddie with her favorite lemon-ginger tea. A plate of Maddie's homemade peanut butter cookies sat between them.

Julia nibbled on one. "I don't recall you doing much baking before you got married."

A wistful smile curled Maddie's lips. "Before Witt came into my life, I had no reason to." She wiggled a brow. "Perhaps there'll be more baking in *your* future soon?"

It was hard to miss the implication. Even harder to ignore her growing feelings for a certain mountain man. "I won't deny there's something between Lane and me, but it's too soon to know what to call it. And whatever it is, you won't find me going all Betty Crocker in the kitchen."

"Fair enough. So let's talk about what we both know is weighing heavily on your mind. I gather your dad's condition will force the retirement issue. How are you handling that?"

"Frankly, I'm at my wits' end. Interviews lately haven't been very promising, and it'll be another few weeks before the doctor we've hired will come on board. We still need an office manager, too."

Maddie touched Julia's arm. "I didn't mean just logistically. It must be hard to imagine being the only Dr. Frasier at the clinic."

Tears welled again as thoughts of Steven rose, along with all her dreams and plans for working alongside him. "Oh, Maddie, there are so many things I could—*should*—have done differently—as a daughter, a wife, a mother. Can God really forgive me for all my mistakes?"

"He already has." Maddie smiled. There was a faraway look in her eyes. "Something I've learned since first meeting Witt is that looking back should serve only three main purposes— to keep us from repeating our mistakes, to remind us how far we've come and to turn our hearts to God."

Julia scoffed. "I'm not sure I've come very far at all. But I do know I'm way past trying to make it on my own strength." She gazed at her friend through tear-filled eyes. "Can you help me find my way back to God?"

Joy sparked in Maddie's expression. She took Julia's hands in her own. "He never left you, sweetie. Just talk to Him. Tell Him what's on your heart."

It seemed both too easy and too hard. But she tried anyway. In fits and starts, she confessed the many times and ways she'd shut God out. She thanked Him for never giving up on her. She asked for the strength to relinquish control, and for the faith to turn full authority over her life to the Lord.

By the time her prayers died away, she and Maddie had both been reduced to a puddle of tears. "I know I still have a lot to work out," she said, "but I no longer feel like everything depends on me."

"That's exactly how I felt when Witt helped me find my faith again. For so many years, I prided myself in not needing anyone…until I discovered how much more beautiful life is when you're sharing it with someone who loves you." Maddie offered a knowing smile. "With someone you love in return."

"I have a feeling we're not just talking about God anymore." Julia gave her friend a hug. "I'm so happy you and Witt found each other."

Maddie gripped Julia's shoulders. "Oh, honey, we are *definitely* still talking about God. Do you think Witt and I would ever have gotten together without Him? And Lane and your sweet little grandson showing up when they did… If that isn't God's doing, I don't know what is."

She hadn't thought of it quite that way. Much as she'd come to cherish every moment she spent with Tate, when Lane first strode into her office with the news that they shared a grandson, in some ways it had felt like one more complication to work into her already too-complicated life.

And now these baffling feelings for Lane that she'd never in a million years expected. Talk about complications!

Needing space, she went to refill her coffee mug. She leaned against the counter and sipped slowly, thoughtfully. "How did you know with Witt? How'd you know it was the real thing?"

Maddie laughed. "I didn't, not at first. I only knew how he made me feel inside, how he gave me courage and made me want to hope again." Her gaze grew wistful. "Then, when we had our misunderstanding and he disappeared for a while, I didn't know how to go on. I think that's when I knew for certain, when I realized how desolate I felt without him."

Julia was definitely becoming a different person around Lane. A better version of herself, perhaps? Someone who didn't have to be perfectly in control. Someone who could enjoy a snowfall or a fireside cup of decaf or watching a boy and dog at play without continually rehashing everything she'd left undone and every problem she had yet to tackle.

Head tilted, Maddie studied her. "Why, Julia Frasier. You're falling in love."

She scoffed. "Whatever gave you that idea?"

"Because I recognize that silly smile," her friend replied with a wink and a grin. "It's the same one I see every time I happen to glance in the mirror while thinking of Witt."

Heat spread through Julia's chest and crept upward, warming her face. She'd sworn off romantic love the day she'd admitted her marriage was over. Dare she hope for a happily-ever-after this time around?

CHAPTER TEN

AFTER HIS CONVERSATION with Witt and Pastor Peters, Lane had a lot to think about—ideas and emotions he was better off wrestling with alone for a few days. Except he missed Julia something fierce. He wanted so badly to share with her all the insights bursting in his brain and heart. But she was likely preoccupied with her father and managing the clinic, and as intense as things had gotten last weekend, a little breathing room for both of them seemed advisable.

They did text a few times. He learned her father had been released from the hospital on Tuesday and was grudgingly accepting the inevitability of retirement. In the meantime, Julia had more interviews scheduled with applicants for the office manager and associate veterinarian positions.

Which meant she couldn't break free to accompany Lane on Thursday for Tate's first visit with his mom since she'd been admitted. It was a sunny September day that had warmed quickly, even more so down in the valley. Since dogs weren't allowed inside the hospital, Dr. Yoshida arranged for them to gather on the back lawn, so Shannon could watch her active little boy at play.

Rowena served as a big furry go-between, easing some of the discomfort lingering between Lane and his daughter. Shannon's medications, though somewhat sedating, seemed to have lifted the depression slightly. It was good to hear her laughter as Tate and Rowena entertained them all with their antics. Eventually, Tate began to tucker out and crawled into Shannon's lap.

"There's my sweet boy," she murmured, snuggling him beneath her chin. She offered Lane a cautious smile. "He's growing so fast."

"He is." Lane strove for an upbeat tone. This might be his best chance to earn Shannon's approval for temporary guardianship. "He's a happy little guy, too, no trouble at all. You can see what great pals he and Rowena are."

"I just wish…" She glanced toward the building and back at Lane. "Isn't Julia coming?"

"No, honey. I told you, she's tied up at the

clinic." He strove for patience in his tone. This was at least the fourth time since he'd arrived that Shannon had asked about Julia.

Swiping at an errand blond curl, she pursed her lips. "Sorry, I'm a little fuzzy-headed these days. It's my meds."

"I'm just glad you're doing better." Lane edged his lawn chair a little closer. "I… I've been praying for you, honey."

Her brow furrowed. "Really? I didn't think you…"

"Believed?" He released a self-conscious chuckle. "My faith is still about as small as the proverbial mustard seed, but I'm working on growing it."

"That's…that's good." Shannon's voice trailed off as she grew mesmerized by the swirl of hair at Tate's crown. The little guy had begun to doze in her arms.

Lane cleared his throat. "Honey, we need to talk about some stuff." When she looked up with a sleepy smile, he continued, "While you're here getting well, someone should have the legal authority to manage your financial affairs and to do whatever's necessary for Tate."

She studied him for a moment as if trying to make sense of his words. "Oh. Yes. Dr. Yoshida said you and Julia could both be Tate's temporary guardians."

His mouth went dry. He'd informed the doctor about his findings to the contrary, but apparently Shannon hadn't understood. "Uh, no, honey, I'm afraid it can't work that way." Briefly, he explained the legalities, as well as Julia's current personal difficulties. "So—on paper, anyway—it'd just be me as Tate's guardian."

Before he'd finished speaking, he could see Shannon's resistance mounting. "No, Dad. No. It could be a long time until I—until—" Her voice was trembling now, and tears slid down her cheeks. She clutched Tate against her chest and rocked frantically. "I won't have you raising my son up there on that lonely mountain. I won't!"

Startled from his nap, Tate squirmed and began to cry. Before Lane could intervene, Rowena was pawing at Shannon's leg and pushing against her arm with her snout. The dog's actions alerted hospital staff as well, and Tate was quickly back in Lane's arms while a nurse attempted to calm Shannon.

The kid had seen his mother at her worst too many times already, and Lane decided to remove Tate from the chaos. He snatched up Rowena's leash and made for the side exit.

Someone must have summoned Dr. Yoshida, because she met him on her way out. "I take it your visit didn't end well."

"I thought you were going to help her understand about the guardianship arrangements." He couldn't hold back the irritation in his tone.

"I brought it up several times in our sessions, but I can't be sure how much she grasped." She cast Lane a sympathetic frown. "Considering her fragile state, it may be necessary for you to take other measures."

In other words, having her declared legally incapacitated. He'd hoped with all his heart it wouldn't come to that.

How did the visit go?

Julia's text showed up a few minutes after Lane had tucked Tate in bed for the night. He wished he had strong enough cell service for a voice call. Maybe if he went out to the deck...

Two whole bars showed up—a gift—so he gave it a try.

She answered right away. "Lane? Where are you?"

"At the cabin. The wind must be just right."

"You sound tired."

Gaze drifting to the starry sky, he muffled a groan. "It's been a tough day."

"Did something happen with Shannon?"

"I tried to bring up the guardianship issues, but she reacted so badly that she scared Tate, and we had to leave." He pounded a fist on the deck rail. "She didn't leave me a choice, Julia. My attorney's taking action to get her declared legally incapacitated."

"Oh, no. Are you sure she can't be reasoned with?"

"Not now. Not like this. And Dr. Yoshida won't make any predictions about how long Shannon's recovery will take. It could be several months before she's well enough to manage her own life, let alone be responsible for Tate."

Julia didn't reply right away. "You know doing this without her consent could permanently damage your relationship."

He bristled. "What else am I supposed to do?"

Her sharp exhalation sounded in his ear. "I guess this is one of those times when we're supposed to trust God, huh?"

"Guess so." The tightness in his chest eased. "I wish you could have heard Tate's bedtime prayer tonight. He asked God to make his mommy happy again and be nicer to his gampy."

Julia laughed, then murmured shyly, "I've been praying this week, too. I can't tell if God's actually listening, but talking to Him is helping me feel more hopeful."

He smiled into the night and imagined God watching from somewhere up there. "It's kind of nice to know we're dipping our toes in this faith thing together."

"I heard you went with Witt to talk with their pastor."

"So now you've got your spies checking on me?" He said it in a teasing tone.

"I told you, Maddie's my best friend. We look out for each other."

He decided to go out on a limb. "So, uh, what would you say to meeting me at their church on Sunday?"

She hesitated. "You mean for worship?"

"Sorry, too much too fast. I get it."

"No, I... I think I might actually like that."

He squeezed his eyes shut. How was it possible at his age to feel like a gawky eighth-grader who'd just asked the prettiest girl in school for a date—and she'd said yes?

"Wow. Okay. Guess I'll see you—" Static crackled. "Julia? Are you there?"

"La— Can't—"

A series of tones sounded, then nothing. He still had one bar, so he typed a quick text: Sorry, lost service.

Julia: Sorry too. Nice we could talk tho.

Lane: On for Sunday then?

Julia replied with a thumbs-up and two praying hands emojis.

Only after he went inside did he realize he hadn't asked about her father's health or things at work. They also hadn't discussed whether she'd be driving up to the cabin Saturday afternoon for what was becoming her usual extended visit with Tate.

Maybe he could change things up this weekend. Rather than expecting her to drive an hour plus each way, he could take Tate and Rowena to her place and make dinner there. She'd had a rough week, and it would feel good to do something nice for her.

Face it, Bromley. You'd jump at any excuse to be near the woman.

JULIA HOPED THE Lord wouldn't frown upon the fact that her overriding motivation to actually set foot in a church again was Lane, because if not for his invitation, she might have required a whole lot more convincing. True, her parents had continued their gentle nudges, which typically increased around Christmas and Easter. Eventually, she'd let them know that she was exploring her faith again. But until she made more progress, she didn't need them looking over her shoulder.

With Dad out of commission and Mom helping him adjust to his new reality, Julia had been managing the clinic mostly on her own and working late into the evening most days. On Friday, though, the ideal office manager candidate showed up like an answered prayer—*thank You, Lord!*—and Julia hired him on the spot.

On Saturday evening, seeing Lane smile across her kitchen table as she sampled his homemade lasagna was a blessed escape. He'd taken her completely by surprise with his text about bringing Tate to her house and cooking dinner. What with extending Saturday clinic hours to serve patients who'd had to be rescheduled, she couldn't possibly have made it to the cabin that afternoon.

She savored a tender bite, the tomato, cheese and basil flavors bursting across her tongue. "This is amazing."

His grin widened. "Thanks. It's another of my specialties—with credit to Lila Vernon and her pasta-making skills. And did I mention my specially seasoned elk sausage?"

"It's all delicious." Furniture making, cooking, horticulture… Was there anything this man *couldn't* do?

"Auntie Lila nice," Tate chimed in as he scooped a spoonful of mashed lasagna into his mouth.

Julia caught a morsel off his chin before it could hit the floor and become fair game for Daisy or Dash. Rowena had the good manners not to beg at the table. "I'd like to meet the Vernons one of these days. They sound like lovely people."

"They've been almost like second parents to me." Stabbing a cucumber on his salad plate, Lane softly cleared his throat. "I look forward to introducing you."

When they finished eating, Lane insisted on doing the dishes and sent Julia to the den for some one-on-one time with Tate. After they played for a bit, Julia pulled him onto her lap and picked up the storybook she'd recently come across in a box of Steven's childhood mementos. *My Little Golden Book About God* was a children's classic, and it held even more meaning for Julia now. Tate fell asleep about halfway through, but she softly read on, letting the words seep into her heart.

As she turned a page, she looked up to see Lane watching from the doorway.

"Don't stop," he said. "I want to hear the rest."

By the time she reached the end, the words had blurred. She quietly closed the book and wiped her eyes. "I'd all but forgotten how much Steven loved this book. I'm glad I saved it."

"Me, too." Coming closer, Lane smoothed back Tate's hair. "Guess I should get this little guy home. I still have evening chores to do."

Julia helped him slip Tate's arms into his tiny gray fleece jacket and walked them to the door. "Thanks again for dinner. It... It meant a lot."

"To me, too." Stepping onto the porch, he turned, his eyes darkening. "Julia, I—"

Tate lifted his head and whimpered. "Mama?"

"Go back to sleep, Tater Tot." Lane soothed him with a pat while casting Julia a regretful frown. "We'd better go."

And just when she'd thought Lane might kiss her good-night. She held back a sigh. "See you at church in the morning?"

"We'll be there." He snickered as he glanced down at Rowena. "All of us, most likely, since these two are practically inseparable."

"You've met Witt's dog, Ranger, so you know it won't be a problem."

She watched Lane drive away and then closed the door to find Daisy and Dash glaring up at her as if it was all her fault their giant playmate had left. If she'd known how well the three of them would get along, she might not have worked so hard to convince Lane to take Rowena. Still, she had no regrets. Tate and "Weena" would be lifelong companions.

It was only a little past seven o'clock, but with fatigue taking its toll, she was ready to fall into bed.

Before she made it down the hall, her phone rang. It was her mother, sounding overwrought. "Honey, we need some help. Can you come right over?"

She arrived at her parents' house to find her father collapsed on the living room floor and without the physical strength to get himself up. But would the prideful, stubborn man let Mom call 9-1-1, or even ask their brawny next-door neighbor for assistance? Not a chance.

That left it up to Julia and her mother to

wrestle him into the recliner. Julia wouldn't leave until he'd rested and regained some muscle control. With threats and negotiations, they persuaded him to use the walker he despised so they could help him to the bedroom. It was almost midnight by then, and Julia was ready to collapse.

"You can't continue taking care of him alone, Mom." Julia gathered her things. "Not as fast as the Parkinson's is progressing."

Looking drained, Mom pressed a hand to her forehead. "I know, I know. We're still figuring this out."

"Well, don't take too long, or you'll only destroy your own health."

"And what about yours?" Her mother's lips thinned in a concerned frown. "I feel awful about the burden all this has placed on you at the clinic."

"I'm managing. Amy and Dylan are helping to pick up the slack." She wouldn't mention losing a few patients to other veterinary practices. If too many more jumped ship, she wouldn't need to worry about hiring a third veterinarian. They might even have to let a couple of their part-time techs go.

At the door, Mom drew her into a hug. "If

your dad's illness is teaching me anything, it's that there are more important things in life than keeping the family business going. If and when you feel it's time to let the practice go, so be it."

Julia pulled away with a gasp. "Mom, no—"

"I mean it, honey. You have a grandson now, Steven's precious little boy." Sniffling, she found a tissue in her pocket and dabbed her cheeks. "Don't let a false sense of obligation deprive you of the time you could be spending with him."

"But I love the clinic. I'm proud of what we do there. I'm proud every time I glimpse the Frasier name on the front door."

"Of course you are." Mom motioned in the direction of the bedroom. Voice breaking, she went on, "But you see what it's cost your father—cost all of us. Whatever decisions you make, be sure they're for the right reasons."

THE NEXT MORNING, Julia was sleeping more soundly than she had in weeks. Only Daisy's and Dash's strident barks, combined with the two of them leaping back and forth across her on the bed, finally roused her. And no wonder they were so anxious—the bedside clock read 10:34.

"Okay, okay, kiddos." She grabbed her robe and jammed her feet into slippers. "Outside first, and then I'll get your breakfast."

From another part of the house came the muffled ring of her cell phone. Hoping it wasn't Mom with another urgent Dad problem, she jostled her foggy brain into remembering where she'd dropped her things after getting home last night. She traced the sound to the pocket of the hoodie she'd worn and answered without looking at the display.

"Julia?" Lane's voice. Praise music played in the background. "Did you change your mind?"

She slammed a palm to her forehead. "I'm so sorry. I never set my alarm." Explaining about rushing over to help her parents last night, she apologized again.

"Don't worry about it. I understand." Other voices sounded close by. Lane excused himself for a moment, and Julia heard him speaking to someone else. Then he came back on the line. "Maddie wants to talk to you. I'm putting her on."

"Hey, Jules. You take it easy, okay? I'll bring a meal over later."

"You don't have to do that. Really, I'm fine."

"No, you're not, so don't argue. I'm hanging up now. Bye!"

The last thing Julia heard before the line went silent was Tate's excited "Yay! Dis Jesus house!"

If not for the dancing dachshunds at her feet, she'd have plopped into the nearest chair and sobbed out her shame and disappointment. She used to believe she was a lot stronger than this, but tears came too easily these days. "I'm sorry about church, God," she whispered with a skyward glance as she opened the back door for the dogs. "Do good intentions count?"

Later, fortified by two large mugs of extra-strong dark roast, she tossed in a load of laundry and sat down at the kitchen table with her laptop to check email and pay bills.

She was just finishing when Daisy and Dash broke out in excited yips and raced for the front door two whole seconds before the doorbell rang. She marched to the foyer and maneuvered past them.

A peek through the peephole revealed the source of their anticipation. Rowena and Ranger were both sniffing at the other side of the door. Witt, Maddie, Lane and Tate waited on the porch behind the dogs.

Knowing she'd never win at holding her pups back, she stepped out of the way before opening the door. The four canines greeted one another with a lot of sniffing and prancing, and somehow, the four adult humans managed to herd the dogs to the backyard.

Once the house was semi-quiet again, Julia turned to the others. "You guys! What are you doing here?"

"I told you I'd bring a meal." Maddie set two large brown restaurant bags on the kitchen counter. "After church, we stopped by the Smith Family Hometown Café and ordered takeout."

Aromas were already teasing Julia's senses. "Does one of those bags happen to contain my favorite chicken potpie?"

"Of course." Maddie was already pulling plates from Julia's cupboard. "We thought we'd join you, if that's okay."

How could she say no to her thoughtful and generous friend? "That'd be great."

While Maddie and Witt set out the food, Julia stepped outside to where Lane was keeping a close eye on Tate as he romped with the dogs.

He offered a tentative smile. "Sorry if we intruded on your plans for a quiet afternoon."

"It's fine. And I still feel awful about standing you up this morning. I'd really wanted to be there—*needed* to be there." Here came those annoying tears again. She sniffed and swallowed.

"So we'll try again next week." Lane's fingers brushed hers, and she let her hand slide into his. So warm, so reassuring, so...*right*.

In the yard, the little dogs were weaving through the big dogs' legs while a giggling Tate tried to do the same. Rowena was tall enough that he barely had to stoop. Ranger's legs weren't nearly as long, so Tate dropped to his hands and knees.

Laughing out loud, Lane pulled his phone from his pocket. "I need to video this to show Shannon."

"She'll love it." Julia chuckled as he recorded several seconds of dog-and-toddler mayhem. When he lowered his phone, she asked, "Are you still going through with having Shannon declared incapacitated?"

"It's in the works. Under the circumstances, my attorney thinks he can get a judge to act on it pretty quickly." He grimaced. "I know you have reservations. I do, too, but it's the only way to ensure my right to make decisions on their behalf."

Before Julia could respond, the back door opened. "Lunch is on the table," Maddie called. "Come get it while it's hot."

Lane tucked away his phone. "Let's go eat, Tater Tot."

"Not before you wash your hands, little guy." Julia ushered him inside and down the hall to the bathroom.

On the way, she couldn't help recalling the first time she'd met Shannon, nor the young mother's desperate plea for Julia to make sure Tate wouldn't spend his childhood on the mountain.

Yes, Lane's place was remote. But the more time Julia spent there, the more at peace she felt. The clean air, the breathtaking views, the sense of time slowing down and the real world melting away... She'd come to cherish her trips up to the cabin. After the week she'd just had, she needed that sense of tranquility all the more.

She needed Lane.

Who was she kidding? Despite what her mother had said, she did feel a responsibility to the family business. And she did love her work. Not to mention, her parents would need her more than ever now. And Steven's death had certainly taught her the utter futility of imagining a perfect future.

God, if You're really listening, give me strength for today and help me trust the future to You.

CHAPTER ELEVEN

Dr. Yoshida had given the okay for Lane to bring Tate and Rowena for another visit. Lane almost wished he could come up with an excuse not to go. He didn't know how his daughter would react when she learned a judge had granted him emergency temporary guardianship of Tate while his petitions were further examined.

He didn't know how to help her understand that even though he'd made mistakes, his deepest motivation had always been love.

He arrived at Mercy Cottage on Thursday around midmorning. Tate was much more energetic this time of day, but he'd start getting hungry closer to noon, which would give Lane an easy out if things with Shannon got uncomfortable.

Hopefully by now, Dr. Yoshida had reassured her that the legal arrangements he'd made were for the best and would remain in place only until she'd recovered. He sent up yet another prayer—unpracticed as he was—asking the Lord not only to soften his daughter's heart toward him, but to grant her healing in mind and spirit.

The visit began well, with Shannon seeming more clearheaded. They chatted for a few minutes about inconsequential things, and then Tate needed a diaper change. Before taking the boy inside to the visitors' restroom, Lane left his phone with Shannon so she could watch the video of Tate playing with the four dogs in Julia's backyard.

When he returned, he suggested they take a walk around the grounds so Tate could burn off some energy. Gripping Rowena's leash, the boy trotted ahead. Along the way, Shannon slowed to pick up a bronze-tinted leaf. As she studied it with a pensive frown, Lane took the opportunity to ease into the subject he'd been dreading.

His daughter surprised him with her quick assent. "I get it, Dad. No need to explain." She twirled the leaf stem between her fingers. "I'll sign whatever papers you need me to."

"That's... That's great." Relief swept through him at not having to pursue the "legally incapacitated" route after all. "I promise, honey, this is only temporary."

She smiled and nodded. "Tate, sweetie, wait for Mommy!"

Wow. Maybe he should simply be thankful and move on, but…had this been a tiny bit *too* easy?

Before leaving later, he asked for a moment of Dr. Yoshida's time. She met him on the front sidewalk after he'd settled Tate and the dog in the truck. "Are you sure Shannon's okay with everything?"

"She understands the importance of ensuring her own as well as her son's welfare. In fact, I'm so encouraged by her overall improvement that I'm considering an overnight furlough soon. It would be good for Shannon to spend quality time with her little boy away from the hospital. Would you be up for that?"

"Definitely."

Anxious to share the news with Julia, he headed to the veterinary clinic in hopes of catching her between patients. He figured she'd probably work through lunch, so he stopped on the way to pick up a burger, a grilled chicken salad and a kids' meal. He wasn't averse to locking her in her office if it would force her to take five minutes to sit down and eat something.

As soon as he walked in the door, a young woman in purple scrubs burst from behind the counter. Over her shoulder, she called, "Rowena's here!"

Soon she was joined by two more vet techs. All of them fawned over the big dog, who was literally lapping up the attention.

Julia entered from the corridor. "I wondered what all the commotion was about."

"Gammy!" Tate ran to her, arms upraised for her to hold him.

"Hi there, sweetheart." Lifting him onto her hip, she cast Lane a curious grin. "This is a nice surprise."

He held up the fast-food bag. "I brought lunch. Can I steal you away for a few minutes?"

"Go on, Dr. J," the purple-clad tech said. "We've got things covered."

"Thanks, Amy. Why don't you take Rowena to the back and get her vitals? I'll give her a quick exam while she's here."

In Julia's office, Lane set out the food he'd brought, only to have Julia snatch up the burger he'd intended for himself. Guess he'd have to settle for the chicken salad. He pulled a chair closer, balancing Tate on one knee while the kid scarfed down grilled chicken nuggets and ignored the fruit cup.

Between bites, Lane described his visit with Shannon. "If I weren't so relieved, I'd be suspicious."

"Your daughter's improving. Maybe just accept it for the good news it is." Julia dabbed mustard from the corner of her mouth before taking a sip of diet cola. "So what happens next?"

"On the way over, I called Harry, my lawyer. He's finalizing the details."

Smiling, Julia took another monstrous bite from the hamburger. Seemed she had every intention of keeping this a five-minute lunch break. After another swig of cola, she shoved her chair back. "Stay here and finish. Sorry, but I've got to get back to my patients. And thanks again for lunch. Now I may actually survive the afternoon."

"Julia—"

"Oh, yes, Rowena. I'll have Amy bring her to you as soon as we're done." The door banged shut behind her.

Tate looked up with a frown. "Gammy go bye-bye?"

"Grammy's a busy lady."

Should Lane be suspicious of her, too? Her texts since last Sunday had taken on a different tone. Less chatty, more… What else could he call it but polite? And just when he'd thought something meaningful was happening between them. He'd like to believe she was merely preoccupied. Who could blame her, what with all the complications she was dealing with?

He only hoped her work stress would ease off soon, because with every minute he spent with her, he grew increasingly certain he wanted to be much more to Julia Frasier than Tate's other grandparent.

UNTIL SHE'D CAUGHT a whiff of the juicy burger Lane had brought, Julia hadn't realized how hungry she was.

Now the meal sat like a rock in her stomach. She'd gulped it down entirely too quickly, partly because she really did need to stay on schedule today, but also because she was afraid if she spent too much time in Lane's presence, her resolve to slow things down between them would wither.

Yes, her attempt to stop trying to control everything was failing miserably. But these feelings for Lane seemed like the one thing she most needed to keep under control. Otherwise, she risked losing her focus—which in turn could mean losing the clinic she and her parents had invested so much of themselves in.

Her examination of Rowena proved the big dog healthy in every respect. Her injured leg was mending well. Julia had Amy return the dog to Lane, and she made sure to be in an exam room with a patient when they left.

Later that afternoon, she had a Zoom interview with another candidate for associate veterinarian. Nikki Ramirez, three years out of veterinary college, was currently on staff at a twenty-four-hour emergency vet clinic but wanted a position with regular daytime hours. The young woman was personable, came with solid references and could start the end of next week. Julia scheduled an in-person interview and clinic tour on Saturday afternoon.

Which meant she'd once again leave work too late to make the drive up to Lane's cabin. She texted him Friday evening to let him know.

Good news and bad news, I guess? he replied. How about trying church again on Sunday?

That was something she'd told herself she needed to do no matter what. Definitely. This time I'll set TWO alarms.

The Saturday interview went well, and before the young doctor left, they'd inked an employment contract. A go-getter new office manager who was already proving his worth, two impressive new vets soon to join the staff—was she finally seeing light at the end of this particular tunnel? For the first time in too long to remember, the chronic tension between her shoulder blades had begun to ease.

The world looked even brighter Sunday morning after her best night's sleep in ages. She made it to Elk Valley Community of Faith with ten minutes to spare.

Maddie and Witt arrived at almost the same time. Maddie rushed over to give Julia a welcoming hug. "You made it. I'm so glad."

Julia snorted a self-deprecating laugh. "After how this week turned out, I thought God deserved a proper thank-you." On their way to the building, she told her friend about filling all the staff positions. "I'll soon be able to slow down and hopefully spend more time with my grandson."

"And a certain ruggedly handsome mountain man, too?" Maddie winked, then looked over her shoulder as a big maroon truck turned into the parking area. "Speaking of whom…"

Julia's stomach twisted. "Please, you're jumping to conclusions. Lane and I are just—"

"Don't you dare say *just friends*." Maddie speared her with an icy turquoise stare, though her tone was tender. "Have you forgotten how long we've known each other? Your feelings for this man are written all over your face."

She glanced past Maddie to see Lane ambling their way with Tate propped on his hip. Rowena tugged on the leash in her excitement to greet Ranger. Maybe she should have stayed home after all, because she could read in Lane's warm smile and the hopeful look in his eyes exactly how much he was beginning to care for her.

"Gammy!" Tate practically flew from Lane's arms into hers.

Huffing a startled laugh, she caught her balance. "Careful there, fella."

Lane steadied them both. "He kept asking me all the way here if you were really coming today. How'd the interview go?"

"Great. We're now fully staffed—or will be, once everyone reports in."

"So just a couple more weeks?" His words ended on an expectant note.

"Yes, a couple more weeks." Behind her, the

church doors opened, releasing a burst of praise music. "We should go find seats." Preferably near the back, and not right next to Lane. Her feelings for him remained a bit too complex for comfort.

Having a squirming Tate planted between them helped minimally. Julia chuckled to herself when she noticed the dogs had better church manners, both of them stretched out between the pews for naps.

In fact, it appeared Witt and Ranger had started a trend. Julia counted at least six other canines of various sizes and breeds among the congregants. The sight wrapped around her heart like a warm, fuzzy sweater.

It could have been the dogs, or it could have been the pastor's message based on the New Testament scripture about "the peace of God, which passeth all understanding"—or more likely both—but when Julia stepped out into the midday sun an hour later, her spirit felt ten times lighter. She would have asked God where He'd been the last twenty-plus years, but she already knew the answer. He'd been right there with her the whole time, if only her eyes of faith had been open to see.

Maddie and Witt had taken charge of Tate

and the dogs, leaving Julia to follow behind with Lane. He leaned toward her ear. "You look happier than I've seen you recently."

A shiver went through her. She cast him an appraising smile. "I could say the same about you."

"It's been an encouraging week in many ways." His voice softened. "Any chance that opens the door a little wider for…us?"

She didn't answer right away—she *couldn't*, considering the staccato drumming of her heart. After a hard swallow, she murmured, "Ask me again in a week or two, okay?"

His mouth flattened into a smug smile. "I'll do that."

GUESS HE COULDN'T blame her for leaving their relationship in limbo for the time being. After how quickly Julia had scurried out of her office on Thursday, Lane had fretted all the way back home that she'd both literally and figuratively closed the door on him.

Today, though, he sensed her heart inching open again, and it made him ridiculously giddy—a fact he had to work extra hard to conceal.

Since she'd been tied up all day yesterday,

he'd hoped she'd be free to spend this afternoon with him and Tate.

"I wish I could," she told him as they stood beside her SUV. "But my mom has been looking after my dad almost 24/7 since he came home from the hospital, and I promised her I'd stay with him for a few hours today so she could have some time to herself."

"Tate and I could join you," Lane offered. "A visit with his great-grandson could be good for your dad."

Julia scrunched her brows together. "It's a little too soon, I think. Dad is still coming to terms with his diagnosis, plus adjusting to new meds, and Mom says he hasn't been very pleasant to be around."

"Another time, then." Moving a step closer, he took her hand and felt her shiver. "I'm here for you, Julia. And while you're consumed with running the clinic and helping your parents, don't neglect taking care of *you*."

The emotion in her eyes when she looked up at him spoke of long-ago hurt and stifled hope. It made him wonder what kind of a creep she'd once been married to that had made her believe she could rely on no one but herself.

When she glanced away, he gently cupped

her cheek and turned her face toward his. "I mean it, Julia. You can count on me. Always."

"Gampy!" came Tate's impatient shout. He'd been walking Rowena on the lawn with Witt, Maddie and Ranger. "Go now!"

Lane chuckled softly. "Somebody wants lunch. Guess I should be going."

"Guess so." A tiny smile curled Julia's lips as she covered his hand with her own. "Thank you. Your… Your friendship means more than I can say."

Was it only wishful thinking, or had she imbued that ordinary term *friendship* with something more? It might be too soon to call what they had a *relationship*, romantically speaking, but he hoped with all his heart they were headed that way.

OVER THE NEXT couple of weeks, the texts from Julia began sounding more positive. She really liked the office manager she'd hired, and now that one of the new veterinarians had joined the staff, her workload was easing.

On the downside, her father had been complicating things by insisting on a supervisory role at the clinic. She explained that she could hardly tell him no, since it would be depriving him of what little dignity and sense of purpose he had left.

Lane could understand. He saw something similar during his regular Thursday visits with Shannon. Each week, when Tate rushed headlong into her arms with a loud "Miss you, Mama!" a spark of life lit her eyes, as if being needed by her little son were all the medicine she required just then. Even so, Dr. Yoshida reported there continued to be difficult days, when grief and sadness took Shannon to places so dark and remote that no one seemed able to reach her.

Fall temperatures continued their downward trend. Since Rowena wasn't allowed inside at Mercy Cottage, Lane left the dog at the cabin when he took Tate to visit Shannon the first Thursday in October. Tate wasn't happy about leaving his doggy pal behind, but when his mother cheerfully joined him on the floor with crayons and drawing paper, the boy was soon busily sketching line-and-circle figures he claimed were Lane, Shannon, Rowena and himself.

Then Tate proudly announced one of his unrecognizable drawings was "Gammy." There was even something vaguely resembling a stethoscope around what Lane assumed was the figure's neck. Laughing, Lane decided Julia should see it. He gave her a call as he was leaving.

"I know it's last minute," he said, "but any chance you could break free to meet us for lunch?"

"You know what? I think I can actually say yes." She gave a lighthearted laugh, a sound he'd rarely heard from her, and it made his own heart lift.

"That's great. Name a place close to your clinic, and we'll meet you there."

Half an hour later, they were seated in a booth at a pub-style sandwich shop, Lane and Julia across from each other, and Tate in a tall wooden booster chair pushed up to the open end of the table. While they waited for their order, Lane unfolded Tate's drawing and pushed it across to Julia.

"Oh, yes, that's definitely me," she said with mock seriousness. "See? There's my bedhead first thing in the morning, and my frazzled brain leaking out, and my long, *long* arms—" she stretched them to encircle Tate "—so that I can give my Tater Tot even bigger hugs!"

He giggled and squirmed. "Gammy, no tickle me!"

The server brought their orders, and conversation ebbed while Lane got Tate situated with his triangle-cut grilled cheese sandwich and orange wedges.

After a bite of her chicken club, Julia asked, "So the visit with Shannon went well?"

"It did. She really looks forward to spending time with Tate every week. She's hoping you can visit again soon, too."

"Now that my life is settling down a bit, I plan to." She sipped her iced tea. "And the legal stuff? Still no pushback?"

"None at all. Papers are signed and on the way to being finalized." Frowning, Lane gave his head a brisk shake. "To be honest, I'm kind of in shock. I never expected Shannon would be this agreeable."

"It has to be a positive sign, don't you think?"

"I want to believe so, but…something feels off about it." He gnawed off a mouthful of his Reuben and then had to mop sauerkraut off his chin.

"Surely she's not just pretending to go along with the arrangements? What would be the point?"

"True." Lane gave a rueful laugh. "If I really am at the point of trusting God with all this, then I ought to quit overthinking Shannon's reaction and just be grateful."

"Easier said than done, as I know all too well." Helping Tate get a better grip on his sippy cup, Julia cast Lane a sideways glance. "Don't ask me how I'm doing with putting my parents in the Lord's hands. It's taking a conscious effort every day."

"At least we're trying, which—for me, anyway—is a marvel in and of itself."

Julia smirked. "A month ago, I'd have said nothing short of a wedding or a funeral would get me back inside a church." She paused, a faraway look in her eyes. "Maybe people like us need to reach the end of our own strength before we can admit how desperately we need God."

They fell into a thoughtful silence and continued eating, chuckling now and then over something silly Tate did with his food. The kid was learning all the right moves to divert his grandparents' attention and get them to smile.

After finishing her sandwich, Julia checked her watch and let out a gasp. "I totally lost track of time. I have to get back to the clinic." Scooting out of the booth, she pulled her wallet from her purse and began tugging out bills. "Here, this should cover—"

"Put your money away." Lane stuffed the cash back into her hand, his fingers closing around her fist. "I invited you. This is my treat."

"But—"

"We promised to cut back on the arguments, remember? So consider this your chance to practice." He winked. "Give me five seconds— or maybe ten—to get the munchkin cleaned up, and we'll walk out with you."

His estimate was on the low side for wiping Tate's face and hands and working that wiggly little body into a jacket. Julia's tense posture said she was anxious to be on her way, but she waited by the door while Lane paid their bill. As they walked out, she muttered a reluctant thank-you.

Fingers closing around her elbow, he compelled her to face him. "Be honest with me, Julia. Was my treating you to lunch so hard for you because you'd rather not feel obligated, or because it felt too much like a date?"

"I... I don't know." She grimaced. "Both, I suppose."

"Well, how about I clarify the situation once and for all?" Shifting Tate to his other hip, he slid his free hand beneath her ponytail. Gently but firmly, he pulled her to him for a kiss he hoped would leave no doubt as to his deepening feelings.

"Oh, my…" A smile teased up the corners of her lips. Her stunned stare reminded him of the glassy-eyed mule deer he'd caught in his headlights the other night.

Tate chortled. "Gampy kiss Gammy! Again, do again!"

Hands lifted, she put more space between them and released a shaky laugh. "How am I supposed to blithely move through the rest of my workday after *that*?"

Her discomfiture pleased Lane in ways he couldn't even describe. "I'm sure you'll find a way."

CHAPTER TWELVE

WHEN JULIA RETURNED to work after lunch, she found her father holding court in the clinic kitchen. Apparently, he'd been regaling any available staff member with stories of his early years as a veterinarian.

Sidling into the room, Julia was relieved to see Dad's fancy new walker beside his chair. He'd been embarrassed about using it at first, but Mom had insisted early on—either he agreed to faithfully use his walker, or she wouldn't let him leave the house.

Julia's mother skirted the two junior techs taking their lunch break and joined her at the door.

"He's winding down, I think," Mom said. "Then I'll…" Her voice trailed off as she studied Julia with a furrowed brow. "Honey, you're positively *glowing*."

"What? No!" Turning away slightly, she gave her head a brisk shake.

"Don't pretend with me. I know you met Lane for lunch. Did he…" She gasped and dropped her tone to a whisper. "Did he kiss you?"

Julia scurried into the corridor. One hand pressed to the side of her rapidly warming face, she collapsed against the wall.

Her mother followed, a gleeful grin brightening her eyes. "He did! Oh, honey, I'm so happy for you."

"Stop, Mom." She gripped her mother's fluttering hands. "It's all too new, and I'm not sure I'm ready for—for—"

"For falling in love? My dearest daughter—"

"Your *only* daughter."

"Which means I cherish you all the more. You've waited so long to put yourself first. Isn't it about time?"

Just then, Amy peeked out of an exam room. "Your next patient's waiting, Dr. J."

"Be right there." With a forced smile, she ducked into her office to grab her lab coat.

She hadn't known how to answer her mother's question. Or maybe she was afraid she'd been putting herself first all along. This wall she'd erected around her heart, her efforts to control every situation—weren't those merely a form of selfishness?

Somehow she made it through the afternoon. Several routine appointments plus an emergency procedure to suture a dog's ear after a tussle with his housemate helped to distract her from thoughts of Lane and that amazing—and extremely persuasive—kiss.

Catching up with desk work after closing time, she reviewed the next day's schedule. Her first appointment wasn't until 9:45, and Dr. Ramirez could cover any early walk-ins. This might be her best chance to see Shannon.

First thing Friday morning, she phoned Mercy Cottage to ask if she could visit. A few minutes later, Dr. Yoshida's secretary called back with a yes. She drove right over and was escorted to Shannon's room.

The young woman greeted her with a hug. "When they told me you were coming again, I could hardly wait."

"I meant to visit sooner, but work's been so hectic." Julia's smile warmed as she smoothed back one of Shannon's blond curls. "You look like you're feeling a little better."

"I'm trying—really, really trying." Taking

Julia's hand, Shannon drew her toward a small table and chairs by the window. As they sat, she continued, "I have to get well for Tate. And that's the main reason I've been wanting to see you so badly."

A warning twinge tightened Julia's stomach. "If you're having reservations about your dad's guardianship…"

"I know it's for the best right now." Shannon waved dismissively. "Let's talk about something else. Do you have any new photos of Tate?"

They spent a few minutes flipping through the photos on Julia's phone, and then Julia asked how Shannon's week had been.

Anticipation lit the girl's eyes. "Did you know I'll be getting a furlough soon?"

"Your dad mentioned you might be allowed to spend a weekend at home with Tate. That sounds wonderful."

"There's just one problem." Shannon's lower lip trembled. "I… I don't think I can face going back to my dad's cabin."

Julia reached across the table to cover Shannon's hand. "I understand it was hard for you growing up there, but it'll be different now. Besides, it's so peaceful in the mountains, so…

healing. Every time I'm there, it's like the cares of my everyday world melt away."

She wouldn't mention that being near Lane in his element sparked a whole different kind of tension.

Heaving a frustrated sigh, Shannon turned her gaze toward the window. "I can't. There are too many bad memories."

"But your dad loves you so much. Let this be a time to make new memories—happier memories."

"I'm just not ready yet." Shannon sniffled and swiped at a tear. She cast Julia a pleading look. "But if you'd let me stay with you…"

"For your furlough weekend?" Julia wasn't sure how Lane would take to the idea, but it could be a viable compromise. "It's a possibility, but—"

Shannon nearly toppled the table in her rush to wrap her arms around Julia. "Thank you! I've been praying so hard about this, and I knew I could count on you."

"Okay, honey, okay." Julia tamped down a nagging sense of unease as she gently guided Shannon back to her chair. The girl seemed a little too jubilant over the whole idea. "We'll need to clear this with your doctor first."

"I'm sure she'll be fine with it. So you'll arrange with my dad to have Tate at your house for the weekend, right?"

"Yes—again, with Dr. Yoshida's approval." She checked the time, almost relieved she had to be on her way. Rising, she gathered her coat and purse. "I need to get to work, honey, but I promise I'll look into this."

Between appointments later, she phoned Mercy Cottage and requested a callback from Dr. Yoshida. The doctor returned her call as she was finishing up for the day.

After supplying the gist of her conversation with Shannon, she went on, "It isn't that I wouldn't love to have her stay with me for a weekend. I'm just concerned she's using me as an excuse to avoid facing her issues with her father."

"Highly likely," the doctor acknowledged. "We're continuing to work through those issues in therapy, but in the meantime, I still believe it would be extremely beneficial for her to have some time with her son away from the hospital. If you're agreeable, I'd like to plan for a week from this Saturday. It would be just one night, and you would need to commit to staying with her the entire time."

Julia consulted her calendar. By then, Dr. Kruger would have joined the practice and they'd be fully staffed. If any questions arose, she could always be reached by phone. "I'm sure that can be arranged," she said. "I'll do anything I can to help in Shannon's recovery."

"YOU WHAT?" LANE nearly dropped an armful of logs on his toe. Good thing Julia had kept Tate and Rowena well away from the wood-shed opening.

"Shannon's doctor agreed to the idea." Her nose and cheeks were red from the cold, but the determination in her eyes shone like embers.

After stacking more logs in the utility wagon, he started hauling it through the snow toward the cabin. Yes, he could see the logic of not bringing Shannon to the mountain for her first overnight away from the hospital, but it hurt nonetheless. He wanted to make amends with his daughter, and since the home where he'd raised her was their only tangible point of connection, how else could he hope to reach her?

"Go Mama?" Tate said.

"Not today, sweetie. Lane, wait up." Julia grunted like she'd just lifted something heavy—

Tate, no doubt—and her steps crunched behind his.

Without looking back, he hefted an armful of logs and marched up the deck steps. It would be a frigid night with more snow predicted, so he needed to fill his firewood rack with enough to last through the weekend.

"Lane." Julia was breathing hard as she reached the top step.

He dusted his gloved hands and rolled his shoulders before turning toward her. "Shut the gate, please."

"I *know*." Her glare could have melted the icicles off the eaves. With precise movements, she closed the thigh-high gate Lane had installed to bar Tate's access to the deck stairs. After testing the latch with a quick shake, she set Tate down.

Lips in a twist, Tate moved between them and held up his hands like a referee in a boxing match. "Gammy Gampy no fight!"

Rowena gave a punctuating bark.

Julia rolled her eyes. "Truce?"

"Truce." Lane marched to the cabin door and held it open while the woman, boy and dog trooped inside. After stripping off his jacket and gloves, he helped Tate out of his winter things, took Julia's coat from her and draped everything on hooks behind the door.

In the meantime, the aroma of brewing coffee enticed Julia to the kitchen. As soon as she'd texted she was heading his way, he'd set the coffeemaker to start exactly one hour later. He knew all too well how she loved her fully caffeinated dark roast.

Leaving Tate and Rowena playing ball on the living room carpet, he joined Julia at the counter and filled a mug for himself. "I shouldn't have jumped down your throat like that."

"And I could have used a bit more tact when I broke the news."

"Well, you did sound a wee bit smug about the whole thing."

She carried her mug to the table and sank into a chair. "I didn't mean to, honestly."

Taking the chair kitty-corner from hers, he set down his coffee and reached for her hands. Soft and fine-boned, they were warm from cradling her mug and fit so comfortably into his work-roughened grip. He grew so entranced holding her hands that for a moment, he forgot what they'd been talking about.

"I'm really sorry," she murmured. "I know how much it would mean to you to have Shannon home again. Maybe by her next furlough, she'll be ready."

Tate traipsed into the kitchen, his wise-be-yond-his-years glance darting between them. "Gammy Gampy aw better?"

"Yes," Lane assured. "Grammy and Grampy are all better."

Arms akimbo, the boy nodded and grinned. "Otay, den. Kiss."

Heat shot up Lane's neck. Forcing a swallow, he lifted his gaze to Julia's. "Would that be okay with you?"

Mischief lit her eyes. "Can we dare risk disobeying a direct order?"

"That would be extremely dangerous, in my opinion." He stood, then pulled her to him and planted a whopper of a kiss on her surprised lips.

"Yay!" Tate clapped his hands and laughed. "Yay, yay, yay!"

Ending the kiss, Lane felt like celebrating, too. He grinned down at Julia and savored her languidly happy expression. "If all our arguments could end like this, I'd be picking fights with you every hour on the hour."

"Actually, I'd prefer to skip the arguing and get straight to the making-up part." She interlaced her fingers behind his neck and tilted her head, clearly waiting for another kiss.

He wouldn't let the moment slip by.

LANE HAD RESIGNED himself to the fact that Shannon would spend the weekend at Julia's house. However, since he'd be making the trip into town anyway to bring Tate to Julia's, he made arrangements with the Mercy Cottage staff to pick up his daughter on the way.

Shortly before eight o'clock on Saturday morning, he loaded Tate and Rowena into the truck along with enough clothing, diapers and dog food to last until Sunday evening. Shannon was packed and ready to go when he arrived. Dr. Yoshida escorted her out to the truck, and while she climbed in and got situated, the doctor handed Lane a zippered pouch containing Shannon's meds and a page of instructions.

"It's very important for Shannon to have her medications on schedule," the doctor said, "so be sure you and Julia are both clear about everything on the information sheet. My cell phone number is included, and I can be reached all weekend, day or night. If for any reason you cannot get through to me, call the Mercy Cottage emergency number."

The urgency in her tone made him feel slightly panicky. "Is there any reason to think something could go wrong?"

"No, I'm only being thorough." Smiling, Dr. Yoshida gave his arm a reassuring pat. "I've been preparing Shannon for today, and she's ready. She also understands she needs to maintain her routine and rest when she needs to. With proper supervision and the love of her family, this should be a positive experience all around."

What else could he do but trust the doctor? Thanking her, he tucked the pouch into his coat pocket and got in behind the wheel.

Shannon had been leaning between the seats to play patty-cake with a giggling Tate. She swiveled and fastened her seat belt. "I'm ready. Let's go."

He tried not to be overly concerned about the almost manic glint in her eyes. Why shouldn't she be excited about her first foray into normal life since he'd checked her in to the hospital?

Julia was watching for them from her front porch and strode out to the truck as soon as he parked in her driveway. While she helped Shannon get Tate and the dog from the back seat, Lane hefted the luggage and pet supplies. Following the women inside, he felt pretty much like an afterthought. When Rowena looked back from the porch as if waiting for him, he wanted to believe the dog actually cared about his feelings, but more than likely, she only wanted to make sure he hadn't forgotten her bag of kibble.

Inside, Julia relieved him of the dog supplies and directed him to the guest room with Shannon's and Tate's things. When he returned, he found everyone in the den. Shannon sat on the floor with Tate on her lap, both laughing while the dachshunds entertained them with a game of tug-of-war. Rowena seemed to understand she was too big and ungainly to join in. Instead, she parked herself as close as she could get to Tate without being in the way.

Julia came over to stand by Lane. "They're having a great time already. Just look at the smile on Shannon's face."

"I know. It makes me nervous."

"I'm a bit nervous about this weekend, too. But maybe we should just be happy about her improvement."

"I am." He crossed his arms. "Or I would be, if it all didn't seem so... I don't know..." With no idea how to put his misgivings into words, he could only shrug. He pulled the zippered pouch from his coat pocket. "Before I forget, Dr. Yoshida sent this along. It's Shannon's meds and instructions for the weekend."

"Oh, right. She said you'd be bringing it." Julia took the information page from the packet. Reading silently, she nodded.

Lane peered over her shoulder. "Anything I should know?"

"Only that she needs to be returned to Mercy Cottage no later than six o'clock tomorrow evening. If you'd rather not make the drive again, I'm happy to take her."

"No problem. I'll need to pick up Tate and Rowena anyway."

Disappointment flickered across her expression. "Of course. I forgot." She went back to perusing the instructions, then checked her watch. "Looks like it's almost time for one of Shannon's meds. Would you mind getting her a glass of water?"

He did as she asked.

After Shannon dutifully swallowed her meds, Julia started to the kitchen with the empty glass. Crossing in front of Lane, she smiled. "We'll be fine here if there's anything else you need to be doing."

He'd been debating whether to stick around—Shannon *was* his daughter, after all—or head back to the cabin and catch up on some work. Guess that answered his question.

JULIA SENSED LANE'S DILEMMA, and she felt bad for him. Maybe she should have invited him to stay awhile, but with Shannon utterly ignoring him, the whole situation felt too strained.

Instead, she made up her mind to provide Shannon with plenty of support and encouragement while subtly inserting enough of the right things into their conversations to soften the girl's heart toward her dad and the home she'd grown up in.

It wasn't long before Shannon's efforts at remaining cheerful began to waver. She lost patience with Tate when he had a minor meltdown over misplacing a toy, and again during lunch when he repeatedly tried to feed part of his tortilla rollup to the dogs. Julia had to intervene by ushering the animals out to the backyard, then took Tate onto her lap and coaxed him to finish his meal. When mother and son retreated to the bedroom for an afternoon nap, Julia felt like she needed one herself. She let the dogs inside and stretched out on the den sofa.

She hadn't realized she'd fallen asleep until a pudgy finger poked her cheek. Blinking, she rolled onto her side. "Hi, Tater Tot." Apparently, the boy had figured out how to escape the portable crib. "Did you have a good nap?"

"Uh-huh. I wake now." Nudging Daisy and Dash from their comfy nest by her feet, he crawled up beside them at the end of the sofa. Moments later, Rowena came over to rest her chin on Tate's knees.

The ring of Julia's cell phone sounded from down the hall. She thought she'd left her phone on the charger in the kitchen. When had she taken it to her room? Easing upright, she shook off her grogginess and reached for Tate's hand. "Better come with Grammy while I find my phone."

Reaching the hallway, she nearly ran into Shannon.

"I, um…" The girl wore a frozen look as if she'd been caught shoplifting. She swallowed and handed Julia the ringing phone. "I wanted to set an alarm so I didn't sleep too long."

"That's fine. Thanks." She read her mother's name on the screen and excused herself to answer. "Hi, Mom. Is everything okay?"

"That's what I was going to ask you. How's the visit going?"

Keeping a smile on her face, she waited while Shannon and Tate continued on to the den. "Mostly good." She lowered her voice to a whisper. "I'm probably overcompensating, but I feel like I need to be hyperalert."

"It was brave of you to take on this responsibility."

"Not really." She peeked into the den, finding Shannon and Tate snuggled in an easy chair and paging through a storybook. "I just hope it helps."

The rest of the afternoon passed without incident, with Shannon seeming more settled as the day went on. Occasionally, a glazed look would come into her eyes, as if melancholy was setting in, but she'd eventually find her smile again and return to playing with her son.

Tate was eating up the attention, too, giggling and doing silly dances and rolling on the floor with the dogs. In another sense, it was as if he was trying every trick he knew to keep his mother's spirits up.

Later, Julia served a simple supper of lemon-pepper chicken with rice pilaf and green beans. After dinner, she helped Shannon give Tate his bath. With the boy clad in footed jammies and smelling like lavender-scented baby wash, Julia left mother and son propped in the guest bed reading a bedtime story while she went to get Shannon's evening meds and a glass of water.

When she returned, both of them had drifted off. The book lay open atop the coverlet, and Rowena snoozed on her blanket at the foot of the bed. After transferring Tate to the portable crib, she roused Shannon long enough to swallow her meds, then turned out the lights and pulled the door partway closed.

Retreating to the den, she decided Lane would appreciate an update and sent him a text: A few ups and downs but overall a good day. Both are sound asleep now.

Several minutes passed before he responded with a brief Thanks. See you tomorrow afternoon.

Apparently, he was still feeling the sting of rejection, and she couldn't blame him. I hate how she snubbed you this morning, she texted back. We can both stretch our faith muscles and pray for things to go better next time.

He shot her a thumbs-up and the praying hands emoji.

Too bad they couldn't talk in real time and reassure each other, perhaps even pray together.

She laughed to herself. A month ago, she'd never have imagined she'd turn to God in prayer—least of all with a man she was beginning to care for more than she'd ever intended to.

More than she'd ever thought possible.

Those were thoughts best set aside for another time. Yawning, she decided an early bedtime was a good idea after the day she'd had. On her way through the kitchen to let Daisy and Dash have a quick trip outside, she remembered her phone had never finished charging, so she plugged it in.

After making sure the house was secure, she peeked in on Shannon and Tate once more. Leaving her bedroom door ajar so she could hear them if they needed anything, she crawled into bed.

It felt as if she'd barely closed her eyes when Daisy's and Dash's frantic yipping jolted her awake. Sitting up, she fumbled for the switch on the bedside lamp and squinted as her eyes adjusted. Both dogs were racing from the bed to the closed door and back, while Rowena's deep-throated barks came from the other side.

"What in the world..." Grabbing her robe, she yanked open her door and hurried across the hall to the darkened guest room. She flipped the light switch. "Shannon? Are you—"

The room was empty.

"Shannon! Tate!" Choking on her own panicked cry, she spun around and almost tripped over Rowena. When the panting, wide-eyed dog spun around and galloped toward the front door, Julia darted after her.

Gripping Rowena's collar to keep the dog from running out, she pulled open the door. Just then, headlights flashed across the lawn as a car roared away. It took all Julia's strength to keep Rowena from tearing off after it.

Which told her one thing. Tate was in that car, and now he was gone.

CHAPTER THIRTEEN

LANE HAD NEVER driven down the mountain so fast in his life.

Julia's text had come through just past midnight, startling him as he sat in the living room trying to lose himself in a suspense novel. Alone in the cabin for the first night since Shannon had shown up with his surprise grandson, he'd found sleep elusive.

Please, God. Please, God. Please, God. It wasn't much of a prayer, but he was desperate. Desperate to make it to Julia's in one piece, hopefully without leaving any roadkill in his wake. And desperate to learn exactly how a mentally ill young mother and her toddler son could so easily have disappeared into the night.

Screeching to a stop in Julia's driveway, he bolted from the truck. He found her barefoot and coatless on the front porch, shivering as much from worry as from the cold.

"I'm sorry. I'm so sorry," she repeated through half-frozen lips.

Part of him knew he should try to reassure her, but his terrified rage wouldn't let him. He took her by the shoulders and turned her toward the door. "You're chilled to the bone. Let's go inside."

Three anxious dogs blocked their passage. Rowena whined and paced as the dachshunds wove between her long legs.

Once they got past the tangle of canines, Lane demanded to see the note Julia had found. She fetched it from beneath her cell phone on the kitchen counter and handed it to him with trembling fingers. He skimmed quickly, then read the note again, each word like an ice shard to his heart:

I know what my dad's trying to do. I'll NEVER let him have my son. This was the only way we could get away. Remember, I told you the first time we met that you were the answer to my prayer? I realize now this chance you've given me is why. Shannon

He drew a pained breath and faced Julia. "You were supposed to be looking after them. How could you let this happen?"

"How was I to know what she was planning?" An indignant spark flashed in her eyes. "Maybe you should be asking yourself where she got the idea that you intended to take Tate away from her permanently."

"But I wouldn't—" He swallowed. Was it possible something he'd said about the guardianship arrangements had given his daughter the wrong impression?

"Lane, I'm sorry. I know you'd never have threatened her with anything like that." A sob caught in Julia's throat. Convulsing, she felt her way to a chair. "You're right, this is my fault. I should have been paying better attention. I should have seen the signs—"

"Stop, stop." Moving behind her, he massaged her shoulders while attempting to corral his racing thoughts. "We're not helping anything by blaming each other or ourselves. Did you call Dr. Yoshida?"

"I was too scared and embarrassed." She shifted to look up at him. "Oh, Lane, this is awful. How can I tell her I let Shannon run away with Tate?"

"First of all, you didn't *let* Shannon run away." He pulled her to her feet and held her trembling body against his chest. How could he be upset with her when he had years to atone for? "We'll find them, Julia. I'll call the doctor and explain what happened, and then...somehow...we'll find them."

His call roused the doctor from sleep, but once she grasped the situation, she came quickly alert.

"I have you on speaker," he told her, positioning the phone on the table between Julia and himself. "Should we call the police? Go looking for her ourselves?"

"First of all, try not to panic," Dr. Yoshida said.

"Too late for that."

"I understand, but it won't help." The doctor took a deep breath. "Shannon left of her own volition, correct?"

"Yes, but—"

"She is an adult. *And* she voluntarily committed herself for mental health treatment. Those factors alone mean she isn't, legally speaking, a missing person. However, you were granted emergency temporary custody of her son, and that puts her actions in a completely different light."

Julia drew her brows together. "Which means...what?"

Lane's jaw clenched. "It means this could be considered a kidnapping."

"That's true," the doctor said. "So unless you have some idea about where Shannon could have gone, you may want to bring in the police."

"I can't do that to my daughter." Lane firmly shook his head. "Treating her like a criminal would turn her against me forever."

Dr. Yoshida sighed. "I sympathize with your predicament. But you must also think of your grandson and what's best for him—especially considering Shannon's current emotional state."

Julia gripped Lane's hand. "You know Shannon would never intentionally hurt Tate. It's why she brought him home to you in the first place."

Lane lowered his head and groaned. "Then what should we do, Doctor? What *can* we do?"

"You could start by reaching out to any of Shannon's friends or acquaintances, anyone she might have called on to help her with this plan."

He racked his brain. "She left home so long ago that I wouldn't know where to begin."

"Julia?" the doctor said. "Can you think of

any of your late son's friends she might still have contact with?"

"I… I can try."

"Good. You work on that, and I will review Shannon's session notes for anything relevant she may have mentioned. Call me if you have any news at all."

"We will," Lane said. "Thank you."

"There's one more thing you can do," Dr. Yoshida added, her tone softening. "Pray."

Lane thanked the doctor again and ended the call. Scooting his chair closer to Julia's, he took her hands. "Pray with me?"

She nodded.

"Dear God," he began, head bowed. His throat closed, and he couldn't continue. From somewhere in his far distant memories of church and Sunday school came fragments of a Bible passage, something about the Spirit interceding when words wouldn't come. He hoped it was true, that God already knew his deepest longings, the unutterable pleas swelling his chest until the only sound he could make was an anguished moan.

Silently, Julia moved onto his lap and wrapped her arms around his neck. As she wept into the folds of his shirt, he pressed her close and gave in to his own tumble of emotions.

Soon, a furry muzzle nosed between them. Rowena whimpered as if to say, *Enough already. Find my boy!*

The interruption was enough to spur him into action. Spying a tissue box, he snatched a handful and pressed them into Julia's hand while easing her onto her own chair. After grabbing a tissue for himself and blowing his nose, he said, "Are you ready to do some brainstorming?"

"I think so." She glanced around as if getting her bearings. "I never shut down Steven's Facebook account after…" She shuddered. "It's likely at least a few of his friends knew about Shannon."

"Then let's start there."

JULIA SITUATED HER laptop on the table so she and Lane could both see the screen. It took a megadose of willpower to open Facebook and click on Steven's profile.

When his smiling, bright-eyed image came up, she nearly collapsed.

Lane's strong arms surrounded her, giving her strength. "Hang in there, Julia. You can do this."

After several shaky breaths and a few more tissues, she tried again. Steven's feed contained a seemingly endless string of his friends' posts expressing sorrow over his death and sharing photos and memories. The only way she could push through was to remind herself their goal was to find where Shannon had taken Tate.

"Tell me again when Steven and Shannon got married?"

Lane gave her the date, and she scrolled rapidly backward until she reached posts from that year. The only pictures she found of Shannon also included others in Steven's circle of friends, and in situations that hadn't suggested to Julia that he was in a serious relationship.

"That photo with Shannon and Steven at the lake," Lane said, pointing at the screen. "Do you know the other couple they're with?"

She took a closer look. In hindsight, it became all too clear that when this photo was taken, Steven and Shannon were already much more than friends. Had Julia seen only what she'd wanted to see—a young man following his mother's admonition to keep relationships platonic and focus on his studies?

You don't have time for this. Not with her grandson's well-being at stake.

Swallowing hard, she focused on the image. "That's Eric Davison. He was one of Steven's best friends."

"And the girl?"

Julia scanned the tags. "Claudia Garza. I remember now that she and Eric got engaged not long after this picture was taken."

After which, she'd cautioned Steven again about avoiding romantic entanglements and keeping his eye on the goal. *Her* goal, she admitted with a pinch to her heart.

She clicked over to Eric's Facebook profile. Since she wasn't in his friends list, she couldn't dig any deeper, but his cover photo of a wedding party in front of a church indicated he and Claudia had gotten married.

"Wait, that's Shannon." Lane leaned closer. "See? The last girl on the right. She's one of the bridesmaids."

Julia recognized her now. She was reed-thin and looked as if she'd had to dredge her smile from the depths of her being, and for only as long as it would take to snap the photo. "This had to be after Steven…" Her throat clenched. "After Tate was born."

Lane gently squeezed her shoulder. "If Shannon was in the wedding party, she and Claudia must have been close. They could still be in touch. Do you know how to reach Claudia? Or her husband?"

"I only knew them through Steven, and not well at all." She vaguely remembered accepting Eric's condolences at the funeral. "I don't even recall where Eric is from."

Lane's frustrated sigh whispered past her ear. "Can you maybe post a message or something? I have no idea how Facebook works."

Sinking into the chair, she rubbed her temples. "I can, but since I'm not on Eric's or Claudia's friends list, they may not see the message for days or weeks or…ever."

He shoved to his feet and stalked to the counter. "I can't think anymore without coffee."

"I'll make some." She went to the cupboard for the canister. "What time is it, anyway?"

"A little past five."

Had they been at this that long already? No wonder her eyes felt like sandpaper.

Lane filled the reservoir while she measured coffee grounds. "We should eat something, too," he said. "I can scramble some eggs."

"I couldn't." Her stomach heaved at the mere suggestion of food. That meant full-strength java wasn't going to sit very well, but she'd done it before when in crunch mode.

The dogs, who'd settled down a bit as the night wore on, now paced at the kitchen door. Julia released them into the yard and then scooped kibble into their bowls. They weren't likely to complain about an early breakfast.

Daisy and Dash didn't, anyway. After Julia let the dogs back inside, Rowena turned up her nose at the bowl and lay staring at the front door as if Tate were sure to return through it any moment now.

The dog's sullen posture only increased Julia's burden of guilt. She'd convinced Lane that having Shannon stay with her would work out for the best. Could she have been more wrong?

"Julia." Lane touched her arm. "Coffee's ready. I'm making myself some toast. Sure you don't want some?"

She waved away the offer and filled two mugs while Lane buttered his toast. Returning to the computer, she composed messages to both Eric and Claudia that she hoped wouldn't come across as too alarming or desperate. *Please contact me if you hear from Shannon*, she concluded. *I only want to help.*

"It's done," she said, closing her laptop.

"So now we wait." Legs extended under the

table, Lane nursed his coffee and gazed into the distance. After only one or two bites, his toast remained untouched.

Real or imagined, she felt his judgment. "If I could think of anyone else to reach out to, don't you think I would? After Steven died, it would have cost me too much emotional pain to try to stay in touch with any of his friends. I never even opened most of the sympathy cards. I just stuffed them in the bottom drawer of my desk."

Casting a glance her way, he gave a humorless laugh. "About three years after Tessa's funeral, I came across the shoebox where I'd stashed the cards I'd received. I tossed the whole box into the recycle bin without opening a single one."

"Oh, Lane, that's so sad. Now you'll never know what people who knew and loved your wife wanted to share with you."

He lifted one shoulder in a weak sign of agreement. "All I cared about then was forgetting the past and starting over." Sliding his hand over hers, he asked, "Are *you* at the point where you could bear to read those cards and letters? Will you ever be?"

"Maybe not yet," she replied softly, "but I want to be. Because that's when I'll know I'm finally coming out on the other side of my grief."

THE OTHER SIDE of grief. Lane wondered if he could pinpoint exactly when thoughts of Tessa hadn't made him want to double over from the pain ripping through his gut. Having a growing daughter to focus on had helped, and he still believed he'd done the right thing by ditching his former life and career and starting from scratch in the mountains.

Well…mostly. He never should have taken it to such isolating extremes. All through Shannon's childhood, the Vernons had tried to tell him she needed so much more than a lonely, sheltered life on the mountain. Why hadn't he listened?

After two more mugs of coffee, he was ready to climb out of his skin. Tired as he was—he hadn't slept since dawn yesterday—he couldn't allow himself to sit still long enough to grab a quick nap. Not while his daughter and grandson were missing.

Over the past hour or so, Julia had posted messages to three or four other friends of Steven's who might also know Shannon. Returning to the table, he asked, "Did you check for replies again?"

"I just did ten minutes ago." Elbows resting on either side of her laptop, she rubbed her eyes. "It's only a little past seven on a Sunday morning. Sensible people are still sound asleep."

"Can you think of anyone else you could contact? Judging from Steven's Facebook page, he didn't lack for friends." He immediately regretted his impatient tone. Drawing a chair closer to hers, he shifted her to face him. "I didn't mean to snap. But I feel like I'm going to lose it if we don't get answers soon."

"I know. Me, too." She lifted red-rimmed eyes to his before turning back to her computer. "I'll look through Steven's timeline again. Maybe more names will jump out at me."

"No. Stop. You've done all you can for now. You're exhausted." He pulled her to her feet and propelled her to the den sofa with an arm around her waist. "Close your eyes. Try to get some rest."

"Only if you do the same."

Pulling out his phone, he nodded and sank into the easy chair. "Okay, one hour. I'm setting my alarm."

And so the day went. He and Julia took turns catnapping between checking her laptop for replies. When they'd heard nothing by late afternoon, he had no choice but to head home and take care of his livestock. He couldn't expect the Vernons to cover for him indefinitely.

He hated to leave Julia, though. Her haggard look worried him, and he was at a loss for anything more he could say or do to convince her she wasn't to blame.

"At least let me call Maddie and Witt," he said, smoothing her tangled hair off her face. "Besides, they're probably wondering why we didn't make it to church this morning."

He'd hardly spoken the words when Julia's cell phone rang. She spun away to grab it. Shoulders collapsing as she read the caller's name, she cast Lane a weary smile. "It's Maddie. She must have read your mind."

He supported her with an arm around her waist as she tearfully described what had happened. When the call ended, she pivoted and sank against Lane's chest. "Maddie and Witt are coming over," she said. "I couldn't talk them out of it."

"I'm glad." He kissed the top of her head. "You shouldn't be alone."

"I wish I could go to the cabin with you."

"Me, too. But you know how bad cell and internet service is up there." Stepping back, he hooked his index finger under her chin and searched her face. "Hey, convince me the tough, tenacious Julia Frasier I know and love is still in there."

She gave a trembling nod. "I'll try."

He stayed with her until the Wittenbauers arrived, and he promised he'd return first thing in the morning—or sooner, if word came. Making his way up the winding mountain roads, he prayed as he never had before. For Shannon. For Tate. And for the woman he'd come to care for at a depth he'd never expected to feel again.

MADDIE'S FIRST QUESTION after Lane had left was, "What have you eaten today?"

"Not much," Julia admitted. "I haven't felt like I could keep anything down."

"That won't do. Mind if I snoop in your pantry?"

Hunched over the computer again, she gave a dismissive flick of her fingers. She already missed Lane's comforting embrace, his confidence, his strength.

She missed everything about him.

The tough, tenacious Julia Frasier I know and love…

She wasn't feeling particularly tough or tenacious at the moment. And had he meant to use the word *love*…or had it merely been an offhand remark? Because over the course of the past few weeks, her feelings toward him had been inching toward the *L* word.

Inching? How about moving at the speed of light?

But would he ever forgive her—ever truly be able to love her—if they never found Shannon and Tate?

Witt pulled over a chair and wrapped her icy fingers in his. "In the Book of Luke, Jesus says, 'For the Son of man is come to seek and to save that which was lost.' It's a truth I can vouch for firsthand. So believe me when I say that wherever Shannon and her little boy are right now, God is watching over them."

All she could do was nod.

While Witt sat praying with her, a savory aroma wafted from the stove. Shortly, Maddie brought a steaming bowl of chicken noodle soup to the table. Nudging Julia's laptop aside, she set the bowl in front of her along with a napkin and spoon. "This should go down easy. And after you've eaten, you're going to bed. Witt and I will monitor your computer and phone for any messages."

"But I—"

"That was a direct order, not a suggestion." Maddie had used her schoolteacher tone, but her smile conveyed tender concern.

It took only one spoonful of soup for Julia to realize how hungry she was. She ate slowly, giving the warm, flavorful broth ample time to settle in her stomach. Afterward, fatigue overwhelming her, she gave in to Maddie's directive and retreated to her bedroom. She fell into a sound sleep the moment her head hit the pillow and didn't know another thing until a shaft of sun pierced her eyelids.

Morning already? She jolted upright. Still wearing yesterday's yoga pants and sweatshirt, she hurried to the kitchen. Witt was just letting the dogs in from the backyard, and Maddie was stirring something on the stove. When they looked her way, she didn't have to ask the question hovering on her lips. Their apologetic smiles told her there'd been no news.

Realizing they'd been here all night, she immediately grew concerned about their sanctuary dogs.

"They're being looked after," Maddie assured. "Two of my best volunteers stepped in."

She added a dash of pepper to the pan. "By the way, your mother called a few minutes ago. I gathered she doesn't know what's happened, so I didn't tell her. I just said we came over because you were feeling a little under the weather."

"Thanks. Mom doesn't need anything else to worry about." Julia sank into a chair and began scrolling through email and messages.

It dawned on her that it was Monday, and she should be on her way to the clinic. But how could she possibly concentrate on work?

Because that's what you do. What she'd always done. Becoming adept at compartmentalizing her life was how she'd managed to survive divorce, single parenthood, the loss of her son, her father's illness...

It was how she'd survive this crisis, too.

She closed her laptop. Maddie or Witt had started coffee, so she went to the cupboard for her favorite travel mug. "I'll be taking this to go, just as soon as I clean up and change."

"Change for what?" Maddie demanded.

"Work, of course." Snapping on the lid, she started from the kitchen.

Maddie sucked in a breath. "Are you serious?"

Continuing on, she said over her shoulder, "I

can check for messages at my office as easily as I can here. And besides, at least at the clinic I'll feel like I'm accomplishing something."

CHAPTER FOURTEEN

LANE HAD RISEN before dawn to tend the live-stock and deal with the usual morning chores. He'd wanted to text Julia first thing but put it off in hopes that with Witt and Maddie there, she'd been able to get some sleep.

When she replied to his 8:14 a.m. message by saying she was on her way to the clinic, he was more than a little surprised.

Left Rowena with D&D at my house, she texted. I sent M&W home to take care of their own animals. Obviously no news or I would have let you know right away.

Obviously.

He'd prayed for Julia to find her inner strength, but was she striving *too* hard to regain some control?

Once he'd taken care of things at home, he drove to the clinic. Dylan greeted him at the front desk and said Julia had just gone into surgery—routine, he stated, so it shouldn't take long. Lane made himself a coffee and claimed one of the doughnuts someone had brought. He grabbed a fishing magazine from the coffee table and went to Julia's office to wait.

He'd read the magazine from cover to cover twice by the time she strode in forty-five minutes later.

She went straight into his arms. "I was so happy when they told me you were here."

"How are you holding up?" He inhaled the fruity scent of her freshly washed hair. "You could have taken the day off, you know."

"This is where I needed to be." Heaving a tired sigh, she nestled closer. "Where I'm needed."

I need you, too, he wanted to say. "Promise me you won't overdo it. This could turn into a marathon, not a sprint."

"Which is another reason I have to keep working." She left his arms and moved behind her desk. "While I'm between patients, I should check for messages."

Lane pulled a chair around to join her. When she found no replies from any of Steven's friends, he said, "We should call Dr. Yoshida.

Even if she hasn't come up with any new leads, I'd like her input on where we go from here."

What the doctor had to say wasn't reassuring. She left them with the same choices: wait it out while hoping and praying, or take legal action and risk further alienating Shannon…or worse.

It was the *or worse* that held Lane back. He firmly believed his daughter would never endanger her son. But would she fall so far into that deep, dark hole that she'd harm herself? He'd rather never see her or his grandson again than push her toward an act of desperation she could never return from.

"So," he said, "I guess we wait."

Eyes filled with understanding, Julia laced her fingers through his. "I guess we wait."

She was about to return to work when her desk intercom buzzed. Dylan's voice came over the speaker: "Dr. J, you have a call on line two from someone named Eric."

With an anxious glance at Lane, she grabbed the receiver. "Eric? Hello!"

"Hi, Dr. Frasier. Claudia was looking at Facebook this morning and saw your message. She told me I should call you right away. Is everything okay?"

"No, Eric, it isn't. May I put you on speaker?

I'm with someone who needs to hear our conversation." At his assent, she introduced Lane and told Eric in as few words as possible why she'd reached out. "We're hoping one of Steven's friends might know where Shannon could have gone."

Eric remained silent for several seconds. "Sorry, but no. We haven't heard from her. Honestly, until just now, I wasn't sure if you'd ever found out Steven got married. He wanted to tell you, right up until the end, but…"

"Then why—" Julia's voice broke. She closed her eyes and swallowed hard. "Why didn't he?"

Heart aching for her, Lane took her hand and gave it an encouraging squeeze.

Eric cleared his throat. "I'm not sure I should say anything, but since Steven can't anymore…"

"Please, just tell me." Julia gave a hard sniff. "Not knowing is destroying me."

Haltingly, Eric admitted what Steven had confided in him nearly four years ago. He'd begun to feel pressure about joining the family veterinary practice, and he'd concluded it wasn't the right path for him.

"He never wanted to let you down, and he struggled a long time with how and when to break the news to you." He paused and inhaled deeply. "This may be more than you want to hear, Dr. Frasier, but the day of his accident, he was on his way home to tell you everything."

Silent tears slid down her face. Lane swiveled her chair toward him and pulled her into his arms. Speaking toward the phone, he said roughly, "Thank you, Eric. If Shannon does happen to contact you, please let us know."

"I will, sir. Wish I could have been more helpful."

Lane pressed the disconnect button. He cradled Julia on his lap and smoothed back her hair while she sobbed.

Face buried in his shoulder, she murmured through her tears, "How could my son imagine I'd ever be disappointed in him? I thought he *wanted* to become a vet. If I'd only known sooner—"

"Hush, don't do this to yourself." He made her sit up and look at him. "You think I haven't asked myself a million times how I could have been a better father for Shannon? But we're only human. No matter how hard we try to do the right thing, we'll still make mistakes."

"I know, but—"

"But nothing." Truth dawning, he gave in to a crooked smile. "I think I'm finally getting what Witt and Pastor Peters tried to tell me the first time I met with them. God knows we're helpless, self-centered, mistake-prone human beings, but He loves us anyway. It's the whole reason He sent us Jesus, so we can quit wallowing in our guilt and start living—*really* living."

Julia slid back into her own chair and pulled a handful of tissues from a desk drawer. Dabbing her eyes, she said, "You make it sound too easy."

"I thought the same thing at first. But reading the Bible again has reminded me that God's ways are so much higher than ours. I think He *wants* to make it easy for us to come to Him." He lifted his hand to her cheek and thumbed away a teardrop she'd missed. "He just asks us to believe. The rest will follow."

LONG AFTER LANE had gone, his words played through Julia's mind. Just as with every other area of her life, had she been attempting to manage her interaction with God instead of simply letting Him in? She imagined God's amusement over the disconnect between her intentions and her follow-through. What good were promises to trust Him if she continually resorted to doing things her own way?

She recalled years ago hearing an inspirational speaker pose the question, "Are you a human *being*, or a human *doing*?"

At the time, she'd smothered an annoyed chuckle, because what did sitting around and waiting accomplish? Her ex-husband's irresponsibility had ingrained in her the value—no, the *necessity*—of direct action, because if she didn't do something, whether taking care of the house or raising their son or bringing home a regular paycheck, it didn't get done.

But the events of last weekend were driving home a truth she continually tried to sidestep.

You are not in control, Julia, and you never were.

Leaving an exam room, she offered a brief smile to Dr. Ramirez as she strode her way. The young veterinarian was already proving her worth, as was Dr. Kruger. In fact, the clients had taken well to all three new staff members. Julia paused and dipped her chin in silent gratitude. God had sent her two skilled vets and a competent office manager exactly when she needed them.

"Dr. Frasier?" Nikki Ramirez lightly touched her arm. "Are you okay?"

"Yes—actually, no." She suddenly found herself unwilling to pretend otherwise. "I—I'm dealing with some personal issues." Gaze softening, she tilted her head. "And I know I've said you can call me Julia."

"Sorry, it's hard when I have so much respect for you... *Julia.*" Nikki gave a self-conscious laugh before growing serious. "If you need to take care of something, Dr. Kruger and I can cover the rest of today's appointments."

"Thanks, but things are in kind of a holding pattern. There's nothing to be done right now."

"Except possibly to take a little time for yourself? You've been going almost nonstop since your visitor left this morning."

At the mention of Lane, her heart flipped. She'd like nothing better than to head straight to the cabin and into his arms.

But no, she needed to stay in town where she could be reached if any of the contacts she'd made responded with news.

She flicked a loose strand of hair off her forehead. "I appreciate your concern, Nikki, but staying busy keeps my mind off the things I have no control over." With a rueful smile, she added, "Which I'm learning is pretty much everything."

A midafternoon coffee break kept her going long enough to finish the day. Before leaving that morning, Lane had asked if he could pick up Rowena and take her back to the cabin with him, so she came home to just Daisy and Dash, who happily cuddled in her lap for a few minutes. She zapped a frozen meal for herself, and after the dogs had their supper, they trotted between the front and back doors as if missing their giant-size playmate as much as she missed Lane.

Deciding it was time to let her parents know what was going on, she called her mother. Mom was stunned but supportive, saying she could get a neighbor to sit with Dad for a day or two if Julia needed her at the clinic. She assured her mother she was coping for now but wouldn't hesitate to ask for help if things changed.

Next, she called Maddie, only to say there'd been no news as of yet. As they said goodbye, a text came through from Lane, and they spent the next half hour texting back and forth about how their days had gone and generally attempting to keep each other's spirits up. Lane signed off with a texted prayer that brought a lump to Julia's throat.

Getting ready for bed later, she wondered if she'd ever have rediscovered her faith if not for everything that had happened since Lane had come into her life. As frightening and difficult as the past few days had been, she didn't know how she'd get through this ordeal without Lane's support combined with the love and provision of a sovereign God.

TUESDAY PASSED MUCH the same. Then Wednesday and Thursday, still with no word from Shannon or anyone she may have reached out to. Julia made it through each day only by the power of prayer and the faith that wherever Shannon and Tate had disappeared to, God watched over them.

Early Friday morning, while she stood shivering on the patio and waited for Daisy and Dash to take care of business, her cell phone chimed in the pocket of her velour robe. She'd been carrying it with her at all times, but after so many days with no news, she assumed it was her mother's regular call.

Herding the dogs inside, she answered without looking at the display. "Good morning, Mom."

"J-Julia?" The stammering, panicked voice was definitely not her mother's. "Please, y-you've got to help me!"

Her stomach clenched. Kicking the door

shut, she pressed the phone hard against her ear. "Shannon. Where are you?"

"I—I can't—" The girl sounded like she was hyperventilating. Tate's incessant crying sounded in the background.

"What's wrong with Tate?" Julia demanded. "Is he sick? Is he hurt?"

"No, but he won't stop crying, and I—" Shannon's voice rose with every word until she was practically screaming. "He just wants his dog, and he won't shut up about it!"

Julia inhaled slowly, deeply. *Please, Lord, give me the words.* "Shannon, honey, I need you to try to calm down and listen, okay? Because your anxiety isn't helping Tate." She tried for a light laugh. "I remember when Steven used to obsess over something, and if I let him upset me, too, it was a lot harder to quiet him."

"Okay…okay…" Shannon expelled a tremulous gust of air, while nearby, Tate's sobs grew louder. "But could we just come get the dog? Because I can't take this crying anymore. I just can't!"

It didn't take a mental health pro to realize the girl was spiraling. Maybe Julia could use this to her advantage. "If you tell me where you are, I could—"

"No. I'd rather come there. My friend can watch Tate till I get back."

So that strategy wasn't going to work. "The thing is, Rowena isn't at my house anymore. Your dad took her home to the cabin."

Shannon grew silent except for her strained breathing.

Tate's howls continued. "Want Weena! "P'ease, Mama, now!"

Julia's heart broke over the little boy's despairing cries. She had to think of something. "Shannon, listen. I know how you feel about seeing your dad again, but if you want to get the dog, I'm afraid you'll have to go to the cabin. I can meet you there, though. You'd hardly have to see your dad at all, just get Rowena and leave."

A sniffle. "Really?"

"Yes, really. I'd just ask one thing of you, though."

"Wh-what's that?"

She sent up a silent prayer that her request wouldn't slam the door on this discussion. "Bring Tate with you so your dad can tell him a final goodbye. Please. You can spare him that much compassion."

Shannon's silence stretched thin, until she finally murmured, "I... I guess so."

Eyes squeezed shut, Julia pressed a hand to her racing heart. "Thank you." She lowered the phone long enough to make sure it showed the number Shannon had called from. "Can I text you back at this same number when I've arranged a time to meet?"

"Yes, okay. Soon, though." Speaking away from the phone, she said, "It'll be all right, sweetie. Mama's going to get your doggy for you."

A little boy's hiccuping cry was the last thing Julia heard before the line went dead.

She immediately sent a text to Lane: **Heard from Shannon! Working on a plan. Can you come over?**

His reply came seconds later: **See you in an hour.**

A quick call to the clinic caught Amy tending to preopening duties. "Something's come up, and I can't make it in today. If things get too backed up, my mom has offered to be on call."

"Don't worry about a thing, Dr. J. We've got your back."

She thanked the Lord again for the caring and dependable staff He'd given her.

After feeding the dogs and starting coffee,

she phoned her mother to fill her in and asked her to please pray the plan worked.

 AFTER NEARLY A week of waiting and wondering, could they be close to getting Tate and Shannon back? *Please, Lord,* Lane prayed as he rushed through his morning chores, *whatever Julia has in mind, let it work.*

Shortly after eight thirty, he parked in her driveway. She met him at the door with the hug he'd been craving and then ushered him to the kitchen. Dressed in jeans, a turtleneck and a fleece vest, she looked more beautiful—and more hopeful—than he'd seen her in days.

"Don't keep me in suspense," he said as he accepted a mug of strong coffee. "What did Shannon say? And what's this plan you're working on?"

She gave him the gist of Shannon's phone call. His chest squeezed as he pictured his distraught grandson.

"The first thing we need to do," she said, "is talk to Dr. Yoshida. She should be there when Shannon brings Tate to the cabin."

"I see where you're going with this." He tweaked his chin. "Like an intervention?"

"Exactly. We need to lovingly convince her

that running away isn't the solution. That she must go back into treatment. She may not trust either of us right now, but I believe she trusts her doctor enough to listen."

Dr. Yoshida agreed the plan had merit. They talked through the timing and decided to ask Shannon to come that afternoon at three o'clock. Dr. Yoshida would arrive an hour earlier so they could discuss any last-minute details.

After Julia called her parents with another update, Lane followed her to their house to drop off Daisy and Dash in case this turned into a longer day than anticipated.

At the cabin, Lane parked in his usual spot under the deck, and Julia pulled in behind him. Her lime-green SUV would be in plain sight to assure Shannon that she'd kept her promise to be there. He'd have Dr. Yoshida park out of sight.

Over a lunch of Lane's homemade vegetable soup neither of them had much appetite for, they reviewed every possibility—good, bad or downright horrible—as to how the afternoon could go. The initial excitement quickly wore thin, replaced by nerves and doubt. For Julia's sake, Lane fought to stay positive, but all he could think about was what he'd do if they didn't convince his daughter to leave Tate with him and return to the hospital.

Dr. Yoshida arrived a few minutes after two. While Julia showed her inside, Lane took her keys and moved her car to the other side of the barn.

The doctor's serenely confident demeanor allayed some of their anxiety. She reminded them to remain calm no matter how Shannon reacted, and above all, to trust the Holy Spirit for the words to speak.

As it neared three o'clock, Lane's pulse ramped up. According to plan, he took Rowena upstairs and shut her in the bedroom. She wasn't happy about it, but it was one more stalling tactic to keep Shannon from bolting.

Back downstairs, he distracted himself with a sudoku puzzle while Julia watched from the living room window. At five after three, she called him over as a blue sedan slowly approached the open gate and turned in. A woman he didn't recognize was driving. Shannon sat in the passenger seat.

He turned toward Dr. Yoshida. "She's here."

Julia hauled in a deep breath and started for the door. "That's my cue."

"Wait." Lane cut her off and wrapped her in his arms. "I'll be praying. For all of us."

"I'm counting on it." Casting him a shaky smile, she reluctantly slipped from his embrace and stepped out to the deck.

Lane returned to the window he'd left open slightly so he could hear what was said. Dr. Yoshida joined him, both of them staying out of view while peering around the curtain.

The blue car eased to a stop next to Julia's SUV, and now Lane could make out the top of Tate's head in a child's seat in the back. He dipped his chin in a sigh of relief. His greatest worry was that his daughter would decide not to bring Tate after all, and if this intervention didn't work, how would they ever find him?

After a moment's hesitation, Shannon opened the passenger door, her gaze nervously skimming the area as she stood beside the car. "Where's the dog?"

"In the cabin," Julia replied calmly. "It's okay. I've talked with your dad, and he understands what you want. We'd both be so grateful if we could spend a little time with Tate before you go."

Arms crossed, Shannon glanced over her

shoulder. "Well…just for a few minutes. I don't want to be here any longer than I have to."

"Of course." Julia edged closer, all smiles. "Can I help you get him out of the car?"

"No, I'll do it." Leaning into the rear seat to unbuckle Tate, Shannon said something to the driver, who nodded.

When she emerged with the little boy, his lips were trembling and his face was blotchy from crying. Lane would have charged out the door to grab him if Dr. Yoshida hadn't held him in place with her amazingly strong grip.

"Remember what we talked about," she reminded him. "Whatever you're feeling right now, don't let Shannon see anything but her loving, concerned father." She gave his arm a final pat and slipped out to the kitchen, where she'd stay until Shannon and Tate were settled in the living room.

When Julia and Shannon started up the outer stairs, Lane swallowed his mounting anxiety and crossed to the other side of the room. He'd give his daughter plenty of space so she wouldn't feel cornered.

The door opened. Julia entered first, casting Lane a subtle nod. As they'd agreed, once Shannon and Tate passed through the door, Julia closed it and reached up to silently secure the safety latch. It wouldn't keep Shannon from bolting if she decided to, but it might slow her getaway.

"Me down!" Tate demanded. He wriggled in Shannon's arms until she had no choice but to release him. He ran to Rowena's empty bed near the woodstove and swung his gaze in all directions. "Weena? Weena!"

"It's okay, Tater Tot." Lane knelt and held out his arms to the whimpering boy. Judging from the muted scratching and whining coming from upstairs, Rowena sensed her best pal was near, but she'd have to wait a little longer. "I'll get her for you in a few minutes. We just need to talk to Mama first."

"I'm not here to talk." Rushing over, Shannon grabbed Tate's hand before Lane could scoop him up. She raised her glance toward the noises and then turned to Julia. Her voice shook as she stated, "Y-you promised we could get the dog and leave."

"Yes, and you also promised we could have a little time with our grandson. Please. Just five minutes." The smile never left Julia's face.

Lane didn't know how she managed, because he was about to lose it big-time. Pushing to his

feet, he prayed for a measure of Julia's self-control. "How about we all sit down? Hey, I have
some of that cocoa mix you always liked. Can
I fix you a cup?"

Breath coming in quick gasps, Shannon appeared on the edge of a full-blown breakdown.
"I—I just want—"

Dr. Yoshida quietly entered the room. "Hello,
Shannon."

Her chin dropped. "Wh-what are you doing
here?"

"I thought you might need a friendly face."
The doctor moved closer, one hand extended.
"Will you let me help?"

"Mama?" Tate tugged on his mother's hand,
his little face turned up and his lower lip pushed
out in a pleading look. "It be otay."

That broke her completely. Sobbing, she collapsed into the rocking chair and pulled her son
into her lap. Dr. Yoshida knelt in front of her,
speaking so softly that Lane couldn't hear. Shannon nodded, her expression compliant, and that
had to be a good sign.

Thank You, Lord!

CHAPTER FIFTEEN

A FULL TWO weeks had gone by since Shannon had returned to Mercy Cottage—voluntarily, for which Julia gave thanks every single day. Back on the meds Shannon had neglected to take while in hiding, the young mom was slowly stabilizing. In the meantime, Tate was safe and secure at the cabin with his grandpa and his faithful dog.

That was all well and good—wonderful, in fact—but it left Julia with one significant problem. With things returning to a semblance of normal, including her work at the clinic, weekends were her only real chance to see her grandson.

And Lane. She couldn't forget Lane.

Too distracted by everything that had happened recently, they'd both been avoiding a closer examination of their relationship. Julia's heart was telling her she wanted it to be more…

but did Lane still feel the same? Or, now that his focus had returned to taking care of Tate and monitoring Shannon's improvement, would it be easier all around if they scaled things back to the friendship level?

She hoped to get a sense of his feelings soon—possibly even today.

Leaving Drs. Ramirez and Kruger to cover the Saturday morning clinic appointments, Julia aimed her SUV up the winding mountain road to Lane's cabin. The first weekend in November had turned decidedly colder, but the sky remained a clear wintry blue. The comforting scent of woodsmoke seeped through the air vents as she passed other homesteads on the way up. She pictured Lane's cozy living room, the red-orange glow of his stove, Rowena stretched out on her bed nearby and Tate stacking blocks on the nubby carpet.

She imagined walking into Lane's arms and inhaling his manly scents of piney aftershave and flannel.

She imagined his kiss…

Jerking her attention back to the road, she gave herself a mental talking-to. No point in getting her hopes up in case recent events had permanently cooled things between them. Lane may have forgiven her for her part in Shannon's disappearance, and he'd shown nothing but kindness and reassurance ever since. But shared hugs and chaste kisses didn't tell the whole story. A man who'd chosen to hide away from the world for twenty-plus years after the death of his wife could just as easily decide that giving his heart again wasn't worth the risk.

It was half past nine when she braked outside his ranch gate. Stepping from her car to open the gate, she inhaled a bracing breath of clean mountain air. Something cold and wet brushed her cheek, and she looked skyward to see a few tiny snowflakes swirling in the breeze. The clouds creeping in didn't appear too heavy, but this was Montana in the mountains, and the weather could change quickly.

Not *too* quickly today—*please, Lord*—because she was counting on a full day's visit with her grandson.

And with Lane.

"Julia." His husky voice startled her. "I didn't expect you until this afternoon."

She looked up to see him striding down the driveway, Tate propped on his hip. Rowena trotted beside them, still favoring her cast rear leg.

Pushing open the gate, Julia tried for a casual smile. "I had a chance to get on the road early. If you have other stuff to do, I can keep Tate entertained and out of your way."

Mouth in a twist, he glanced toward his workshop. "I do need to finish a project I've been working on."

"Perfect." She came just close enough to plant a kiss on Tate's cheek and then took a giant step back. Keeping her smile bright, she said, "Let me get parked at the cabin, and I can take over with the little guy."

After she drove forward, Lane closed the gate and met her at the cabin steps. He had an edginess in his posture that she hadn't noticed the past couple of weekends when she'd either driven up to spend a couple of hours with Tate or they'd met at church on Sunday mornings.

She cocked her head. "If I've come at an inconvenient time—"

"It isn't that. I, uh…"

"Gampy." Tate pinched Lane's chin between his pudgy thumb and fingers, forcing him to make eye contact. The boy's expression was as insistent as Julia had ever seen it. "No wait. Show Gammy."

She narrowed her eyes. "Show me what, Tater Tot?"

"In there." He pointed to the workshop. "Gampy make su'pwise."

"A surprise? For Grammy?" She cast Lane a questioning glance as her heart gave a stutter.

"It isn't ready yet. I was hoping to finish it before you got here." Annoyance filled his tone. His puckered frown reminded her of Tate's when he didn't get his way.

"Well…like I said, Tate and I can go inside and play by ourselves while you…do whatever it is you need to do."

"No, Gampy. Show now!" Tate wriggled so much that Lane had to set him on the ground. He grabbed Lane's fingers and tugged him in the direction of the workshop.

Planting his feet, Lane struggled to keep his balance. "Tate—"

"Now, Gampy!" The boy grunted and pulled harder on Lane's hand. Rowena barked and pranced, her own excitement bubbling over.

He hung his head in defeat. "Okay, okay. But this isn't how I wanted today to go."

Julia almost felt bad for him, but she was too interested to see what her surprise was to let him off the hook. Besides, if he'd gone to all this trouble, it had to mean something about his feelings for her...didn't it?

NOPE, THIS WAS not at all the way Lane had pictured today going. Julia *never* managed to break away from the clinic on Saturdays early enough to spend the whole day with him and Tate. He'd assumed he'd have at least four or five more hours to put the finishing touches on his project. Then he'd planned to spruce up the cabin before running over to Lila's to pick up the rhubarb pie she was making for tonight's dessert. Lila had even volunteered to keep Tate at her house during dinner so Lane and Julia could have a bit of privacy.

And all this to—he hoped—convince Julia exactly how much she meant to him. Since Shannon had returned to the hospital, they'd been idling in neutral, as if Julia felt as insecure as he did about looking deeper at where they went from here.

"Gampy. C'mon." Tate's tug on his fingers hadn't let up.

"I'm coming, kiddo." Wincing, he motioned for Julia to follow. "I'd intended to save this for later, but I guess we're doing it now."

She caught up and grabbed Tate's other hand. "You made something for me in your workshop?"

His anticipation rose as he imagined her reaction. "Like I said, it's not all the way done yet." He still needed to apply the last coat of varnish. By late afternoon, it would have been dry enough for the unveiling.

When they were still several steps away, Tate trotted ahead and then stood with his back to the workshop door and stretched out his arms. "Gammy, close eyes."

"Okay." She cast Lane an uncertain glance. "But someone will have to take my hand and guide me."

"Happy to do the honors. Wait right here while I get the door." He couldn't believe how his heart had begun to pound. Would she like it? Or would she see it as either too sentimental or too presumptuous? Or both?

He eased open the door, releasing aromas of sawdust, oil, wood stain and varnish.

Tate bounced on his toes and clapped his hands. "Otay, Gammy. Come see!"

Lane returned to link her arm through his. "Keep your eyes closed. I'll tell you when to look."

Her breaths became quick and shallow as he led her inside.

When he'd positioned her directly in front of his creation, he stepped aside. "You can open your eyes now."

She blinked a few times, gasped and pressed both hands to her heart. "Oh, Lane, how beautiful!"

"Don't touch it yet. I still need to apply another coat." Watching her expression as she examined every inch of the high-backed oak rocking chair, he warmed with pride.

"Lane, is that..." She extended her hand toward the designs he'd carved into the scrolled upper back. "It is! It's the rose of Sharon like my great-grandmother's ring."

"Since you were kind enough to let Shannon keep it, I thought you might like a remembrance."

"It's... It's perfect." A tear slipped down her cheek, and she blotted it with the back of her glove.

Tate sidled up beside her leg and tugged on her jacket. "Gammy like?"

"I sure do, honey. So very much." She scooped him into her arms. "And look there between the roses. That spells 'Grammy.'"

"Gammy!" He clapped his hands. Rowena barked and wagged her tail.

After giving Julia a few more minutes to admire the chair from various angles, Lane suggested she take Tate to the cabin while he applied more varnish. "It won't be ready to take home until it's completely dry, but I could bring it over in a few days."

She pulled her lips between her teeth, her gaze turning thoughtful. "Maybe. We'll see…"

Her remark punctured his enthusiasm. "Hey, I get it. I should have matched it better to your decor—"

"No, I wouldn't change a thing. It's just—" Drawing a quick breath, she brightened her smile. "We can talk about it later. Tater Tot, let's take Rowena to the house. We can play or read a story while we wait for Gramps."

He watched for a moment as they plodded across the yard. Then he latched the door to keep from losing any more warmth from his shop heater.

Great. Now he was left to ponder where he'd gone wrong. Because how did gushing, teary-eyed appreciation do a complete U-turn toward *We'll see* in a matter of seconds?

An hour later, he put away his tools and supplies, slipped into his jacket and closed up the shop. Outside, the clouds had thickened, and the wind had picked up. Before he reached the cabin steps, his coat sleeves looked like they'd been sprinkled with powdered sugar.

So much for his dinner plans. Julia would likely decide to cut her visit short before the weather got any worse.

Inside, he found all three of them—Julia, Tate and Rowena—camped out near the stove on the giant-size fleece-covered dog bed.

Julia looked up from the storybook she'd been reading to Tate. "I helped myself to the rest of your coffee, so I started a fresh pot. It should be ready."

"Thanks. I could use some warming up." It was a convenient excuse to put off a discussion he wasn't sure how to begin. Trying not to think about how beautiful she looked in the red-gold glow of the firelight, he started for the kitchen. "By the way, the snow's picking up. You might want to head home before it gets too heavy."

"Yes, I noticed," she said, startling him. He hadn't realized she'd gotten up to follow. "But your guest room's still available, isn't it?"

His stomach somersaulted. He swallowed hard before swiveling to face her. "It is. But are you sure—"

"I'm sure I'm not ready to leave so soon."

Her tentative smile made his mouth go dry. He returned his attention to what he'd come to the kitchen for, but in his current emotional state, he feared he'd either drop his mug or spill coffee all over the counter and himself.

"Here, let me." She nudged him out of the way and reached for the carafe. "Tate's going to be hungry for lunch soon, and then he'll need a nap. While he's sleeping, I was hoping we could…talk about a few things."

"Talk?" The word came out in a squeak. He cleared his throat. "I mean, sure. That sounds like a good idea."

This was it. She was breaking up with him.

Breaking up? How was that even possible when they'd never officially declared themselves a couple?

And how many mixed messages could one woman give in the space of a few hours?

Before he could take a sip from the mug she'd handed him, his cell phone signaled a text. He pulled it from his hip pocket and read the message. It was Lila, telling him he could come over for the pie any time.

"I have an errand to run." He gingerly set

his mug on the counter. "Shouldn't take more than twenty minutes."

Without waiting for a reply, he rushed to the front door, grabbing his jacket and truck keys on the way.

Maybe by the time he got back, he'd have figured out what he could say to keep her in his life as more—*much more*—than merely a friend and Tate's other grandparent.

COULD THINGS GET any weirder between them?

Arms folded, Julia watched from the living room window as Lane's truck disappeared from view. And what sort of errand could be so urgent but required less than half an hour to complete?

Tate nudged his way between her and the window and peered over the sill. "Where Gampy go?"

"Good question. Want some lunch while we wait?" The sooner the little guy went upstairs for a nap, the sooner she could sit Lane down for their long-overdue heart-to-heart.

She found Tate's usual tortillas, hummus and sliced turkey in the fridge. He was swallowing his last sip of milk when she heard Lane coming in the front door.

"In the kitchen," she called.

He strode through the archway carrying what looked like a pie and set it on the counter.

Julia hiked a brow. "*That* was your errand?"

"Yep. Fresh from Lila Vernon's oven." He shrugged out of his jacket. Apparently, that was all he had to say on the subject.

Tate scrubbed the sleeve of his sweatshirt across his mouth. "Yay, pie!"

Using a dampened cloth, Julia cleaned the remnants of Tate's lunch from his fingers and face. "Nap time, fella."

Leaving Lane to deal with his pie and whatever else he had going on, she herded her grandson upstairs. He talked her into reading him one more story but fell asleep before she finished. After covering him with a blanket, she stepped away from the crib with a sigh. He was growing so fast. Another month or two, and he'd be ready for a toddler bed.

And where would *she* be in another month or two? Where did she *want* to be?

Time for that talk with Lane.

Enticing aromas—tomatoes and toasting bread?—drew her back to the kitchen. Lane stood at the stove, a wooden spoon in one hand and a spatula in the other. He shot a quick smile over his shoulder. "Didn't look like you'd eaten yet, and I'm starved. Hope tomato soup and grilled cheese sandwiches work for you."

Another stalling tactic? She shrugged. "I'll set the table."

They managed a few sentences of small talk over lunch. When Lane rose to wash dishes afterward, she stopped him. "Those can wait, can't they? I'd really like us to talk before Tate wakes up."

He nodded slowly. "Coffee first?"

Giving it a moment's thought, she said, "No, thanks."

"All right, then." Seeming to understand she was ready to get this conversation started, he gestured toward the living room.

They took opposite ends of the sofa, not too close, not too far apart, and angled slightly toward each other.

"If I did something—" Lane began.

"I've been wanting to tell you—" she said at the same time.

He lifted one hand. "Please. Say what you need to say."

She paused for a slow breath, her glance drifting toward the window. The snow was falling heavily now. If this conversation didn't go as hoped, she could be stuck here through an extremely uncomfortable weekend.

Directing a silent prayer heavenward, she marshaled her courage and faced him squarely. "The fact is, Lane, I think I'm in love with you, and I—"

He barked out a laugh. "You… You are?"

She flinched. "I don't see what's funny about it."

"No, I'm just relieved." Grinning, he shook his head. "I mean, considering how you left things this morning, I was afraid you were about to tell me the exact opposite."

Brow furrowed, she tried to recall what she'd said earlier. "It was only because…" Then her brain keyed in on a word he'd just used, and her pulse sped up. "Wait…you're *relieved*?"

"I am." He reached across the space between them to take her hand. His voice roughened as he said, "Because I've been trying for days to figure out how to let you know I'm falling for you, too. In a very big way. In fact," he went on with a nod toward the window, "since it looks like you'll be staying over tonight, you have every right to blame it on my prayers."

It was her turn to laugh. "You *prayed* we'd get snowed in?"

"Only if the conversation we're having right now went the way I hoped."

Warmth spread through her chest. "And did it?"

"So far...except for one small detail." Scooting closer, he drew her into his arms. With one hand cradling the back of her neck, he pressed his lips to hers in a kiss that erased any doubt whatsoever about his feelings...or her own.

When the kiss ended and she could breathe again, she snuggled against his chest. "I was worried you were still holding too tightly to your memories."

"Of Tessa? She'll always be a part of me. I can't change that. But she'd hate how I turned my back on life in a misguided effort to shield our daughter—and myself—from the world. And I know she'd want me to be happy again." He kissed her forehead and hugged her closer. "To *love* again."

It would have been easy to rest there in his arms and dwell in the moment, but Julia hadn't yet shared everything on her heart. She gave his chest a pat and straightened but stayed close, her fingers weaving through his. "You should know why I reacted the way I did when you mentioned bringing the rocking chair to my house."

He stiffened slightly. "Okay..."

"It was because I don't know how much longer I want to live there."

"I don't understand. You want to move?"

"Lane." Heart ready to burst, she eased sideways to palm his cheek. "I want to make my home with you. Right here, where I've never felt more at peace."

He stared in disbelief. "But the clinic. Your work. How would you manage?"

Thoughts spinning, she realized the possibilities had been brewing in her subconscious since her first visit to the cabin. Abruptly, she rose and paced to the window. She returned to stand in front of him, but her gaze was fixed on the future. *Their* future.

Plopping down again, she clasped her hands between her knees. "I've been stressed and anxious for so long, believing that after my parents retired, the success of Frasier Veterinary Clinic would land solely on my shoulders. After Steven died, that burden only grew heavier, because he wouldn't be running the family business at my side."

Lane caressed her shoulder. "I can only imagine."

"Then, to learn it was only *my* dream, not

his… It's changed my whole perspective." She sniffed back a tear. "We have two highly skilled doctors on board now, plus our excellent vet techs and a fantastic new office manager. The clinic has never run more efficiently."

"So…what are you saying?"

"I'm saying I'm ready to ease back, to take time for myself—for *us*." She cast him a watery gaze, her smile hopeful. "To create some new dreams with the man I love beyond imagining."

His lips skewed into a crooked smile. "Hmm, if you're contemplating spending most of your days…and nights…right here with me, we should probably make it official."

"That's what I was thinking." The look in his eyes sent warm tingles up her spine. She locked her fingers behind his neck, bringing them nose to nose. "Lane Bromley," she murmured, "will you marry me?"

His throaty chuckle tickled her face. "How does Monday work for you? Because that's the earliest we can get a license."

"Monday can't get here soon enough."

EPILOGUE

Five months later

LANE CAST HIS gaze around Julia's kitchen—actually, Shannon's kitchen now. "Are you sure you have everything you need?"

"Yes, Dad, I'm sure. Thanks to you and Julia, there's plenty in the pantry and fridge to last until I get my first paycheck in two weeks."

"And your meds—you won't forget those, will you?"

"Dad. Stop fussing." His grinning daughter patted his cheek before setting another plate in the dishwasher. "I hear Tate waking up from his nap. Why don't you get him into his snowsuit and take him and Rowena out back to build a snowman? He's been begging to ever since he saw it snowed last night. By tomorrow, it'll all be gone, and I've been too busy settling in."

He shouldn't worry so much, but he couldn't

help it. Shannon had been released from Mercy Cottage three weeks ago—praise God! She'd stayed with him and Julia at the cabin temporarily while reconnecting with "normal" life and with her little boy.

Yesterday, they'd moved her, Tate and the dog into Julia's house so she could be close to the new job she'd begin on Monday as part-time receptionist at Frasier Veterinary Clinic. Julia's mother had already volunteered—actually, she'd *demanded*—to watch Tate while Shannon was at work.

Later, watching his grandson pat mounds of wet snow into two lumps resembling a misshapen human and a legless dog, Lane's heart swelled with wonder and gratitude. How his life had changed in a matter of months! Yes, they'd experienced a few setbacks since Shannon had shown up at the cabin with her precious little boy, but he'd never been happier than he was at this moment.

Well, except for an unforgettable Monday evening five months ago when he and Julia had stood before Pastor Peters with their hours-old marriage license and pledged their love before God, Witt and Maddie, and the pastor and his wife.

The familiar rumble of Julia's SUV drew his attention to the driveway. Giving a wave, she climbed out and started through the side gate. After greeting Rowena with a scratch behind the ears, she sidled up next to Lane. "You guys look like you're having fun."

Grinning, he drew her into a one-armed hug while concealing the snow he'd scooped up with his other hand. "It's about to get a lot more fun."

"What— *Aaaagh!*" She yanked free, furiously brushing at the icy clump he'd shoved down the back of her collar. "You're in for it now, Gramps!" She grabbed a fistful of snow and aimed it at Lane's face.

He ducked just in time, but momentum sent him toppling sideways—right on top of Tate's snow figures.

"Gampy! Oh, no!"

"Oops. Sorry, Tater Tot." Lane scrambled onto his knees. "Grammy and I will help you fix them."

The back door opened and Shannon stepped onto the porch with her cell phone. Laughing, she snapped several photos while Lane and Julia attempted to rebuild Tate's masterpieces.

When they'd done all they could, Lane

helped Julia to her feet. Studying their lop-sided handiwork, he frowned. "Looks like we should keep our day jobs. Which reminds me." He planted a kiss on his wife's temple. "How'd your surgeries go today?"

"Both patients are recovering nicely. And in other news…" She turned to wrap both arms around his torso. "Dr. Kruger is ready to sign the partnership papers, *and* he has a colleague who's very interested in joining the practice."

Lane cast her a hopeful grin. "Does this mean you'll be cutting back on your hours even more?"

"I'd probably come in two days a week, just to keep an eye on things and stay in touch with my favorite patients."

"I can live with that…if you can." He studied her, wanting to be sure she wasn't hiding any reservations about the changes she'd been making. But all he saw were the eyes of love looking back at him.

And all he could do was lift his face heavenward in silent praise to God for giving him a grandson, for restoring his daughter, and—most especially—for filling his arms and heart with this bright, beautiful and utterly amazing woman.

IT WAS WELL past sunset when Julia and Lane arrived back at the cabin. They'd have three whole days together before she'd head down the mountain again to see to things at the clinic. While he stoked the woodstove, she found some leftovers in the fridge to reheat for a light supper. While the food warmed, she brewed a pot of decaf for later.

With the dishes done, they carried their mugs to the living room, where Lane had positioned their rocking chairs facing the stove. As they sipped and rocked in companionable silence, with Daisy and Dash cuddled together on the plush bed near their feet, Julia savored the deepest peace she'd ever known.

She still couldn't quite believe they'd married so quickly, but neither of them had been willing to wait a moment longer to begin building a life together. Hadn't they both been lonely long enough? Their pastor, closest friends and Julia's parents had given their blessing as well.

And in this tranquil place, supported by her husband and dwelling in God's Word, she was coming to terms not only with the loss of her son, but with lost dreams as well. She'd always miss Steven, always regret the mistakes she'd made, but she was learning day by day to rest in God's forgiveness. Even more so, to forgive herself.

Lane reached for her hand. "Happy?"

"Incredibly." She glanced over at him, his features burnished by the fire's glow. "I thought the cabin might feel too quiet after the kids moved into my place. But now I'm more than ready for it to be just us."

"I miss them, but I'm happy for them." He drew her fingertips to his lips. "For *us*."

A tingle raced up her arm even as languid warmth spread through her limbs. "I know it's still early, but what if we let the dogs out once more and then head upstairs?"

He grinned. "That's the best suggestion I've heard all day."

★ ★ ★ ★ ★

His Neighbour's Secret
Lillian Warner

MILLS & BOON

Lillian Warner earned a master of arts in professional writing from the University of Massachusetts. After she retired from her federal career as an editor and webmaster, her next goal was to become a published author. She was thrilled when her book was picked up through a Love Inspired blitz! When she's not writing, Lillian is active as a performer and director in community theater on Cape Cod, where she lives with her husband and several rescue cats.

Visit the Author Profile page
at millsandboon.com.au for more titles.

I sought the Lord, and he heard me,
and delivered me from all my fears.
—*Psalm* 34:4

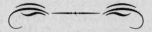

DEDICATION

To my husband, Glenn, who has been with me
throughout my writing journey.

CHAPTER ONE

SQUASHING THE URGE to collapse onto her desk, Mackenzie Reid scanned the spacious room with critical eyes. It was the first classroom she'd ever set up and she wanted to get it as perfect as possible.

Kenzie had prepared each area for a different creative activity suitable for first through fifth grades. Cheerful colors bloomed on all sides. Pots of bright paint lined the shelves next to several easels in one corner. Fairy-tale puppets hung in a row near the miniature stage. Dress-up clothes spilled from a trunk. Another space boasted sturdy musical instruments surrounded by room for dancing.

Her young students would have fun while they experimented with the arts in preparation for the school's first ever performance, scheduled for October. And that was all that mattered. The headmistress knew that Kenzie hadn't taught since her student teaching days over ten years ago, when she was working on her bachelor's degree in early childhood education. She was still amazed that she'd gotten this job and wanted to do her absolute best, especially given everything that had gone wrong over the past couple of years.

She wouldn't allow herself to take a single step into the past. It was like walking into quicksand. The only way to look was forward. Now she was the creative arts teacher at the Good Shepherd Academy, a small private school in the heart of Massachusetts's beautiful Berkshire Mountains. She had a whole new life, so different from the old one she had no idea what to expect. This was an adventure. It was exciting. It was challenging.

It was exhausting. And she hadn't even started yet.

She took comfort in knowing the room had once been used for Sunday school classes. The school had started up in the old church building a few years ago when the new chapel was built, right across the parking lot.

For the past two years, faith and her little daughter, Pippa, had been the only things that made it possible for her to keep going.

Glancing at the oversize clock on the wall, she was surprised to see that it was already a quarter to one. She had to pull herself together and get to her first faculty meeting on time if she wanted to make a good first impression.

Which she desperately needed to do.

In a hurry to push the thought aside, Kenzie rose too hastily and had to grab the desk as the room spun around her. Squeezing her eyes shut, she took deep, slow breaths and waited for her brain and stomach to settle.

"You're fine," she whispered. "You're perfectly fine. There's absolutely nothing wrong with you."

That was what all the Boston doctors had said, and that was what she tried to believe, in spite of the strange array of symptoms that had assailed her after a week on Martha's Vineyard two years ago. She firmly believed it was Lyme disease but the doctors didn't agree.

Maybe out in the country it would be easier to find a doctor who would listen to her. She hoped so, anyway.

Her eyes opened. The room had stilled, although it was a bit out of focus. Kenzie raised her chin and strode toward the door to the unlit hallway. Her still-unsteady feet caught on the threshold, and boom, she was on the floor.

"Whoa! Are you all right?"

The man's voice came out of nowhere, forceful enough to echo through the empty corridor. Startled, Kenzie looked up, trying to blink the darkness away. "I'm fine. Just…the floor is slippery, and I was rushing to get to the faculty meeting."

"No rush. They never get these things started on time."

Something in his booming voice with its slight Boston accent stirred her memory. She peered harder at his face, a shadowed blur in the dark hall.

"Good to know." Kenzie struggled to get back on her feet with her modesty intact. Not so easy in a dress.

"Let me help." A firm hand took hold of her wrist.

"I'm fine. I can manage," she huffed.

The hand released her. "Yipes. Sorry."

After some more ungraceful flailing, Kenzie stumbled to her feet and sighed. "No, I'm sorry. I'm just so embarrassed. Not the introduction I was hoping for."

The man laughed, a pleasant, hearty sound. "You must be the new creative arts teacher."

Kenzie took a deep breath to tamp down the dizziness. "Yup, that's me."

"I'm right across the hall, in the old rec room. It's my second year teaching health and safety. Which is just a fancy name for phys ed." The big, warm hand took hold of Kenzie's and shook it. "I'm Mr. Raymond."

Kenzie felt her throat go dry.

It couldn't possibly be Jonah. Could it?

He kept talking, oblivious to Kenzie's silence. "Anyway, we should head on up there and grab some coffee before it's all gone."

She followed numbly as he guided her toward the stairs, where the lighting was better. When she took another quick glance up, her fears were confirmed.

Kenzie's heart clunked into her stomach.

Even though silver was starting to invade his thick, dark hair, even though the lines around his eyes and mouth were etched more deeply and his muscular physique showed the beginnings of dad bod, even after not seeing him for many years, Kenzie would have known him anywhere.

Jonah Raymond. The man she'd been in love

with back in grad school, eight years ago. The man she'd been ready to marry the minute he asked. And when he didn't ask, the man she'd left behind for a job on the other side of the country.

Then discovered she was pregnant.

He was talking away in his hearty, cheerful voice, but Kenzie hadn't heard a word. It took her a moment to find her voice. When she did, it came out hoarse. "Jonah?"

He turned to look at her, surprised, then confused. "I'm sorry. Do I know you?"

Kenzie winced internally. She knew she'd changed but hadn't realized how much. Forcing a smile, she said, "It was a while ago. About eight years, in Boston?"

She watched recognition dawn in Jonah's eyes, followed by dismay. "Kenzie? What—what on earth are you doing here?"

His tone reminded Kenzie that their parting hadn't been bittersweet, just bitter. "I could ask you the same thing."

Jonah seemed frozen in place, one foot on the first step of the staircase. His lips barely moved when he spoke. "I've been here over a year. Moved here from Boston. You?"

"I just moved here a week ago. From Cambridge, actually."

"Really?" The crow's-feet deepened around his eyes. He was only a few years older than Kenzie, in his midthirties, but he looked older than that. "How'd you end up in Chapelton?"

"Because I got this job." Kenzie's heart was beating way too fast. Her brain spun like a Tilt-A-Whirl. With deliberate nonchalance, she held on to the stair rail to steady herself. As she did, she took a casual glance down at Jonah's left hand.

There was no missing that thick gold ring on his third finger.

"What happened to the big career? Last I knew, you were some kind of big shot in kids' TV." Jonah sounded indignant, as if he thought she'd come here on purpose to upset him.

"Oh, you know, things change." Skirting the subject of the disastrous end of her career in educational television, she cleared her throat. "Last I knew, you were a Boston cop. What happened to that?"

"Oh, you know, things change." Jonah echoed her words in a sardonic tone.

After a tense pause, Kenzie started up the stairs, still grasping the railing to keep herself steady. "Well, I don't want to be late, even if they don't start on time."

She heard a heavy sigh behind her, then Jonah's footsteps. At the top of the stairs she kept going straight.

"Do you know where the meeting is?" Jonah sounded cautious.

"I'll find it."

"Not that way, you won't."

Careful not to move too quickly, Kenzie turned back to look at him. The sight of his amused smile made her insides shiver, but she kept her face neutral. "Where, then?"

"This way." Jonah crooked a thumb in the opposite direction. "Meetings are usually held in the old sanctuary. I'll show you."

"Thanks." Kenzie held herself stiffly as they walked down the hall together. She sensed that he was looking at her, but kept her own eyes riveted ahead.

"You're welcome." His chilly inflection made it clear to Kenzie that he hadn't forgiven her.

She didn't blame him. But she had every reason to be even less forgiving. And he didn't seem to realize or acknowledge that.

Frustration tightened Kenzie's throat and threatened to strangle her. What a mess. This was the only job she had managed to get since her health took a downturn, her television career had crashed and burned, and her husband deserted her for another woman. The pay wasn't great, but at least her ex paid child support and alimony. Plus, life in this village was far more affordable than in the city. And since she was faculty, Pippa got free tuition to this small but reputable private school.

The health insurance would kick in soon and she could resume her quest for a diagnosis. Lyme disease was very common in the Berkshires, so local doctors might be more likely to listen to her.

Kenzie needed this job for her own and Pippa's sake. She had no choice but to make this work. No way was she going to let Jonah Raymond spoil it for her.

"Look." Kenzie stopped dead in the middle of the hall and glanced around to make sure no one would overhear. To be safe, she slipped into a nearby nook and gestured for Jonah to join her. In an urgent undertone she continued, "I'm not happy about this, and obviously you aren't either. But this is a new start for me and I need to make the best of it."

Jonah blinked. "O…kay…"

"So here's the deal." Kenzie summoned every ounce of determination and laser-focused her eyes on Jonah's. "Let's keep things at a distance, okay? I mean, let's be civil but not…not interact much unless we have to. Okay?"

A corner of his mouth quirked as if amused by her bossy tone. "Are you serious?"

A pleading note crept into her voice as she went on. "Absolutely serious. I think it'll be better for both of us, don't you?" When he didn't respond right away, Kenzie closed her eyes and added, "Please?"

When Kenzie opened her eyes again, bewilderment mixed with sympathy had softened Jonah's expression. "Yeah. Okay. I agree."

"Thanks," she whispered. Giving him a quick, grateful smile, she turned away and started toward the sanctuary again.

JONAH RAYMOND FELT like he'd been stabbed in the heart and then crushed by a freight train crammed full of uncomfortable emotions. Running into Kenzie and finding out they were colleagues swept him into a state of unreality. Joy turned quickly into bitterness, which morphed into a bout of nostalgia. And that led to memories of being overwhelmed by hurt and despair.

He'd certainly never expected to see her at Good Shepherd Academy. After all, the last he'd known, she'd been a children's television producer in San Francisco. And he hadn't recognized her at first.

He found himself wondering how long it would have taken him to realize it was Kenzie if she hadn't said something. Her face had lost its cherubic roundness and the sparkle of her eyes had dimmed. Her once plump but muscular body seemed to have shrunk. Her curly strawberry blond bob was now a mass of copper waves that trailed well past her shoulder blades, bundled into a careless ponytail. Her vibrant teal dress, typical of the bold colors Kenzie favored, seemed to overwhelm her thin frame.

Strangest of all, she walked slowly and carefully, as if afraid she might fall again. Where was the purposeful stride that had been her trademark? Back when they were together, Jonah used to joke that "Getouttamyway" was Kenzie's middle name.

What had happened to her to cause such a dramatic change? And why on earth did she want to keep him at a distance? After all, she'd been the one to break up with him, not the other way around.

By now they'd reached the door to the sanctuary, which was propped open with a battered hymnal. The old-fashioned, high-ceilinged chapel buzzed with conversation and laughter as faculty members greeted one another after the long summer break.

Fighting to keep his voice neutral, Jonah turned to Kenzie. "Here we are."

Kenzie stood frozen a few feet from the door, her face so pale her freckles stood out, her blue eyes wide as if with fear.

From the corner of his eye, Jonah studied her in surprise. The Kenzie he remembered was larger-than-life, bold and adventurous. Nothing daunted her.

Again he asked himself how she'd gone from that daredevil girl to this pale, anxious woman.

As he watched, she drew in a deep breath, raised her chin and put on a brave smile.

That gesture punched Jonah right in the heart. He'd seen it many times all those years ago. It was part of Kenzie's preparation when she was about to do something she'd never done before, like giving a speech at a crowded conference, or going for a television interview, or that time he taught her how to ski and she went right for the steepest slope.

A faculty meeting at Good Shepherd Academy was nothing to be afraid of, but Jonah could see clearly that she was intimidated.

Chin up, she strode past him with her oddly hesitant gait and headed for the table sporting a colorful sign that declared it "The Caffeination Station." Puzzled, Jonah stood behind her and watched as she seized a cardboard cup and pumped decaf into it. It took her three tries to pry the top from a creamer.

As Jonah grabbed his own cup and filled it, he continued to observe Kenzie from the corner of his vision. Her hand was unsteady, her lips pursed, her eyes focused and determined as she tried and failed to put a lid on her coffee cup. Her expression became more stubborn and she tossed the recalcitrant lid into the trash before turning to face the room.

His cup filled to the brim with high-test black coffee, Jonah also turned. The Good Shepherd staff comprised only a dozen teachers, but they made enough noise for at least twice as many. Happy voices rang through the old chapel, bright as the sunshine that made the stained glass windows glow.

"They're a friendly bunch," he assured Kenzie. She jumped at the sound of his voice, sloshing coffee out of her lidless cup and onto her hand. "Ouch!"

Jonah quickly grabbed a napkin and patted her hand dry. "Didn't mean to startle you."

"Sorry, that was clumsy," she murmured, setting her coffee on the table with trembling fingers.

"Are you okay?"

He could hear Kenzie's deep inhalation as she raised her head, proud and feisty. "Of course I am. I'm perfectly fine." She flashed him a bright smile that didn't mask the anxiety in her eyes. "Everything is great." And she started to move away.

Before he could say anything else, Mick D'Angelo jumped between him and Kenzie. "Hey, I'm Mick. I teach science. You must be the arts teacher?"

Kenzie smiled and took Mick's proffered hand. "Kenzie. Nice to meet you."

Mick turned to Jonah. "Hey, buddy, how's it going?"

"Hey, Mick. All good," he auto-responded.

"Yeah? How are the kids?" It wasn't just a casual question. Worry creased Mick's high forehead. "I know it's been over a year since you lost your wife, so hopefully they're coping okay now?"

Jonah couldn't help glancing at Kenzie, who registered Mick's words with surprise. "Excuse me," she muttered, then made her way to the back of the hall.

Jonah shrugged. "Jolie is great. Obviously she was way too young to have Elena's death affect her much, if at all. Frankie's up and down, though." He chewed his lower lip. "I thought we had a pretty good summer, all things considered, but recently he's gotten quiet and started having nightmares again."

Mick clapped him on the arm. "These things take time. For grown-ups as well as kids, so don't leave yourself out of the equation."

Jonah blinked away a sudden stinging in his eyes that Mick's words provoked. Elena and Frankie had shared a special bond. Their foster child had been so lost since she died. He didn't know what they'd do without his sister and her husband, who had forced Jonah to move in with them.

"So that new teacher?" Mick nodded toward the pew where Kenzie sat alone. "She's pretty cute, right? Maybe it's time for you to get back out there." He gave Jonah a wink. "Better go sit down. Enid's about to kick things off." Waggling his heavy eyebrows, Mick added, "Maybe sit next to that new teacher. She looks lonesome."

Once Mick sat in the front row and started talking to the English teacher, Jonah glanced back toward Kenzie and caught her staring at him. Right away she switched her gaze to another part of the room, embarrassed but defiant. Should he go sit next to her? Did she look lonely?

No, that wasn't Kenzie's sad face. That was her *don't come near me* expression. Jonah knew her well enough to keep his distance, so he plunked down next to Mick with a shrug.

As the headmistress called the meeting to order, Jonah couldn't stop wondering what had happened to the joyful, intrepid love of his life, the woman who'd ripped his heart out and thrown it away for a shiny job in children's television on the other side of the country. When he'd thought of her after they split up, which was way too often, he imagined her soaring high in her career, or skydiving, or belting out boisterous karaoke at a party.

Taking a quick glance at the clock on the wall at the back of the sanctuary, Jonah found himself worrying about how Frankie was doing in day care. He hadn't done much socializing with other children over the summer, preferring to spend time with his family or wander around the farm they owned. Not surprising, considering the trauma he'd endured before Jonah and Elena had started fostering him. The little boy enjoyed exploring nature, which was fine but gave him far too much time alone.

Jonah sighed. His own proclivity for solitude had increased since his wife's death shortly after Jolie was born. He knew he wasn't setting a good example for his foster son by giving in to grief for so long.

Mick was right. He needed to get out there again. Not dating—no way was he ready for that, and certainly not with Kenzie—but he should make an effort to be more social. After all, he was closer to forty than thirty. It had been over a year since Elena died. Maybe if he pushed himself to be more social, Frankie would follow suit.

It was time for both of them to move on.

CHAPTER TWO

KENZIE SAT UPRIGHT in the hard pew, seemingly attentive and focused as the headmistress welcomed the staff to a new school year. What she really wanted to do was lie down and close her eyes to shut out all the sensory input. She'd spent so much time at home over the past couple of years because of all her weird symptoms, it was going to take time to get used to being around people again. Right now the noise, the crowd, the light and, most of all, Jonah Raymond threatened to overwhelm her.

Jonah hadn't recognized her at first, which in itself was devastating. To her, the change had been gradual, but the last time Jonah had seen her she'd been at least twenty well-muscled pounds heavier, with short curly hair and boundless energy. Kenzie knew she'd aged more than the eight years that had passed since then, and her fighting spirit was threadbare at best.

Despite what the Boston doctors said, she was sure her decline was due to a single tiny tick bite two years ago. But until she could find a local doctor, she had to power through.

Kenzie checked the time on her phone. Soon she'd be able to pick up Pippa from the church's day care center and go back to their motel. The one-room efficiency, a weekly rental, was within their budget as long as they didn't have to stay too long.

She suppressed a groan at the thought that she still needed to find them a place to live that was both large enough and cheap enough. And another week's rent on the efficiency was due today.

The sound of her own name interrupted her worrying. "Mrs. Reid, would you mind standing up and introducing yourself?" The school's headmistress, Dr. Enid Mullin, a regal African American who could have been anywhere from forty to seventy, was beaming at Kenzie from the podium.

Masking her dismay, Kenzie hauled herself to her feet using the back of the pew in front of her. Her brain kicked into autopilot and words flowed out in her old, fearless voice.

"Hi! I'm Mackenzie Reid, but you can call

me Kenzie. After I got my master's in communication and arts education, I worked as a creative director in educational television. This is a pretty big change for me. I'm so excited to be kicking off your new creative arts department. My little Pippa will be entering second grade here. We're both looking forward to getting to know you all."

"Kenzie will be spearheading our school's first public performances, the first one in October," Dr. Mullin told the staff. "Kenzie, could you tell us anything about your plans for that?"

Fortunately, Kenzie had given that job requirement a lot of thought over the past few weeks. "The October performance will be a harvest pageant. Since classes are divided up by grade, I'll assign each group a different piece of the program. There'll be a lot of singing and a bit of dance and drama. And all classes will help make bits of scenery and costumes. It should be a lot of fun but also instructional."

With a beaming smile, Kenzie dropped back down onto the pew and breathed a sigh of relief.

When she'd mentioned her daughter, it had taken all her might to keep from glancing at Jonah to see his reaction. Did he even remember her desperate messages from eight years ago?

Did he even know he was Pippa's father, or had he been so angry with her that he hadn't bothered to read any of her letters or emails? Part of her wanted to ask him outright, while another part wanted to let sleeping dogs lie.

Twenty minutes later the meeting ended. Before anyone could come over to introduce themselves and welcome her, Kenzie ducked out the back door and down the steps to the parking lot.

Once she reached the ground she paused for a moment to drink in the beauty of the late New England summer. In Boston it would be uncomfortably hot and sticky, but in the Berkshire Mountains of Western Massachusetts a gentle breeze kept things pleasant. She'd never seen a sky so blue or grass and trees such a vibrant green. As she made her way across the parking lot toward the church, Kenzie found herself feeling hopeful, despite the shock of Jonah appearing out of nowhere.

The church was just across the parking lot from the school it sponsored, but after her unusually strenuous day, the twenty-five or so yards felt like as many miles to Kenzie. A few years ago she would have sprinted across the lot in no time flat, but now it might as well have been one of the marathons she used to run.

She paused in the vestibule to catch her breath and take a peek into the sanctuary where she was to stage the harvest pageant and other performances. The Good Shepherd Academy was housed in the old clapboard church that had been built in the late 1800s. The new church wasn't glaringly modern or huge, just a bright, modest structure with lots of windows. Kenzie fully intended to go to services as soon as she and Pippa had found a place to live.

Smiling in spite of her difficulties, she turned right and followed the hallway to a good-sized, cheerful room. Several small children played with blocks and other toys, including her own little girl. A plump baby giggled in a bouncer, slapping at the tray.

"Hi there!" Diane, the day care lady, called to her with a wave. "Are you done with the meeting already?"

"Just finished. The other teachers should be along soon."

"Mommy!"

Her seven-year-old's boisterous bellow made Kenzie laugh out loud. The sturdy little red-head sporting a wild mass of curls flung herself into Kenzie's arms, causing her mother to gasp. "Oof!"

"I missed you!" Pippa hopped on her toes to peck at Kenzie's face. "Guess what! I made a friend!"

Kenzie kissed her girl back with an affectionate laugh. "I'm not surprised. Can I meet her?"

"It's a him!" Pippa was dragging her mother across the room to where a small boy sat on the floor, a pad of paper in his hands and crayons scattered all around him. "This is Frankie!"

The boy looked up at Kenzie shyly, then right back down again. He had huge dark eyes, floppy brown hair and a sweetly waifish face. Absolutely adorable.

"Hi, Frankie." Kenzie knelt down next to him. "I'm Kenzie."

When he looked uncomfortable, she got back to her feet with an effort. "He doesn't talk much," Pippa explained, "but he draws real good." At her mother's raised eyebrow, she amended, "I mean, he's a really good draw-er." Pippa sat down next to the boy and watched him coloring, her eyes rapt.

"Your girl is very outgoing."

Kenzie turned to find Diane standing next to her. "Don't I know it," she chuckled.

"I hope I'll be seeing you and Pippa at church," the petite brunette said.

"Me too." Kenzie frowned. "Hopefully soon. We're living in a motel until we find somewhere to live."

"The one out on Route 20, right?" Diane grimaced. "Not a very reputable spot, I'm afraid. But Pippa mentioned you were looking for a place, and I might have the perfect one."

"Really?" Kenzie's hopes flared up, but she squashed them back down. Too many recent disappointments forced her to be wary. "Where?"

"My house!" Diane beamed at her. "We have a couple of apartments downstairs. My brother and his kids live in one, but the smaller one is empty."

Kenzie sent up a silent prayer as she asked, "How small?"

"Oh, it's two bedrooms!" Diane assured her. "We renovated a big old farmhouse that's belonged to my family for ages. There's a ton of space, plus quite a few acres. Lots of room for kids to play!"

"Out in the country?" Although she loved the fresh air and beautiful scenery, nature held something of a horror for Kenzie.

Diane's deep brown eyes gleamed. "It's only about a stone's throw from the village. You could easily walk to school from there on a nice day." As if sensing Kenzie's hesitation, she added, "It's a Christmas tree farm, and we also have a big pumpkin patch and an apple orchard and lots of vegetables. Great place for kids, believe me."

Kenzie held her breath and prayed again. It sounded too good to be true, but Diane seemed honest and kind. Plus, she'd looked at about a dozen places in the past week, all of which were either unsuitable or too expensive for her modest teaching salary. "How much is the rent?"

The price Diane named clinched it. She didn't even need to look at the place.

"I'll take it."

WITH HIS HEAD still reeling from seeing Kenzie after so many years, Jonah had to force himself to make small talk with his teaching colleagues. More than one of them asked if he was okay, which meant he wasn't entirely succeeding.

"Where are you today, Jonah?" Dr. Enid Mullin's aristocratic eyebrows lifted high with curiosity. "I've asked you the same question three times and you've given me three different answers, none of which make sense."

Embarrassed, Jonah gave his head a shake to clear it of thoughts of Kenzie. "Sorry. Just getting readjusted to being here, I guess."

"I was saying we miss seeing you and the kids at church. My husband keeps asking after you." The wise woman pierced him with her gaze. "Are you planning to join us again soon?"

"Um…" He groped for a way to explain his dilemma and came up empty. "Maybe?"

Jonah had attended the Good Shepherd Church across the parking lot dutifully all of last year, his first year of teaching. He'd felt indebted to the headmistress and her husband, the pastor of the church, for giving him a position he didn't feel qualified for, having spent the previous sixteen years serving as a police officer in Boston. But he'd earned a teaching certification while working on his master's in community education, and based on his work experience and interest in fitness, they felt he was a perfect fit for the position.

Enid kept studying him with that all-knowing expression. "Are you having some struggles with your faith? That's not surprising, given what you and your family have been through."

As usual, the headmistress had hit the issue on the head. Jonah sighed. "It's not so much about me, but I can't help wondering why God would let all that horrible stuff happen to Frankie," he admitted. "I mean, to lose his real mother when he was just a baby, then his foster mother. He adored Elena."

A line formed between Enid's eyebrows as she nodded. "I get it. He's just a helpless, innocent child. It's not easy to understand when things like that happen to someone who in no way deserves it."

Sudden anger pulsed through Jonah's veins. "Elena was helping him deal with his issues, and he was doing so well. Now he's a mess again."

Enid nodded. "And you're left alone to clean it up."

"I thought he was starting to do better over the summer, but now he's back to having night terrors. And he's gone quiet again."

"Which explains why you look like you haven't slept," she commented dryly. "But I'm sure your sister and her husband pitch in."

The remark made Jonah feel like an ungrateful brother. "They do all they can, but I'm his parent. It's on me to be there for him as much as possible."

Enid put her hand on his arm. "Jonah, you were left alone with a tiny baby and a very troubled foster child. I think you're entitled to take advantage of all the help you can get. And Diane and Paul are right there and they adore those babies. I'm sure they don't see it as a burden."

Jonah knew she was right, but that didn't lessen his guilt about not being as good with Frankie as Elena had been. His late wife had been the definition of unconditional love and Frankie had flourished under her care. Since her death, at times the six-year-old seemed to regress four years when he was upset. Back to when Jonah and Elena, then partners in the Boston PD, answered a call about a crying child and found the toddler sobbing next to the body of his biological mother.

"Are you listening to me?" Enid asked gently.

"Yeah, sorry," Jonah mumbled.

"Don't be sorry. I just want to be sure you're getting what you need." Lips pursed, she gave his arm an encouraging squeeze. "You know I'm here to sit and talk anytime you like. And the same goes for Pastor Mullin. You know my husband's office is right across the parking lot, and we're both only a phone call away."

Jonah dredged up a smile that didn't quite make it to his eyes. "Thanks, Enid. I appreciate that."

She shook her head. "No man is an island, Jonah. Remember you're surrounded by people ready and willing to help you and pray with you. Come back to church and you'll see."

"Soon." Under the headmistress's steely gaze, Jonah couldn't lie. "Maybe."

"We'll keep on praying for you and your family. Don't be a stranger." With that, Enid gave him a final pat on the arm and moved on to talk to another teacher.

Jonah hastily slipped out the back door of the sanctuary, following the same path Kenzie had taken. He scanned the parking lot hoping to see her, but all he spotted was a battered red Volvo station wagon pulling out onto the road. Was that Kenzie at the wheel? He squinted against the late summer sunlight but couldn't see through the car window.

Heaving another sigh, Jonah trudged down the stone steps to the parking lot and headed to the Good Shepherd Church's day care center. His younger sister, Diane, ruled the roost, rejoicing in caring for other people's children while praying fervently to have one of her own.

The beauty of the brilliant cerulean sky overhead, the lush green grass of the grounds and the rich cyan of the Berkshire Mountains couldn't distract him from his thoughts. All he could see was Mackenzie Reid's once vibrant face, now so thin and faded he'd barely recognized her.

He'd heard she'd gotten married shortly after moving to San Francisco, to the guy she'd been dating before she met him. He remembered Greg Halloran as short and deeply serious, the latter being a strange quality for a man who worked in children's television. Although he'd clearly been disappointed, Greg had been very gracious about being thrown over for Jonah. He must have been thrilled to get her back, and she must have been eager to reunite. Maybe that had been the reason behind her breaking up with him and moving so far away at a moment's notice.

Feeling the old bitterness bubbling up inside him, Jonah stood still for a moment and fought it back down. He needed to be calm and upbeat when he picked up the kids. Little Jolie had a happy disposition, but Frankie was an emotional sponge. And the boy had more than enough feelings of his own. The last thing he needed was to add his father's heartaches to the mix.

Once he'd applied enough emotional Novocain, Jonah entered the church and walked down the hallway to the day care room.

"Hey, big bro!" As usual, Diane's effervescent greeting lifted his spirits. She stood in the center of the room, bouncing Jolie in her arms and blowing on her face as the baby laughed and squealed.

"Hey, lil' sis." Jonah spotted Frankie sitting on the floor, surrounded by discarded drawings and what looked like a thousand crayons. He squatted next to the boy. "Hey, buddy. Whatcha drawing?"

Frankie crouched closer to his artwork and muttered, "I'm not drawing. I'm coloring."

"I stand corrected. Whatcha coloring?"

"Stuff."

"What kinda stuff?"

His son lifted his shoulders in a shrug. "Whatever."

Jonah stifled a sigh. "Okay, Mr. Whatever. Can you pick up all these crayons and put them away neatly for Auntie Di?" When he leaned in to pat Frankie's head, the boy ducked.

"Thanks, Frankie!" Diane sang out.

Jonah stood up and moved back to his sister to take the baby. "Hoo-boy, someone's in a mood today," he whispered.

Diane released Jolie into Jonah's arms. "Unfortunately, it seems to be aimed at you. He was actually interacting with some of the other kids today, especially—"

Jolie interrupted her with a deafening shriek. Her distress wasn't allayed by Jonah's attempts to soothe and distract her. "I think she's teething again." He bellowed to be heard over her crying, which made the baby wail even more loudly.

"Yikes—don't break her tiny eardrums with that gym teacher voice." Diane ran for the medicine cabinet and pulled out a tube of ointment. She took advantage of Jolie's wide-open mouth to dab some on her gums. Surprised, the little girl stopped howling and stuck a fat finger between her lips to explore. "How'd the faculty thing go?"

"Pretty good, although…" Jonah paused as he debated sharing the shock of seeing Kenzie Reid again. Diane had been on an overseas mission throughout their relationship, so she'd never met Kenzie. She'd only seen the aftermath, when her brother had been a thundercloud of self-pity for far longer than was justifiable.

"Although?" Diane prompted.

Deciding against telling her, he shrugged. "You know. Lots of work getting things set up the way I want. I'm pretty beat." He glanced over to see that Frankie had just finished loading crayons into the Tupperware container. "Hey, good job, buddy. You ready to go?"

Setting the container on a shelf, Frankie moped his way over to his father. "I guess."

"We're off to run a few errands. See you around suppertime." Jonah pecked his sister on the cheek and, Jolie in his arms, headed outside. When he turned to make sure Frankie was following, he shifted his daughter to one shoulder and held out a hand to the little boy.

Frankie looked at Jonah's big hand and stopped in his tracks, then stuffed both his own hands in his pockets and trudged to the car.

With a deep sigh, Jonah kept walking. There was no point in pushing Frankie to trust him the way he'd trusted Elena, but the dismissive gesture still bruised his heart.

After all the little boy had been through, how could Jonah possibly make Frankie feel safe and loved again?

CHAPTER THREE

"COME ON, BABY GIRL. Just a few more boxes!"

Somehow Kenzie managed to inject encouragement into her voice when what she really felt like doing was collapsing on the sofa. But not spending another night in the motel was a priority, and once they had unloaded the last box she could get some rest.

"I'm not a baby!" Pippa underscored her protest with a stamp of her foot.

"You most certainly are not," Kenzie agreed, "and that's why you're going to pick up that box of toys and bring it inside."

"But I'm sooooo tired!"

Pippa's melodramatic tone made Kenzie shake her head. Only seven years old, the girl had the makings of an actress. "So am I, Pip," Kenzie said in a gentle voice. "But we're almost done. Then you can go look at the pond and the pretty trees, okay?"

Pippa's sulking turned to curiosity. "Mommy, why do they grow Christmas trees? I thought you got them from the store."

"We got ours from the store when we lived in the city," Kenzie explained. "But out in the country you get them from places like this."

"But they're trees!" Pippa protested. "I mean, real actual trees!"

Kenzie laughed. "In the city we got the kind that don't drop pine needles everywhere, because Daddy didn't like the mess. But I don't mind sweeping them up when they're so pretty and smell so good."

"They smell?" Pippa's astonished face made her mother laugh even more.

"They smell wonderful." Kenzie sighed, remembering childhood Christmases with her parents. Then it was just her mother, then Greg and Pippa. She swallowed, refusing to let the past in any further. "As soon as we're done bringing in the boxes, you should go sniff the one closest to the house. Then you'll see what I mean."

Intrigued, Pippa seized the box of toys and ran into the house.

Their new apartment took up half the ground floor of a sizable farmhouse overlooking a good-sized pond. The surrounding land boasted neat rows of dark green fir trees, which Kenzie figured were the Christmas trees Diane had mentioned. The sign at the top of the drive read Holiday Farm, and a smaller sign tacked underneath announced that apple-picking season was coming and pumpkins would be on sale October through November.

As soon as Pippa spotted the pond, she'd been wildly excited, so Kenzie knew she'd been right to take it. Plus, it was perfect: two bedrooms, a big living/dining area with a fireplace, a sweet little galley kitchen and—best of all—a wraparound porch with swings and rockers.

It amazed her that something she'd accepted sight unseen had turned out to be so perfect. The apartment was not at all what she'd expected when Diane handed her a key without mentioning a lease. The place was gleaming with polished wood floors and paneling, bright with fresh paint, and filled with simple, comfortable furniture.

Kenzie couldn't help feeling that God had a hand in this. It was far better than anything she'd looked at, and the rent was more than manageable.

They shared the front entrance with their

neighbors across the hall, the landlady's brother and his family. The hallway separating the two apartments was more like a foyer, wide and welcoming, with a carpeted staircase leading to the owners' residence on the second story.

"Is this my room?" Pippa was staring in amazement at the loft bed with a desk and bookcase cleverly built in underneath.

The room was much smaller than what Pippa had enjoyed in the homes Greg had provided. Kenzie braced herself for an argument. "I'd say it's made for you, don't you think?"

Pippa surprised her by giving a joyful whoop, running over to the bed and clambering up the ladder. "I love it! Can I have sleepovers with my new friends?"

Kenzie smiled at her girl's habitual optimism. "Of course you can, once we're settled in."

"It's going to be so cool to study here!" Pippa climbed back down to the floor and admired the desk. "I like that it's little. It'll be easier to keep neat."

"If I'd known that was all the motivation you needed, I'd've made sure you had a tiny bedroom years ago," Kenzie teased.

As she and Pippa hauled the last boxes inside, Kenzie heaved another sigh and looked around the living room. The squashy-looking brown sofa under the picture window was calling her name. The matching chairs looked almost as inviting. She imagined sitting there, looking out at the backyard with the picturesque pond and stately fir trees, a steaming mug of coffee resting on the pine coffee table.

Despite her exhaustion, she thanked God again for this beautiful place that seemed to have fallen into her lap.

And it was an excellent distraction from obsessing about having to work with Jonah Raymond. *God, please help me to forgive him for ignoring my messages.*

"Mommy, are you praying?" Pippa asked.

Kenzie opened her eyes. "How'd you know?"

"You had your God face on. Like this." Pippa closed her eyes and folded her hands. Then her big brown eyes—so like Jonah's—popped open again. "Is Daddy going to come visit?"

Trying not to grimace, Kenzie said, "Maybe. It's only a couple of hours from Boston." She examined her daughter's face, which showed more curiosity than sadness. Greg had never acted very fatherly to Pippa, probably because she wasn't his child. And since he'd remarried and his new wife was expecting their first child,

Kenzie thought it unlikely that they'd ever see him again. "Do you miss him?"

Pippa seemed to think this over, then shrugged. "Not really. I just wondered."

"Well, he's busy with work and getting ready for the new baby, settling in with Camilla." She made herself say the name of her replacement as calmly as possible. Greg's new wife was certainly nice enough and seemed genuinely contrite about breaking up their home.

"But he's my daddy." Pippa's forehead wrinkled with confusion. "And his new baby isn't even borned yet."

Kenzie pulled Pippa into a hug. "Once we've gotten everything sorted and put away, we can ask him to visit. Okay?"

"Okay." Pippa pulled away, immediately focused on something else. "Can I go see the pond now?"

"Of course, sweetie. Just don't get too close to the water."

Pippa shot out the apartment door, through the hall and down the front steps, pelting as fast as she could go toward the rockbound pond. Kenzie gazed out the window to watch her intrepid little girl standing a few yards from the water, peering at something on the ground.

Hopefully not a snake. Kenzie shuddered at the thought. Pippa was fearless and adored all of God's creatures, no matter how creepy.

Finally giving in to her fatigue, Kenzie sank onto the big comfy sofa. As she kept a watchful eye on Pippa, she heard a car pull into the driveway out front and a man's voice calling something she couldn't make out.

Suddenly a small boy darted past the window and headed for the pond. His dark, floppy hair reminded Kenzie of the little boy Pippa had befriended earlier in the day care room. He stopped in his tracks when he saw Pippa, who had turned her head at the noise and started waving at him. She scrambled up the rocks and greeted the boy with her wide, gap-toothed grin, seemingly thrilled to see him.

That's my girl, Kenzie thought with a loving smile. Her daughter would grow up to be an ambassador if she wasn't an actress.

Another figure appeared outside the window and called out in a big, resonant voice. A tall man with dark hair, holding a squirming toddler in his arms. And for the second time that day, Kenzie's heart slid into her stomach.

Jonah Raymond. Again. What was he doing here? Could he possibly be the widowed brother Diane had said lived across the hall? His friend at the faculty meeting had said his wife had died recently, so it seemed all too possible.

With a reluctant groan, Kenzie pried herself from the sofa and hurried outdoors to join the little group.

"Mommy! Mommy!" Pippa was jumping up and down. "Remember Frankie from the day care? He's our neighbor and he goes to our school! And this is his daddy." She looked up at Jonah. "I don't know his name yet."

"Jonah," Frankie piped up.

Pippa's eyes were enormous. "Like the guy who got ate by the fish?"

"What?" Frankie looked alarmed.

"In the Bible. A fish eats this guy named Jonah." With a sage nod, Pippa added, "Some people say it was a whale, but whales can't eat people."

Jonah's booming laugh stopped abruptly when he turned and saw Kenzie. "Oh. Um. Hi again." He didn't sound pleased. "Uh…what are you doing here?"

"That's my mom," Pippa announced, then pointed to the baby in Jonah's arms. "And, Mommy, that's…" Furrowing her brow, she turned to Frankie. "Um, what's your sister's name again?"

Frankie scowled. "Jolena. We call her Jolie."

Pippa studied the chubby baby with adoration. "She's so cute! It must be so fun to have a little sister. I always wanted a little brother or sister."

Frankie kicked at a stone near his feet. "She's dumb."

"Franklin, be nice!" Jonah said sternly.

When Kenzie finally managed to talk, she couldn't keep the dismay out of her voice. "You're our neighbor?" A sudden memory came to her of Jonah talking about his sister, Diane, who'd been on a long-term mission in Haiti back when they were dating.

"Really?" Pippa, who'd been whispering to Frankie, turned back to Kenzie. "Mommy, Frankie's going to show me a snapping turtle that lives by the pond."

Kenzie shot an anxious glance at Jonah, who quickly reassured her. "It's fine. Frankie knows to keep his distance. Don't you, buddy?"

Frankie gave his father a wary look. Without a word he turned and led Pippa back toward the pond.

Jonah watched his son with a worried expression. "He's not my biggest fan today, but he sure took to your girl right away. I'm surprised. Frankie's pretty shy."

Kenzie had to swallow hard before she could respond. "Pippa has that effect on people. She's always so friendly and outgoing."

When she looked at Jonah he was smiling sadly. "Takes after her mother, I guess."

Jolie had stopped squirming in her father's arms and was staring at Kenzie with a wide, drooly grin. Then her chubby arms reached out as she leaned toward Kenzie, clearly begging to be held. Without a second thought Kenzie took the girl in her arms, where she proceeded to inspect Kenzie's curls with sticky fingers.

Jonah watched in surprise. "Guess you and your girl are magnets for my kids. Never seen Jolie do that with anyone else. Not that quick, anyway."

"Her name's Jolena?" Kenzie put her face against the baby's and reveled in the sweet scent, temporarily forgetting how awkward the situation was. "I've never met a Jolena before. What an unusual name, and so pretty."

"Elena's idea."

Startled, Kenzie's eyes shot back to Jonah. "Elena? But—" She stopped herself before she could go any further.

Elena had been the name of Jonah's partner in

the Boston PD, and she'd never taken to Kenzie. Had he married her?

Jonah continued. "It's one of those— What do you call them? Hybrid names." At Kenzie's puzzled look, he explained, "Jonah and Elena, so she came up with Jolena. But we just call her Jolie. Elena said it's French for *pretty* or *sweet*."

Kenzie felt her throat tighten with longing as Jolie nestled against her. "She's very sweet." Her voice was a husky rasp.

Jonah was studying her, his face stoic. "So you named your girl Pippa."

"Philippa, actually. Pippa for short."

"Your grandmother's name." His tone had darkened with a touch of bitterness. "One of the names on our list, as I recall."

Kenzie froze, swallowed again. Was it possible that he'd deliberately ignored her increasingly desperate messages eight years ago because he was so angry with her for breaking up with him?

She knew he'd received the certified letter she'd sent as her final message. The letter informing him that he was going to be a father. She'd gotten the return receipt and held her breath waiting to hear back from him.

He never responded. Maybe he wanted to

punish her. Or maybe he'd signed for the letter but thrown it away without reading it when he saw who it was from.

Was it possible that Jonah had no idea he was Pippa's father?

THE LOOK OF shock on Kenzie's face made Jonah immediately regret his bitter words. After all, it was almost a decade ago that they'd been talking about baby names. And they hadn't even been engaged, so it was more like a game than anything to be taken seriously.

He forced brightness into his voice. "Your little girl looks so much like you."

That was an understatement. Pippa was a perfect duplicate of Kenzie, with her wild strawberry blond curls, fair skin and dusting of freckles across her nose. The only aberration was the little girl's eyes, which were a deep brown instead of vivid blue like Kenzie's. Pippa must have gotten those from her father, although Jonah could barely remember what Greg Halloran looked like.

But more telling than the physical resemblance between mother and daughter was the attitude: spunky, friendly and funny. All the things he remembered Kenzie being back when they were a couple. All the things that seemed to have disappeared from her personality over the intervening years.

At least she was smiling right now. It looked a bit threadbare, but she was trying. "You'd better take this baby before I drop her. She's a hefty little thing."

Jonah jumped to Kenzie's rescue, grabbing Jolie and hoisting her to his shoulder. When she started to wail in protest, he swooped her up into the air until she burst out with gleeful baby laughter.

A side-glance at Kenzie showed she was watching them with a genuine smile, and something else. A wistfulness. A hunger. A loss.

What had happened to that happy-go-lucky woman Jonah had adored? He tried to think of a way to ask that wouldn't be too intrusive but he came up empty.

A third car pulled into the driveway and stopped. As the door opened, a woman's voice called out, "Hey there!"

"Hey, sis!" Jonah answered with relief.

Diane trotted up to them, her dark eyes sparkling with excitement. "I see you guys have met!" She glanced back and forth from Jonah to Kenzie as if checking to see how they were getting along, then reached her arms out for Jolie. "Give me that baby this minute! Auntie Di needs a welcome-home smooch!"

Jolie squealed with joy as Diane covered her with kisses, although Jonah could see that his sister kept glancing at him and Kenzie. What was she looking for? Was she trying to set them up?

This was way too much of a coincidence.

Jonah narrowed his eyes and cocked an eyebrow at Diane until she noticed. She froze, looking guilty.

"We're all moved in," Kenzie was saying. "It's absolutely perfect. I can't thank you enough for offering it to me like that!"

"Like what?" Jonah asked.

Kenzie turned to Jonah. "When I went to pick up Pippa at day care, I mentioned that we were looking for a place to live and Diane told me she had an apartment ready to move into."

"Wow. That's truly an amazing coincidence." He tried to keep the sarcasm out of his voice but didn't entirely succeed.

Diane was grinning. "Wasn't it, though?"

Kenzie looked at them, probably puzzled by the vibe, then shrugged. "I'd better rescue Pippa from the snapping turtles and get her dinner ready." She shot Jonah a tight-lipped smile. "It was nice to see you again." With that, she started walking tentatively toward the pond to find her daughter.

Jonah turned to Diane, preparing to grill her. "So, when did your guest suite become a rental?"

Unfazed, Diane bounced Jolie in her arms. "When I saw this adorable redheaded lady with an adorable little redheaded girl who needed a place to live."

"And she told you her name was Mackenzie and you remembered I once had a redheaded girlfriend by that name?"

"That's not what happened at all." Diane's eyes widened. "That's your Kenzie? Really? Because you know I never met her, right?"

"Right, but still, this is a bit much of a coincidence."

Diane was shaking her head. "I honestly had no idea." At his stern glare, she amended, "Okay, maybe just a little idea, but it was kind of a long shot. Pippa was in day care today. She told me they were living in that awful motel out on Route 20, so when her mother came to pick her up…"

"Do you know we're also teaching right across the hallway from each other?" Jonah demanded.

"On the same floor? Wow, that's a surprise." Her smile widened as if this was good news. "I mean, obviously I knew you were both teaching at the school, but…"

"She suggested that we avoid each other as much as possible." It came out sharper than he'd intended. "Which is going to be interesting if we're both living and teaching in close proximity."

"Oh!" Diane's smile disappeared with almost comical rapidity. "I had no idea—I mean, why would she want that?"

Trying to ignore the ache in his chest, Jonah shook his head. "I honestly don't know. It was her idea to break up and move across the country before her graduation. I'd been planning to propose to her after the ceremony, but…" His eyes started to sting. Embarrassed, he turned so Diane couldn't see his face. "I must have done something to upset her, but she never told me what it was."

"Well, you could ask," Diane suggested.

"No." The word came out more sad than resolute, but Jonah knew it was true. "You never met her, so you don't know what I'm up against here."

They watched as Kenzie and Pippa walked by them on their way to the porch steps. Pippa gave an energetic wave and smile but Kenzie barely looked at them.

"You could at least try…" Diane started again as soon as Kenzie was out of earshot.

"No. Diane, you don't get it. Trust me on this." Jonah sighed deeply as he took Jolie from his sister. "Once Mackenzie Reid makes up her mind about something, there's absolutely no changing it."

CHAPTER FOUR

UNTIL THE LAST few students waved goodbye as they left her classroom, Kenzie kept a big, warm smile plastered on her face. But as soon as she heard the final footsteps receding up the stairs, she finally let herself relax.

Which meant collapsing face-forward onto her desk with a groan. *Thank You, God. I could never have done this without You.*

There was no doubt in her mind that God had gotten her through her first full week of teaching. She'd made a start in assigning groups tasks for the harvest pageant, which most of the children seemed excited about. All her careful planning had paid off, although she'd had to improvise a few times with kids who'd called some projects boring or were too shy to participate in group activities.

Jonah's son, Frankie, was the most extreme case of the latter group. He hung back, standing apart from the other kids, seeming almost to disappear inside himself if Kenzie tried to coax him. Once she learned how much Frankie loved to draw and color, she let him stay in the art corner as much as he liked. In other words, every single creative arts class period for the entire week.

Just today during the first grade's period, she'd tried to convince the boy to spread his wings. "Wouldn't you like to try something different today? Maybe play the bongo drums or make a mask for the harvest pageant? Your grade is the parade of farm animals. Maybe you could make a horse mask?" But Frankie only shook his head decisively and headed for his favorite easel.

Tessa Adams, a fellow first grader—a pushy little girl with pigtails and braces—had tugged Kenzie's elbow. "Frankie is stupid. He doesn't like to do anything fun."

"Never call anyone stupid, Tessa," Kenzie had scolded. "It's mean. Frankie may not enjoy the same things you enjoy, but that's absolutely fine."

"All he ever does is draw pictures like a baby," Tessa said scornfully.

"Drawing is hard and Frankie does it very

well." It was true. Frankie's pictures showed innate skill surprising in a six-year-old.

Tessa had scowled and stomped away to the puppet theater, muttering something under her breath about stupid art. That was how she'd earned herself Kenzie's first time-out and made the new teacher wonder if Frankie could be getting bullied. It didn't seem possible at such a small school, but it might explain why he drew back from group activities.

Kenzie knew she should discuss it with Jonah. As much as she might wish to avoid him, there was no getting around the fact that he was the father of an apparently troubled child.

Frankie's diffidence also made her wonder about what was behind it. He certainly seemed to have a solid home with a loving father, happy little sister and doting aunt. Losing his mother so recently had to be a factor in Frankie's behavior, but it seemed to Kenzie that something more was going on.

She remembered Elena Medeiros as a strong-willed beauty in her late twenties. In the time she and Jonah dated, Kenzie had only met his partner on a couple of occasions, but those fleeting encounters had been enough to convince Kenzie that Elena had some very strong feelings for Jonah. He, of course, was oblivious.

Kenzie had been careful to avoid Jonah as much as possible, both at school and at the farm. It wasn't easy, given that they worked and lived right across from each other. Even harder since their kids had become fast friends. For the first week she'd managed to avoid him pretty well, but those days were numbered, for sure.

"Hey! Congratulations!"

Kenzie jumped a mile as the boisterous male voice rang through the room. Her eyes shot to the door to find Jonah standing there grinning at her. Her heart was already hammering from being startled, and that once familiar smile didn't slow it down any.

"You okay?" His face creased with worry as he looked at her. "Didn't mean to scare you. Sometimes I forget how loud I can be, especially after a day of teaching in a gym."

Kenzie managed a weak chuckle. "Yeah, just having a minor collapse. At least the week is over."

"That's why I wanted to congratulate you." Jonah came closer to the desk and looked down at her, concern still etched into his forehead.

"You made it through your first week with flying colors. The kids absolutely love you."

"Really?" Her eyes stung at the unexpected news. Or was it the gentleness in Jonah's warm brown eyes, the kindness in his voice? Kenzie shoved down the emotion welling up inside her. It was not okay to react like that to a fellow teacher, especially one she'd been so much in love with years ago, whose child she'd been raising without him.

"Yeah, really." Jonah's smile was back, stirring something she'd buried deep inside her. She forced herself to look away. "They talk about Mrs. Reid all the time, how cool you are, how much fun they have in your class, how excited they are about the harvest pageant. And my Frankie is your biggest fan."

"Wow. I'm surprised to hear that." Kenzie ignored her aching joints and stood up. "He doesn't seem very interested in most of the class projects."

A line formed above Jonah's nose as he nodded. "He's a bit of a loner, but you're taking the right approach with him. He really loves to draw. You're letting him be himself and not pushing him to socialize."

Kenzie looked straight at Jonah. It was the

perfect opportunity to express her concern and find out more about Frankie. "I'm not sure I should be encouraging that, but anytime I try to get him involved in a group project, he freezes up. Is there anything I should know about him?"

Jonah studied her for a moment, glanced at the clock on the wall. "I just sent him up to the office to drop off some papers for me. Dr. Mullin will undoubtedly spend some time talking to him, so we have a few minutes."

Kenzie nodded. "Pippa's in the library, looking for another pile of books to read this weekend."

Jonah pulled a chair next to Kenzie's desk and sat. "You should probably sit back down."

"Okay." Suppressing a sigh of relief, Kenzie plopped back into her chair. "I've been worried about him. I mean, I know he has a loving home." Actually, she didn't know that for sure. She just assumed it.

Jonah held up a hand. "Not always. I mean, not originally."

"But I've seen you with him," she persisted, then hesitated before adding, "I mean, I know your wife passed away, but…"

Looking perplexed, he cut her off again. "Let

me start from the beginning, okay? It's a pretty convoluted story."

"Of course. I'm sorry." Kenzie propped her chin in her hand to look at Jonah. She couldn't help wondering what was behind his sorrowful expression as she tried to push down the tug of nostalgia. "I won't interrupt."

He leaned forward, folding his hands on her desk, and gave her a wistful smile that made her wonder if he was having a similar struggle. "It's okay. You never were patient when it came to long stories."

Their eyes met and Kenzie felt her cheeks growing red. Ignoring the complex twist of emotion in her stomach, she managed to give a little shrug. "Please go on." At his puzzled reaction, she prompted, "About Frankie?"

"Oh! Of course." Jonah chuckled, shaking his head. "Brain like a sieve." He folded his arms across his broad chest and cleared his throat. "About four years ago—"

Pippa chose that moment to burst through the classroom door with an armload of books and Jonah's son trailing behind her. "Mommy, can Frankie and me camp out in the backyard this weekend?"

Jonah gave Kenzie a comical half smile that

she remembered so well from their time together. Maybe he was remembering their own disastrous camping expedition, which was about the last thing Kenzie wanted to think about. Pushing the memory aside, she said, "Camping?"

Jonah reached for Frankie, who twitched away from him. "It's something we did during the summer."

Kenzie couldn't help feeling a jab of alarm. "But is it safe? I mean, there's a lot of wildlife around the farm, isn't there?"

"It's perfectly safe. I pitch the tent near the back door of the house so if it rains or someone gets scared, they can run right indoors." He pulled Frankie into a one-armed hug. "Right, buddy?"

Frankie leaned away from his father's embrace. Pippa let go of her friend's hand and bounced up and down in front of her mother. "So, can we, Mom? I've never camped out in my whole entire life and it sounds so cool! Frankie says there's like a zillion stars and bugs that light up and…" Her eyes grew huge. "And singing frogs!"

The look of alarm on Kenzie's face made Jonah burst out laughing. "Such a city girl!" he teased.

Kenzie's heart flipped over at the familiar old taunt. Although Jonah had become a police officer in Boston, he'd grown up in the New England countryside and loved to tease Kenzie about her "big city" ways. As the daughter of two college professors, she'd led a pretty sophisticated life, full of the arts and devoid of nature unless it was under a microscope.

"Um…let me think about it," she stammered, horrified at the thought of her little girl outside at night with nothing but a tent to protect her. What if a fox or coyote came along? She'd heard that there were coyotes in Massachusetts. And even bears.

"Please, Mommy? Please, please, please?" Hands clasped under her chin, Pippa hopped up and down with excitement.

"I said let me think," Kenzie repeated firmly. "Right now we need to head to the grocery store."

"Booooo-ring!" Pippa singsonged, then tacked on a quick "Sorry!" when Kenzie shot her a reproving look.

Feeling exhausted at the mere thought of doing anything at all, Kenzie slapped on a bright smile and got to her feet again. She turned to Jonah and said in a brusque, professional tone,

"Thanks for the encouragement, by the way. I needed it."

"You're welcome." The weary smile he gave her tugged at her heart. "I'll see you back at the house. Maybe we can have our talk then."

ON THE DRIVE HOME, Jonah glanced in the rear-view mirror and tried to catch his son's eye. "So you like Mrs. Reid?"

"Yeah."

"You excited about doing the pageant?"

Staring straight ahead at the back of the seat in front of him, Frankie shrugged. Next to him, Jolie let out a squeak of pure happiness.

"What's your sister doing back there?" Jonah asked.

Frankie made an impatient sound. "She's not my sister."

Jonah couldn't help sighing at the return of their on-again, off-again argument. "Yes, she is, buddy. You're my son, she's my daughter, therefore she's your sister."

"You're not my father." The statement held more misery than a six-year-old should ever feel.

Careful to keep his tone gentle, Jonah said, "I am your father in every way that counts. Who do you live with? Who takes care of you? Who comes to your room and comforts you when you have nightmares?"

"That doesn't make you my father," Frankie muttered. Sometimes he sounded an awful lot like a teenager, which made Jonah dread the day he actually became one.

"If you want a fight, I'm not giving it to you, buddy. As far as I'm concerned, I'm your father." After a pause, Jonah added, "And I love you."

"No, you don't."

The little boy's voice quavered and Jonah felt his throat thicken. Sometimes Frankie could be a real chore, fretful and angry and obstinate, but all Jonah had to do was remind himself of where the boy had come from and everything he'd had to overcome just to function from day to day.

Elena had worked hard with Frankie and he'd come such a long way in the few years she'd been a part of his life. After her death last year, it wasn't surprising that the boy had regressed. Jonah was doing his best, but he didn't have his wife's tireless energy and endless patience.

He tried. He didn't always succeed, but God knew he tried.

But does God know? Jonah asked himself. He wasn't sure what he believed anymore. The questions he'd asked Dr. Mullin after last week's staff meeting came back to him. Why would God put Frankie through the horrors of his early childhood? Why would God take Elena away after Frankie had learned to trust again?

Swallowing the lump in his throat, Jonah pulled into the drive past the Holiday Farm sign. Apple-picking days were in full swing and he and Frankie helped out on busy Saturdays. Then the pumpkin patch would open, followed closely by Christmas tree season. Maybe Kenzie and Pippa would want to pitch in. There was always plenty of work to be done around the farm, but autumn was especially busy.

With a sigh, he parked by the farmhouse, hopped out of the car and went to Frankie's door to unstrap him. When the boy started to run off, Jonah took his hand and wouldn't let it go when he struggled.

"Listen to me, Frank. Whether you believe it or not, I consider myself your father and I love you like crazy. And when you're done being mad at me, I'll still be here."

Frankie turned his face away, but Jonah could

still see a fat tear roll down his cheek. "No, you won't," he whispered.

The words broke Jonah's heart. "Yes, I will. I promise. And that's final." He gave Frankie's hand a squeeze before letting go. The kid shot away like a rocket, pelting down the path to the pond before Jonah could stop him. Feeling like he had a boulder in his chest in place of his heart, he went to the other side of the car to get Jolie.

"Hey, big bro!"

Diane's greeting sounded less jolly than usual. She stepped off the porch and walked up to her brother gingerly, without the usual bounce in her step.

"You okay?" he asked.

She wrinkled her nose. "A little stomach upset. Probably something I ate, but you'd better keep the baby away from me just in case."

"Should you see a doctor?" Given his sister's excellent health, Jonah couldn't help feeling concerned.

Diane's hand rested on her stomach. "I'm much better, really. A few hours ago it was barf-o-rama, which is why I had to come home from work and leave Leah in charge of the kids. Now I'm just a bit sore."

"When's Paul getting home? Any update?" Diane's husband, a general practitioner, spent every September on an overseas mission. This year he was in Kenya.

"Not for a week or so." She nodded toward Frankie, who was looking under a rock at the edge of the pond. "How's he doing?"

"He's having a rough day. I think he's afraid I'm going to leave him or disappear or something."

Sympathy flooded Diane's eyes. "Poor little guy. It's hard for him to feel safe after all he's been through."

Jonah nodded, bouncing his daughter gently as she nestled into his shoulder. "Yeah. I promised him I wasn't going anywhere, but... I mean, I have no right to make that promise. I could get hit by a bus tomorrow or find out I'm fatally ill."

Diane winced. "I wish you wouldn't think like that. Frankie's not the only one who'd be lost without you."

"Sorry, but..." Jonah gazed off at the small figure trying to skip stones across the pond. Such an idyllic scene that didn't give a hint about the little boy's traumatic history. "Life is unpredictable. Horrible things happen out of nowhere. People disappear from your life without warning. Is it fair to promise I'll always be here?"

Diane studied her brother with worried eyes. "I think you had to say those words. That's what he needs to hear."

Jonah's heart ached for Frankie. "I thought he was doing okay for a while this summer, but now he seems to be struggling again."

Diane shook her head. "You've got to expect ups and downs, given what happened." Eyeing her brother, she added, "I'm sure you've been having them, too. It hasn't been that long since Elena's accident."

"She wouldn't have been in an accident if she hadn't taken those pills."

The sudden bitterness in Jonah's voice made Diane peer at him more closely. "And you haven't forgiven her for that," she said softly.

"How could she do that to us?" Jonah exploded. "Especially to Frankie. She knew what he'd been through. What was she thinking?"

"She wasn't." His sister put a calming hand on his arm. "Jonah, postpartum depression is not logical. When she took the pills, Elena was probably just thinking about feeling less pain. Most likely she felt overwhelmed and not up to the task of caring for two small children, which could also be why she left them alone to go for a drive."

"Why didn't she let me know how sad she was? Why didn't she get help?" He choked out one last question, this one more painful than the ones before. "How did I not see it?"

Frightened by her father's ragged tone, Jolie started to sniffle. He hugged her close and kissed her soft brown hair until she calmed down.

"You haven't forgiven her, but you also haven't forgiven yourself," Diane said softly. "God will help you if you let Him."

Careful not to upset Jolie, Jonah murmured, "I don't know if I trust God at all anymore."

"I know. But I'm praying for you, and I know you'll find your way back to Him." Diane smiled lovingly, then grimaced. "I'm still not feeling a hundred percent, so I'm going upstairs to lie down for a bit. Come on up later if you want company and help with the kiddos." She blew him a kiss and hurried back into the house.

As Jonah started down the path to the pond, he heard a car pull into the driveway behind him. Turning, he saw Kenzie's beat-up Volvo wagon pull into a parking spot under the ancient oaks. When she got out of the car, it was instantly clear to Jonah that she was worn out.

He secured his squirming daughter into the baby swing on the front porch. "Here, Jolie. Daddy'll be right back." Jolie kicked her fat little legs and babbled happily.

"Need some help?" he called out as Kenzie and Pippa pulled grocery bags out of the way-back.

"Nope, we're good." Somehow Kenzie's overly bright smile didn't convince Jonah.

Pippa ran up to Jonah and handed him one of the bags she was holding. "Yes, please, Mr. Raymond. We would very much like your help, thank you."

Despite his mood, Jonah couldn't help chuckling. "Well, Miss Philippa, you are very welcome. I'm most happy to help," he responded.

"Hey, how'd you know my name was Philippa?" the little girl demanded.

Jonah glanced toward Kenzie. She slammed the rear door of the wagon shut, her arms draped with several bags of groceries. "Your mom told me."

Pippa spotted Frankie down at the pond, shoved her other bag into Jonah's arms and raced down the path toward the pond. "Hey, Frankie! I'm home!" Her bellow echoed throughout the property.

Noticing how wobbly Kenzie seemed, Jonah hurried over to take some of the bags from her. "Your daughter said my help is very much appreciated."

"She's right," Kenzie admitted as they walked up the porch steps.

"Are you all right? You seem kind of unsteady."

Kenzie had frozen on the top step, blinking rapidly. She grabbed the railing, the color draining from her cheeks. "I'm just tired."

Alarmed, Jonah set the groceries on the porch and leaned in closer to study Kenzie. "You are way more than tired, Kenz. What's going on?"

She took a breath and swallowed, squeezing her eyes shut. "No big deal. It's just a headache," she admitted. "It came on very suddenly while we were shopping. Those fluorescent lights…" She winced and swallowed again. "Sometimes they bother me."

Without waiting for her permission, Jonah helped Kenzie into the house, relieved to find the door to her apartment unlocked. He guided her inside and made her lie down on the sofa. Then he pulled down the shades.

"Do you have anything you can take? Tylenol? Aspirin?" As he asked, he remembered Kenzie's extreme sensitivity to any kind of medication, her insistence that "walking it off" was her preferred choice of dealing with pain after a marathon because even over-the-counter stuff made her dizzy and sick.

One arm over her eyes, Kenzie whispered, "I'll be okay soon. I just need to be still for a bit." With a wavering smile, she added, "Thank you."

As quickly and quietly as possible, Jonah brought in the rest of the groceries and put them away in the little kitchen. Back in the living room he asked softly, "Is there anything else I can do?"

He could barely hear Kenzie's response. "It's getting better. I guess I just needed to rest a minute." The words sounded forced as she pushed herself upright.

"You should keep resting. I'll be out on the back porch if you need me. And I'll watch out for the kids, so don't worry about Pippa."

"No, no," she insisted. "I can see them from the window. It's fine."

"Well, I need to get out there 'cause Jolie's in the bouncer."

"I'll come with you."

Jonah sighed to himself as he watched Kenzie rise. Too many obstinate people today, first his son, now his...whatever Kenzie was. Neighbor. Fellow teacher. Ex-girlfriend.

Love of his life, until she'd yanked the rug out from under him for no apparent reason.

His protective feelings vanished as the old bitterness returned. He studied Kenzie with critical eyes. She stood stock-still for a moment as if finding her balance, then gave him a tremulous smile. "See? Much better."

"If you say so."

He strode to the door, leaving Kenzie behind. Despite the surge of anger, he found himself wondering for the millionth time what had happened to her. If you weren't used to it, a week of teaching could be exhausting. But it shouldn't affect anyone that severely.

What was she hiding?

After he grabbed Jolie from the bouncer, he headed to the back of the house to keep an eye on the other kids. When Frankie wasn't talking about Mrs. Reid, he was talking about Pippa. Jonah was grateful that the little girl had befriended his son and seemed so happy to spend time with him.

If only she wasn't Kenzie's daughter.

It was embarrassing how much it galled him to think of Kenzie having a child with someone else. On one of the sleepless nights years ago he'd googled her and discovered she'd married Greg Halloran suspiciously soon after moving to San Francisco. If Pippa was seven, that meant she'd been born within a year of their wedding. Probably less.

Maybe that was why they got married so fast.

"I'm going to sit on the swing."

Kenzie's breathy declaration roused Jonah from his reverie. The back porch offered a selection of wooden rocking chairs and a couple of old-fashioned porch swings. Kenzie dropped onto the nearest swing and leaned back with a sigh. "What an incredible view!"

Lowering Jolie to the porch so she could stomp her little feet, Jonah glanced out at the rows of green-hued firs that he'd need to prune this weekend to make sure they kept their Christmas tree shape. The rich blue pond reflected the clear sky, and the first touch of autumn colored the leaves on the trees swooping up into the towering mountains. "I never get tired of looking at that," he murmured.

"I've never seen anything so beautiful in my life."

Kenzie's comment surprised him, but he refrained from calling her "city girl" again. It was too evocative of their time as a couple. Guiding Jolie's stumbling feet over to a rocking chair, Jonah sat. After a moment's thought he asked, "So whatever happened to your big TV career?"

He heard her take in a surprised breath. Not surprising, considering his resentful tone.

But he forced himself to stay focused on Jolie, whose hands clutched his index fingers as she rocked back and forth.

Eventually Kenzie said, "You know I married Greg Halloran, right?"

Jonah had to tamp down another surge of bitterness. "Yeah, I heard."

She seemed to be thinking about what to say next. "We worked together in San Francisco. Then he got an offer from a Boston production company, so we moved back here. I... I was having some health issues, so I ended up not working for a while. Then Greg met Camilla and that was that."

Still focused on his daughter, Jonah suppressed a feeling of guilty triumph. "So that's why you're divorced."

Kenzie closed her eyes and sank deeper onto the swing. "I thought we were going to talk about Frankie." When he gave her a blank look, she added, "You know, continue the conversation we started at school?"

"Oh! Of course." Jonah shook his head. "Like I said, brain like a sieve."

"Understandable, given that you're raising two little kids on your own."

Taken aback by her directness, Jonah stammered, "Well, yeah, but I have my sister."

"You said your wife's name was Elena. Your partner when you were a cop, right?"

He pulled Jolie onto his lap and turned his eyes to Kenzie. "Yes, that's right. We got married four years back, and she died last year."

Kenzie held his gaze. "What happened? Was she sick?"

He shook his head. "She had a pretty rough pregnancy with this one. Lots of complications."

Kenzie's blue eyes brimmed with sympathy. "And that's what she died from? The complications?"

Pulling Jolie into a hug, he kissed the top of her head. "Yes, more or less."

"That's so…" The sound of children's voices drawing nearer interrupted Kenzie. "Uh-oh, here comes trouble!" she laughed.

"Mommy! Mommy! When is supper?" Pippa charged up the porch steps and pretended to faint on one of the rockers. "I'm starving to death!"

The swing bounced as Kenzie got to her feet. "Then I think we'd better have supper right away, don't you?"

"Yes!" Pippa jumped up. "Bye, Frankie!" she bellowed as she crashed through the door.

"Whoa!" Diane's voice came from just inside the door. "Guess someone's in a rush."

Kenzie called out, "Pippa, come here and say sorry to Miss Diane!"

"Sorry, Miss Diane!" Pippa yelled. "I'm starving!"

Frankie sat quietly next to Jonah and started playing with his little sister, much to Jonah's surprise. Diane stepped out onto the porch.

"Feeling better?" he asked.

"Yes, thank goodness." She leaned against the door frame. "But Kenzie doesn't look too good."

Jonah glanced at Frankie. "Hey, buddy, how about you take Jolie over to the other swing?"

"So you and Auntie Di can talk?" But Frankie's question didn't sound sarcastic. He even smiled at his father as he led Jolie to the other end of the porch.

Once they were settled on the swing, Jonah nodded at his sister. "Yeah, she said she had a headache."

"Ugh. Poor thing." Diane traced a line on the porch with the toe of her shoe. "I thought she was an athlete." When Jonah didn't respond, she added, "Didn't you guys meet doing charity runs or something like that?"

"Yes, that's right." Jonah shook his head, baffled once again by the huge change in Kenzie. "We met at a 10K to raise money for the Red Cross. She shot past me at the finish line, then turned to apologize." He smiled at the memory, temporarily forgetting his anger. "That did it."

Diane's face was puzzled. "Now I don't know if she could walk a mile without collapsing."

"She was in incredible shape when we were together, had always been an athlete, the epitome of health." He watched his kids swinging gently on the other side of the porch. "I can't imagine what happened to make such a drastic change."

"It's sad, for sure." Diane sat down next to

him. "I don't think I ever really understood why you guys broke up."

"Same here." Jonah's response was sharp. "She ended things with me out of nowhere. And I'd just gone to see Mom and get Grandma's engagement ring."

Diane took a sharp breath. "Whoa! I had no idea you were going to propose."

"Honestly, I'd been ready to marry her about a month after we met." His heart ached at the memory of how much he'd adored Kenzie, how crushed he'd been when she'd broken up with him. "I don't know what happened. When I left to go see Mom I thought we both felt the same way. But when I came back, she'd accepted this incredible job offer in San Francisco and was moving there right away, with or without me."

Diane's eyebrows drew together in puzzlement. "So she asked you to move there with her?"

Jonah nodded. "And when I said I couldn't move that far away from my family, she told me we were through." Hurt and anger surged through his veins as he relived the scene. "I mean, she'd told me about the offer over the phone a couple of days before but didn't tell me she was going to take it. When I got back it was a done deal. She was packing up all her stuff and would barely look at me."

Frowning, Diane said, "That's strange."

"Maybe not so strange." Jonah scowled. "Turns out her ex worked at the station that hired her. They got married a few months after she moved. So I'm pretty sure Greg Halloran had a lot to do with her sudden change of heart."

CHAPTER FIVE

KENZIE WAS IMPRESSED by Holiday Farm's brisk apple-picking business. Diane and Jonah were tied up after school and on Saturdays. Frankie and Pippa pitched in. Pumpkins would go on sale in early October and the Christmas trees in November, so they all helped to keep the farm in good shape so they'd be ready in time.

Kenzie started to feel stronger as she got used to the routine and learned to pace herself. To her relief, she was having a great time teaching, especially working on preparation for the harvest pageant.

The fourth and fifth graders, comprising twelve children, including the very first class when the school was founded just a few years ago, were busy creating costumes and memorizing verses for their appearance as farmers and their families. The second and third graders—eighteen of them, including Pippa—

were learning songs about farming and hymns of gratitude, while the nineteen first graders, including Frankie, made farm animal masks and learned a simple dance for the procession down the aisle.

Kenzie had the most difficulty teaching the dance—not only because she had two left feet, but because the movement made her dizzy. Jonah walked in one day while she was trying to teach the kids. He was alarmed to see her grab her desk, pale and breathless, after a few steps.

"Hey, can the gym teacher help out?" Jonah's voice was casual and friendly, but his face expressed concern.

Kenzie automatically started to tell him she was fine, but the expression on his face blunted her refusal. Then a memory of dancing with Jonah on one of their early dates wafted into her head. He was a much better dancer than she'd ever been, and it made sense for the phys ed teacher to help.

"Actually, that would be great," she admitted.

A smile briefly lit his face, but he quickly turned businesslike. "Delighted to help."

Jonah caught on to the steps right away and made the dance into a sort of game. Soon the entire class was moving together as if they'd been dancing all their lives. When the dismissal bell rang and the kids ran off to their next class, Jonah gave Kenzie a terse smile. "I'd be happy to collaborate with you on the pageant, especially the physical aspect. I mean dancing, but also set stuff if you need anything built."

As much as she wanted to avoid spending more time with Jonah, Kenzie knew it would be best to have another teacher involved. Jonah was right across the hall, and given his subject area, he was the obvious choice. So instead of turning him down, she forced herself to say, "That'd be great. I'm sure the kids would love having your help."

He nodded. "Thanks. It'll be fun." For a moment he hesitated as if he wanted to say something else, but finally he just sketched a wave and left.

Kenzie sighed and sank into her chair. She thought she'd gotten used to seeing Jonah every day. Well, kind of. She'd tried to steer clear of him because she wasn't prepared to deal with the jumble of feelings he awoke in her. Although she fed her long-held anger by reminding herself of what had happened all those years ago, his moments of kindness threatened to undo her resolve. It was easier to stay aloof than to endanger herself emotionally.

She was a coward.

No, she was protecting herself. Jonah had never even acknowledged her desperate emails eight years ago, including the certified letter he'd signed for. She was right to be cautious. It seemed as if he were completely oblivious to the effect of his actions—or lack thereof—or he had forgotten all about it.

Whenever she felt herself responding to Jonah's warm brown eyes or kind smile, she reminded herself of the turmoil she'd gone through after finding she was pregnant. She was grateful not to have gone through it alone, thanks to Greg Halloran coming to her rescue and marrying her. Although in retrospect that marriage probably hadn't been the best decision.

One brilliant September afternoon, Kenzie lazed on one of the back porch swings watching Pippa and Frankie pretend they were horses galloping around the yard. When she heard someone come out of the door behind her, she prayed for it to be Diane.

"Hey there," Jonah said. "Getting some rest?"

Kenzie slipped to her feet. "I was just about to go in and start getting dinner ready."

As she made her way past Jonah and Jolie, he took her arm gently with his free hand. "Wait a minute, okay?"

She tried to pull away. "But it's already getting late."

"Why do you always take off when I show up?"

Something in his tone made her hesitate before saying, "I have some things to do, so just a few minutes, okay?"

Jonah studied her face, then shook his head and shrugged. "Okay. I just came out to see if you and Pippa want to join us for a bonfire tonight." When she started to object, he cut her off. "It's Friday, so you'll have a couple of days to get things done before school starts up again."

Pippa and Frankie had come barreling up the porch steps in time to overhear Jonah's invitation. "What's a bonfire?" Pippa demanded.

Frankie pointed toward a spot in the backyard where a few thick logs and stones circled a charred-looking mass. "It's a big fire we make over there. We cook hot dogs and marshmallows and make s'mores. We had lots of them last summer."

Pippa's eyes grew saucer-big and she turned to her mother. "Mommy? Can we? Can we *please*? We never got to sleep out because you were scared about animals."

Kenzie frowned but had to admit Pippa was right. She'd been too worried about wildlife predators to let her daughter sleep outdoors, no matter how safe Jonah and Diane insisted it was. With a sigh, she capitulated. "Okay, but you're not staying up any later than eight o'clock."

Pippa opened her mouth to protest, but at Kenzie's stern expression she snapped it shut and put on her best butter-wouldn't-melt look. "Okay, Mommy."

Then she and Frankie took off, racing each other around the house.

When Kenzie turned, she found Jonah studying her with admiration. "You need to teach me how you do that."

"Do what?"

"Get my kid to behave just by looking that way."

Kenzie couldn't suppress a chuckle. "Sorry, it's an innate talent that can't be taught. You either have it or you don't."

Jolie wrestled out of her father's arms as he set her on the porch. After teetering on unsteady feet for a few seconds, she dropped to her padded bottom and burst out laughing and clapping.

Jonah gazed down at his daughter with wistful fondness. "Elena had that talent, for sure."

As he bent over to take Jolie's hands, Kenzie said softly, "You must miss her a lot."

"I do." Jonah sighed. "We were good friends for years before we got married. I mean, we were partners in the police department, and we…" After a moment of apparent consideration, he went on. "We started spending more and more time together. Elena…she stood by me through…a lot." He shot a meaningful glance at Kenzie. "She saw me at my worst and was always there for me."

Knowing Jonah was referring to their breakup, Kenzie swallowed hard and tried to sound like his words didn't cut deep. "No wonder you fell in love with her."

Jolie threw her pudgy arms around her daddy's neck. For a moment his face was hidden behind the baby. Then he looked up at Kenzie with sorrowful eyes.

"Yes. That kind of devotion is rare, and Elena had it in spades." He choked a little as he finished speaking. Without another word, he hefted his daughter up into his arms and went back into the house.

Kenzie stared after him, squashing down a wave of sympathy. After all, this was the man who'd ignored her pleas to get in touch with her. In her emails and letters she admitted she'd made a mistake in breaking up with him. She'd told him she wanted to come back and be with him.

And he'd either ignored all those messages or chosen not to respond.

With a sigh, Kenzie recalled her first and only camping trip. Jonah had proposed the trip as a mental break before her final week of grad school, but she'd hated every minute of the chilly, lumpy, buggy discomfort.

When her tent collapsed during a sudden rainstorm, she'd taken shelter in Jonah's tent.

"Mommy!" Pippa was stomping up the porch steps, panting. "Mommy! Guess what?"

Kenzie instantly switched into mom gear, smiling at her daughter's excited tone. "What is it, Pips?"

Frankie trailed Pippa up the steps and threw himself on one of the wicker chairs. "She didn't even know what s'mores are," he said with six-year-old scorn.

"But now I do! Frankie told me! Mommy, they're made out of graham crackers and chocolate and marshmallows!"

"*Toasted* marshmallows," Frankie corrected. "You put a marshmallow on a stick and hold it over the fire till it gets melty. Then you smoosh it all together."

"And we're having them tonight!" Hands clasped, a big grin showing off her missing front teeth, Pippa bounced up and down. "Mommy, doesn't that sound amazing?"

Kenzie's heart sang at her little girl's overwhelming happiness. Pulling Pippa into a sudden hug, she said, "It sure does, sweetie. I can't wait." She gave the girl a smacking kiss on the cheek that induced giggles. "And guess what?"

"What?"

"You can stay up as late as you like!"

Pippa gasped and stared at her mother as if not believing what she'd just heard. Then she flung her arms around Kenzie's neck and peppered her with kisses. "Mommy! Thank you! I love you so much!"

Kenzie hid her big smile in Pippa's curls. Seeing her little girl so happy eased her discomfort about spending the evening in Jonah's presence.

Watching him interact with his unacknowledged daughter—especially in such a warm family setting—made Kenzie's heart ache.

IN THE COOL dark of Jolie's nursery, Jonah tenderly laid his daughter in her crib and waited for her to stop fidgeting. Soon her soft breathing evened out and he knew she'd be sleeping for at least the next forty-five minutes. Frankie was still out playing with Pippa, and Kenzie was keeping watch, so he finally had a little time to himself.

Which meant he had time to think about Kenzie. Like he wasn't already doing that when he lay awake at night, all too aware of her presence on the other side of the hall. Like he didn't have to stop himself from dropping by her apartment or her classroom a dozen times a day.

Why did she try so hard to avoid being alone with him? She'd been the one to end their relationship.

What had he done to make her so angry? The previous weekend they'd gone on that camping trip. Neither of them had resisted temptation. But was she putting all the blame on him?

A brisk knock on the door yanked Jonah out of his reverie. His heart leaped at the thought that it might be Kenzie until his sister's voice called out. "We should probably get that fire started, don't you think? It's nearly dinnertime and the kids'll want to roast weenies!"

Jonah pushed himself out of his chair with leaden arms. Given what he'd just been thinking about, it wasn't a great idea to spend the evening with Kenzie, but Diane was right. The kids would be hungry and excited to get things going.

"I'll get Jolie up and be right there," he called back in the most cheerful voice he could muster.

An hour later the bonfire was roaring, tossing sparks into the twilight of the warm September evening. Stars began appearing one by one in the deepening blue sky, tiny diamonds on indigo velvet. It was all ridiculously romantic. Jonah took a deep breath and tried not to look at Kenzie, who was sitting on the other side of Pippa and Frankie, next to his sister.

Kenzie had pulled her wild copper curls into a high ponytail, which made her look younger. In fact, despite the new thinness of her face, by the firelight she looked much more like the energetic grad student he'd fallen for the second they met.

The kids had gobbled down fire-roasted hot dogs and melty s'mores in record time. He hadn't spent more than a few minutes with

Pippa before and was pleased that Frankie's new friend was charming, funny and affectionate.

In other words, just what his son needed.

Suddenly Jonah realized that Pippa was standing right in front of him, hands on her hips and a puzzled look on her chocolate-smeared face. "Mr. Raymond?"

He smiled at her. "Miss Halloran?"

Pippa looked surprised, then burst out laughing. "No, silly! You call me Pippa." Her big brown eyes slid toward Kenzie with a mischievous giggle. "Or Philippa Joy, if you're mad at me."

"How could anyone ever be mad at you?" Jonah asked in a mock-horrified voice.

She smiled, showing her dimples and missing front teeth. "Mommy gets mad if I'm naughty. Sometimes she calls me by all three names, which means I'm going to be sent to my room. But that hardly ever happens," Pippa hastened to add. "Anyhow, I wanted to ask you something."

"Sure! Go ahead and ask."

The little girl glanced at Frankie, who stared back at her wide-eyed. The children had some sort of silent communication. Then Pippa nodded and looked boldly at Jonah. "Are you going to get Frankie a new mommy?"

"Pippa!" Kenzie gasped. Next to her, Diane stifled a laugh.

Perplexed, Jonah took his time to answer. "Well, Pippa, that's..."

Kenzie came to his rescue. "That's not something you ask someone."

"Why not? How else am I s'posed to find out?" Pippa asked, folding her arms across her chest.

"It's a very personal question," Kenzie responded. "Getting Frankie a new mommy means that Mr. Raymond would have to get married."

Forehead creased with consternation, Pippa persisted. "But that would be nice, wouldn't it?"

All three adults fell silent, unsure of how to answer Pippa's questions. Fortunately, Frankie chose that moment to speak up.

"Daddy, can Pippa and me go looking for fireflies?"

Jonah tried to hide his surprise and pleasure at being called Daddy. That hadn't happened for a couple of months, not since Jolie's first birthday.

He cleared his throat and gave Frankie a loving smile, careful to keep his big voice gentle. "It might be too late in the year for fireflies, but you might find something just as good."

"Singing frogs?" Pippa squealed, jumping up and down.

"It's too late for peepers, too," Jonah laughed. "But you might see possums or raccoons."

Kenzie had snapped into alert-mom mode. "Don't go too far, and stay away from the edge of the pond, okay?"

Jonah took one look at her worried face and stood. "I'll go along and keep an eye on them. Just to be sure they don't find a skunk." He gave Kenzie a reassuring smile and trailed after the kids, who were already out of earshot.

It was hard to keep his imagination from wandering to a brighter future, full of hope. Maybe Frankie was starting to heal again, now that they'd gotten past the first anniversary of Elena's death. Maybe he'd just needed a little time to realize that Jonah still loved him as if he were his own son. Maybe even though Elena was gone, everything would be okay after all.

And maybe Kenzie would come around and realize he wasn't the enemy. Maybe, in spite of their history, they could be friends.

"Daddy! Why'd you stop?"

Frankie's question snapped Jonah out of his reverie and made him realize he'd stopped in his tracks. He rubbed at his eyes, which suddenly stung, and cleared his throat.

"I'm coming, son!"

CHAPTER SIX

NEXT TO THE crackling embers of the bonfire, Kenzie was trying not to worry about the two children roaming around the dark farm. Her heart warmed with gratitude that Jonah had gone with them. As much as he used to kid her about being a city girl, he understood that her worries were real and made sure she didn't get too anxious.

It made her wonder again if he'd actually read the messages she'd sent eight years ago, pleading with him to talk to her and finally telling him she was pregnant. The idea of Jonah heartlessly ignoring her news didn't jibe with how gentle he was with her and Pippa. The conversation he'd had with their daughter a few moments earlier had stirred up mixed feelings in Kenzie.

"What a sorry bunch of singletons we are." Sitting on the log next to Kenzie, Diane sighed and glanced at little Jolie nodding off in her well-padded carrier. "I know it's whiny, given what you and my brother have been through, but I miss Paul so much. He really loves bonfires and he's so great with Jonah's kids. He will absolutely adore your little girl."

"I thought he was supposed to be home this week," Kenzie said. After hearing Frankie rave about his fun-loving uncle, she was eager to meet Diane's husband.

"His flights got messed up. It happens." Diane's face brightened. "But he should be here in a week or so if the latest plans work out."

"I hope it does. I think it's incredibly generous of you to let him go on a mission every year."

Diane was shaking her head. "I doubt I could stop him. And God knows they need his expertise. But sometimes I'm a bit worried about where they send him."

The fear in Diane's voice gave Kenzie a pang. "I'm sure you are. I'll pray extra hard for his safety."

Diane squeezed Kenzie's hand. "Would you? Thank you so much!"

Kenzie squeezed back. "Of course I will. Since I moved here, I find myself praying more and more. I'm not sure why." After a moment of thought, she shyly added, "I only rediscovered my faith a couple of years ago, during a really difficult time in Boston. I think I feel even closer to God here."

Smiling, Diane nodded. "It's so easy to see the beauty of His creation here, isn't it?"

"Honestly, I don't see how people can miss it," Kenzie agreed.

"You know something?" Diane put her head on Kenzie's shoulder. "I knew you were a sister the minute I saw you. I don't know why, but I feel like God had a hand in your coming to live here."

"I feel the same way!" Kenzie hadn't realized how much she missed having a close friend. She couldn't imagine a better one than Diane, even if she was Jonah's sister. "I'd been praying so hard for a good place to live."

"And here you are!" Diane gave Kenzie an impetuous hug. They both stared into the fire for a minute. Then Diane peered around through the dark as if to make sure they were alone. Her voice dropped to a whisper. "Can I tell you something I haven't told a single soul yet?"

"Sure! Do I need to swear myself to secrecy?"

Diane nudged her playfully. "I trust you.

Maybe because…" She bit her lip. "Well, Pippa said something to me that made me think you'll understand."

Kenzie suppressed a jolt of alarm. "What did Pippa say?"

"Just that…well, she thought she was going to get a little brother or sister a while ago, but they never came."

Swallowing, Kenzie closed her eyes. "Greg and I tried for kids, but I couldn't seem to carry for more than a month or so."

"I'm so sorry." She felt Diane's arm slip around her shoulders. "But you have Pippa."

Kenzie fought the urge to tell her friend that Greg wasn't Pippa's father, and that Diane was actually her daughter's aunt. But if Jonah didn't want his sister to know, Kenzie wasn't going to tell her. She forced her mind back to the moment at hand.

"Yes. Of course. But we wanted more. Like three or four." Kenzie smiled wanly. "Greg was an only child and hated it. So we kept trying, but…well, none of them survived past the first month." Her throat tightened at the memory of those three little lives. She'd loved every one of them and grieved them so intensely it had affected her health.

Or so the doctors believed, refusing to acknowledge the possibility that it might have been the other way around. Kenzie was convinced that her mysterious illness had caused her to miscarry.

"Paul and I have tried, too. For years. And when we finally succeeded…" Diane's voice broke. "Well, like yours, they didn't stay around long." A huge smile lit up her face. "But now…"

The way Diane glowed had nothing to do with the firelight and told her secret better than words. "You're pregnant!" Kenzie whispered, excited for her friend.

Diane nodded. "I've made it through the first trimester for the first time, and the doctor says everything looks great. I haven't even told Paul because I didn't want to get his hopes up and have him worry about being away if something goes wrong. But the minute he gets home I'm yelling it from the rooftops."

Kenzie threw her arms around Diane. "I'm so happy for you!"

But she found her happiness for Diane tempered with something else, something bitter and sad. This was Jonah's sister, her own little girl's aunt, pregnant with Pippa's first cousin. And as much as she felt her new friend deserved this blessing, as sincerely as she meant her congratulations, Kenzie felt a familiar wave of sorrow deep inside.

The sound of approaching voices made the two women sit up and try to appear normal. Diane giggled a little as she put a finger to her lips.

Pippa staggered over to her mother and collapsed onto her lap with an enormous yawn. "How late is it, Mommy?" she asked sleepily.

"Pretty late. Way past your usual bedtime." Kenzie pulled her daughter close and kissed the top of her head.

Jonah sat down next to them with Frankie in his arms. "This little guy's almost out," he said. "How's Jolie holding up?"

Diane smiled lovingly at the baby next to her. "She's been asleep since you left."

"Guess it's time to get these kiddos to bed." Jonah shifted Frankie up onto his shoulder and started to stand.

"I don't want to go to bed," Pippa mumbled.

Frankie yawned and burrowed deeper into Jonah's shoulder. "Me neither."

"Tell you what." Diane got to her feet. "I'll put Jolie down while you guys stay up a little longer."

Kenzie tried to stand, but the weight of Pippa on her lap kept her seated. "No, I need to…"

"Don't be silly." Grabbing the handle of Jolie's carrier, Diane shot Kenzie a conspiratorial look. "Enjoy the last little bit of the fire." With that, she headed up the porch steps and disappeared into the house.

Kenzie stared into the glowing orange embers, trying not to focus on the thought that she was holding Jonah's first child on her lap, while right next to her he was holding the little brother Pippa had always wanted. The idea made her heart ache, made her want to ask the man sitting beside her if he'd gotten her messages all those years ago.

But her—*their*—little girl was fast asleep now, and the last thing Kenzie wanted to do was wake her up. So she let a few minutes pass in silence, then sniffed back her tears and shoved down her questions before turning to Jonah. "She's fallen asleep. I'd better take her inside."

He gave her a regretful shrug. "Yeah, this little guy's down for the count, too. Guess we wore them out." He grinned. "At least they should sleep well, huh?"

They both rose at the same time. Jonah went ahead and opened the door to the house, then the door to her apartment so she wouldn't have to let go of Pippa. With a nod of thanks, Kenzie slipped inside. He closed the door gently behind her.

As she changed her sleeping child into a nightie, Kenzie kept wondering why Jonah hadn't called her the second he read the final letter. The secret Diane had shared with her had revived all those feelings of hurt and resentment. In all of her messages, Kenzie had apologized, said she wanted to come back to Boston and be with him again. He'd been so heartbroken by the breakup she felt sure he'd be thrilled to have her back. She'd waited and waited, her hope waning with every passing hour.

His lack of response spoke louder than any words, especially given the contents of her last letter. Or so it seemed at the time. But maybe there was something else behind his silence. Elena had made no secret of her dislike of Kenzie, and according to Jonah, she'd jumped in as soon as Kenzie was gone.

Could Elena have intercepted Kenzie's messages and gotten rid of them before Jonah could see them?

Even if she had, how on earth could Kenzie ask Jonah about it? Grilling him about his late wife's possible duplicity sounded like a terrible thing to do. He clearly loved Elena and was still grieving her.

But if that was what had happened, it meant Jonah hadn't simply ignored Kenzie.

And it meant he had no idea Pippa was his child.

With a sigh of frustration, Kenzie tucked Pippa in and kissed her forehead. "Night, sweet girl," she whispered before tiptoeing out of the room.

But she couldn't settle down. If she sat on the sofa, she sprang up again a second later and sat in one of the chairs. If she turned on the TV, all she did was flip unseeing through the channels. She thought about going to bed but knew she'd just end up lying there wide awake.

Finally she strode outside to the back porch, figuring she could look at the stars and pray for peace. Pippa's window faced the porch and was open enough that Kenzie would hear if she called out. That seemed unlikely, given what a sound sleeper Pippa was.

Back in the cool night air, Kenzie leaned against a column next to the porch steps and looked up at the sky. The sheer number of stars took her breath away. It was impossible to see them in the city, where the glaring lights obscured them. But out here in the country they filled the heavens on a clear night like this one, and they actually seemed to sparkle.

As she studied them in breathless wonder, Kenzie felt peace wash through her heart and soul. *Thank You, dear Lord, for this wonderful new home*, she prayed silently.

"Beautiful, isn't it?"

Kenzie almost jumped out of her skin at the voice behind her. She stifled a shriek so she wouldn't wake Pippa and whirled around to find Jonah sitting on the porch swing. "I—I didn't see you there!" she stammered.

He got up and moved toward her, standing next to her at the top of the steps and gazing upward. "Sorry. Didn't expect anyone to join me. I come out here a lot at night, just to look at the sky. The kids' rooms are right there, so I can hear if they call."

He was standing so close to Kenzie she could feel the warmth coming from him. Maybe because of the questions she'd been entertaining a few moments ago, she felt differently toward Jonah. Something she should know better than to feel for this man.

She tried to move away without being too obvious about it, but the porch post was in the way. She could either go down the steps into the darkness or walk backward to get to the door, which would look silly. So she stayed put, filled with conflicting emotions, her arms folded across her chest like a protective barrier.

Finally she dredged up what seemed like an appropriate response, awkwardly indicating the window behind her. "Pippa's room is right there, too." *Your other daughter,* she added silently.

He didn't respond for a moment, just stood there staring up at the starry canopy. "Seemed like she had a good time tonight."

Despite her discomfort, Kenzie couldn't suppress a smile at the memory of her daughter's happiness. "She had a ball. Guess she's a country mouse at heart." She stopped herself before she could add, *Just like her father.*

"Wonder where she gets that from?" Jonah chuckled.

Kenzie turned her head and studied him, looking for some kind of sign that he knew he was Pippa's father. His face showed only humor and kindness. Perplexed, Kenzie turned her gaze back to the heavens. "I'm sure I have no idea."

"I'm impressed with how much you've taken

to country living." Jonah seemed oblivious to her confusion. "I wasn't sure you'd be able to stick it out, given how squeamish you were during that camping trip we took."

Kenzie whipped her head around in surprise. She could feel her face heating up with embarrassment. "Um…"

It was obvious that Jonah realized he'd made a mistake. He scrunched up his face. "I'm sorry. I… I guess maybe you'd rather forget that trip."

Kenzie kept her eyes glued to his face until he looked at her. Despite the darkness, she could see the blush cover his cheeks as that night in the tent came back to him.

"Kenz… I'm such an idiot. I'm so sorry." He took her by the wrist. "Please forgive me."

She peered up at him, trying to figure out how to react, but the mournful brown eyes looking down at her dissolved her confusion. All she could think of was how much she'd loved him all those years ago, and how foolish she'd been to end things the way she did.

She'd been furious that he hadn't proposed after what happened on the camping trip. Instead, he'd run off to spend a week with his mother and had hardly been in touch with Kenzie. She'd felt ignored, rejected. The hurt festered out of proportion until he returned. Then she'd said mean, ugly things that she couldn't unsay. In just a few minutes she'd destroyed what they had. Maybe she had a few things to apologize for as well.

Jonah was still holding on to her wrist, his face wistful and tender. Suddenly Kenzie couldn't bear to look at him for another second. But instead of looking away, she fell forward against him, burying her face in his chest.

Mistake.

The scent of him, the warmth of him, the sensation of his heart pounding next to her ear, all filled her with a rush of regret. She knew she should pull away, but something kept her from moving a muscle. All she could do was rest against him and wish she could go back eight years.

After a stunned moment, she felt Jonah's arms creep around her and pull her closer. Kenzie didn't resist. She still couldn't move. She just wanted to sink into this sweet, comforting moment and stay there.

"Kenzie," Jonah whispered into her hair. He pulled back slightly and put a finger under her chin, lifting her head so they could look at each other.

Kenzie held her breath and gazed steadily at that face, once the dearest thing in the world to her. Too much time had passed since they'd been this close. His thick brown hair had more than a few silver threads, his laugh lines had deepened, but he was still the man she'd been sure she was going to marry.

And whether he knew it or not, she'd had his child. That was a bond like no other.

Jonah stroked her cheek, tucked a curl behind her ear. "Kenzie," he said again, "I…"

An ear-shattering shriek pierced the silence, followed by a series of little screams and hysterical sobbing. Kenzie jumped a mile, but Jonah steadied her with his firm hand and spoke quickly. "Frankie. He's having night terrors."

He was gone like a shot, leaving Kenzie breathless on the porch, feeling as if she'd been turned inside out.

"WHAT FRIGHTENED YOU, BUDDY? Was it another bad dream?"

Although he was deeply disappointed at having his moment with Kenzie interrupted, Jonah wasn't sorry to be holding his son and comforting him. These days, anything that strengthened their tenuous connection was precious, even if it was a nightmare.

"There was a bad man," Frankie choked out. "He wanted to hurt Mommy."

"That is scary." Knowing his naturally loud voice sometimes frightened the boy, Jonah focused on keeping his tone low and calming. "But it was just a dream, right?"

Frankie whimpered and sniffled. "I don't know. He was mad at Mommy and was yelling at her real loud."

Jonah hugged his son more tightly. "You know a man didn't hurt Mommy, don't you?"

The boy looked up at him with huge, terrified eyes. "It wasn't Mommy Elena. It was my real mommy."

Jonah had to grit his teeth and push down anger against his late wife for telling their son he wasn't really their child. She'd done it soon after Jolena was born, probably already under the influence of postpartum depression and pain medication. But why she'd done it at all confounded Jonah. They'd discussed telling Frankie at some point, but not when he was only five years old and still fragile from his early trauma. Unfortunately, Frankie hadn't mentioned it to

Jonah until after Elena's death, so he couldn't ask her what she'd been thinking.

Forcing himself to go still inside, Jonah met his son's gaze. "Do you remember your real mommy?"

Frankie's eyebrows met in a confused arch. "I don't know. Sometimes. Did she have kind of yellow hair like Miss Thorsen at school?"

Jonah held his breath. Lana Tiffman had had unnaturally blond hair with several inches of dark roots. The long, scraggly tresses had spread out around her head like a halo as she lay unresponsive next to her hysterical toddler. Did the boy actually have that memory? He'd only been two years old at the time, but it was possible.

Had the memories just started coming back to Frankie? Was that the reason for his recent regression?

"Yes, buddy. She had yellow hair."

"Why was the bad man yelling so loud?"

"I don't know, son. But he shouldn't have been yelling. I'm sorry he scared you."

But he couldn't help mulling over Frankie's nightmare. Although he'd left the force well over a year ago, being a cop was still in Jonah's blood.

As her death had presented more like an overdose than a murder, the investigation into Lana Tiffman's demise had been cursory. Had there been a "bad man" that two-year-old Frankie saw yelling at his mother? If so, did he have anything to do with Lana's death? And could he possibly have been Frankie's father?

But what was the point of all these questions? No one they'd spoken to had any idea who Lana's boyfriend or Frankie's father was. According to the neighbors, she had lots of male friends. No policeman in his right mind would ask to reopen the investigation based on a traumatized little boy's nightmare.

No point in thinking about that right now. Jonah kissed the top of Frankie's head and tucked him back under the covers. Once his son had drifted back to sleep, Jonah tiptoed out of the bedroom to sit in his recliner and relive that sweet, brief moment with Kenzie.

A soft tap on the door roused him from his thoughts. His heart filled with hope that it was Kenzie, Jonah launched himself from the chair and opened the door.

His face must have registered his disappointment, because Diane laughed as she stepped inside. "Hoping I was your other neighbor, were you?"

Jonah gave his sister a rueful shrug. "Am I that transparent?"

They headed to the area by the fireplace and sat side by side on the sofa. "I saw some sparks tonight that weren't from the bonfire," Diane chuckled. "And now you're blushing." When he didn't laugh, she added, "I guess I shouldn't tease you."

He stood abruptly and walked to the fireplace, looking at the photos on the mantelpiece. Most were pictures of himself, Elena and Frankie. There was only a single photo of Jolena, taken at the hospital shortly after she'd left the NICU. He hadn't wanted a picture of her in the incubator, hooked up to all kinds of scary contraptions. The difficult labor and birth had nearly killed both mother and child, but excellent medical care had brought them through.

When they got home, Elena refused to let him take pictures of her with the baby, claiming she was fat and ugly. Despite the fulfillment of her long-held wish of motherhood, she didn't dote on Jolena, didn't interact with her the way a new mother usually did. She saw to the baby's needs in an almost robotic fashion. She'd practically ignored Frankie, who thought she'd suddenly stopped loving him because of the baby. Jonah had chalked Elena's behavior up to the aftereffects of the traumatic birth and the anesthetic they'd given her for the emergency C-section.

He should have paid more attention. He should have asked questions. He should have taken her to see someone.

He should have known something was very, very wrong.

"You must miss her terribly."

Diane's words jarred him. He'd almost forgotten she was there. "Of course I miss her. And so do the kids."

"I heard Frankie screaming a little while ago. That seems to be happening more often lately."

With a sigh, Jonah sank back onto the sofa. "The nightmares are back and they're escalating. I don't know why."

"Do you know what they're about?"

Covering his face with his hands, Jonah shook his head. "He says it's about his real mom and some bad man who hurt her. He was only a toddler but I suppose it's possible."

Diane leaned back, a worried expression on her face. "So much for a little guy to handle, losing two mothers. It's no wonder he's afraid he'll be abandoned."

Jonah sat very still for a moment, head in hands. Finally, in a very soft voice, he said, "It's my fault she died."

"What?" Diane's disbelief was clear in her sharp response.

He dragged himself to a more upright position, guilt gnawing at his stomach. "I should have known something was wrong. She wasn't acting like herself. Of course, I knew she was on medication, but I never imagined she'd take it, then leave the kids alone and go for a drive."

He felt his sister's hand on his shoulder. "You were working a ton of hours and picking up the slack with the kids while Elena recovered."

Jonah closed his eyes and grimaced at the memory. "I should have taken more family medical leave so I could keep a better eye on things while she healed. She seemed calmer, so I thought she was getting better, not worse."

Diane squeezed his shoulder. "Maybe she thought she was getting better, too. You know she hated to worry you."

"I should have noticed how she was neglecting Frankie." He turned miserable, haunted eyes to his sister. "That was completely out of character. And she started snapping at me, which she'd never done before. But I chalked it up to what she'd just been through."

"That's surprising," Diane admitted. "I'd never seen a woman so in love, even the first time I met her, before you met Kenzie." When Jonah shot her a questioning look, she continued. "Just before I left for Haiti, remember? I came to Boston to stay with you and we all had dinner together. I could tell she was totally smitten but was doing her best to keep things professional." Diane gave her brother a reproving shake of the head. "Next thing I knew, you were raving about this little redhead."

Jonah slumped against the back of the sofa, processing the information his sister had just given him. "That far back? Really?"

"I had a feeling you were oblivious." Diane grinned. "I'm sure Elena was relieved once Kenzie was out of the picture."

He mulled over Diane's revelation. "She started hanging around a lot right after Kenzie left, making sure I was okay. I was a mess for a while. I got the feeling she was trying to protect me, in some way."

"Yeah, you were a barrel of laughs. But Elena was great. I was thrilled when you finally realized what a wonderful person she was. I was over the moon when you got married and took Frankie in." Diane's sigh was weighted with sorrow. "I never imagined it would end so tragically."

Jonah slung an arm around his sister and pulled her close. "Did I ever tell you she's the one who proposed?"

Diane laughed. "No, but I'm not surprised to hear it. That girl knew what she wanted and made no bones about going for it."

Despite the subject, Jonah felt himself smiling. "Yup, that was Elena. She didn't exactly ask me to marry her—she told me to. Said we were great together, and if we got married, we'd have a better chance of adopting Frankie." His voice thickened. "Said she liked me enough to put up with me for the rest of her life."

"Oh, Jonah," Diane breathed. "Don't make me cry."

"Within a year we were fostering Frankie and starting the adoption process. Then she was pregnant." Overwhelmed just thinking about everything that had happened, he blinked and shook his head rapidly. "Then…"

Diane wrapped her arm around her brother's shoulders. "No one could have predicted that Elena would try to drive after taking opioids.

I mean, she was a former cop. She knew what that stuff could do."

"But I should have noticed. I could have done something."

Diane embraced her brother as his body went rigid with the effort of holding back tears. "You can't blame yourself, sweetie," she pleaded.

After a moment he pulled away. "But I have to be honest with myself." Jonah rubbed his eyes on his sleeve and cleared his throat. "So please don't expect me to move on or encourage me to think about Kenzie again. I know that's what you were doing tonight, leaving us together by the bonfire."

Diane shook her head in violent disagreement. "But—"

"But nothing." Jonah glanced back toward the hallway where the kids' bedrooms were. "I need to focus on my children. It's what Elena would have wanted." With a sad smile he added, "And having put me back together after the breakup, she definitely would not have wanted me to go chasing after Kenzie Reid again."

CHAPTER SEVEN

THE MOMENT ON the porch with Jonah had left Kenzie dazed. After he ran inside to take care of Frankie, she wandered back into her apartment in a stupor, bewildered by what had happened, by her involuntary display of vulnerability.

It almost seemed as if Jonah had wanted to kiss her.

And maybe she had wanted him to.

Despite all of her long-term anger, she'd practically fallen into Jonah Raymond's arms. And it had happened only a few feet from their sleeping daughter's bedroom window.

The daughter he still hadn't acknowledged.

Why wasn't she furious with him or with herself? Instead, she was moping around reliving that moment and hoping for more.

And what would have happened if Frankie hadn't had a nightmare?

Kenzie found herself blushing. Even though

no one was there to witness the extent of her stupidity, she collapsed in an embarrassed heap on the sofa and buried her face in the cushions.

Maybe it was time to mend things instead of pretending they'd never happened.

As soon as that thought crossed her mind, she stomped on it as if it were a cockroach. Okay, so they'd embraced. It had been quick, meaningless. Right?

But it sure hadn't felt meaningless. The moment had been fraught with complex emotions.

She couldn't reach back eight years and prevent herself from getting so worked up she couldn't think straight, but she could stop being such a coward and tell the poor guy exactly why she'd broken up with him. In retrospect her reasoning seemed childish, rooted in hurt pride. Right after their camping trip he'd gone to see his family for a week and had hardly been in touch with her. She was still reeling from what had happened and interpreted his withdrawal as a loss of interest in her.

But what if he actually didn't want to interrupt her while she was studying? He'd known she was going to have an exceptionally busy, intense week. What if he was just trying to give her space?

There was still the question of why he hadn't responded to her frantic emails and letters. But what if he hadn't read them?

What if he had no idea he was Pippa's father?

Kenzie suddenly realized she was pacing her apartment, excited by the thought of resolving long-buried problems. She would ask Jonah why he'd never responded to all her apologies, requests to get back together, and finally her pregnancy. Maybe that would make him realize that Kenzie regretted her abrupt end to their relationship.

Kenzie knew she had to talk to Jonah. The sooner the better.

Since Holiday Farm was closed on Sunday, Jonah and Diane bundled the children into her car and headed to church. Jonah noted that Kenzie's car was gone and wondered if he'd see her there. He'd been avoiding her since their embrace on Friday night, which wasn't hard because the farm was overrun with apple pickers all day Saturday.

Sure enough, when they pulled into the parking lot, Kenzie's station wagon was already there. He and Diane noticed it at the same time and exchanged a glance.

"Everything okay with you two?" Diane asked. "You've been a bit distracted."

Jonah sighed and shook his head. "Everything's fine." He turned to the back seat. "Okay, Frankie, unbuckle your sister." When Frankie obeyed without objection, Jonah sighed again, this time with relief.

In the sunlit sanctuary, Jonah immediately spotted Kenzie's and Pippa's curly mops, shiny copper and bright strawberry blond side by side in a pew near the back. As Diane took the kids to the Sunday school room, Jonah debated the wisdom of going up to them after the resolution he'd made Friday night. Fortunately, his dilemma was interrupted by Enid and her husband, Pastor Mullin.

"Jonah! How wonderful to see you here again." Enid embraced him warmly with her long arms.

"Welcome back, son." The stout little pastor gave him a firm handshake, grinning from ear to ear. "We've missed you, as I'm sure my beautiful wife let you know."

Cheered by their sincere greeting, Jonah returned their smiles. "It's time to get our lives back on track."

"You picked a good place to start, if I do say

so myself." Pastor Mullin chuckled, and then his face grew serious. "How's little Frankie doing these days?"

"He's up and down," Jonah admitted. "I never know what to expect."

Enid nodded, her face solemn. "You're doing a wonderful job, Jonah. I can't imagine how hard it must be."

Pastor Mullin's iron gray eyebrows furrowed with concern. "It's a very heavy burden to bear, but you know we're here to help whenever we can. Please don't hesitate to call on us."

Jonah felt his throat tighten with gratitude. "Thanks, both of you," he whispered.

"We should have him over to dinner, don't you think?" Enid asked her husband.

"Absolutely. Especially if that means you'll make your wonderful stew," Pastor Mullin added with a mischievous grin. "With lots of biscuits, of course."

"Oh, you." Enid gave her husband a playful push, then noticed Kenzie and her daughter sitting nearby. "Henry, that's our new arts teacher. We'd better go say hello before you take the pulpit." She beamed at Jonah. "I'll get back to you about dinner. Maybe this week?"

When Jonah nodded, she and the pastor hurried away to greet Kenzie.

Suddenly feeling melancholy, Jonah watched them talk to Kenzie and Pippa. The Mullins were the happiest couple he'd ever known, married over forty years and still apparently in love and content. He'd thought he and Elena had a shot at something like that, even though he hadn't been in love with her at first.

Love grew. Then she was gone.

Before Elena, he'd been sure he'd found the love of his life in Kenzie. Then that camping trip seemed to ruin everything.

If only she'd talked to him about what had upset her so much, instead of breaking up with him. He'd gone to see his mother to tell her he wanted to marry Kenzie, and to get the antique engagement ring that had belonged to his grandmother. It had been in his pocket while Kenzie stomped around and told him she was moving to the other side of the country. Instead of a fiancée, he'd gotten a broken heart.

"Penny for them." Diane appeared at his elbow. "And if you stare any harder at Kenzie, you might set her on fire."

Ignoring her comments, Jonah headed for the pew on the other side of the aisle from Kenzie.

Pippa jumped up and ran off, presumably to go to Sunday school. Frankie would be happy to have her there.

Jonah sighed as he opened his hymnal. Maybe he should confront Kenzie instead of avoiding her. Maybe it was time for him to ask what had happened eight years ago that made her break his heart without warning.

Would she tell him the truth?

There was only one way to find out.

AFTER THE SERVICE, the congregation gathered in the large fellowship hall for coffee and treats. Kenzie and Pippa found themselves surrounded by friendly faces welcoming them, Pastor and Dr. Mullin the friendliest.

Enid enfolded Kenzie in her arms, then pulled away to beam at her. "I'm so pleased to see you two in our flock!"

Beaming back, Kenzie exclaimed, "It was a lovely service! I've never been to such a spirited church."

The pastor threw back his head and laughed. "We do love to sing to the Lord, at the tops of our lungs."

"We sang a bunch in Sunday school, too," Pippa said eagerly. "It was so much fun. Can we come back, Mommy?" Standing next to Pippa, Frankie studied her curiously but didn't say anything. Pippa seized his hand. "Frankie's too shy to sing, but I think he should do it anyway because it's fun."

Kenzie hadn't noticed Jonah standing behind Frankie until he spoke. "That was a wonderful message, Pastor. And one I needed to hear."

The pastor nodded. "We all need to be reminded of the two greatest commandments now and then. If you love God with all your heart, loving your neighbor comes naturally."

Kenzie glanced at Jonah to find him looking at her. Blushing, she looked away.

Enid was patting her husband's arm. "Yes, dear, we don't need an encore," she laughed. Turning to Kenzie, she said, "We'd love to have you over to dinner some night this week. How's Wednesday?"

"That sounds great," Kenzie agreed happily.

Pastor Mullin's eyes lit up. "Before the service we were talking about having Jonah and his brood over. Maybe we could have a little dinner party!"

Kenzie thought she caught an uneasy look on Enid's face at her husband's suggestion, but it vanished quickly. "Of course! That's a wonderful idea." She smiled at Jonah. "We'll make it nice and early for the children, of course. Five o'clock?"

Jonah glanced worriedly at Kenzie before saying, "Okay. Yes. We'll be there."

CHAPTER EIGHT

THAT AFTERNOON, KENZIE was trying to relax on the back porch swing as she geared herself up for talking to Jonah. Half of her was watching Pippa and Frankie play a hilarious two-person version of softball that involved making up a lot of rules on the spot. The other half still hadn't stopped reliving Friday night's encounter.

What had she been thinking?

Truth was, she hadn't been thinking. Not at all. If she had, there was no way she would have let herself literally fall into his arms. But that didn't stop her heart from fluttering like a fledgling bird when she thought back to that night: the sky crammed full of shimmering stars, Jonah standing close beside her, waves of nostalgia washing through her.

Why had she given in to her emotions and leaned against him? Why hadn't she said goodnight and gone inside like a sane human being?

Now she had not only those treacherous old feelings to contend with, but also a fresh memory of being in his embrace again.

And she'd talked herself into having a very difficult conversation with him. She knew she had to do it as soon as possible, before she lost her nerve.

Next to her head she heard the screen door creak open. Kenzie's radar was so tuned up she knew it was Jonah without even looking. His voice, gentled down from its full power, confirmed it.

"Hey."

When he sat next to her without asking, Kenzie sat up straight and almost ran away. A big hand on her arm stopped her. "Please don't leave."

Looking at him was a terrible idea, but Kenzie made herself turn her head. There he was in jeans and a sweatshirt, holding little Jolie to his shoulder as she slept. It was way too adorable, designed to make a woman melt, so she cranked up her inner icebox and forced out the most dreaded words in the English language.

"We need to talk."

Jonah groaned. "What have I done now?"

Kenzie scrambled to find a good answer but

couldn't come up with a thing. "N-nothing," she stammered. "It's just…"

"We hugged," Jonah finished for her. "Right over there, a couple of nights ago."

"I know, but—"

"Don't worry about it."

That was not the response she'd been expecting, and it made what she'd planned to say feel even more awkward and out of place. "Don't worry about it?" she echoed lamely.

Rubbing Jolie's back, he nodded. "It was a mistake. It won't happen again. So please don't yell at me." He gave her a whimsical grin that softened his words a bit.

Thoroughly confused, Kenzie blinked at him. "O…kay."

"You're right. It's a bad idea. We're both completely different people now, and we have other things to think about." He gave her a knowing side-glance. "That's more or less what you were going to say, right?"

"Um…" He was completely wrong, but Kenzie couldn't find the words to set him straight. "Yeah, I guess."

"Great!" Jonah sat there a moment longer, looking as if he had more to say. But Jolie stirred in her sleep, then opened her big brown eyes and smiled at her father. Jonah smiled back and kissed the tip of her nose, apparently forgetting Kenzie's existence.

Bewildered, Kenzie got up from the porch swing and went inside, back to the comfort of her apartment. Keeping her eye on the kids through the picture window, she curled up on the sofa and picked up her reverie where Jonah had interrupted it.

But he hadn't just interrupted it, had he? He'd completely changed the tone of her thinking with that "don't worry about it" remark. She'd been trying to figure out how to tell him she'd made a mistake all those years ago, and ask him why he'd ignored her urgent, apologetic messages.

Now she was upset that he'd told her their brief embrace was a mistake.

Shouldn't she be relieved? Yes, she should. But she wasn't. Instead, her feelings were hurt.

What was wrong with her? How could she possibly still have feelings for Jonah? Again she reminded herself that after their camping trip, he'd run off to his family the next day. She'd hardly heard from him for days. What kind of guy did that?

Sighing, Kenzie forced herself to be honest. She'd known he was close to his widowed mother and visited her as often as possible. And he tended to get busy with fixing things for her and spending time with his family and old friends when he was there. He was probably too distracted to think much about what had happened that weekend.

But to Kenzie it had felt like desertion. She'd fervently hoped that when Jonah returned, he'd propose. Especially after she told him about the job in San Franciso that she'd accepted. It was the best offer she'd received by far, an exceptional position for someone just out of grad school. She would have been a fool to turn it down.

Jonah hadn't proposed. Even when she suggested they both might relocate to San Francisco. Together. Hint, hint.

Nope. Jonah had given her the basset-hound eyes and said, "Kenz, you know I need to stay around New England. I want to be near my family."

Kenzie's heart broke and her feelings of hurt and rejection had taken over. Without waiting to hear another word, she'd shut him down and flown off to the West Coast, vowing never to speak to Jonah Raymond again. He'd blown it. His loss.

Then, a few weeks after her move, nausea and fatigue hit. The home pregnancy test came up positive and was confirmed by a doctor.

When Jonah ghosted her, marrying Greg Halloran had seemed like the best choice. He was a good guy, he adored her, and she enjoyed his company. They worked together in the studio and it turned out he was behind her landing the job of her dreams. Shortly after they'd moved back to Boston, the weird symptoms hit. Kenzie had felt so sick she couldn't function well, could barely think straight. No doctor she saw could tell her what was wrong. Every one of them referred her to someone else who couldn't tell her what was wrong. She ended up with diagnoses of fibromyalgia, chronic fatigue and migraines. The only treatments they recommended were pain medications, which she refused to take.

She lost her job. She lost three babies. Then Greg had confessed he was in love with someone else, and she was pregnant. He wanted a divorce so he could marry Camilla.

Kenzie yanked her mind back to the present.

She had traveled way too far down a dark road. Time to take some positive steps.

She'd promised Pippa that she'd invite Greg to visit once they were settled. Pushing herself upright, Kenzie grabbed her laptop and typed an email to invite her ex to Chapelton some weekend afternoon. She knew he was wrapped up in his new wife and offspring-to-be, but surely he could spend a few hours visiting the little girl he'd helped Kenzie raise even though she wasn't his own.

Kenzie hoped so, anyway. If the disconnect went on much longer, Pippa would be hurt. Greg had never been Father of the Year, but he was the only father her daughter had ever known. As little as Kenzie wanted to see her ex, there was nothing she wouldn't do for Pippa.

The thoughts made her wonder how Pippa would react if she knew Jonah was her real father. Shocked, no doubt, and full of potentially embarrassing questions. But she seemed to like Jonah, and she definitely adored Frankie and Jolie. What if...?

Kenzie shook herself, finished the email and sent it to Greg. Despite that sweet moment they'd shared the other night, Jonah had made it clear that it had meant nothing.

And wasn't that what she'd told him she wanted?

IF JONAH HAD made up his mind for sure that holding Kenzie in his arms would never happen again, why did he feel so miserable about it?

He'd thought he was saying what he'd decided to say to Kenzie. He'd thought he was saying what she wanted him to say. Given her determination to avoid him, surely she'd want to pretend that embrace had never happened. And given all the things he'd told himself, he wanted to forget it as well.

Didn't he?

"Da! Da! Da! Da!"

Jolie's insistent cries to get his attention finally penetrated Jonah's emotional fog. He got back to spooning lunch into her food-smeared face as she slapped at the high chair tray, spraying peas and carrots in all directions.

Frankie spoke from one side of his mouth, like a gangster. "She's gross."

Jonah started to correct his son but stopped

himself. "Yeah, she can be kind of messy," he agreed. "But that's because she's just a baby."

"And she stinks." Frankie demonstrated his point by holding his nose.

Jonah frowned at his son. "That isn't a very nice thing to say."

"You always say to be honest."

Jonah took a breath and thought carefully before responding in a level, kind tone. "But we think before we speak, right, buddy? We don't say something hurtful even if we think it's the truth."

"She can't understand what anyone is saying, so it doesn't hurt her." Frankie took a bite of his grilled cheese sandwich. "I bet Pippa doesn't get in trouble for saying things like that."

Mentally counting to ten, Jonah told himself to respond calmly. Frankie was sometimes startled by Jonah's naturally loud voice, so he'd been making an effort to speak more softly. "That's up to Pippa's mother, Frankie. And maybe Jolie stinks sometimes, but again, she's just a baby."

Frankie scowled. "Jolie gets away with everything because she's a baby. It's not fair."

In spite of himself, Jonah smiled at the boy's observation. "Maybe it doesn't seem fair, but she really is too little to help it."

"I bet if I threw my food all over the place and made a mess in my pants, I'd get in trouble."

Jonah chuckled and tousled his son's hair. "I'd be disappointed because you're a big boy and know better. But when you were Jolie's age, you were pretty gross, too."

Frankie jerked away. If his lower lip stuck out any farther, it would be resting on the table. He glared at his father. "Pippa says she's always wanted a little brother and she's going to ask her mommy if they can 'dopt me."

Despite the hurt that knifed his heart, Jonah kept his face as neutral as he could manage. "Don't you want me to be your daddy anymore?"

Frankie's eyes filled with tears, making Jonah realize that this acting-out came from a place of pain, not anger. "I don't like when you shout."

"Do you think I shout a lot?" Jonah couldn't keep the surprise out of his tone. He'd been so careful to speak gently to Frankie, although at times his frustration broke through. "Buddy, you know I have a loud voice. Do you think I'm mad at you?"

Frankie scrubbed his eyes with his palms. "Sometimes. It's scary."

"I'm sorry, son. I don't mean to be scary." Jonah frantically tried to think back to the last time he'd been angry with Frankie. "I was a policeman and sometimes I had to yell to stop the bad guys. Now I teach in a gym, which also means I have to yell just to be heard. But I'm not being loud because I'm angry, okay? I'm just…loud."

"It sounds like yelling." Frankie crossed his arms and furrowed his brow.

"I'm sorry," Jonah repeated. "I honestly don't mean to yell or make you think I'm angry." He felt his throat close as he pushed his chair closer to Frankie, leaving Jolie to grind the rest of her lunch into the tray. "I love you, son. I hope you know that."

But when he tried to put an arm around the boy, Frankie drew back. "I'm not your son."

"Frankie," Jonah choked out.

"Do you know who my real daddy is?"

So many emotions were swirling around inside Jonah that he felt off-balance. Frankie's words winded him as if he'd been punched in the stomach.

Jonah took an extra deep breath to quell the pain in his chest and spoke as gently as he could. "Don't you want me to adopt you anymore?"

The little boy's eyebrows furrowed as tears spilled down his cheeks. He sniffled furiously. "I want to be Pippa's little brother."

Tamping down the heartache, Jonah tried to hug Frankie again. To his relief, the boy didn't pull away this time, although he tensed up a bit. "Pippa may not be your big sister, but she's your best friend, isn't she?"

Frankie nodded and sniffled again. "But if you married Pippa's mommy, she'd be my big sister for real."

Jonah didn't know whether to laugh or cry, so he hugged his son closer.

CHAPTER NINE

"MOMMY, COME *ON!*"

Pippa's exasperated cry didn't help at all. Kenzie stood at the bottom of the outdoor stairs that led to the parsonage, one foot on the first step, hand gripping the banister. Try as she might, she was finding it hard to overcome the headache and vertigo enough to take another step.

"In a minute, baby girl." She hoped her reassuring tone masked her uncertainty. "I might have left something behind in the car."

"What?" Pippa demanded. "I have the pie."

"I'm trying to think." Kenzie looked up at her impatient daughter and pushed a smile onto her face. "Why don't you go ahead? I'll catch up with you once I've checked, okay?"

Her daughter didn't need further encouragement. She flew up the last few steps, holding the blueberry pie at a dangerous angle, and knocked on the parsonage door. When it opened, she announced, "Mommy's coming! She might have forgot something, so she has to think about it."

Once Pippa had squeezed through, Pastor Mullin waved from the doorway and called out, "Is there anything I can help with, dear heart?"

Warmed by his kindness, Kenzie replied with a smile, "Nope, all good! Just left something in the car. I'll be right there!"

The pastor nodded and stepped back into the parsonage. Trying to appear casual, Kenzie went back to the car, opened her purse and took out the untouched bottle of painkillers. She'd tossed the vial in her purse as an afterthought because of the persistent headache. Would taking half of one make it possible for her to get through the evening without betraying how much her head hurt?

But she hadn't overcome her trepidation about taking the pain medication. Throughout her athletic years she'd been a big advocate of "walk it off." Although "walking it off" didn't seem even remotely possible at the moment. With grim determination, she put the vial back in her purse and took two aspirin instead.

Two aspirin. Years ago, just one used to make her fall asleep. She hoped Enid had made a big pot of strong coffee.

It would take at least twenty minutes for the aspirin to kick in, but she could fake it in the meantime. Determined, she got out of the car and put her foot on the bottom step again.

Taking a deep breath and blowing it out slowly, Kenzie grasped the banister tightly with both hands and pulled herself up to the next step. Then the next, going hand over hand, pausing on each step to rest, coaching herself under her breath—*you can do this, you're fine, everything's fine.* Finally she reached the top.

On the porch she took a moment to compose herself. Lately she'd been having more trouble managing stairs, among other things. Her head spun if she moved too quickly, and the fatigue never seemed to let up.

Every symptom she looked up pointed to Lyme disease, in spite of what the Boston doctors and tests said. She knew the pain couldn't possibly be in her imagination or caused by depression. She knew what depression felt like, having suffered from it after every miscarriage. Yes, it was exhausting and it could make you ache, but what Kenzie was dealing with now went way beyond what emotional pain had done to her.

She wasn't sick because she was depressed. She was depressed because she was sick.

"Hey, everything okay?"

Kenzie jumped at the sound of the voice in front of her. She'd been holding on to the railing with her eyes closed, completely distracted by how she felt, and hadn't heard Jonah open the parsonage door. When she tried to look up at him, her neck spasmed and she gasped at the sudden, stabbing pain. But she still managed to smile. "Yup, everything's just fine."

Joining her on the porch, Jonah studied her, clearly unconvinced. "You look like you're in pain again."

Kenzie lifted a shoulder, trying to appear carefree. "Nope, absolutely fine. Did Pippa get the pie there in one piece?"

She let go of the railing and took a step but couldn't suppress a wince as her head throbbed. Jonah was at her side in an instant, taking her arm and peering into her face with deep concern. "You are not fine, by any stretch of the imagination."

As the pain calmed down, she tried to laugh it off. "It was just a little twinge."

Jonah shook his head. "Don't forget, I know

you. I've seen you keep smiling right after you pulled a muscle. What's going on, Kenz?"

"Is she okay?" A booming voice came from behind Jonah as a substantial, bearded man stepped out of the door and onto the porch. "Did she hurt herself?" The man shouldered Jonah aside to take a closer look. "I'm Diane's husband, by the way. Dr. Paul Solomon. And you must be Kenzie."

Struggling to appear normal, Kenzie spoke in a bright tone. "I know Diane was off to pick you up at Logan, but I had no idea you'd be here tonight. You must be tired after such a long flight!"

"I'm just fine," Paul said, "but you don't look like you're doing so well."

"She's in pain a lot," Jonah explained. "But she won't say what it is, other than headaches."

Paul frowned. "Does she have a headache? Could it be a migraine?"

Kenzie scowled at the men hovering over her. "Hello? I'm right here. I can answer any questions you may have about my okay-ness."

"Yes, but will you answer them truthfully?"

Jonah's tone pushed the wrong buttons, putting Kenzie on the defensive. "Even if I do, will you believe me, or will you decide you know better?"

Paul gave Jonah a wry smile. "Maybe you should go back inside," he advised. "Leave the medical stuff to me."

With another glance at Kenzie, Jonah shrugged. "I'm only worried about you, Kenzie, because you don't seem to be getting better. In fact, if anything, you seem worse." He turned and disappeared into the parsonage.

"Have you seen a doctor about this?" Paul spoke to Kenzie directly this time.

"I've seen just about every doctor in the world over the past two years," she admitted.

He smiled sympathetically. "Well, there's one doctor you haven't seen."

Puzzled, she shook her head. "I didn't mean it literally, but…who?"

"Me."

Kenzie balked. "I'd rather not see someone I know."

He nodded his shaggy head. "I get it, but— well, not to be immodest, I'm one heck of a diagnostician. And even more importantly, I listen to my patients."

Still unwilling to agree, Kenzie didn't have the energy to argue. "I'll think about it," she lied. "Right now we should get inside, shouldn't we?"

The sumptuous meal was over in less than an hour. Now they all lay around the comfortable living room, stuffed and groaning, protesting that they couldn't possibly even think about having dessert.

The evening might have gotten off to a rocky start health-wise, but the aspirin Kenzie had taken eventually kicked in and dulled the pain enough to allow her to enjoy herself. Dinner with the Mullins and Jonah's family was the way she'd always imagined a family dinner should be. Pippa was having the time of her life experiencing what a relaxed meal with good friends could be like.

With her ex-husband's insistence on everything being perfect, from the table setting to the food presentation, their dinner parties had always been subdued affairs that were more about style and networking than friendship. Even when she'd been in the best of health, Kenzie had found entertaining exhausting.

"How are you doing?"

Kenzie jumped at Jonah's voice right next to her. She'd been so absorbed by her thoughts that she'd missed whatever everyone was laughing at. Jonah must have noticed how distracted she was.

Forcing a smile, she said, "Yeah, I'm fine. Just spaced out for a minute."

"You seem to be feeling a bit better." Jonah's return smile was tinged with sadness. "I hope you're having a good time."

"Yes!" Kenzie's emphatic response surprised even her. "It's so great to see Diane and Paul together at last and have such a fun meal. I'm used to dinners being very formal."

His eyebrows quirked up. "You've never had a fun family dinner?"

"Well…" She thought back to meals with her late parents, then with her husband and Pippa. "Both my mother and my ex were perfection-ists. You remember Greg Halloran, right? I think you met him a couple of times."

Jonah lifted a shoulder. "He seemed very nice, if a bit tightly wound."

"He could be very exacting, wanting every-thing to be just so. Which is a great quality in a television producer but can be a bit stressful when it comes to entertaining."

"That's too bad."

Frowning slightly, Kenzie called to mind the last dinner party she and Greg had given. "He has a firmly fixed idea of what things should look like. It was kind of like he wanted to create a set rather than a good time." She gave her head a rueful shake. "Even our family vacations were more about how things looked than how much we enjoyed ourselves." Glancing around the room at the laughing group, she couldn't suppress a huge smile. "He would never have gone for this. Way too laid-back. But Pippa's having a great time."

"And what about you, Kenz?"

His gentle concern created a rush of affection that she quickly stomped on. "Good! I'm good. If Pip's happy, I'm happy."

Was it her imagination, or did Jonah move a bit closer to her? Her knee felt warm where he brushed against it. "She seems very happy here, don't you think?"

"Yes, she does. She adores your family."

Without thinking, Kenzie gave Jonah a sweetly affectionate smile. His eyes widened with surprise, and then he returned the smile and touched her arm gently. "I hope you do, too."

Kenzie's internal alarm went off. Her smile drooped and she jumped to her feet. "I—I should circulate."

WITH THAT, KENZIE wandered over to the group gathered around the spinet piano, which Paul played with impressive ease. Jonah saw Pippa run to her mother and drag her closer to the piano. Then the little girl came up to Jonah. "Why aren't you singing, Mr. Raymond?"

"I'm a terrible singer," he admitted. "Everyone is better off if I'm just the audience."

"But—" Pippa hesitated. "But you don't have to be a good singer. Singing is fun." She glanced back at the group clustered around the piano. "Frankie won't sing either, but I know he likes it when we sing together, when we're playing."

"Sometimes he's shy, especially with a lot of people around."

"But why?" Pippa's face grew more concerned. "How did he get shy?"

Smiling, Jonah took her hands in his. "You don't know what it's like to feel shy, do you?"

She shook her head. "It seems... I don't know, like it doesn't really help anything. But Frankie..." Pippa looked back toward the group, where Frankie stood just outside of the circle, staring at the floor. "It just seems sad."

Jonah noticed Kenzie glancing in their direction, her face worried. Did she not like Pippa talking to him? "Maybe you should go back over there."

But Pippa obviously had something on her mind. "Mr. Raymond, why is Frankie sad?"

Jonah tried not to let his emotion show on his face. "Didn't he tell you why?"

"I mean, a little, but he's so lucky." Pippa sighed. "He has you and Jolie and Miss Diane and Mr. Paul. That's…" She paused to count on her fingers. "That's four whole people, and they're all his family!" Throwing her arms around his neck, Pippa whispered in his ear. "I wish you were my family."

Then she flew over to Frankie without looking back.

Enid slipped next to Jonah on the sofa. "I haven't had a chance to talk to you yet. How are you doing, Jonah?"

"Okay," he said automatically. "How are you?"

Enid shook her head. "Watching your interchange with Kenzie and Pippa just now made me wonder."

Jonah felt himself tense up. "About what?"

"About our talk the other day." She put a gentle hand on his forearm. "I know it must be hard when you work and live so close to each other. Are you sure you're going to be able to keep your distance?"

Jonah gave a vehement nod. "Yes. In fact, we've discussed it and we both agree that there's no way we'd get back together."

Enid pursed her lips. "I don't know, Jonah. From what I saw just now, you still care about her very much."

His throat tightened and he had to clear it to respond. "Okay, maybe I care a bit. I mean, she was the love of my life—"

Enid inhaled audibly. "The love of your life? I'd thought that was Elena."

Frustrated, Jonah studied his hands. "It's a long, complicated story. I wanted to marry Kenzie, but she got mad at me about something and took a job in California. Elena stood by me for years before she convinced me we should get married and adopt Frankie. I did love her, but not the same way I'd loved Kenzie."

Enid started to respond, but Paul's big, hearty voice cut her off.

"Do you little guys know this one?" he asked, his big hands rippling gracefully over the keys to tease out a familiar hymn. "It's about thanking God for blessings."

Pippa nodded. "Mommy thanks God all the time. And she taught me to do it, too."

Paul beamed at Pippa and ruffled her curls. "Good for your mommy for teaching you to pray."

Brows furrowed, Frankie scowled at his uncle. "Praying is dumb."

"Franklin!" Jonah's tone held a warning.

Paul had turned to his nephew with simple curiosity. "Why do you say that, buddy?"

"'Cause it's dumb. It doesn't work."

Diane moved over to the boy. "It works if it brings us closer to God."

To Jonah's surprise, Frankie pulled away from his beloved aunt. "It's dumb."

"Franklin!" This time Jonah's voice was louder, making Kenzie jump as he took hold of Frankie's arm.

Pippa wheeled around and glared up at Jonah. "Don't yell at him!" Her own voice could probably be heard for miles.

It was Kenzie's turn to rush to her child and take her by the arm. "Philippa, don't you ever speak to anyone like that, especially not a grown-up!"

Pippa frowned at her mother. "But he yelled first!" The little girl pulled herself free, went to

Frankie and grabbed his hand. "Mommy, can't we 'dopt Frankie? Please? He really wants us to 'cause you're nice and he wants a mommy."

Jonah's grip on Frankie loosened and he knelt down next to the boy. His anger changed to sorrow. "Buddy, do you really not want me to adopt you anymore?"

"Can we, Mommy? Please?" Pippa tugged her mother's sleeve. "You told me I was going to have a little brother or sister soon, but it was a really long time ago now and it never happened. And I love Frankie. Can't he be my little brother?"

"No, baby girl," Kenzie whispered. "Frankie already has a daddy and a little sister."

"But he wants a mommy! His mommy died." Pippa's dark eyes were solemn as an owl's.

Kenzie shook her head and frowned Pippa into silence.

"You're never gonna 'dopt me," Frankie growled at his father.

"Yes, I am." Astonished and grieved by the accusation, Jonah felt as if the bottom had dropped out of his world. "It takes time, buddy."

"They won't let you 'cause Mommy died." The boy dragged his sleeve across his eyes and scowled harder. "And I don't want you to, anyway. I want a mommy."

Enid came up behind Frankie and placed her hands on his shoulders. "Frankie, we all love you. Not just the family you live with, but your whole church family."

Diane knelt in front of the little boy and took his hands in hers. "You know how much we love you, right?"

When his face threatened to crumple, Frankie pulled away. His voice came out tight and tiny. "But you're going to have a baby and then you're not going to love me anymore."

The anguish in his son's voice ripped Jonah's heart in two. He reached out to take the boy in his arms again, but Frankie held himself rigid.

"Of course I will!" Diane insisted in her warmest tone. "There's always enough love for everyone. It doesn't get used up."

"That's right, son," Pastor Mullin agreed. "Love just keeps on growing."

Suddenly Frankie became aware of all the eyes fixed on him. Embarrassed, he raced to the door.

Jonah followed him and seized him in a fierce hug. Then, without another word, he lifted the boy off his feet, walked out the door and carried him down the steps to a little bench.

Jonah sat on the bench holding Frankie close and letting him cry his heart out. Jonah was tempted to bawl along with him. His own heart broke over and over at the memory of his son's words.

How had he not realized the root of Frankie's fear? The boy had assumed Jonah was not going to adopt him since Elena had died, while in reality the paperwork had gotten held up after her death but was still in process.

Closing his eyes and holding Frankie close, he prayed silently to a God he was no longer sure was listening to him.

Lord, this is beyond me. Let me know how to comfort my poor little boy. I'm lost and I need You. Help me to find You again.

CHAPTER TEN

IN LATE SEPTEMBER the countryside burst with flaming golds, reds and oranges. Kenzie had often heard the term "leaf peepers" but had never figured out why people would drive around New England just to look at trees. Now she got it. The colors were intense, and right around the backyard pond they were the most breathtaking, a stunning contrast to the deep green of the nearby Christmas trees.

Kenzie's downhill slide continued. Her energy dropped, the physical pain increased and the headaches returned with a vengeance.

She and Jonah sometimes combined their classes so they could work on the harvest pageant together. Set pieces were constructed and painted, costumes pulled together and made festive, and songs of gratitude rang through the downstairs hallway. The first graders worked on perfecting their dance for the farm animal procession.

It was all coming together beautifully despite her conflicted feelings about Jonah, and Kenzie had to admit there was no way she could have done all this coordination without him.

Toward the end of most school days she fought with all her might to stay focused and engaged with the kids. She must have been succeeding because only Jonah seemed to notice that she was anything other than perfectly healthy, and he'd learned to keep his opinion to himself. If he said anything, Kenzie made a point of just smiling and saying she was fine.

Not only was Kenzie feeling sick again, but she was eaten up with worry. What would happen to Pippa if Kenzie fell apart? In the agreement resulting from their divorce, Kenzie had full custody, and Greg seemed to have little interest in exercising his visitation rights. No doubt he was absorbed with his new wife and their impending offspring.

Kenzie had postponed asking Jonah about her messages for so long that she felt awkward about it. Plus, her exhausted brain couldn't figure out how to start that conversation. But given her health issues, she had to find a way soon to ask if he knew he was Pippa's father.

Although Paul was home from his mission

and working at his medical practice in the village, Kenzie didn't want to confide in him. Besides, he and Diane were busy with the farm. Anytime they weren't at their regular jobs, they were finishing up the apple harvest, working in the pumpkin patch or tending to the Christmas trees. So she found another local doctor who listened to her concerns, looked at her blood work and shook his head, clearly puzzled.

"There doesn't appear to be anything wrong. All your tests came back normal, or at least within the normal range."

Kenzie's hope of finding an answer deflated. Dr. Alden's words echoed those of doctors she'd seen in Boston, who had insisted that her symptoms were psychosomatic and had labeled her as a hypochondriac. She wondered if those labels had traveled with her to her new home.

"Well, this pain is real whether the tests show a reason or not. I wish someone could figure out what's wrong with me," she sighed.

"You do have a diagnosis of fibromyalgia and possibly chronic fatigue."

"But all these symptoms came on practically overnight," Kenzie explained. "At the same time that I had a huge rash on my right side that started with some kind of insect bite. Is there any way that the Lyme disease test results could be wrong?"

"You've had several Lyme tests over the past couple of years and they all came back negative. But I'm not an infectious disease specialist and it's an extremely controversial illness." Alden squinted at her chart and pursed his lips. "Your liver enzymes are a bit elevated. Do you take a lot of over-the-counter painkillers? Tylenol, aspirin, ibuprofen?"

Kenzie shook her head. "I tend to have a strong reaction to most medications, so I only take something if I'm in really bad shape."

That made him look at her as if she were some rare species. "Even with the constant pain and headaches?" When she shook her head, he set down the paperwork and pressed his fingers into her neck. "Any swollen glands?"

"I had swollen lymph nodes after that bug bite, but they went away." She shrugged. "Sometimes they feel sore, but not swollen."

The doctor picked up her folder again and tapped his pen thoughtfully against the paperwork. "Given your symptoms and the liver count, you may have had mononucleosis recently." At her surprised reaction he added, "Or a similar virus."

"Would that explain all the headaches?" Kenzie asked, pressing her fingers against her throbbing temples.

He nodded. "It could. How long have you had the current one?"

"About a week." She grimaced. "They usually last at least a few days, but lately it's been longer. And light and sound make them worse, which isn't great when you're teaching young children."

The doctor studied her with growing concern. "Are you willing to try prescription medication?" he asked gently.

"At this point I'm willing to try anything," Kenzie admitted.

Dr. Alden nodded. "Good. We need to break you out of this cycle. Then we can talk about how to manage your headaches and pain in the future. Does that sound good?" When she agreed, he tapped the keys of his computer. "I'm giving you three prescriptions. One is for the general, all-over pain, one for insomnia, and one is specifically for your headaches, which definitely sound like migraines." The little printer next to his computer whizzed and spit out a few slips of paper, which he signed with a scribble and handed to Kenzie. "Get these filled at the pharmacy in town right away, as soon as you're out of here."

Kenzie felt a pang of trepidation. "How strong are they? Like I said, I'm pretty sensitive even to over-the-counter stuff."

"The painkillers and sleeping pills are moderate, but the migraine meds are pretty strong. But you need something strong to break the cycle." The doctor swiveled his chair around to face her again. "I want you to take a migraine pill as soon as possible."

"Okay. Thanks." Kenzie slid off the examination table.

"You're going to need to take some time off from teaching," the doctor advised her. "You need complete rest and quiet to deal with the persistent headaches and get rid of any lingering virus. Once you've picked up the prescriptions, go straight home, take a migraine pill and go to bed."

Kenzie didn't respond. He didn't need to know that she was on her lunch break and was planning to go back to school for the afternoon. She needed some extra time to pick up the prescriptions first, so she texted Jonah, asking him if he'd mind pulling her second graders into the first grade gym class until she got back. He responded right away with a simple thumbs-up, to her relief.

She hated to ask Jonah for favors. Since that night on the porch and the conversation at the Mullins' dinner party, they'd been walking on eggshells around each other at the house, ridiculously polite and aloof. At school their relationship was strictly professional.

The wait at the pharmacy was even longer than she'd feared, but eventually she had a white bag with three identical bottles of pills. Desperate to stop the headache enough to get through the rest of the school day, Kenzie picked out the bottle with the word *migraine* on the label. She washed a pill down in the car outside the pharmacy before driving to the school as quickly as was legal.

Squinting against the sunlight, Kenzie pulled into the school parking lot. The medicine hadn't worked so far, but it had only been about five minutes. She hurriedly parked the Volvo, ran into the building and headed down the stairs.

When Kenzie poked her head into the spacious gym, she found the two classes playing a game of volleyball. Pippa was in the midst of the action, apparently having a wonderful time, her wild red curls bouncing as she jumped and smacked the ball over the net. Kenzie felt a swell of pride in her gregarious, athletic daughter. *I used to be just like that*, she thought with a twist of sadness.

On the other hand, Frankie hung back and watched everyone else play. Even when Pippa trotted over to him, grabbed his hand and tried to coax him out onto the floor, he shook his head and stepped farther back. With a shrug, Pippa ran off to rejoin the game.

Jonah spotted Kenzie and jogged to the doorway. Kenzie couldn't help but notice how his T-shirt showed off his well-muscled arms and chest. She looked away, trying not to blush.

He stood next to her, panting a little. "Hey! I hope this was okay, but it was the only way I could really keep an eye on everyone. I couldn't work on the animal dance because that would leave the second graders with nothing to do."

"No, it's fine. Thanks." When Kenzie turned to look back at him, suddenly she felt her brain spin inside her head. She grabbed the doorjamb to steady herself.

"Whoa!" Jonah reached out and grabbed her arm. "You okay? You look awfully pale."

Embarrassed, Kenzie forced a laugh. "Just a bit of a headache, but I'm sure it'll go away soon."

"Another headache?" Jonah's concern was etched onto his face. "You get a lot of those, don't you?"

Kenzie shrugged and tried to look nonchalant, although she was starting to feel very strange. "Probably the change in the weather."

"Have you seen a doctor?" he persisted.

"Yup. Actually, I just saw one," she answered as cheerfully as she could. "He gave me a prescription, so I'll be fine."

Jonah was leaning in close. Uncomfortably close. He seemed to be studying her mouth. "Are you sure you're okay? You're kind of slurring your words."

Kenzie tried to laugh but the room was getting weirdly dark, as if storm clouds were gathering inside the gym. When she tried to look around to see what was causing the darkness, her vision narrowed to a tunnel. There was a loud buzzing in her ears as everything disappeared.

Jonah tried to catch Kenzie before she hit the floor, but only managed to break her fall a little so she didn't land too hard. She appeared to have passed out cold and he had no idea why.

Behind him kids were panicking at the sight of their beloved Mrs. Reid lying on the floor.

Jonah himself stared in horror for a few seconds before kneeling next to her.

"Mommy!" Pippa shrieked. Before Jonah could stop her, she'd flung herself at Kenzie and was shaking her.

Jonah gently pulled Pippa away from her mother. "Stay back, sweetie. She just fainted. I'm sure she'll be fine, but she needs breathing room, okay?"

As calmly as he could manage, he checked Kenzie's pulse. It was strong but fast, so it probably wasn't a blood pressure drop that had caused her to faint. Her eyes were opening and she seemed to be surprised to find herself on the floor. "What happened?"

"How are you feeling?"

"Embarrassed. Did I actually faint?" Her voice was breathless but the words were clear, so at least she wasn't slurring anymore.

Jonah turned to reassure the kids and discovered Frankie standing frozen next to him, staring at Kenzie with wide, terrified eyes. He appeared to be paralyzed with fear. Maybe somewhere deep in his memory Kenzie's collapse reminded him of sitting beside his unconscious mother when he was a toddler.

Jonah knelt and took his son's hands in his.

"Buddy, it's okay. She just fainted. She's going to be okay."

But Frankie's eyes remained locked on his favorite teacher.

Jonah was torn between keeping his attention on Kenzie and comforting Frankie. Then Pippa put her arms around Frankie and hugged him. "It'll be okay, Frankie. She just fainted. See, she's getting up."

Kenzie was easing herself to a sitting position. "What happened?" she asked again.

"Mommy, you fell over!" Pippa yelped.

Jonah put a hand on Kenzie's arm. "I was going to call an ambulance, but—"

"What?" Kenzie sat up so fast she almost fell back again. "I don't need an ambulance!"

"Maybe I should take you to the ER," Jonah said firmly.

Clearly frustrated, Kenzie huffed and wobbled to her feet. She swayed for a moment before straightening up. "I'm fine. See?"

"Mommy, stop being silly!" Pippa ran to her mother and shook a finger at her like a scolding grown-up. "I don't want you falling over again. You scared Frankie!"

"Oh, no! I'm sorry." Jonah's throat tightened as he watched Kenzie brace herself, walk over to Frankie and give him a hug. "I'm fine, honest! I just got dizzy for a minute. Probably because I skipped lunch."

"See?" Pippa said. "I told you so. She's fine."

At that moment Dr. Mullin hustled through the gym door looking worried. "I was walking by the stairs and heard an uproar. What's going on?" she demanded in her clear, strong voice.

Kenzie tried to look bright and alert. "Nothing."

"Mrs. Reid fell over!" a few kids volunteered, excited now that they knew she was out of danger.

The headmistress hurried over to Kenzie and studied her face, then turned to Jonah. "Go ahead and tell the kids to change. It's almost time for seventh period."

Jonah clapped his hands and yelled, "Okay, kids, class is over. Get your civvies on, pronto!"

The gym magically cleared of six-and seven-year-olds as they ran for the locker rooms, with the exception of Pippa and Frankie. Pippa looked up at Jonah, solemn with worry. "Mr. Raymond, Frankie won't move," she whispered.

Jonah dropped to his knees again and noted that Frankie was standing frozen in the same place, his thumb jammed into his mouth. He'd started that habit again when Elena died but hadn't done it for a few months. He seemed oblivious of his surroundings.

The headmistress joined the little group. "Is he all right?" she asked softly.

Jonah shook his head. "He shuts down when something frightens him, but he'll be okay in a bit. Diane's not working today, so I'll ask her to come get him." He addressed Frankie. "Would you like Auntie Di to take you home? She can let you watch a show or something. Would that make you feel better, son?"

The little boy blinked and focused on his father, still glassy-eyed, and gave a brief nod. Then he seemed to realize he was still sucking his thumb. Quickly he pulled it out of his mouth and hid his hand behind his back, clearly embarrassed.

As Jonah sent a quick text to his sister, Pippa squeezed Frankie's free hand and whispered loudly enough for the adults to hear, "Don't tell my mommy, but when we first moved into your house, I was scared at night, so I sucked my thumb so I could go to sleep."

"Honest?" Frankie's face relaxed when Pippa nodded.

Jonah was deeply touched at how Pippa reassured his son. He almost felt jealous at how Frankie trusted her and responded to her kindness. No wonder he wanted her to be his sister.

His phone buzzed and he glanced at the words on the screen. "Auntie Diane will be here in a few minutes. Can Pippa go home with him?" He looked at Kenzie, who nodded. "Would you like that, buddy?"

"Yes!"

Jonah felt a whoosh of relief when Frankie almost smiled.

The other kids were crowding each other as they ran from the locker rooms. Tessa Adams stopped when she saw Frankie and Pippa huddled together. She burst into derisive laughter, so loud the other children turned to see what she was laughing at.

"Pippa and Frankie sitting in a tree!" Tessa sang. "Pippa, your boyfriend is a baby who sucks his thumb!"

Furious, Pippa stamped her feet and bellowed at the top of her lungs. "Stop being so mean, Tessa Adams! You're one to talk. I saw you picking your nose in science class last week."

All laughter ceased. All eyes turned to Tessa, who looked mortified but lashed right back. "Liar! No, you didn't. You're just embarrassed because your boyfriend is a baby."

Three firm hand claps resonated through the gym. "That's quite enough, children!" Dr. Mullin glared down at Tessa and Pippa. "Miss Adams, you know better than to make fun of people. And, Miss Halloran, it's kind of you to defend Frankie, but we don't do that by making someone else feel bad, do we?"

While Tessa looked cowed by the headmistress's reprimand, Pippa stared up at her defiantly. "She's always mean to him. She's a bully."

Kenzie seemed to have recovered from her fainting spell. Her voice was firm as she chastised her daughter. "Pippa, apologize to Tessa."

"But, Mommy—"

"This. Minute."

Pippa crossed her arms and stamped her foot in a way all too familiar to Jonah.

She looked like a miniature version of Kenzie eight years ago, furious with him for reasons he still didn't understand, telling him they were through.

CHAPTER ELEVEN

ONCE SHE WAS satisfied that Kenzie's fainting spell didn't warrant a trip to the ER, the head-mistress took charge. "You don't have a class next period, so you go ahead and take Mrs. Reid's class," she told Jonah, then turned to Kenzie. "You and I are going to have a talk."

When they entered her comfortable, unpretentious office, Dr. Mullin indicated a small sofa and sat next to Kenzie rather than behind her desk. "I'm sure you need a bit of time to sit and feel better. I've been meaning to schedule a meeting with you, and now's as good a time as any."

Although her headache was gone, Kenzie still felt dizzy and unsteady. The vertigo worsened at Dr. Mullin's words and she felt herself turn paler. What if her job was in danger? "Uh-oh."

"No, no! Absolutely no need to worry. You're doing a fine job, by all accounts. I just wanted to offer you some encouragement." Beaming, the headmistress leaned forward to give Kenzie a reassuring smile. "The kids love you and are very engaged with the pageant project, and from what I can see, you're sneaking in a lot of good lessons while they have fun."

Kenzie breathed a sigh of relief. "Thank you, Dr. Mullin."

"Oh, please. Call me Enid. Everyone else does."

"Okay, well, thank you, Enid," Kenzie amended.

"Just a couple of things." Kenzie grimaced at the headmistress's words, causing her to chuckle kindly. "Not about your teaching, by any means," Enid reassured her. "But I have two concerns. Maybe I'm being nosy, but it's important to me to know you're happy." She paused. "And healthy."

A niggle of worry squirmed in Kenzie's stomach. Even on her worst days she tried so hard to act normal, even peppy. But after the medication and fainting spell, she was feeling especially fatigued, and Enid's piercing brown eyes probably didn't miss a trick.

She should have listened to the doctor and gone straight home to rest. And she shouldn't have taken that medication and gone to school until she knew how it would affect her. But the last thing she wanted was to "sick out" so early in her new career. She would power through somehow.

"I just got dizzy for a moment. I should have had lunch." Kenzie managed a rueful smile.

The headmistress studied Kenzie for a moment. "I can see you're a fighter and I'm sure you can fool most people, but it's clear to me that some days you're really struggling."

Kenzie stiffened her spine and raised her chin. "I'm fine. There's absolutely nothing wrong with me." She noticed she was back to quoting what several Boston doctors had told her, which she had adopted as a mantra despite the fact that she didn't believe it.

"Do you have a condition?" Enid asked, ignoring Kenzie's protest. "I know you put on a very brave face, but to me it seems like you're tolerating a lot of physical pain and fatigue. And sometimes you seem a bit unsteady." She put a gentle hand on Kenzie's arm. "Have you seen a doctor, dear heart?"

"I just saw one!" The admission burst out of her. "He couldn't find anything. Just like all the others." Despite her determination to be unemotional, she could feel frustration bubbling up inside her.

Frowning, Enid moved her hand to Kenzie's knee. "Why don't you take a big breath and tell me all about it?"

"I'm sorry," Kenzie choked out. "It's just—I've already seen every doctor in Boston and none of them could figure out what's wrong with me. All the tests came back normal. They finally gave up, told me it's all in my head and to go see a psychiatrist."

"Doctors don't know everything," Enid murmured. "Some of them sure like to think they do, though."

"You can say that again." Shaking her head, Kenzie thought back to how her illness had started. "The thing is that it happened so suddenly. I'd always been super healthy and athletic. Then boom, I became a total wimp."

"You are most certainly not a wimp!" Enid protested.

"Well, I mean, suddenly I started having these weird pains, felt exhausted most of the time, started getting headaches. I'm positive I was bitten by a tick, but the Lyme tests keep coming back negative, so…" She thumped the sofa arm with her fist, dismayed to realize that she was about to start crying.

"Breathe, baby," the headmistress whispered. "What happened with the doctor you saw today?"

Kenzie blew out a tight breath. "He gave me some medication for the headaches and pain, so hopefully that will help."

"Prayer helps, too." Enid offered Kenzie a tissue from a box on the end table.

"I know. At times I've been in so much pain, all I can do is pray." Her mind drifted back to days in Boston when she'd felt so awful she could hardly move, and the wonder of knowing that God was right there with her. "I... I think sometimes God used my weakness to draw me back to Him. Not that He made me ill, but that He saw how much I needed Him."

Enid nodded, her face full of understanding. "The Lord is close to the brokenhearted. Psalm 34. You should read that when you get home. One of my favorites."

Kenzie dabbed at her eyes and blew her nose. "I strayed for a while," she confessed. "When I was in college I kind of gave up on God. But I'm so glad He never gave up on me."

"He's always with us, child," the headmistress murmured. "We turn our backs on Him at times, but He never turns away from us. All we have to do is listen for His voice."

At the sound of the last bell of the school day, Kenzie glanced at the clock. "I should probably get home." She started to get up but Enid stopped her.

"I said I had a couple of things, didn't I?" Kenzie sat back down as Enid stepped to the door and closed it. "I hate to pry, but I have to ask you about your relationship with Jonah Raymond."

That comment gave Kenzie a jolt. "Relationship?"

Enid sat back down, leaning toward Kenzie and keeping her voice low. "Or whatever you want to call it. Sometimes it seems like there's some kind of, I don't know, tension between the two of you."

Kenzie shook her head vehemently. "No, ma'am. There's nothing between us." When Enid kept looking at her, she amended, "Well, there hasn't been anything for a long time."

Enid chuckled and whispered, "Then why are you blushing?" She leaned back and folded her arms. "Funny. Jonah had the same reaction when I asked him that question."

"You—you asked him?" Kenzie swallowed. "And what did he say?"

"He told me that you'd been a couple years

ago, but things had ended when you got a job on the West Coast." She lifted her shoulders. "That's all."

"That's correct," Kenzie said quickly.

"Here's the thing." Enid leaned forward again. "I'm not a big fan of romance in the workplace. I just want to make that clear. It tends to get messy and can be very distracting, especially if things go wrong. And it's not great for the kids."

Now that she'd recovered from the surprise, Kenzie made herself speak without emotion. "It's not a problem. On the very first day, Jonah and I agreed to leave the past in the past. Things didn't end well, so there's no chance we'll ever want to start seeing each other again."

Enid was nodding her approval. "That's good, then. He said the same thing. I'm certainly glad I don't need to worry about any drama!"

"No, ma'am," Kenzie assured her, then hastened to add, "Although you probably should know he's working with me on the harvest pageant."

Enid clapped her hands like an excited child. "Oh my goodness! I'll need to stop in and see what you've come up with."

Kenzie felt a surge of pride. "We have each

class working on a different part of the pageant. We'll add a few after-school rehearsals soon, if that's all right."

"Wonderful! And how is Mr. Raymond helping?"

Kenzie couldn't help grinning at the memory of tall, brawny Jonah leading the tiny first graders in their cute dance. "He's working on the farm animals' procession and overseeing the set pieces. And of course, everyone is helping to paint sets and pull costumes together."

Enid clapped again, clearly delighted. "Oh my word, I'm so excited! We're finally having a performance at our little school, and it sounds marvelous!"

"I hope so!" Kenzie glanced at the clock again. "But I really should get going, if we're done for now."

"Absolutely." Enid stood and opened the door. "Thank you for the talk, Mackenzie. Now you go have yourself some time with that precious little girl of yours."

THE MINUTE THE final bell rang, Jonah hurried to the headmistress's office to wait for Kenzie. He knew she'd drive herself home unless he took some drastic action, and since Frankie and

Pippa had already gone home with Diane, he decided to lie in wait and insist she ride home with him instead of driving herself.

As he stood in the hallway by the closed door, he could hear the rise and fall of voices. It was easy to distinguish Kenzie's quick speech from Enid's more deliberate tones, but he couldn't make out any words. He was tempted to move closer to the door and eavesdrop but decided that would not be right. Instead, he leaned against the wall a few feet away and tried to distract himself by checking for messages on his phone.

It didn't work. Not even the text from his sister saying Jolie was napping and Frankie was happily playing with Pippa could mitigate his worry over Kenzie. Was she all right? She'd been in there with Enid for a long time.

At last the door creaked open and Kenzie came out, spotting him right away. "Oh! What are you doing here?"

Was it his imagination or did she look guilty? What on earth had the two ladies been talking about in there?

Jonah's response came out like a teenage boy asking a girl on a date. "Um…so I thought maybe I should give you a ride home."

He could almost hear her armor clank into place. "That's sweet, but not necessary. My car is here."

"I realize that, but I don't think you should drive after passing out like that."

"That was over an hour ago. I'm fine now." And she headed for the door to the parking lot.

Jonah stayed on her heels and took her gently by the arm before she could open the door. "I'm sorry, but I can't allow you to drive."

She shook her head. "But I'm perfectly—"

Enid's resonant voice cut through Kenzie's retort. "Mackenzie, I'm afraid I'll have to agree with Jonah."

The headmistress stood partway through the door to her office, obviously having heard their argument and come out to see what was going on.

"But, Dr. Mullin—I mean, Enid—" Kenzie started to object.

"There are no buts in this situation," the headmistress said firmly. "You passed out cold an hour ago. There is absolutely no way you should be driving." When Kenzie opened her mouth, Enid cut her off again. "And that's final."

With a stern look, the headmistress went back inside her office and closed the door.

Jonah tried hard not to smirk with triumph. "You heard the boss. Let's go."

They walked out to the parking lot together. As soon as they reached their cars, Kenzie demonstrated where her daughter got her defiant attitude by fishing her keys from her purse. "Thanks for walking me to my car. Now I'll be driving myself home."

Jonah deftly grabbed the keys from her hand and held them aloft. "Oh, no, you don't." She whirled around to face him and would have lost her balance if he hadn't caught her. "See that? You're still not steady on your feet. And besides, I'm the health and safety officer for the school." He couldn't help sounding smug as he reminded her of that fact. "It's my responsibility to see that you don't endanger yourself or others. So I forbid you to get in that car."

Jonah should have known that was the wrong thing to say to Mackenzie Reid. She stepped toward him, eyes sparking. "I am perfectly fine. Ask any doctor in Boston."

The statement gave Jonah pause. "Wait—how many doctors have you seen?"

"A lot!" She delivered her answer as if it were a good thing. "And they know more than a school health and safety officer."

Slowly, Jonah shook his head. "If you've seen that many doctors, and you saw another one today who gave you prescriptions, it sounds to me like maybe you have some serious health issues."

Realizing her mistake, Kenzie scowled. She took a moment to think before continuing her argument. "The doctor today gave me medication. I told you I took it for the first time just before I got back to school. That's why I fainted." Even she seemed to recognize the weakness of her words. Her eyes dropped to the pavement at her feet.

Jonah couldn't help being moved by Kenzie's determination. She was trying so hard to be as strong and feisty as her younger self, to rise above whatever was ailing her. He was still holding on to her arm. Without thinking, he slid his hand down and took her hand. "Kenzie, I'm sorry I was so bossy, but it's absolutely true that I need to look after possibly dangerous situations. That includes students and staff who are sick."

"There's nothing wrong with me," she said in a broken whisper.

"Maybe not, but given that you fainted only an hour ago and you're taking some new medication, I don't think it's wise for you to drive. Do you?" Head still hanging, she didn't answer. "What would happen to Pippa if you got in an accident?"

When she looked up at him, the anguish in her eyes almost undid him. He swallowed hard and took her other hand.

"So please let me drive you home. Please. For me." His voice went husky. "I couldn't stand it if something happened to you."

Whoa, where had that come from? He was supposed to be keeping his distance. Instead, he'd basically told her he still cared about her.

She was staring at him, stunned by his words. At least she'd stopped objecting. With uncharacteristic meekness, she slipped into the passenger seat of his car when he opened the door.

As he carefully pulled out of the parking lot, he chuckled. "I can see where your daughter gets her stubbornness."

When he glanced over at Kenzie, she had a very odd expression on her face. "How do you know she doesn't get it from her father?"

From what Jonah could remember of Greg Halloran, he thought it more likely that Pippa would have inherited a chronic case of fussiness from him. But he could feel frost forming in the air between them, so he backtracked hastily. "Hey, I was kidding. Sorry. I know you've had a rough day. I was just trying to lighten things up, that's all."

After a moment, Kenzie sighed and leaned back in her seat. "It's okay." After a moment she added, "But you should know, I'm not the only one responsible for Pippa's personality."

CHAPTER TWELVE

OCTOBER'S THREE-DAY WEEKEND could not come soon enough for Kenzie. Her exhaustion and pain seemed to increase every day, no matter how much rest she got. In the mornings she woke up feeling like she'd gotten no sleep at all, but so far she was still able to keep working and acting normal enough not to arouse suspicion.

Dr. Alden's advice to take time off to recover was simply not an option. She'd had the teaching job for such a short time there was no way she could take sick leave, which at this point would be unpaid. The last thing she needed was to lose the one job she'd managed to land. If she'd had no one except herself to worry about, things might have been different, but she needed security for Pippa. Sometimes that was the only thought that kept her going.

Also, work on the harvest pageant was ramping up. So Kenzie kept going, kept working with Jonah to build up the different parts of the pageant so everyone would be ready when they started full rehearsals after the long weekend.

Friday afternoon was the absolute worst. Kenzie barely managed to keep a cheerful facade as she dismissed her final restless class of first graders, walked to the car with Pippa and headed home.

As soon as they'd pulled past the Holiday Farm sign and rolled to a stop in front of the house, Pippa went whooping out of the car to jump in crispy piles of leaves with Frankie. Kenzie meandered into their apartment and sank onto the sofa, vowing not to move again until absolutely necessary.

She thought about the painkillers in her nightstand. A few times lately when the pain had been extra severe and a sleeping pill didn't help, she'd thought about taking half of one painkiller just to reduce the pain enough for her to get to sleep. But given her sensitivity to medication, Kenzie remained determined to stay away from those pills. She knew they held dangers that outweighed their advantages. Right now she felt optimistic that having some quiet time on the sofa would get her through the rest of the day.

Tomorrow she'd chart out a schedule for the final pageant rehearsals, in time for their performance the last week in October. But until then, she could take advantage of the holiday and get some much-needed rest.

She started to flop back on the sofa, but a jarring spasm seized her spine. The pain was so unexpected and intense she unintentionally cried out, then gripped the edge of the sofa with both hands and took harsh, tight breaths to will it away. After a minute her breathing eased a bit and she tried to move, which made her cry out again.

What on earth was happening now?

The apartment door burst open and Pippa galloped into the room with Frankie. "Mommy! Can Frankie come over and play?"

Desperately masking her agony, Kenzie gave her daughter a gentle smile. "I don't think now's a good time. I need a little rest."

Pippa pouted. "You're always sick. It's boring."

Although her daughter needed correction, Kenzie couldn't even summon enough energy for her *don't cross that line* look. "I don't do it on purpose, Pip," she murmured. "I'd much rather not be boring, believe me. Can you go over to Frankie's to play?"

Pippa consulted Frankie, then turned back to her mother. "Jolie's taking a nap. If we're really, really, really quiet can we play here?"

Kenzie started to shake her head but a spasm in her neck stopped her short. "Ow!"

"Mommy?" Now Pippa was alarmed.

"Sorry, baby girl," Kenzie gasped. "But I can't right now. Play outdoors, okay?"

Frankie peeked out from behind Pippa, a stricken look on his face. "Are you going to die?" he quavered.

The boy seemed terrified. Somehow Kenzie found the energy to give him a reassuring smile, even to laugh a little. "I'm not planning on it. It's just a really bad headache, honest. I need to lie down for a bit. Then I'll be fine."

Keeping the smile on her face, she watched as the children tiptoed out and closed the door with exaggerated care behind them. Then she worked herself incrementally to a half-standing, half-crouching position and inched her way across the floor to the bedroom. Every movement sent her spine and ribs into spasms.

It was unquestionably the worst physical pain she'd been in since this affliction had started a couple of years ago. Combined with the now searing migraine, it was enough to make her think seriously about taking a painkiller.

I'm sorry, Lord, she prayed silently. *Please be with me and help me hold on to You.*

She made it all the way into the cool, dark bedroom, where she carefully eased herself onto the bed. But lying down seemed to make the pain explode. She hadn't thought it could get any worse. Apparently she'd been wrong.

"Help me, God!" she prayed aloud as she groped for the nightstand drawer. Her hand located the bottle of migraine pills. Trying to unscrew the cap was almost too much for her, but she finally managed it. Grasping one of the pills, she bit it in half, dry-swallowed it and flopped back on the bed, waiting for the agony to abate.

As JONAH RAISED his hand to knock on Kenzie's door, Pippa and Frankie came running in from outdoors, their cheeks flushed from playing in the crisp autumn air.

"My mom's asleep." Pippa folded her arms and frowned as if she were a security guard ten times her size. "She said she needs to rest."

Jonah's smile faded. Pippa had been different to him for the past week or so, as if she no longer liked him. Maybe Frankie had told her more stories about how much he yelled, even though Jonah had been more careful than ever to keep his naturally loud voice gentle and soft.

"Okay. I'll try later." With a puzzled glance at Frankie, Jonah started toward their apartment.

A soft click made him turn back. Kenzie's door opened and she peeked out. She looked better than she had earlier at school, although she was still far too pale and had dark circles under her eyes. Her smile seemed unfocused and she held on to the doorjamb for support.

"Oh! Hi, everyone. I thought I heard voices." Her words were a bit slurred, which probably meant she'd taken the migraine medication.

"I told him to go away," Pippa said with a sigh. "But he didn't leave fast enough."

"Pippa! Why on earth would you say something like that?" Although she was scolding her daughter, she sounded as if she were still half asleep.

"He's mean," the little girl replied. When Frankie poked her and shook his head, she shrugged. "What? He is. You said so."

So Jonah was right. His son was still upset about something. Or everything. It was hard to tell lately.

It seemed to take Kenzie an effort to say, "And you are rude, missy. Go to your room right now. Playtime is over."

With a ferocious pout, Pippa stomped into the apartment and disappeared. Frankie turned on his heel and headed across the hall, slamming the door behind him.

"Well, that should wake Jolie up," Jonah muttered.

"Sorry about Pippa." When Kenzie's eyes met Jonah's, she blushed and looked away.

The little moment made his heart skip a beat and he felt a rush of something he shouldn't be feeling. Hadn't he told both himself and Kenzie that getting close would be a mistake? Hadn't he decided he needed to focus on his children?

Then the headmistress's warning from the week before came back to him and Jonah wondered if that was why Kenzie seemed embarrassed.

"Did Enid talk to you about me, by any chance?" he asked.

Kenzie kept her eyes on the floor. "Yes, she did. The day I fainted, actually. I guess she said something to you, too?"

"Yeah." Jonah found his gaze going to the same spot on the floor, between their feet. He tried to lighten the mood by adding, "That wasn't at all awkward."

Kenzie didn't laugh. "I'm glad we said the same thing, anyway."

"Did we?"

"Yeah, you know…it was all over years ago and there's no way we were ever getting back together." She glanced up. "Right?"

Jonah pushed down a twinge of regret. "Yeah, that's what I said." He cleared his throat and looked at her, so pale and vulnerable, so close he wanted to reach out and take her hand. "Anyway, I stopped by because I thought you'd want to talk about the rehearsal schedule."

Kenzie sagged a bit more against the door frame. "Now's really not a good time. Maybe tomorrow?"

"Okay, sure." Jonah moved a little closer and studied her face worriedly. "You look awfully tired, Kenz."

Her eyes moved back to his and he caught his breath at the sadness in her gaze. For a moment neither of them spoke. Jonah had to fight the urge to take her in his arms and comfort her.

Kenzie broke the silence. "I know. I think there's something really wrong with me." A tear rolled down her cheek. "I don't know what to do. I have to keep going, take care of Pip." Her voice shook. "I can't fall apart."

The lump in Jonah's throat made it impossible to say a word. Suddenly he pulled her close. At first she tensed up. Then she relaxed against his chest and allowed him to comfort her. Tenderness washed through him and he felt his own eyes fill. Clearing his throat, he whispered, "Can't your ex take care of Pippa for a while so you can get some rest?"

Her response was muffled by his sweatshirt. "His wife has to be on bed rest for the remainder of her pregnancy, so he's looking after her." With a sniffle, she added, "He seems to have lost interest in Pippa."

A bolt of anger struck Jonah. "How can he possibly—"

Kenzie stiffened and pulled away from him. "It's a long story," she said hastily. "Anyway, I'd better go have a talk with Pippa and get her fed. And I promise we'll talk about the rehearsal schedule tomorrow, okay?" With that, she went back inside her apartment and closed the door softly behind her.

After staring at the door for a while, Jonah shook himself and headed across the hall. He checked on Jolie, who was happily awake and playing in her crib, chattering away at her stuffies. Then he went to Frankie's room, rapping sharply on the closed door before opening it. "Frankie? Buddy, let's talk."

He found the boy sitting sullenly on his bed with a big sketch pad, surrounded by crayons. "I'm busy."

Jonah sat on the bed. "You can keep drawing, but I think you need to let me know why you think I'm mean."

"That's not what I said," Frankie grumbled. "Pippa said it wrong."

"Okay, then what did you say?" When the little boy hesitated, Jonah put a hand on his arm. "This is important to me, Frank. If I'm acting mean or grouchy or whatever, I need to know so I can do better."

Frankie gave him an evasive shrug. "I was talking about the man in my dream who was yelling at my real mommy."

Jonah shook his head. "But you must have said something about me that made Pippa mad at me."

Frankie went completely still, shoulders hunched, eyes fixed on the drawing he was working on. "I told Pippa I wanted you to marry her mommy so she could be my sister, but you said no."

Jonah gave a startled laugh. "Frankie, I can't just go and marry someone because you want me to."

"Why not?" His son looked up at him with innocent, imploring eyes.

Jonah pulled Frankie onto his lap and kissed the top of his head. "Because grown-ups need time to get to know each other before they make that kind of decision."

The little boy looked baffled. "Why? I know I love Pippa, and I met her when you met Mrs. Reid."

Wishing he could be as honest and innocent as a six-year-old, Jonah heaved a sigh. "It's just different for grown-ups, buddy."

CHAPTER THIRTEEN

"MOMMY?"

Pippa's voice sounded uncharacteristically cautious, as if she didn't really want to talk about whatever was on her mind. Kenzie roused herself from her semi-nap on the sofa, prepared to give her daughter her full attention. "What is it, baby girl?"

Pippa sat next to her mother and wrapped her arms around her as she looked up with a hopeful expression. "Did you ask Daddy to come visit?"

Kenzie had been dreading this moment. It had been a while since she'd sent Greg the email asking him to come visit Pippa, but his only response had been terse and dismissive. She needed to find the words to explain the situation to her daughter. Her brain felt soggy from the unrelenting exhaustion and pain, but she was going to have to do her best.

At first she simply said, "Yes, I emailed him, but—"

The little girl sat upright. "When's he coming?"

"I'm not sure he can."

Pippa's face fell. "Why not?"

"Don't be sad, sweetie." Kenzie took her daughter onto her lap and kissed the top of her head. "Camilla's been sick."

Kenzie's sweatshirt muffled Pippa's voice. "I don't want Camilla to come. I want to see Daddy."

"Pips, what did I say about being respectful?" she sighed. "I get that you miss him, but—"

Her daughter straightened up, a puzzled look on her face. "I don't understand why he doesn't come see me. I mean, he's my daddy. Doesn't he miss me at all?"

Kenzie tried to think of a way to explain mandatory bed rest to a seven-year-old. "Sometimes when mommies are going to have babies, they need to lie down a lot, to make sure the baby will be okay. When that happens, daddies need to be around to take care of the mommies."

"But he's my daddy, too!" Pippa insisted. "And I'm already here!"

Kenzie took a deep breath. "I know, Pips. But we're doing great, aren't we? Don't you love living here? You have all those new friends, and Frankie right next door…"

"Frankie comes from Boston, too," Pippa announced excitedly. "That's where he used to live before…" She clapped a hand over her mouth. "I'm not s'posed to talk about that."

"Did Frankie ask you to keep a secret?" Worry niggled at Kenzie's stomach.

Pippa's eyes shifted away from her mother's. "He said Mr. Raymond isn't his real daddy. He's his…um, his foster daddy." Her red-blond eyebrows met over her nose in a puzzled arc. "I don't know what that means. Something between a real daddy and a 'dopted daddy, Frankie said."

"I'm sure Mr. Raymond loves him like a real daddy."

"His real mommy and his 'dopted mommy died." Pippa turned her troubled gaze back to Kenzie. "He said they got sick and died. I don't like you being sick, Mommy."

"Oh, sweetie!" The niggle blossomed into alarm. Kenzie pulled her little girl close and kissed her over and over. "I have a little trouble now and then, but it's nothing serious."

Scrubbing her eyes with her sleeve, Pippa asked, "If you get really sick, will Daddy take care of me?"

Kenzie blinked back tears of her own. Her usually ebullient daughter had some serious worries, so even though Kenzie felt uncomfortable making the assurance, she said what she needed to say to console the distressed child. "Of course, baby girl."

But I'm not saying which daddy, she thought to herself, realizing she really should have that conversation with Jonah as soon as possible.

"So can you please ask him to come visit? Maybe he didn't see the message."

"Of course I can ask, but, Pips, I told you Camilla is sick and he needs to stay home and take care of her."

For a moment Pippa scrunched up her face into an expression Kenzie recognized as stubborn and determined. Then she turned her eyes up to her mother again. "Does Daddy still live in our house?"

"Yes, of course." When Pippa looked satisfied with the answer, Kenzie found herself worrying again. "Why do you ask?"

"No reason. Does Camilla live there, too?"

"Of course she does. She and your daddy are

married." Kenzie put her hand under Pippa's chin and studied her face, which was an interesting mix of sly and innocent. "Why are you asking so many questions?"

With an elaborate shrug, Pippa answered, "I thought maybe we could go visit him there, if he can't come here."

Kenzie considered Pippa's suggestion, then shook her head. "Maybe after the baby is born," she said cautiously, "but I don't think Camilla needs visitors right now." She tickled Pippa to lighten the moment. "Especially a little girl with a big mouth!"

"I do not!" Pippa yelled at the top of her lungs, squealing and kicking.

Kenzie put her hands over her ears playfully. "I rest my case. That was super loud."

"I can be quiet! And you said Mr. Raymond has a big voice, and sometimes it sounds like he's yelling when he isn't even mad. Maybe I'm like that, too."

Her daughter's words froze Kenzie, who found herself wondering if that was where Pippa got her tendency to shout. She was very familiar with the power of Jonah's voice. With the gym right across the hall from her arts classroom, it was hard to ignore. "It's true. Some people have big voices. But they can learn to tone it down, right?"

"Mommy, I'm trying to be less shouty. I know you and Daddy don't like when I'm loud." Pippa gave her shoulders an exaggerated shrug. "Because if you're shouty all the time, how can people tell when you're mad?"

"You've got a point, baby girl." As she spoke, Kenzie felt exhaustion sweep through her body, intensifying the all-over ache that never seemed to go away. Her automatic reaction was to sit up straighter and breathe deeply.

"Mommy?" Pippa peered at her mother with earnest concern. "Are you hurting again?"

"I'm fine, just a little tired."

Kenzie always did her best to hide her symptoms from Pippa, but it had been getting more and more difficult. At the moment it seemed as if every cell of her body was on fire.

In spite of the growing intensity of her pain, she'd steadily resisted even trying one of the painkillers Dr. Alden had prescribed. Taking pain medication while teaching seemed like a terrible idea. Taking pain medication as the single mother of an active child seemed even worse. But she could treat the impending migraine as long as she took only half a pill.

"I just need to take something for my headache," she explained as she struggled up from the sofa. "Then I'll be fine."

"Okay, Mommy." Pippa glanced through the picture window behind the sofa. A big grin spread across her face and she started waving frantically. "May I please go outside and play with Frankie?"

"Yes, but bundle up first and stay close so I can see you from here." Kenzie managed to gasp out the instructions as she hobbled to her bedroom to get a pill.

Once she'd taken half of a migraine pill, she sat quietly on the sofa, watching the kids play. She was amazed at how well they got on together, considering how different their personalities and backgrounds were. Maybe opposites really did attract. After all, she'd married the serious-minded Greg Halloran and their marriage had been fine until she got sick.

And before that, when she and Jonah were a couple, she'd been the loud one. Pippa could easily have gotten her "shouty-ness" from either parent.

But Frankie certainly could be loud, especially at night. She knew he was still having nightmares that made him wake up screaming.

Because of her persistent pain, Kenzie was having so much trouble sleeping that she either woke up or was already awake when the screaming started. So far Pippa had always slept soundly through the noise—nothing woke that girl up once she was out for the night—but Kenzie found the little boy's pitiful screams so harrowing that she couldn't get back to sleep for hours, if at all.

What had he been through that gave him such horrific nightmares? Despite the fact that her mother and the man she assumed was her father had divorced, Pippa had led a relatively protected childhood. It upset Kenzie deeply to think that a small child like Frankie had witnessed anything that would create such a reaction, but she knew plenty of children were exposed to terrible things.

She burned to help Jonah and Frankie, to find some way to guide them through the darkness. God had sustained her through her own darkest days. Maybe she could find a way to share her story with Jonah.

A soft rap on the door roused Kenzie from her musings. The migraine pill hadn't kicked in yet and she didn't feel equal to getting up, so she called out, "It's open. Come on in!"

She knew it was unlikely that Jonah would drop by unless Frankie was there, so she wasn't surprised when Diane's head poked around the door. "Are you up for a visit?"

"Sure!" Not wanting Jonah's sister to worry, Kenzie forced brightness into her voice. "Do you want some coffee or tea?"

Settling next to Kenzie on the sofa, Diane studied her face. "No, thanks. You look beat."

"Just recovering from a week of teaching," Kenzie laughed.

With a sympathetic nod, Diane rested a hand on her stomach. "I don't know how you do it. I know how challenging some of those kids can be."

"They're not so bad." Kenzie made a wry face. "Well, most of them, anyway."

"I haven't even given birth to this one yet and I'm completely wiped out." With a violent yawn she added, "And I have a few more months to go!"

"Pregnancy takes a lot out of you," Kenzie agreed, although her own pregnancy fatigue had been nothing compared to the level of exhaustion she'd experienced over the last two years.

"I'd been told that, but of course I thought I'd be different, being a sturdy farm girl." Diane stifled another yawn, then smiled fondly. "I think Paul would be willing to carry it for me, if that were possible. He's over the moon about being a daddy."

The last word reminded Kenzie of the conversation she'd just had with Pippa. "I don't want to be the proverbial nosy neighbor, and I know this is none of my business…" she started.

"Uh-oh," Diane teased.

"No, really, just tell me to butt out, but what's the story with Frankie?" She made a face at her own bluntness. "I mean, Pippa said both his mothers died. His birth mother and Elena."

Instantly Diane's expression turned to worry. "I didn't think he could possibly remember that, since he was so little."

"Today's the first time Pippa mentioned it to me, but I got the impression they've discussed it more than once."

A line formed over Diane's nose. "Did she say anything more?"

Kenzie frowned, trying to remember the conversation. "I think it was just that his real mother and his foster mother got sick and died."

Worry creased Diane's forehead. "Anything else?"

"Not that I can think of. We were talking

about my ex. Pippa wanted to know when…"
Kenzie paused, remembering that Diane had
no idea Jonah was Pippa's real father. "When
my ex was going to come visit."

"Is he coming?" When Kenzie shrugged,
Diane shook her head. "I'm glad Frankie has
Pippa to talk to. He has a tendency to go in-
ward and get quiet when he's upset. His life has
been awfully traumatic and Jonah's doing his
best, but he really needed a friend."

"Jonah never told me Frankie's whole history, but it sounds horrific."

"Hmm." Diane appeared to be thinking
things over, finding a way to justify sharing the
story with Kenzie. Finally she nodded. "Well,
as Frankie's favorite teacher, you should probably know a bit more about him."

Kenzie felt her headache easing up as the pill
worked its magic. Trying not to appear too
eager to hear the story, she edged a little closer
to Diane on the sofa. "I'd like to hear it, if you
think Jonah won't mind."

"It's pretty rough," Diane warned. "When
they were partners in the Boston PD, he and
Elena got an anonymous call to one of the
seedier parts of the city. Someone complain-
ing that a baby had been screaming and crying

for hours and it was keeping them awake. Nice, right?" Disgusted, she shook her head. "They broke in and found a two-year-old sitting next to his mom's body." Taking a deep breath, she explained, "The cause of death was an opioid overdose."

"That's awful," Kenzie breathed, her heart aching for the little boy Jonah had taken in.

"Horrible," Diane agreed. "He was collateral damage in the opioid epidemic."

Guilt jabbed her midsection as Kenzie thought of the untouched pills in her end table. Maybe just having them there was too much of a temptation. She should probably get rid of them. "Was she taking them for pain?"

Diane's face took on a sorrowful, sympathetic expression. "Not the kind of pain you mean, but I'd say yes, she was taking them for pain." Diane sighed, shaking her head.

"That's horrible. The poor thing." Kenzie felt herself tearing up with empathy for the lost soul who was in so much emotional pain she self-medicated. "But she kept her little boy with her. That couldn't have been easy."

"She probably shouldn't have, but yes, she held on to Frankie."

No matter what happened, Kenzie couldn't

imagine anything that would make her give up Pippa. Then again, she'd never had a drug problem. "That's how Jonah and Elena met him?"

Diane nodded. "Yes, and according to Jonah, it was love at first sight. Elena latched on to the boy and refused to let go. She had friends who worked with the Department of Children and Families and pulled strings so she could foster him."

Slumping back on the sofa, Kenzie blinked. She'd only met Elena a couple of times, but she'd gotten the impression of a very strong-willed person. "So they were a couple when they found Frankie?"

"Nope. Well, not in the traditional sense. They'd been partners and close friends for years. After you broke up with Jonah and moved away, they started hanging out together. A lot." Diane turned to look at Kenzie with a rueful expression. "I'm sorry to bring that up. But Elena was really worried about him after you left, wanted to be sure he was okay. And I think it was a good thing. He…he wasn't in great shape."

"It's okay." Kenzie felt a lump of guilt form in her stomach. "It was stupid and selfish of me to act the way I did."

"We were all really worried about him. He was truly devastated."

"I'm so sorry. I don't know what I was thinking."

"But I'm sure Elena was over the moon when you quit the field." Diane frowned. "I shouldn't talk about her like that. I mean, they had a good marriage. She was a good wife and a great mother to Frankie, and Jonah seemed happy."

"And they had Jolena."

"Yes, but sadly, that's where it started to go downhill." Changing positions to face Kenzie, Diane leaned forward. "The pregnancy was rough on Elena. Not so much physically as emotionally. She was a mess."

"I can identify." Kenzie smiled, remembering her own mood swings when she was carrying Pippa.

"I bet you were a dream compared to Elena. We'd get phone calls from Jonah three, four times a week, just begging for advice." Diane winced and fidgeted her way to a more comfortable position. "They still lived in Boston and he was still working as a policeman, plus my husband was working a million hours a week because of a doctor shortage, so it wasn't easy for us to drive to Boston and see what was going on for ourselves." Rubbing her belly, she added, "Then the birth was a nightmare. Elena and Jolie were both in danger of not making it."

"That must have been terrifying." Kenzie thought gratefully of her own relatively easy childbirth.

"The upshot was, they told Elena she couldn't have another baby, and she went into one heck of a depression." Diane paused as if thinking whether she should share anything else with Kenzie. After a deep breath, she went on. "Then one day while Jonah was working, she went for a drive, leaving the kids home alone."

Kenzie couldn't stifle a gasp. "Oh, no."

"Oh, yes," Diane confirmed grimly. "Jonah got a call at work that she'd been in a bad accident. Blood tests showed she had taken a few painkillers and probably fell asleep at the wheel. She died the next day."

Kenzie closed her eyes, imagining the horror that Jonah had faced alone. "Poor Frankie."

"Yeah. You can't help thinking it's going to take years for him to overcome what he's been through." Diane blinked back sudden tears. "I can't tell you how much I pray for that boy."

"No wonder he gets so angry," Kenzie whispered.

"The minute we heard, Paul and I ran to Boston and told Jonah they were moving in with us, end of story. He couldn't go on being a city cop when he was left alone with two little kids. I knew a new health and safety position was opening up at the school. It was a no-brainer."

Feeling as if she were in a state of shock and her mouth was on autopilot, Kenzie said, "He's so blessed to have you. They're all so fortunate."

"I guess." Diane made a wry face. "But the last thing I'd call any of them is fortunate."

Stunned with all these new and upsetting details about Jonah and Frankie, Kenzie stared straight ahead of herself without saying a word. Finally Diane reached over and patted her knee, then struggled to her feet. "You look exhausted and I've just given you information overload. I'm going to check in with Jonah, let you get some rest."

Kenzie barely registered Diane leaving the apartment and closing the door softly behind her.

JONAH ANSWERED THE quick tap on his door knowing it was Diane. Paul was at work in the ER, and Kenzie had never gotten into the habit of dropping by unless she knew Pippa was there playing with Frankie and wanted her to come home. He opened the door with a welcoming smile for his sister.

"Hey." His smile faded at Diane's worried face as she slipped under his arm, closing the door behind her. "Are you all right?"

"Me? Yeah, I'm great!" Placing a hand on her baby bump, she gave him a reassuring grin before making her way over to the living area. "But…well, I was just talking to Kenzie."

Although he couldn't stop his heart from leaping at the mention of Kenzie's name, he also couldn't keep from feeling a jolt of worry. "Uh-oh. What did I do now?"

Diane eased herself onto the sofa with a groan and gave a sigh of contentment as she settled into the deep cushions. "Nothing, as far as I know. But Frankie's been talking to Pippa, who in turn talked to her mother."

"And?" Jonah asked when she paused.

Once her brother was seated in the well-worn recliner, she said, "And he's been telling her that both his mommies got sick and died. Did you tell him about his bio mom?"

Jonah sighed heavily. "No, never. But I think he's remembered a bit. He asked if she had yellow hair."

"And did she?"

He nodded. "Her real hair was dark, almost black. She'd dyed it a bright blond color, but she had a couple inches of dark roots. Is that all he said?"

Diane shrugged. "That's all Pippa said to Kenzie. I guess they were talking about asking the ex to visit and somehow that came up."

Jonah closed his eyes and rested his head on the back of the recliner. "Do you think I should sit him down and let him ask whatever he wants? I mean, he has a right to know about his birth mother." He sighed again, shaking his head. "I wish Elena hadn't told him he wasn't ours."

Diane spoke cautiously. "It's unfortunate, but there's no putting that genie back in the bottle. Maybe you could tell him you knew the minute you saw him that you wanted to be his daddy?"

"That would be the truth, at any rate." In spite of his worries, Jonah felt his heart warming. "And the way Elena took to that boy pretty much saved his life."

His sister reached over to touch his arm. "She had a big heart. And she loved you both fiercely."

"I know. She was a lioness, that's for sure." Blinking back a sudden threat of tears, Jonah studied the ceiling. "But Frankie only just started asking questions. Maybe the memories only just started coming back. Or maybe he started thinking more about Elena telling him he was a foster kid." He glanced back at his sister, shaking his head sadly. "Why she decided to tell that to a messed-up five-year-old, I'll never understand."

"Maybe because she was pretty messed up herself at that point," Diane suggested.

"True," Jonah agreed. "But why is he remembering now? She definitely didn't tell him what happened to his mom."

"Maybe he saw something on TV that jogged his memory?"

"You know I do my best to protect him from all of that stuff, but I can't control what another kid might show him. He spends a lot of time with Pippa these days."

"I very much doubt that Pippa would be allowed to show him much of anything," Diane said gently. "From what I've seen, Kenzie is a very vigilant mother. It's probably just a recovered memory. Maybe he blocked it for a while, but now that he knows he's safe and loved, it's coming back."

"I'm not so sure how safe he feels." Jonah

sagged back into the recliner. "I know he feels I'm letting him down because the adoption process is dragging on and on. I've tried to explain it, but it gets a bit messy since it's because of Elena's death."

"So he actually thinks you don't want to adopt him?"

Heart aching, Jonah nodded. "Sometimes it's pretty clear that that's what he believes. That's what his meltdown was about at the Mullins' dinner."

"Not surprising," Diane said gently. "He may be afraid of losing you, like he's lost his other parents."

"He says over and over that he wants a mom," Jonah murmured. "In fact, he pretty much ordered me to marry Kenzie so Pippa could be his sister."

Diane's eyes gleamed with mischief. "Yes, he seems very fond of our neighbor." She shot him a playful wink. "And so do you."

Jonah ran his hands through his hair. "Stop it. That ship sailed about eight years ago. And besides, I need to focus on the kids. I told you that."

"Easier to do when you have a helpmate, don't ya think?" When Jonah started to retort,

Diane cut him off. "Okay, so you guys had a bad breakup eight years ago. Now you've both had time to grow up and get over it, maybe you could at least try dating each other again and see what happens. What's the problem?"

"The problem is I don't think she likes me very much. Sometimes I think she hates my guts."

"Are you kidding me?" Diane reached over again, this time to punch Jonah's arm. "She's just putting on an act."

"It's one very convincing act."

"Well, you're a clueless guy. I'm female, she's female. I'm on to all those little things we do to pretend we're not madly in love with some guy. And that includes acting like we hate your guts when, in fact, we're seriously crazy about your guts."

Jonah burst out laughing. "Well, that sounds gross."

"It's not gross. It's human nature."

"Di, trust me. Kenzie wants nothing to do with me. She's made it clear again and again."

"That just proves what I'm saying," Diane insisted. "If she didn't care, she wouldn't protest so much."

Jonah was deep in thought. "I wish I knew what I did that made her so mad."

"What? When?"

He shook his head. "Eight years ago, when she just dumped me out of nowhere."

"Did you ask her?"

"I did at the time, but she seemed to think I should know what I'd done."

"Okay." Diane folded her arms across her chest. "Tell me everything."

Jonah turned to her as he thought back. "We'd gone camping the weekend before. It was her first time. She hated it, and I couldn't blame her. The weather turned awful, it was cold and wet, and she was miserable."

"But she didn't dump you then? 'Cause I would've."

He grimaced as he recalled that ill-advised trip. "We had separate tents, but when it started raining hers collapsed. So she came in with me, and..." Jonah could feel his face heating up.

Diane didn't miss a trick. Her mouth dropped open. "Whoa. Okay, this is new information. And it could explain a lot. Then what?"

"As soon as we got back, I dropped Kenzie at her place and took off for Mom's to get Grandma's engagement ring."

Diane's mouth formed an O. "Did Kenzie know what you were up to?"

"Of course not! I stayed a week because Mom needed some stuff done around the house, and...well, I didn't talk to Kenzie much." When Diane gave him a look, Jonah added, "She was getting through her last round of tests and interviewing for jobs, so I didn't want to interrupt her."

Comprehension dawned on Diane's face. "Ah. Now I'm starting to see where you may have messed up, dear brother."

Jonah looked perplexed. "Well, please enlighten me, dear sister."

"Seriously? You really are clueless." Diane counted off his sins on her fingers. "One, you drag the girl off on a camping trip that she hates. Two, you take things to a new level, right?" Jonah nodded. "Three, you take off for a week and hardly ever call."

"Um...well, more or less," Jonah muttered.

"Wow. And all she did was dump you?" Diane burst out laughing. "Do you know anything about women at all?"

Before he could answer, there was a loud, frantic banging on the door. A feeling of foreboding made Jonah leap to his feet and run to open it. When he did, Kenzie collapsed against him as if her legs had given out.

"The kids," she gasped. "They're gone. I can't see them anywhere."

CHAPTER FOURTEEN

EVEN BEFORE KENZIE had finished speaking, Jonah and Diane had both run past her into the foyer. Jonah knew the kids sometimes played in a part of the yard that wasn't visible from Kenzie's place, so he ran out the back door. Craning his neck, he peered all around the area near the porch, certain he'd spot Frankie's bright red coat.

Nothing.

As he hurried down the steps to the yard, Diane and Kenzie came panting around the corner. "No sign of them out front," Diane huffed.

"The pond!" Kenzie pointed a shaking finger toward the path leading to the pond before she started her wobbly way down.

Jonah turned to his sister. "You go inside and check all around the house, okay? I'll go to the pond, too." Without waiting for a response, he ran after Kenzie.

Despite her obvious unsteadiness, Kenzie was making her way down the path with that old familiar look of determination. "It's my fault," she choked out, slipping on wet leaves. "I should have been watching."

Jonah took her arm to keep her from falling, then kept holding on to her as they approached the pond's edge. His stomach filled with dread. He'd always been so careful to warn Frankie to keep his distance, but lately the boy's moods had been unpredictable.

Although a stunning landscape for much of the year, the pond was gray and bleak on this overcast day. Brown reeds poked through the dead leaves, which covered the boulders scattered along the edge of the water.

Scanning the expanse for signs of the children, he didn't speak his fears out loud, but his heart sank into his shoes. The pond had boulders sticking out that might look very tempting as stepping stones to a six-and seven-year-old. It would be all too easy to slip and fall into the water, which was very deep in places. He held his breath and kept looking around the little pond, praying harder than he'd ever prayed in his life.

Dear Lord, please keep our children safe. Please have them be hiding somewhere nearby. Please, God, please...

"I don't see any footprints in the mud," Kenzie whispered. "That's good, right?"

Jonah realized he had put his arm around her shoulders in a protective gesture. He gave her a reassuring squeeze as he recognized that she was right. No footprints. No sign that the kids had been here recently. "Yes, that's good."

He felt her sag against him again. "Then where are they?"

Fighting off the surge of fear that threatened to overwhelm him, Jonah guided Kenzie back to the house. He couldn't let her go by herself, given how shaky she was. It seemed as if she could barely hold herself upright, let alone navigate the muddy path without slipping. "Let's see if Diane found them. If not, I'll take a walk around the whole property in case they just wandered somewhere we can't see."

But as Jonah helped Kenzie up the porch steps, Diane appeared at the back door with Jolie in her arms. "They're nowhere in the house. I've been everywhere, calling their names."

Jonah hadn't thought he could feel any more distressed. Somehow he kept his voice calm and authoritative. "Call the police. Now. I'll keep looking around the yard." He went back down the steps and started his search, terrified of what he might find.

Or not find.

"I WAS SITTING on the sofa, watching them through the window. I told them not to leave my sight. But I must have dozed off. When I looked out again they were gone."

Kenzie could hardly recognize the emotion-free words coming from her mouth. She felt like she was a million miles away, listening to some robot drone at the policewoman taking her statement.

"Then you say you looked all around the property, ma'am?" Officer Brooks asked.

"All four of us did, yes."

Kenzie, Diane, Jonah and Paul were gathered around the table in Jonah's eat-in kitchen for the interview. The vibrant yellow walls, the refrigerator covered with Frankie's colorful art-work—the whole atmosphere was at odds with the horror of the situation. In her high chair, Jolie kicked her bootee'd feet and picked at the

Cheerios on the tray, cheerfully oblivious to the drama.

"And you two are the kids' parents?" The officer indicated Kenzie and Jonah.

"Yes." Raw with emotion, the single syllable eloquently conveyed Jonah's stress level.

"I'm the little girl's mother, and he's the boy's father," Kenzie explained in that eerie monotone. "We're neighbors."

"Yes, ma'am, I understand that. You didn't see anyone come into the yard?" Studying the officer's elaborately braided hair, Kenzie shook her head. "And you didn't see the kids leave, obviously."

"No."

Brooks leaned forward and tried to catch Kenzie's eyes. "Are you okay, ma'am?"

"Yes, I'm fine, thank you." Actually, she felt numb, as if her entire body had been injected with Novocain. Maybe she shouldn't have taken that migraine pill. It had made her doze off and now the kids were missing and it was all her fault.

Suddenly she became aware that the police officer was asking her a question, her intense brown eyes boring into Kenzie's unfocused ones. "Ma'am, have you been drinking, or have you taken any drugs?"

Jonah exploded. "Are you kidding me? Can we please talk about the missing children?"

Brooks turned to him with a sympathetic look. "Mr. Raymond, you know we have an Amber Alert out and officers are looking throughout the village. We're doing everything we can. The more information we have, the better our chances of finding them." She turned back to Kenzie. "I'm only asking because you seem pretty out of it, to tell the truth. Now, I don't smell alcohol on your breath, but have you taken anything at all? Maybe an antihistamine, something that might make you sleepy?"

"I took part of a migraine pill, but…" Kenzie shook her head, dazed. "I feel really weird."

Paul cut her off. "As a doctor, I'd say she's in shock." He gave her an encouraging squeeze on the shoulder. "She feels terrible for losing sight of the kids. When I got here she was frantic, worried sick. Then she just kinda shut down."

Still peering into Kenzie's face, Brooks shook her head. "She seems like she's ready to fall asleep. And frankly, she doesn't seem all that worried."

When Paul joined the officer in her study of Kenzie, she noticed a flicker of doubt flash through his eyes. But when he straightened up again, he said, "Like I said, she's shut down emotionally, gone into shock. It's a method of coping with extreme stress and grief. So as Jonah says, let's focus on what matters."

Rousing herself to appear more normal, Kenzie mumbled through lips that didn't want to work. "We should be out there looking for them."

But Brooks shook her head again, slow but decisive. "No, ma'am, we need you and Mr. Raymond to stay put, in case the kids come home. You don't want them coming back to an empty house, do you?"

The thought of Pippa coming home and not finding her mother pierced some part of Kenzie's protective layer. A sob escaped her. When Jonah slipped his arm around her shoulders, she fell against him, crying so hard she was shaking.

"I think that's enough for now." Paul made it sound like a suggestion.

"Just one more question, sir." Brooks glanced at Kenzie, struggling to get herself under control, and at Jonah, who kept his arm firmly around her shoulders. "Is there anything the kids said that might indicate where they went? I mean, like maybe they said they wanted candy and decided to walk into the village."

Kenzie dug through the slush of her brain and came up empty. "Pippa knows not to leave the yard, or even play in the front of the house. She knows I need to see her from my window."

"Same goes for Frankie," Jonah agreed. "He knows to stay where we can easily keep an eye on him."

"Boston!" Out of nowhere, Kenzie's brain kicked into gear. "Pippa was just saying this morning she wanted to see her—her father. She asked me if we could go to Boston to see him. And she said something about that being where Frankie used to live." She turned to Jonah. "Do you think…?"

"Boston?" Jonah rubbed his forehead. "How would they get there? They wouldn't hitchhike, would they?"

"We'll check on the main roads leading out of the village, and the bus station downtown." Right away Brooks was on her radio, giving quick instructions to her fellow officers. When she was done, she nodded at the family. "That was good thinking. Thanks, Mrs. Reid."

Kenzie was shaking so hard she could barely stay on her chair. "They couldn't have gotten far without money," she quavered. "Oh, please, God, let them be at the bus station."

As she sat there feeling useless, she squeezed her eyes shut and continued her prayer silently, begging God to find the kids and bring them back safely. *Please, Lord, they're so little. They need Your help to find their way home. I promise I'll never take my eyes off them again if only You'll send them back to us.*

When she looked up, Diane and Paul were gone and Officer Brooks was in the living room, having an incomprehensible, static-filled conversation on her police radio. Jonah was still sitting in the chair next to her, his head bowed over his folded hands. Without realizing she was doing it, Kenzie reached over and took his hands in hers.

They sat that way together, their heads bent over their clasped hands, for several minutes. When Jonah eventually released her hands, she felt a jolt of disappointment. Then he drew her into his arms and whispered, "It's going to be all right."

As he said it, the policewoman's radio crackled in the next room and words muffled by static came out. Brooks acknowledged whatever was said and came into the kitchen.

"Two small children matching the descriptions you gave us were spotted by a clerk at the bus station," she said. "They asked for tickets to Boston, but since they didn't have any money or adults with them, they were turned away."

Kenzie jumped to her feet, ready to sprint into the village. "Where are they now?"

Once again, Brooks gave her head a firm shake and pushed Kenzie back down into her chair. "No one saw them after they tried to get on the bus. The CCTV cameras don't show them leaving the station, so we can assume they're still there." Kenzie tried to get up again, but Brooks held her down with gentle force. "Officers are searching the premises and reviewing what the cameras captured. It's not the best-quality footage and jumps around from location to location, but they are pretty sure they never left the station."

"I'm going there now." Kenzie shook herself free from Brooks and Jonah and headed straight for the door.

The officer followed her, took her arm and guided her right back to the chair. "Best you stay here with your neighbor and wait for the kids at home. I promise I'll keep you informed of every update, and they'll bring the kids straight here as soon as they locate them."

"You mean *if* they locate them!" Kenzie

wailed. Now that the numbness and shock had worn off, her emotions had come roaring back, out of control.

"You need to calm down, ma'am. We have a good solid lead now," Brooks reassured her. "It's only a matter of time before we find them, since we know where they wanted to go. I know it sounds impossible, but please try to be patient and stay put. Getting yourself all worked up isn't going to help anyone, is it?"

Jonah drew in a shaky breath and put his arms around Kenzie again. "She's right, Kenz. Just take some deep breaths and keep praying."

"Listen to your boyfriend," Brooks chuckled. "He knows what he's saying. I'll leave you two alone."

After inhaling and exhaling deeply a few times, Kenzie managed to raise an eyebrow and fix Jonah with a wry look. "Boyfriend?"

"Well, once upon a time, anyway." He leaned his forehead against hers. "Honestly, Kenz, I never understood why you broke up with me, although…" He sighed and pulled her closer. "Well, I was having a little talk with Diane before all hell broke loose, and I guess maybe after what happened on that camping trip I should have been better at staying in touch."

"Ya think?" Kenzie sniffled. "But I don't think now's the time to go into it."

"Actually, I think it's the perfect time to go into it," Jonah countered. "We both could use a distraction."

Kenzie tried to smile, but it fell apart and she ended up sobbing on Jonah's shoulder. "Pippa…"

"She'll be all right, and so will Frankie." His voice was firm with conviction.

"You don't know that!"

Jonah drew in a tight breath. "You're right. I don't. But while we were praying I felt something."

She pulled back to look at him, curious and hopeful. "What? What did you feel?"

"I don't know how to describe it." Frowning, he thought it over. "Like a light going on inside me, I guess. I felt… It felt like God telling me it was going to be all right, not to worry." He paused, and as Kenzie watched him, his eyes grew bright with tears and his voice grew husky. "I haven't felt anything like that for ages, to be honest. I went to church with Elena pretty regularly in Boston. She was a devout Christian and brought me back to the faith of my childhood. But I abandoned my faith after Elena died. Now I realize I should have worked harder to keep it."

Kenzie felt her own eyes fill at Jonah's confession. "It's the only thing that's kept me going for the past couple of years, besides my little girl. But…" Her throat constricted as her eyes overflowed. "I don't know what I'd do if something happened to Pippa."

"There's no point in thinking the worst, Kenz." He pulled her close again and kissed her forehead. "Is there?"

After a long silence interrupted only by an occasional crackle from Officer Brooks's radio, Kenzie finally found the courage to ask the question that had been haunting her for eight years. "Why didn't you answer any of my messages?"

"Messages?" Jonah sounded puzzled. "I sent responses right away."

Kenzie leaned back in her chair. "Then why didn't I get them?"

"You did get them. You answered them!" Jonah gave his head a slight shake. "Don't you remember? You'd ask how my mom was doing, I'd ask how your final week was going…"

"Not those messages," Kenzie said gently.

"The ones I sent from San Francisco, a month or so later."

Now Jonah appeared completely bewildered. "I never got any messages from you after you left."

"I sent you texts, emails, even a certified letter that I know you got because the receipt came back."

Jonah sat back in his chair and stared at her as if she'd lost her mind. "I never saw a single thing from you once you were gone. I would remember, believe me. And I definitely would have answered."

Realizing her suspicions about Elena might be true but reluctant to say anything, Kenzie forced herself to look confused. "I sent at least a dozen, probably more. Then I waited and waited for you to get back to me. I thought you must have blocked me, which is why I finally sent an actual letter. Which you signed for!"

He'd been shaking his head through her entire speech. "I didn't block you, Kenz. I would never do that. Trust me, I was dying to hear from you, but you'd been so clear that you never wanted to hear from me again." He shook his head. "And I never signed for or even saw a letter either."

"I can't imagine what happened," Kenzie protested. "I definitely sent them to the right addresses. I checked and checked because I couldn't understand why you didn't answer."

Brow furrowed, Jonah thought it over. Then suddenly his face lit up with realization.

"Elena. She hung around my place a lot after you were gone. I'm sure she could access my phone and email and block you." His expression darkened again. "She might have signed for the letter with my name, then not given it to me."

Kenzie pretended to be surprised. "Would she have done that?"

Jonah nodded, and his face grew gentle. "I'm pretty sure she would and did. She told me she thought it would be a bad idea for me to be in touch with you."

"Why?" Kenzie didn't bother to disguise her anger.

"Because I was a complete mess," Jonah admitted. "And Elena was there to clean it up. She saw me at my worst, as I told you, and she wanted to protect me."

Kenzie scowled. "She had no business blocking me like that."

"It came from a good place, believe me. I know it sounds a bit extreme, but she did it out of love and care. I can't be angry with her for that." He cocked his head at Kenzie, curious. "What did the messages say?"

Kenzie's head was spinning as she thought about how to answer such a loaded question. And now she knew the truth about why he didn't acknowledge Pippa as his child.

He had no idea he was Pippa's father.

But now didn't seem like the best time to tell him such momentous news. Mentally she floundered around, looking for something to tell him instead of the whole truth. She finally settled on part of the truth, for now.

"Um…well, I wanted to come back to Boston," she started, but Officer Brooks burst into the kitchen with a big smile on her face.

"The kids are fine."

Jonah and Kenzie were on their feet right away, asking in unison, "Where are they?"

"They turned up in the cargo hold of a bus on its way to Boston, while it was stopped in Sturbridge. They're on their way home in a police car right now. Should be here in an hour."

"They're okay?" Kenzie asked anxiously.

Brooks chuckled. "A touch of motion sickness, from what I hear, but otherwise they're perfectly fine. Except they might be a little bit scared about what Mom and Dad are going to say when they get here." She raised an eyebrow at the pair in front of her. "As well they should be. This goes beyond being naughty, I think."

But Jonah and Kenzie were in each other's arms again, oblivious to Officer Brooks and her opinions.

"They're okay!" Kenzie gasped.

"Told ya," Jonah whispered.

CHAPTER FIFTEEN

WITHIN AN HOUR of their discovery, two filthy, slightly green children with hangdog faces were in danger of being hugged to pieces by their respective parents. For now there were no lectures or scolding or punishment, just joy and gratitude that they were safe.

Jonah couldn't remember the last time he'd felt this happy. Probably well over a year ago. Maybe it was just such a huge relief after all the stress of earlier in the day. Or maybe he was thrilled to have his little boy back. And what was more, Frankie seemed thrilled to be back with Jonah.

After a while Kenzie came up for air and held Pippa at arm's length, trying hard to suppress her smile. "Pee-ew, missy, you really stink!"

Pippa scowled at her partner in crime. "It's Frankie's fault! He barfed on me and it made me barf."

"It's Pippa's fault!" Frankie countered. "She dragged me into that dark, smelly place on the bus and it made me sick."

Now that the parents had let go, Paul started to check the kids over with professional efficiency. "I bet it did," he chuckled. "Inhaling diesel fumes is enough to make anyone barf. How are you feeling now?"

"Gross," Pippa said, wrinkling her nose.

Paul put a big hand on her forehead. "Like you're gonna barf some more?"

She shook her head. "No, just really stinky and dirty and slimy. I want a bath."

"What an awfully good idea," Kenzie said dryly. "We'll get you cleaned up. Then Frankie's daddy and I are going to talk to you about what you did." She turned to Jonah. "Right, Frankie's daddy?"

Jonah grinned, then tried to look stern. "You bet, Pippa's mommy."

After Kenzie and Pippa left, Jonah carried Frankie into the bathroom and ran a tub for him while Diane tucked Jolie into her crib. She poked her head into the bathroom. "All okay in here, big bro?"

Jonah looked up from pouring bubble bath

under the faucet as Frankie played with a toy boat. "All good, little sis."

"Well, you know where to find us if anyone starts feeling yucky." Diane gave Frankie a wink, which he tried to return but ended up blinking both his eyes hard. With a laugh, his aunt left to go upstairs and join her husband for dinner.

Jonah gently bathed the little boy, then dried him off and dressed him in clean pajamas. "Are you hungry, buddy?"

Frankie pouted. "No. My head hurts."

"I'm not surprised." Jonah gave him a children's aspirin and some saltines. "You should feel better soon."

Sitting in his recliner and holding his son, Jonah felt a rush of love and sympathy for the little boy. He kissed the top of his head and was rewarded with a trusting snuggle.

"I'm sorry, Daddy," Frankie quavered.

"It's okay now, Frankie. It's okay." He kissed the boy again and whispered, "I love you and I'm so glad to have you back home."

Little arms wrapped around his neck and a warm cheek pressed against his own. "I love you, too."

Tears pricked Jonah's eyes. He hadn't heard those words from Frankie in quite a while, and

he'd been sure he would never hear them again.
Earlier in the day he'd wondered if he'd ever
even see Frankie again, and his heart had been
ready to break, although he'd held his despair
firmly in check.

And God had been merciful.

Thank You, Lord, he prayed silently. Kenzie's
words came back to him, from when they'd
prayed together earlier.

*"It's the only thing that's kept me going for the
past couple of years."*

The sense of something lighting up inside of
him returned. He knew beyond a shadow of a
doubt that God had answered his prayer, even
though Jonah had turned his back on his faith
after Elena's death. Holding Frankie close, he
suddenly realized how much he and his son had
in common.

*Dear Lord, I'm sorry for running away from You.
I should have trusted You all along, no matter how
bad things got.*

Frankie's timid voice interrupted his prayer.
"Daddy?"

"Yes, son?"

"Do you really not know who my real daddy
is?"

Although he didn't feel prepared to have this

conversation after such an exhausting day, Jonah knew he had to be honest and patient with the little boy who called him "Daddy." Gently he cleared his throat and set Frankie on his knee so they could see each other. "No, son, I really don't."

"Why not? Didn't my real mommy tell you?"

Jonah had to think long and hard about how to answer that question. Finally he decided he didn't need to be literal with an emotionally scarred six-year-old, but he wanted to be technically honest. "No, son, because I never really met your mommy."

Frankie's brows came together over his nose as the boy tried to figure that out. "Then how did you meet me?"

Again, Jonah tried not to be angry with Elena for telling the boy things he was too young to understand. "Mommy Elena and I decided we wanted to adopt a little boy. When we met you, we knew you were the little boy we wanted more than any other."

He had the joy of watching Frankie's face light up, which made telling the shaded truth completely worthwhile. "Honest?"

Grinning back, Jonah nodded. "Honest. We

saw you and we knew right away you were supposed to be our little boy."

After a moment Frankie's smile dimmed. "Why did Mommy Elena have to die?"

The boy just couldn't seem to stop throwing the hardest possible questions at him tonight. Jonah tried to think of a reasonable answer, then realized he really could tell the truth this time.

"I don't know."

"But I thought you knew everything!"

"Nope. I don't, and that's the truth." He held Frankie close again and kissed him. "Only God knows everything, son."

MEANWHILE KENZIE HELPED her freshly bathed daughter put on her favorite flannel pajamas, covered with wild horses galloping and rearing. After she'd pulled the top over Pippa's head, she couldn't help throwing her arms around the girl and holding her close. The horror she'd felt at the mere thought of losing Pippa still hadn't worn off.

Pippa often pulled away when her mother was overly demonstrative, but tonight she submitted willingly and even hugged her back. "Are you still sad, Mommy?"

"Not sad at all, sweetie. Just so, so happy you're home safe."

"Are we still going next door?" Pippa asked the question over a huge yawn.

Releasing her daughter and wiping her eyes, Kenzie nodded. "Yes, I think we need to talk all together about what happened. But we'll keep it short so you can go to bed."

Pippa looked up at her mother. "It's okay. I want to be a good girl and do what you tell me."

Kenzie couldn't help laughing. "We'll see how long that lasts."

Together they walked across the softly lit foyer, past the staircase and to Jonah's door. Kenzie tapped lightly. "Jolie is probably sleeping, so let's be very quiet," she whispered to Pippa.

"Come on in!" Jonah's usually boisterous voice was hushed.

She eased the door open to find Jonah sitting in his recliner with Frankie curled up on his lap. She caught her breath at the loving expression on his face as he cuddled the boy, but she managed to speak around the lump in her throat. "Looks like a pajama party."

Pippa bounced up and down on her slippered

feet. "Can we have a pajama party, Mommy?" All Kenzie had to do was raise a single eyebrow and the little girl looked at the floor. "Sorry."

"Have a seat." Jonah nodded to the sofa that was kitty-corner to his recliner in front of the fireplace.

Once Kenzie and Pippa were settled on the sofa, Jonah started the interrogation with kindly firmness. "Now it's our turn to ask questions. We both want to hear from you why you ran away like that."

Frankie's eyes grew big with worry. "It was Pippa's idea."

"But you went along with it," Jonah reminded him.

Pippa frowned. "I came inside to talk to Mommy, but she was sleeping on the sofa. I didn't want to bother her. She's always tired on weekends and I think she took one of her headache pills."

Although Pippa's words struck her with guilt, Kenzie raised an eyebrow again. "So it's my fault you decided to run away because I happened to doze off?"

Her daughter mulled over her mother's suggestion, then nodded vigorously. "Yeah, kinda."

Squashing down another wave of guilt, Kenzie shook her head. "Think again, Pips."

The girl thought longer this time. "Okay, no. I made a bad choice."

"And you made me come with you," Frankie told her.

"I didn't make you!" Pippa snapped. "You said you wanted to find your daddy, remember?"

"Pippa!" Kenzie glared her daughter into submission. "I'm pretty sure this wasn't Frankie's idea. Why did you want to go to Boston?"

Pippa's chin started to tremble. She looked down at her hand as her finger traced around one of the horses on her pajamas. "I thought my daddy would be able to find Frankie's daddy. And I wanted to see my daddy and he wouldn't come here."

Refusing to blame Greg's negligence for Pippa's bad decision, Kenzie asked, "Didn't I tell you why he couldn't come?"

"Yes, so I thought if I went to visit him it would be okay." Tears slid down her freckled cheeks. "But the ticket person said we had to pay a whole lot of money to take the bus and we had to have a grown-up with us. So we sneaked into where they put the luggage when the bus driver wasn't looking." Her face crumpled into a comical expression of disgust. "It was so gross! Then Frankie barfed."

Jonah whispered into Frankie's ear. Frankie nodded and shot his friend a contrite look. "I'm sorry I made you sick, Pippa."

"It was my fault for making you go in there," Pippa admitted.

"What about leaving the yard without permission?" Jonah asked sternly. "Walking all the way to the village without saying anything to either of us?" It was clear to Kenzie that he didn't feel angry anymore and the last thing he wanted to do was scold the boy. But they both knew they needed to make sure it never happened again.

"It was naughty," Frankie whispered.

"It was very naughty."

Jonah's loving expression belied the tone of his deep, stern voice. Kenzie's heart twisted in her chest at the sight, so she turned away to look at Pippa. "And you're a whole year older than Frankie, so even if he went along with you, even if he said he wanted to go, were you right to do this?"

Pippa furrowed her eyebrows and stuck her chin out. "No. I was wrong. But I thought maybe my daddy could find Frankie's daddy since they both live in Boston. And I wanted to see my daddy and I didn't want to go alone."

Kenzie forced her eyes not to stray back toward Jonah as her heart ached at Pippa's words. *Baby girl, your daddy's right here.*

Oblivious, Jonah gently turned his son's head to look at him. "Frankie, I know I haven't been doing the best job since Mommy Elena died, but I promise I'll try as hard as I can from now on. And you tell me if something is wrong or you feel unhappy. Okay?"

"Okay, Daddy."

The little boy snuggled against Jonah, closing his eyes tightly.

Jonah caught his breath as if overwhelmed with the sweetness of the moment. He looked over at Kenzie, who could no longer hold back her tears.

"He told me he thought you were going to send him to an orphanage," Pippa whispered. "He said you don't want to 'dopt him anymore."

"I think he knows that's not true now, sweetie," Kenzie murmured.

Pippa nodded and suddenly burst out crying. "I'm sorry, Mommy. I promise I won't do it ever again."

"You'd better not, or I'll lock you in Rapunzel's tower." Kenzie took the girl's face in her hands and covered it with kisses until she giggled helplessly. "Now it's time for bed. Go across the hall and climb into bed, princess. I'll be there in a few minutes."

Pippa kissed her mother, then went shyly over to Jonah and kissed his cheek. "Night, Mr. Raymond."

A shock went through Kenzie. Her daughter was kissing her real father good-night, and she had no idea.

Clearly taken off guard by the kiss, Jonah took a moment to respond. "Night, Pippa."

Pippa leaned over and kissed Frankie. "Night, Frankie. I'm sorry I made you sick and got you in trouble."

"It's okay, Pippa," Frankie said sleepily. "I'm sorry I threw up on you."

Pippa hesitated a moment longer, then said in a rush, "I love you. I wish you were my little brother." Then she hurried off before anyone had a chance to respond.

Frankie slid off his father's lap. "I'm sleepy. I'm going to bed." As if following Pippa's ex-

ample, he gave Jonah a kiss. "Night, Daddy."
Then he cast a shy look at Kenzie.

Swallowing to open her emotion-choked
throat, she smiled at him. "Don't I get a kiss,
too?"

The little boy flew over to her, wrapped
his arms around her neck and kissed her face.
"Night, Mrs. Reid." Embarrassed, he ran to his
bedroom and closed the door.

As soon as the kids were gone from the room,
a rush of exhaustion almost flattened Kenzie.
She tried to hide the effort it took to push herself to her feet. "I'd better go tuck Pippa in."

Jonah walked her to the door, where they
both stopped and glanced at each other. Then
their eyes locked and they each took a step
closer.

Jonah echoed her words to Frankie. "Don't
I get a kiss, too?"

A parade of conflicting emotions marched
through Kenzie's insides before she gave in.
Carefully she got up on her toes and offered
Jonah her lips.

The kiss was brief, but so tender and full of
affection that they clung to each other afterward.

Although she wanted to stay in his arms forever, Kenzie finally forced herself to let go of him. "I'd better get home."

Gazing down at her with heart-stopping affection, he pushed a stray curl from her cheek. "You get some rest. You must be exhausted from all the stress."

"So must you," Kenzie whispered. "Thank you for being with me and keeping me sane." Remembering how much she'd actually lost it while the children were missing, she made a wry face. "Well, mostly."

"You're welcome. You did the same for me, whether you realize it or not." Jonah leaned down and gave her another quick kiss, this time on the cheek. "Get some rest. I'll see you tomorrow."

CHAPTER SIXTEEN

EMOTIONALLY, KENZIE FELT as if she could fly across the foyer to her apartment. Physically, she could barely drag herself the few yards to her door, every step shooting darts of pain up her legs.

Standing inside the doorway, holding herself up by gripping the frame, she prayed for strength. *Dear Lord, please help me keep fighting so I can be a good mother to my child. Nothing in the world matters as much as she does.*

As that thought crossed her mind, reality seemed to strike her across the face.

Today, as a mother she had failed. Miserably. Her little girl had run away from home in search of the man she believed was her father. Worse, Pippa had basically kidnapped a little boy and endangered both him and herself. Worst of all, both children had disappeared while Kenzie was supposed to be watching them.

It struck her like a lightning bolt: If Pippa was the most important thing in Kenzie's world, wouldn't she be better off with people who could take better care of her?

When she thought about it, she had to admit that everything had happened because something was wrong with her. Whether it was a physical illness or a mental condition, something made her an unfit mother. She was beyond fatigued all the time now. She was in constant pain. She had bouts of vertigo that made driving dangerous. To deal with the symptoms, she was on medications that knocked her out.

None of the doctors she'd seen since then could explain how she'd gone from fiercely energetic and athletic to all but crippled with pain and exhaustion. Despite what they told her, she was sure the Lyme tests were wrong.

But no matter what, no matter who was right and who was wrong, it wasn't getting any better. If anything, it was getting worse. And today proved beyond a shadow of a doubt that she was not up to the task of raising a seven-year-old on her own.

Greg had been a decent, if distant, father. And Camilla was a sweet person. Kenzie had no doubt she'd be an amazing mother to the baby she was now carrying. But trying to foist a strong-willed seven-year-old on a new mother would probably not go over very well. Not to mention that Pippa claimed to dislike her stepmother.

All the joy she'd felt from kissing Jonah whooshed out of her, replaced by despair.

Jonah. He was Pippa's real father, but thanks to Elena's interference, he had no idea.

Kenzie had nearly told him this afternoon, but the timing hadn't been right with all the drama around the kids running away. Should she march—well, stagger—over there right now and finish telling him? Would he take Pippa in as part of his family?

It was an awful lot to ask of the single father to a toddler and a troubled little boy, but at least his sister and brother-in-law were right upstairs. They adored Pippa, and she adored them right back.

As she mulled over these sad thoughts, Kenzie limped to the big comfy couch and collapsed. She'd never felt so completely drained in her life. The pain she'd ignored while the children were missing had gone screeching past the bearable mark. Any kind of stress kicked off all kinds of physical symptoms, which was one reason the doctors had decided her issues were psychosomatic. And today had been nothing if not out-of-control stressful.

Ugh, her brain was fried from all the anxiety. Her eyes did not want to stay open and she could feel a migraine starting up at the base of her skull. There was something she needed to do before she headed to the bedroom. She knew she had to do it quickly, before the headache made looking at a screen impossible.

Dragging her phone from the coffee table, Kenzie typed out a hasty text to Greg.

Please come visit as soon as you can. Pippa ran away with the little boy next door and sneaked on a bus to Boston because she wanted to see you. We need to talk. Hope Camilla is well. xo K

Once she'd sent the text, she dragged herself to the bedroom, put on her pajamas and fell into bed, praying that sleep would come quickly for a change.

She lay completely still, too enervated to move a muscle as the migraine roared to full power. She kept staring at the inside of her eyelids as time ticked by, obsessing about the idea of having Pippa live with someone else. The brain fog didn't allow coherent thoughts. All she could do was go around in circles trying to figure out who would be willing to look after her child.

The migraine pills were right there in her nightstand, along with pills for sleeping, which she should take right now, and pills for pain, which she'd staunchly refused to even try.

Kenzie had no idea how much time had passed when she managed to force her eyelids open, gasping at the overwhelming pain coursing through her body. If she'd thought yesterday was as bad as it was going to get, she was wrong. Very, very wrong.

The breath she took to quell a groan sent spasms through her rib cage and made the migraine throb even harder. The pain was so intense it felt as if someone had whacked her in the back of the head with a sledgehammer. A wave of nausea forced her to haul herself upright, which shot burning arrows throughout her body.

Desperate, she told herself she could handle it. All she had to do was wait for the worst of it to pass.

But the pain didn't die down. If anything, it kept growing, until it was so huge it took up all of Kenzie's mental space. She closed her eyes and made herself focus on the one thing she knew was bigger than her pain.

Lord, please help me bear this. I know You're here with me and You can give me the strength to overcome anything. Please, please, please help me!

Finally she managed to grope for the nightstand and open the drawer where she kept her meds. Turning on the light wasn't an option, so she felt around the drawer blindly. Once she found the migraine vial, it took every bit of determination she had to unscrew the childproof cap, especially in the pitch dark, but she finally managed it.

After dry-swallowing one, she waited for relief.

And waited.

The headache gradually lessened but the body pain did not. It was far too much to allow her to sleep. After waiting as long as she could bear, she groped in the drawer again, this time for the sleeping pills. She wrestled the cap off in the dark and took one. It probably wasn't a great idea to take both pills so close together, but it was hours before Pippa would be up. She'd be fine by then.

Eventually she was drowsy enough to try to snatch bits of sleep.

Stabbing agony in her eye jarred her awake. The migraine was back full force. She reached for another pill. Gradually she relaxed as it made its way into her bloodstream.

With a sigh of gratitude, Kenzie finally drifted into a deep, dreamless sleep.

AROUND NINE THE next morning, while he was cleaning up after breakfast, Jonah heard someone rapping persistently on the door. Puzzled, he listened harder. Diane and Paul wouldn't knock like that. Kenzie? Hoping it was her, he opened the door to find little Pippa looking up at him.

"Well, hi there!" he greeted her.

"Good morning, Mr. Raymond." She tried to peer past him, no doubt looking for Frankie.

"He's getting dressed, but he'll be out in a minute. Come on in."

Pippa followed him into the kitchen and looked longingly at a box of cereal he hadn't put away yet. "Can I have some?"

"Of course." He grabbed a clean bowl and filled it with Cheerios and milk. "Haven't you had your breakfast?"

Shoveling cereal into her mouth as if she'd

been on the brink of starvation, Pippa shook her head.

"How's your mom doing?"

"She's still sleeping," Pippa explained. "I think I made her really tired."

Jonah chuckled at Pippa's insight but tried to look stern. "I think you probably did. I hope you behave yourself today."

"I will," Pippa promised. "We can't even go outside 'cause it's yucky out. But we can play with my horse farm."

"Why don't you stay over here and watch a movie?" he suggested. "Give your mom a break."

Pippa's eyes looked up at him pleadingly. "But Frankie likes to play with my horse farm, and it's all set up in my room. We'll be extra super quiet."

"Okay, but you'd better check with your mom before you do anything," Jonah advised. "Make sure she's okay with what you're doing."

"But she's sleeping!" Pippa objected.

"Just wake her up enough to tell her what you're up to," Jonah insisted. "She'll want to know, believe me, especially after yesterday."

Pippa sighed. "Okay, Mr. Raymond."

Frankie appeared, wearing an enormous football jersey that came down to his feet. "I'm ready! I got dressed all by myself!"

"Hey, isn't that my shirt?" Jonah asked.

"Yeah, but can I borrow it? It's cool!"

"You got a shirt on under there, in case you get too warm?" Jonah smiled as the boy lifted the jersey bottom to show jeans and a shirt underneath. "Good boy. Go ahead and play with Pippa, but keep the noise level way down, okay?"

Jonah kept smiling after the two kids were gone, as he set Jolie down in her playpen. He couldn't seem to stop smiling because he couldn't stop thinking about last night's kiss with Kenzie.

A short, sharp yelp interrupted his reverie. Jonah froze in the middle of wiping down Jolie's high chair tray, wondering where it had come from. Maybe a hawk outside? He listened intently for the sound to repeat, but it didn't.

Then a low, mournful keening started up. A child in distress.

His child.

Grabbing Jolie from her playpen, Jonah sprinted out to the foyer. The wailing grew louder, and it was definitely coming from across the hall.

"Frankie!"

Jonah barged through Kenzie's front door with Jolie tucked under his arm like a football. The kids weren't in the main part of the apartment. The distressed wail was coming from the back of the house, where the bedrooms were. He ran through the open door of the closest room to find both kids standing next to the bed, where Kenzie appeared to be fast asleep.

Frankie stood stock-still, gazing at the sleeping woman, the eerie sound issuing from his mouth.

Jonah knelt and put his free arm around his son. "It's okay, buddy. She's just sleeping."

Pippa turned to him with huge, terrified eyes. "No, Mr. Raymond! I can't wake her up!"

Trying not to show his worry at the situation, Jonah set Jolie on the floor and walked to the bed where Kenzie lay, apparently unconscious. He breathed a sigh of relief when he felt her warm skin and heard her breathing.

"Kenzie?" He shook her gently at first, then a little harder. "Kenzie, wake up!"

"Mommy!" Pippa sobbed. "Mommy, please wake up!"

"Kenzie, it's Jonah. Can you hear me?"

No response at all. Frantic but trying to remain outwardly calm for the children's sake, he glanced around the room for an answer. His gaze landed on the nightstand, its drawer open and showing three vials of prescription medication. He picked them up and scanned the labels. He knew Kenzie took pills for her migraines and sometimes for insomnia, but the third vial stopped his heart.

An opioid for pain. The same medication Frankie's mother had overdosed on. The same medication that Elena had used after her difficult birth, that the medical examiner had found in her bloodstream after her fatal accident.

Not Kenzie. Not her, too. *Please, God, no!*

Forcing himself to act, he pulled out his phone and hit 911, giving terse responses to the operator's questions. Then he texted his sister and her doctor husband to come downstairs ASAP.

"Mommy?" Pippa's voice quavered behind him.

Jonah turned to look at the frightened children, then held his arms out to them. They both ran to him, burying their faces in his shoulder. When he found his voice again, it came out surprisingly calm. "She'll be okay."

Jonah couldn't keep up with his own racing thoughts. How could Kenzie have been so careless? How much medication had she taken?

The sound of heavy footsteps on the hallway stairs meant that Diane and Paul had gotten his text. Diane took one look at the scene and gathered all three children, shepherding them into the next room.

Paul rushed to the bed and checked Kenzie. "Her heart rate and breathing are a bit slow. You called 911?"

Jonah nodded, then wordlessly indicated the pill bottles on the nightstand.

Paul examined the labels. "Migraine meds, insomnia meds…and an opioid?" Worried, he opened the last vial and peered into it. "It doesn't look like she's taken very many at all, so I'm sure it's not an overdose."

Jonah released a breath he hadn't realized he was holding. "Then what happened?"

At that moment the ambulance pulled into the drive and two uniformed EMTs burst into the house. Paul and Jonah moved away to let them check on Kenzie, Jonah pacing anxiously as he stared at the bed.

This couldn't be happening. It couldn't. Paul said she hadn't overdosed based on the number of pills in the bottle, but what if she had another bottle somewhere? And how long had she been taking opioids, anyway? Didn't she know how dangerous they were?

And Frankie. No matter what had happened, Frankie could not deal with the death of another person he loved. Jonah would not let that happen ever again, no matter how he felt about Kenzie.

He realized his thoughts and emotions were spiraling out of control, but he couldn't seem to reel them back. Fury, heartbreak, confusion all warred for dominance.

Striding into the living room, Jonah grabbed Frankie in his arms and held him close. "It's okay, Frankie. She's going to be okay." The boy was shaking so hard he could barely stand. His breath came in quick, gulping gasps. "Hush, son. Take a big, slow breath. It's okay."

Frankie wrapped his arms around Jonah's neck in a stranglehold. "Mommy," he sobbed.

Jonah didn't think his heart could break any more, but Frankie's anguished voice proved him wrong. "I know, son," he whispered. "I know. It'll be all right. I promise."

To himself he added, *I'll make sure of it.*

CHAPTER SEVENTEEN

As SHE WAS gradually jarred to consciousness by a strange bumping sensation, Kenzie dragged open her leaden eyelids. She vaguely registered that she was strapped to some kind of platform inside what appeared to be a van packed with technical-looking equipment.

She couldn't move enough to look around and see if anyone was with her. When she tried to talk, she realized there was something covering her mouth and nose.

So she screamed.

"Well, I guess she's awake now," a dry female voice quipped.

"Hey, hey, Kenzie, it's okay." The male voice was familiar, soothing.

Had someone she knew abducted her? Why on earth would anyone do that?

A big hand appeared in front of her eyes and removed the thing that was covering her mouth. "You're in an ambulance on the way to the ER," the familiar voice said. "We found you unconscious in your bed, so we need to check you out."

This surprising information made Kenzie choke. The ensuing panic had her struggling for breath until the big hand slipped the mask back onto her face. "Breathe."

"Pippa?" she gasped.

Paul's big, bearded face came into view with a reassuring smile. "She's fine. Diane's taking care of her. And I just texted to let them know you're awake now, so she won't be worrying." His trademark, beaming smile expanded. "I decided to come along for the ride. Being a doctor has its privileges."

Kenzie craned her neck to look around. She spotted an EMT sitting on the other side of her gurney. "What happened?"

The ambulance came to a stop. "We'll fill you in soon," Paul promised. "Right now we've got to get you inside and settled. Then we'll order you a whole bunch of fun tests and try to figure out what's going on." He rose as the ambulance doors whooshed open and the EMTs deftly whisked her into the hospital.

As soon as she was settled in the ER and

hooked up to an IV with something to get rid of her headache and nausea, Paul stood next to her bed and checked her vitals. "How many did you take?"

"How many what?" Kenzie couldn't imagine what he was referring to. Her memories of the preceding night were foggy at best and intertwined with disturbing dreams so vivid they seemed real. She needed time to sort through the mess in her head.

Paul gave her a sympathetic look. "There were several prescription drug bottles in your nightstand. One for migraine medication, one for insomnia and one for painkillers. We need to know how many you took from each vial."

Kenzie thought it over and shook her head, which felt as if it were stuffed with feathers. "I remember I took one migraine pill, then a sleeping pill." Her frown deepened as she strained to remember. "I think I took another migraine pill later on. Or maybe it was a sleeping pill. But I've never taken any of the painkillers."

Paul looked relieved. "That's good. I know Jonah will be glad to hear that."

The fog had cleared enough for Kenzie to realize the mistake she must have made. "I'm very sensitive to medication. I should never have taken a second sleeping pill, especially on top of migraine medication."

His face grew concerned. "Why do you keep them next to your bed, rather than in the medicine cabinet?"

"Because of Pippa. She can be very curious, not to say nosy." Kenzie's feeling of dismay increased as she thought about what Paul had said. "She found me? My poor girl!"

Paul's forehead creased. "So you usually just take one sleeping pill?"

"Not very often, but lately…" Sensing his concern, Kenzie blinked back tears. "I was so exhausted last night I could hardly think straight, but I couldn't get to sleep because of that terrible migraine. I honestly thought the meds would wear off well before Pippa got up."

Jotting notes on a yellow legal pad, Paul nodded solemnly. "So you think you took two migraine pills and one sleeping pill?"

Kenzie nodded. "Pretty sure."

"Anything else?"

"I… I don't think so." Her voice came out small. "My brain is so foggy." Suddenly her eyes flooded with tears. "I can't believe I did that. I must have been way out of it."

"Given the day you had yesterday, it's not surprising." Paul blinked down at his notes, then looked back at Kenzie. "I noticed that all the meds, including the painkillers, were prescribed by Dr. Alden not that long ago. What did he prescribe the opioids for?"

"Because I'm in so much pain all the time!" The admission burst out of her. "It's been going on for over two years now, and no one can tell me what's wrong! All they can say is migraines and fibromyalgia, but not one single doctor can tell me why they came on so suddenly, out of nowhere, and won't go away. They just call me a hypochondriac and tell me to see a psychiatrist."

"Wait—did you say over two years?" Paul's eyes widened with surprise.

Wiping her eyes fiercely, Kenzie nodded. "Dr. Alden thought the pills might help me cope with the pain, but when I looked them up online after I got them, I realized what they are and decided to put them aside. Like I said, I'm hypersensitive to even over-the-counter stuff." She couldn't suppress an ironic smile as she remembered her former, healthy self. "A single aspirin used to knock me out for hours."

Paul raised his shaggy eyebrows. "Wow."

"I can only take half of one of the migraine meds at a time. Otherwise I'm out of it for too long, and I can't do that with Pippa to look after. But I took a whole one last night."

"And the insomnia?"

Kenzie nodded and shrugged. "I only take that when I know I'm not going to get to sleep. Like last night. But I've never taken two of either drug in one night."

Paul sat down in a chair next to the bed and leaned in to listen. "You said this all came on suddenly a couple of years ago."

"It was like someone had just flipped a switch on my health." Even though she hadn't wanted to see a doctor she knew personally, it was a relief to Kenzie to talk to someone who knew her about what she'd been battling. "It was a few weeks after we moved back to Boston." Given how the Boston doctors had reacted when she told them about the bug bite and rash, she hesitated to say anything to Paul. Would he just call her crazy, too?

Briefly taking his eyes from her face, Paul jotted another note onto his pad. "How'd it start? Do you remember the first signs or symptoms?"

"Vividly!" She felt more awake now, as the

fog slowly lifted from her brain. "I hardly ever used to get sick, aside from the occasional cold. But one day I woke up with a high fever and terrible headache. I felt sore all over. It was like the flu, except it didn't go away."

Nodding, Paul made another quick note. "Any other symptoms? Swollen glands, maybe?"

Kenzie frowned. "The doctor said I had swollen lymph nodes. Plus, I was so tired I literally couldn't stay awake. They tested me for all kinds of stuff, like MS, lupus, rheumatoid arthritis. Everything came back negative, so they decided I'm a hypochondriac."

Biting his upper lip so his thick mustache flared out, Paul drummed the eraser end of his pencil against the notepad. "Did you ever notice a bug bite or a rash?"

Hope fizzed through Kenzie's veins. Maybe Paul would believe her. "Yes! We spent a week on Martha's Vineyard before going to Boston. I thought I had a spider bite."

"What about Lyme disease? Did they ever test you for that?"

Kenzie was nearly breathless with hope. "A few times, but the test always came back negative."

"False negatives are unfortunately pretty

common with Lyme. The routine tests are notoriously unreliable." Paul studied her thoughtfully. "Martha's Vineyard is a Lyme hot spot. One of the worst in the country. What time of year were you there?"

"We'd rented a cottage for the month of July." Her hope grew. "I set my chair near a patch of long grass while Pippa played on the beach."

Paul huffed out a triumphant breath. "We'll get you tested properly as soon as possible. I'll order a Lyme panel and a PET scan to look at your brain."

"My brain?" Kenzie felt a jolt of dismay. "Something might be wrong with my brain?"

Paul made soothing motions with his hands. "If it's been this long you may have some inflammation, but treatment will help. That would explain the worsening migraine attacks. It'll take a while to get all the results, but my gut says we should start antibiotic treatment right away."

"Should I stop taking any of the meds Dr. Alden prescribed?" Kenzie felt anxious at the idea of giving up her migraine medication since she was still getting those headaches so often. She was relieved when Paul shook his head.

"No, those are fine for treating the symptoms, for now. Just pace yourself better, maybe put them somewhere other than right beside your bed so you have to get up if you need them. It'll make you more aware of how much you're taking." He sprang up from the chair and gave Kenzie a cheerful nod. "The antibiotics should get you back to your old self, but it may take time."

As Paul bounced out the door, Kenzie felt her heart flood with optimism.

Maybe she finally had a diagnosis, which meant she could get the treatment she needed.

Maybe all the pain and exhaustion would be history soon, and she'd be a better mother to Pippa.

And maybe, in spite of the misgivings she'd let in last night, she and Jonah really had a second chance.

FROM THE QUIET of his apartment, with Frankie napping and Jolie upstairs with her aunt, Jonah heard the slamming of car doors when Paul and Kenzie came home from the ER later that day. He heard Pippa's joyful squeak as she thundered down the stairs from Diane's place and ran outside to throw herself at her mother. And when the front door opened, he could hear Kenzie's loving reassurances that she was fine, that the doctors were going to make her all better.

He knew she was lying to reassure Pippa. Whatever was wrong with her, whatever had been so awful that a doctor had given her a potentially dangerous medication to deal with it, could not have been cured by a few hours in the ER.

There was a sharp knock on his door. Praying it wasn't Kenzie, he rushed to open it and put a finger to his lips when he saw his boisterous brother-in-law standing there.

"Frankie's just fallen asleep," Jonah whispered.

"Oops!" Paul clapped a hand over his mouth as he entered. "Sorry about that."

"Jolie's upstairs with Diane. She wanted to give me and Frankie some quiet time together so I could get him calmed down." Jonah indicated the sofa and sagged back onto his recliner. "He'd been having a pretty rough time, but I finally convinced him to lie down, and he fell asleep right away."

Paul was nodding his big head solemnly. "Seeing Kenzie like that had to be a shock, for both of you."

Jonah blew out a tense breath. "That's an understatement."

There was an awkward silence before Paul asked, "Do you want to know how she is?"

"She sounded fine when she came in just now." Jonah's tone was pure ice. When he wasn't soothing a distraught Frankie, he'd spent the last few hours teaching himself to distrust Mackenzie Reid again. The first time she'd broken his heart he'd pined himself sick. Not this time. He couldn't forgive her for making another rash choice, especially given how it affected his son.

"Dude." Paul sounded shocked at Jonah's attitude. "Seriously, she didn't do anything wrong. She made an honest mistake."

But Jonah was already shaking his head before Paul finished speaking. "I'm not putting Frankie through that again. If we have to move out of here, we will, but I don't want him around her anymore."

Scooting to the edge of the sofa, Paul reached a hand to Jonah's arm. "Okay. I get that you're in protective mode. And it makes absolute sense, on the surface."

"The surface is all a traumatized six-year-old can see," Jonah snapped. He closed his eyes and prayed for calm, then opened them to see Paul's worried face. "Sorry, bud. I'm kinda torn up from being with Frankie the past few hours. You have no idea. He was basically catatonic when I got him out of there."

"But—"

"But nothing. My mind is made up." Jonah furrowed his brow to hide the threat of tears. "We can't deal with another death caused by drugs."

"She's not—"

"No, Paul." Jonah's voice was husky with emotion. "No matter what the reason is for Kenzie to have those pills, I absolutely can't take that risk. I need to put Frankie first. It's what Elena would have wanted if she'd been in her right mind."

After a moment, Paul stood and gave Jonah's shoulder a squeeze. "I think you're being unfair to Kenzie and to yourself, but I get where it's coming from. You're doing it out of love for your boy, and there's no better reason in the world. But trust me when I say you're leaping to conclusions. We can talk about it later, when you're less fried. Now maybe you should get some rest yourself."

Paul tiptoed to the door and closed it quietly behind him, leaving Jonah alone with his thoughts once again.

Was he being unfair? Had Kenzie just made a mistake?

Did it matter? She was taking the same kind of drug that had killed Frankie's birth mother and was responsible for his foster mother's fatal accident.

Another knock on the door interrupted his growing head of steam. This one was quiet and polite. Probably his sister, worried after Paul reported back to her, eager to tell him he'd gotten it all wrong and shouldn't judge Kenzie so harshly.

With a grunt Jonah pushed himself out of the recliner and strode to the door, ready to tell Diane to mind her own business.

But when he flung open the door, it wasn't Diane standing on the threshold with a big happy smile.

It was Kenzie.

CHAPTER EIGHTEEN

WHEN KENZIE MOVED forward to enter Jonah's apartment, he took a step back and started to close the door, as if to keep her out. Baffled, Kenzie held on to the door and looked Jonah in the eyes. "What's going on?" she demanded.

His face was a thundercloud as he tried to wrestle the door closed. When Kenzie stuck her foot in the crack, Jonah flung the door open, nudged her out into the foyer and stepped outside, closing the door behind him.

"Frankie's asleep," he informed her in a fierce whisper.

She stared up at him, desperately trying to figure out what had changed since last night. Had she done something she didn't remember while she thought she'd been sleeping? Or was this just Jonah's way, turning his back on her after an emotional encounter?

Whatever it was, Kenzie wasn't having it.

"Excuse me," she stage-whispered back. "I thought maybe you'd want to know how I'm doing."

"I know how you're doing." Icicles hung from Jonah's words. "You're fine."

Stung, furious, Kenzie fought down the tide of hurt that surged in her throat. "Would you at least mind telling me what happened? Why are you suddenly so mad at me?"

He snorted. "Do I really have to tell you?"

"Yes, you do!" She could hardly believe this was the same man who'd been so tender to her last night. "I honestly have no idea what I did. I think you owe me an explanation, at least."

"You think I owe you an explanation, do you?" Jonah's outrage was palpable. "You think I owe you an explanation after my kid finds you unconscious next to a nightstand full of pills?"

His words were a punch in the stomach. Her hand flew up to her mouth as she realized how that must have looked. She moved her eyes back to Jonah's furious face but she couldn't get any words to come out.

"You never told me you were taking anything like that," he went on. "Do you know what happened to my family last year?"

"It's not what you think." Kenzie's voice was tremulous, breathy. "Jonah. I'm so—"

Jonah cut her off. "Don't bother apologizing. I don't want to hear it. I'm done." He took a sharp breath and added in a strangled voice, "And I don't ever want Frankie to see you or Pippa again."

"Why?"

The child's forlorn cry came from behind Kenzie. She turned to see her distressed little girl staring at her and Jonah, bewildered by his angry ultimatum.

At the same time, Frankie opened the door behind Jonah and glared up at his father. "Why are you being mean to my Pippa, Daddy?"

Kenzie pulled herself together for Pippa's sake, summoning righteous indignation to cover her hurt. "Yes, Mr. Raymond, why don't you explain to the children why they can't play together anymore?"

She watched Jonah tamp down his fury with a deep breath, staring at the floor as he fished for an excuse the children would understand. Finally he glanced at Pippa and spoke somewhat sheepishly. "You talked Frankie into running away."

Frankie tugged at Jonah's arm. "No, Daddy, she didn't. We decided to do it together."

"Well…" Pippa looked ashamed but spoke right up. "Frankie, I think I said it first." She glared up at Jonah. "It was a dumb thing to do, but I already said sorry like a million times."

Frankie pushed past his father and took Pippa's hand. "I love Pippa. She's like my big sister. I want to stay friends with her forever. Please, Daddy?"

Kenzie's heart melted at the sight of their innocent affection, but she knew it was up to Jonah. He still had no idea that he was Pippa's father, and under the current circumstances it seemed best to keep him in the dark.

She wiped her eyes and looked at him, fighting to keep her voice neutral and calm. "We'll abide by your decision, Mr. Raymond. It's your call."

The two children gazed up at him with big, pleading eyes. Kenzie had no idea how he could look at them and not relent on the spot. He was staring at the floor again, hiding his expression, and the silence grew unbearably long.

The sound of car tires in the driveway broke the moment. As far as Kenzie knew, everyone who lived in the house was home. Puzzled, she looked toward the front door as it opened and a very familiar man stepped inside.

She heard Pippa gasp. "Daddy!" she shrieked, flinging herself at the intruder.

"Hello, Philippa." Greg Halloran's voice was calm and cool, as if he were greeting a business acquaintance. Kenzie was instantly reminded of his standoffish attitude toward the little girl, despite her unquestioning adoration.

After all, he was the only father she'd ever known.

Frankie was staring in wonder at the stranger. Jonah hissed, "Frankie, let's go inside," but the little boy was too fascinated by Pippa's father to hear him.

Greg turned to Kenzie and nodded. "How are you doing, Mackenzie?" He peered at her through his wire-framed glasses and frowned. "You're still looking a bit peaked. I thought country living might improve your health."

"It's been a weird day," Kenzie answered dryly. "And that's an understatement. I had no idea you were coming."

He gave her a slow, owlish blink. "I answered your text last night. Didn't you see it?"

"Ah, well." Kenzie attempted to laugh.

"I was separated from my phone for a while this morning."

Pippa tugged at Greg's sleeve to get his attention. "Mommy went away in an ambulance! She only just came home."

"An ambulance?" Greg's eyes snapped back to Kenzie. "What happened?"

"It's fine. I'm fine," she assured him. "Just the same old same old, but they might have finally figured out what's wrong with me."

"Well, that's good, I guess." He glanced back down at Pippa as she grabbed Frankie and dragged him over to Greg. "And who might this be?"

"This is my best friend in the whole wide world!" Pippa shot Jonah a triumphant look. "His name is Frankie."

"Is this the little boy you ran away with?" Greg asked. Frankie nodded, embarrassed. "I trust you won't be doing anything that foolish again."

"Of course not, Daddy. Mommy made me promise."

"Me too," Frankie chimed in.

"And that's Frankie's daddy, Mr. Raymond." Pippa pointed at Jonah. "He's being mean right now but he's usually nice."

Kenzie's heart stopped as Greg took a step toward Jonah, hand extended. Would Greg remember Jonah? He'd only met him briefly, a decade ago.

"Glad to meet you, Mr. Raymond." As he shook Jonah's hand, Greg peered at him curiously and Kenzie braced herself. "Wait—I know you. Mr. Raymond. Jonah Raymond?"

"Yes, we met briefly before—"

Greg smiled grimly. "About ten years ago, before you stole my girlfriend." He shot a mock-accusing glance toward Kenzie.

Jonah grimaced. "Well…"

With an affable nod, Greg looked back up at Jonah. "No worries. Water under the bridge. But I do have to ask…"

Greg turned his gaze to Kenzie, who was trying very hard not to sink into the floor. She knew beyond a shadow of a doubt what was coming next. "Greg, maybe not now, okay?" she pleaded.

He talked right over her, reminding Kenzie of far too many moments in their marriage. "Why didn't you tell me you were back with him?"

Through gritted teeth Kenzie managed to say, "I'm not."

"It most certainly looks like you are." Greg studied Jonah through his glasses, then looked back at Kenzie. "Which begs the question, do I need to keep paying child support? We're not exactly rolling in money since I'm paying you alimony and child support. Cami can't work anymore, and with our own baby coming, it's not fair for us to keep paying for your child."

Kenzie had been holding her breath throughout Greg's speech, until she'd gone lightheaded. She tried to flash a message using just her eyes, but Greg continued, oblivious to Kenzie's distress signals. He'd worked himself up into a state of indignation and she knew there was no stopping him. Nevertheless, she gripped the staircase railing to keep from falling over as Greg pointed at Jonah and dropped the bomb.

"What do you want with my money when you've got her real father right here?"

JONAH FELT AS if he'd been launched into an alternate reality. What was happening? Had Kenzie's ex-husband just accused him of being Pippa's father?

Through his dazed state, Jonah located Kenzie's stunned face. She was staring at him, gripping the banister as if it were a lifeline, her eyes wide with dismay.

Greg still stood in front of her, clearly not understanding the impact of what he'd said. His eyes darted from Kenzie to Jonah and back again. "What? Don't tell me he didn't know. You said you'd tried everything to reach him back then."

Baffled by all the adult weirdness, Pippa spread her arms out and raised her shoulders in an exaggerated shrug and exclaimed, "What's going on? What are you guys talking about?"

To Jonah's relief, Frankie looked completely lost. Neither child seemed to have grasped what Greg had said. Jonah could hardly grasp it himself.

He was Pippa's father?

To add to his confusion, Kenzie suddenly burst out laughing, although it sounded forced. Then she punched her ex's arm. "Greg, that's possibly the worst joke you ever made."

"Ow!" Greg grabbed hold of his arm where she'd hit him and rubbed it. "What? What joke? I didn't make a joke!" When Kenzie gave him an over-the-top version of her angry mom face, Greg took the hint and laughed unconvincingly. "Oh! Um, yeah, that was an incredibly silly thing to say." Jonah got the impression he still had no idea what he'd done.

Pippa gave Greg a playful slap on the leg. "Stop being silly, Daddy!" She grabbed his hand, and with a head-spinning change of subject, she added, "Come see where we live!"

"Oh!" Greg looked at Kenzie, who seemed dazed but nodded assent. "Um, show me the way, I guess."

"Can Frankie come, too?" Dropping Greg's hand, Pippa came over to Jonah and looked up, puzzled. "Why do you look so funny, Mr. Raymond? Are you still mad at me?"

Breathless, Jonah gazed down at the little girl as if he'd never seen her before. She was identical to Kenzie in every way. Except the eyes. Instead of intense blue like her mother's, they were a deep chocolate brown.

Like his.

Was she really his child? Only Kenzie could give him the answer, but he had the very strong sense that Greg's announcement had not been a joke.

"Mr. Raymond?" Pippa tugged at his hand. "Can Frankie please come? My daddy is with us, so he'll make sure we don't run away. And I promise we won't anyway. Please?"

Frankie took his other hand. "Please, Daddy? I promise I'll be good."

Jonah's baffled gaze moved to his son. Did he have a big sister? Even though they weren't related by blood, the two children had grown so close and loved each other as much as if they were siblings.

His throat too clogged with emotion to allow him to speak, Jonah simply nodded. Both children hugged his legs, then dragged a clearly reluctant Greg Halloran into Kenzie's apartment.

Which left him and Kenzie alone in the foyer.

They stood in silence for a moment, both studying the floor near their respective feet. Finally Kenzie let go of the banister and moved to him, chin raised and shoulders squared in the attitude he remembered so well.

"Guess we should talk."

Wordless, Jonah pushed open the door to his apartment and went straight to the kitchen table. After pulling out a chair for Kenzie, he sat next to her and waited. She seemed to be at a rare loss for words.

Finally Jonah broke the silence. He had to ask, even though he was pretty sure of the answer.

"Is it true?"

Shoulders still squared in defiance, Kenzie gave him a single, brief nod.

It was the answer he expected, but Jonah's heart leaped at her confirmation. "Is that what was in all the messages and letters I never saw?"

She cleared her throat. "At first I just said we needed to talk ASAP. When you didn't answer, I started saying it was urgent, I missed you and wanted to move back to Boston. Which was the truth." After a hard swallow, she went on. "The certified letter said I was pregnant with your child and needed to know if you wanted to be part of her life."

Jonah had stopped breathing as Kenzie spoke. He inhaled deeply as he realized how much damage Elena's protective interference had done. "And you thought I got the letter because it looked like I signed for it."

Kenzie nodded. "I'd told Greg all about it at work one day. I mean, he was my boss, so… I was freaking out, needless to say. He said if I didn't hear from you within the week, he'd marry me."

Jonah felt a dart of jealousy. "Were you seeing him?"

"Well, you know we were dating when I met you, but I thought he was too serious for me, so I broke it off." She blushed. "When I got to San Francisco and found he was a studio head, I realized why I'd gotten such a great job offer. He said he'd never gotten over me and he'd be the best husband and father if I said yes."

"Which you did, when you didn't hear from me." Jonah felt sickened by the thought of another man marrying Kenzie but forced himself to look at it from her perspective. "You did what you needed to do."

Kenzie shook her head. "I could have gone it alone. Lots of women do. But…well, Greg's a good guy and I thought we'd both be better off. So yes, I married him. And it was good for a few years, but after a while he told me he wanted a family of his own." She shrugged. "Then I got sick and lost every baby we conceived, and he got tired of me being sick all the time. So he moved on."

Jonah couldn't keep the bitterness out of his voice. "Nice."

"Honestly, I can't blame him. And he was completely up-front with me when he and Camilla got involved." Kenzie blinked as if warding off tears. "He's been a decent father to Pippa, if a bit lacking in affection." She leaned back in her chair and mumbled to the table, "Of course, she has no idea he's not really her father."

Another emotion jabbed at Jonah's heart. "She's mine," he whispered.

"Yup." A tear trickled down one freckled cheek as Kenzie tried to smile. "That sassy little troublemaker is fifty percent your doing."

Despite the ache in his chest, Jonah chuckled. "Frankie is going to be thrilled."

"But what about you?" Kenzie's anxious tone belied her defiant expression. "Neither of us is exactly your favorite person right now. Do you want her to know? If so, how do we tell her?"

Kenzie was asking all the right questions, but Jonah didn't feel like he had the answers. He was still reeling from Greg's revelation, so much that his head felt as if it were literally spinning. He didn't notice Kenzie had stood up until she leaned over to speak softly in his ear.

"I know it's a big shock," she whispered. "It's important that you take your time. Give it all the thought you need. When you know what you want, let me know."

"No." Jonah sat up straight, realizing the unfairness of his reaction. "No, that's absurd. Pippa is my daughter. She deserves to know the truth."

As he got to his feet, the front door burst open and Frankie came running in, clearly unhappy. "That mean man made my Pippa cry," he informed Kenzie, "and now he's going away."

CHAPTER NINETEEN

LAUNCHING INTO PROTECTIVE MODE, Kenzie shot out to the foyer and ran smack into Greg, who was pulling on his coat as he headed to the door.

"What did you say to her?" Kenzie demanded.

"I told her I wouldn't be visiting again." Greg seemed pretty calm for a man who'd just devastated a child.

Kenzie had to restrain herself from grabbing her ex and shaking him. "Why on earth would you tell her that?"

Not even deigning to glance at her, Greg buttoned his overcoat and took his car keys out of his pocket. "Because it's time for her to know the truth, Kenzie. I'm not her father." He nodded toward Jonah's apartment, behind her. "Why should we continue the charade when her real father is right there?"

Kenzie felt the color drain from her face.

"Did you tell her that? I thought you'd gotten the message earlier, when I pretended you were joking."

"No, I didn't tell her," Greg said in his most pompous voice. "I'll leave that to the two of you. After all, you've pretty much moved in together, as far as I can tell."

"No, we have not." Jonah's voice made Kenzie jump. She hadn't realized he'd followed her out into the foyer. "And I resent your implying anything like that."

Greg walked over and looked up at Jonah, who seemed to have grown even taller, towering over the spiteful little man. "And I resent you not taking responsibility for your child. It's about time you did, don't you think?"

"I would have been doing it all along if I'd gotten any of Kenzie's messages," Jonah responded in an even tone. "But trust me, I will from now on. If you're so callous that you can tell a seven-year-old who believes you're her father that you'll never see her again, it's best that you get out of her life and stay out."

Greg stiffened, clearly offended. "My sentiments exactly." Kenzie could see that Greg was trying to stay cool, but that Jonah's characterization had rattled him.

"And I certainly hope you're a better father to your new baby than you were to Pippa today."

Greg's lips disappeared. Without another word, he turned on his heel and strode through the front door. A moment later they heard his car crunch its way out of the drive and turn onto the road.

Kenzie looked up at Jonah. "I'd better go see to Pippa."

Jonah nodded. "Frankie's gone back over there with her. Should I come along?"

She had to think about it for a moment, then gave him a quick nod. "Maybe we should talk to her together, now. Maybe it would make her feel better."

Jonah's big, warm hand on her back comforted Kenzie as they entered her apartment, where Pippa sobbed disconsolately on the oversize sofa as Frankie petted her. The boy gave a worried glance at the grown-ups. "She won't stop crying."

Kenzie sat on Pippa's right, Jonah to the left of Frankie, bookending their children. "Baby girl," Kenzie whispered, "I'm so sorry he said that to you."

Pippa half crawled onto her mother's lap and rubbed at her eyes. "Why's he being so mean to me?" she whimpered. "He doesn't want to see me ever again because he's going to have a new baby."

Kenzie took a deep breath. "Pippa, we have something to tell you that might be hard for you to understand. You can ask all the questions you like, but we might not be able to explain everything very well."

Pippa sat up straight, her tear-streaked face solemn and fearful. "Did you find out you're really, really sick, Mommy?"

"What? No!" Kenzie hugged Pippa, horrified at the question. "I'm going to be fine, I promise. What we have to tell you is something good, but it might take you a while to think so."

The little girl's eyes grew enormous looking from Kenzie to Jonah and back. "Is what my daddy said true? I mean…" She paused as if puzzling over how to phrase the question. "Is Mr. Raymond my real daddy?"

Over the children's heads, Kenzie's eyes met Jonah's. So Pippa had caught on after all. Or maybe Greg had just gone ahead and told her, like the clueless person he was. "Yes, Pips. It's true."

They all watched as Pippa processed the idea.

Confusion chased happiness across her thoughtful little face.

"It's okay if you need time to think about it, sweetie," Kenzie murmured. "He only just found out, too."

"But, Pippa." Frankie tugged excitedly at her hand. "That means you're really my big sister!"

Pippa turned her startled brown eyes to Frankie. Joy slowly took over her face and she squealed and threw her arms around her little brother.

Once she'd calmed down, Pippa turned to Kenzie. "So, Mommy, are you going to marry Mr. Raymond?"

Kenzie found herself speechless for a moment, felt her cheeks turning pink. Finally she managed to choke out, "Um…well, no…that's not…" She couldn't look at Jonah.

"But aren't mommies and daddies supposed to be married?"

"Yes!" Frankie seconded. "They definitely have to get married."

Jonah cleared his throat. "Uh… son, remember our talk the other day? It takes time for grown-ups to make big decisions like that."

Frankie's dark eyebrows furrowed. "But—"

Jonah cut him off deftly. "No buts. And no more questions about that, please."

Pippa and Frankie exchanged a puzzled glance. When Pippa's mouth opened, Kenzie gave her the mom look that made her close her mouth immediately.

In a gentle tone, Kenzie said, "Whether we're married or not, he's still your father. And Frankie and Jolie are your little brother and sister."

That made Pippa leap from the sofa and bounce for joy. "Is Jolie still upstairs?" When Jonah nodded, she grabbed Frankie's hand. "Come on! Let's go see our little sister!" She stopped just short of the door and turned back. "What do I call Diane and Paul now?"

Jonah grinned. "Auntie Diane and Uncle Paul. And their baby will be your cousin!"

Pippa's mouth dropped open in amazement. Kenzie's heart warmed at the sight of her little girl's elation. She'd never had any extended family before, since Kenzie was an only child and both her parents had died years ago. Suddenly Pippa's relatives had more than doubled in number. She stood there stunned for a moment. Then she grabbed Frankie's hand and dragged him through the door so she could break the news to her new family.

ALL THREE HOLIDAY FARM families held an impromptu celebration for their newly discovered connections. Kenzie was surprised at how eagerly Pippa adjusted to her change of fathers, maybe because Greg hadn't been part of her life for a while already. He'd certainly never been as affectionate as Jonah, who came with a ready-made little brother and sister for Pippa to dote on.

As the children chatted happily with Paul and Diane in the spacious upstairs living room, Jonah subtly maneuvered Kenzie onto one of the settees.

"I'd call this an eventful day," he observed dryly.

Kenzie looked confused for a moment, then suddenly seemed to recall all that had happened. "Ya think?"

"How are you feeling?"

"Overwhelmed, but in a good way." She met his eyes. "They gave me something at the ER that got rid of the headache and body pain. I guess it's still working."

Her defiant look reminded Jonah of his earlier anger. "I might have overreacted."

Kenzie thought it over, shook her head. "No. I understand how scary that must have been for Frankie and you. But honestly, I never touched one of those pain pills. I thought about it a few times when the pain was horrible, but I always decided against it."

"Then why did you have them right next to your bed?" He couldn't keep the worry out of his voice.

"Because the pain kept getting worse. But the reason I didn't take them was that I know how sensitive I am to medication." Kenzie sighed, looking regretful. "Which is why taking a second pill last night made it extremely hard for me to wake up."

"Ah." Relief lightened Jonah's heart at her explanation.

"When I got home, I gave the vial of painkillers to Paul so he can dispose of them safely."

His heart lightened more. "I'm sorry I flew off the handle."

"I get it." Kenzie gave him a rueful smile. "I remember flying off the handle myself about eight years ago."

"Oh, that?" Jonah grimaced. "I have been

wondering. I mean, I was planning to propose after your graduation ceremony. I was stunned when you blew up at me."

Now Kenzie was staring at him in surprise. "You were going to propose?"

Feigning nonchalance, he lifted his shoulder. "That was my plan."

Kenzie flopped back on the settee, covering her face with her hands. "Unbelievable."

"What?"

"The reason I got myself so worked up and mad that I took that job and moved away is that you didn't propose after our camping trip." She removed her hands to reveal a blush staining her cheeks. "When you didn't—even after I told you about the job—I'm afraid I made a very foolish decision."

"So that's why you were so mad at me?" He chuckled. "And I had gone home specifically to get my grandmother's engagement ring. It was in my pocket when you dumped me."

"What?" Kenzie's expression was a mixture of surprise and regret. "Now I feel even worse!"

Jonah considered her words and remembered his own pointless regrets about Elena. "What happened, happened. Focusing on the past doesn't accomplish anything." He reached for her hand. "But I hope you're still feeling better. I guess last night was pretty bad."

She winced at the memory. "It was the worst."

"I can't believe you felt that ill and didn't ask for my help." Distraught, Jonah squeezed her hand. "I guess you don't trust me enough to do that."

She laced her fingers through his. "It's not that. I'm just so used to being independent, I hate to ask for help. I don't want anyone to know what a mess I am." Glancing down at their entwined hands, she whispered, "Especially you."

"I guess we both have a few things to sort out," Jonah murmured. "I'd love it if we can sort them out together."

Kenzie looked up at him, her eyes bright with hopeful tears. "I would love that, too, but I need some time to process everything."

Jonah sighed. "You're right, of course. I say let's have no regrets and look ahead instead of back."

A smile lit up her face. "Speaking of looking ahead, the harvest pageant is coming up and we still have a lot to do!"

CHAPTER TWENTY

A FEW DAYS before the harvest pageant, Kenzie learned she had been right all along. According to the tests and scans Paul had ordered, she had had Lyme disease for quite a while, long enough for the bacteria to wreak havoc.

By the time she got the results, she'd already been on antibiotics for almost a week, again thanks to Paul. It would take a while to see any significant improvement, but now that she knew what was wrong with her, Jonah noticed that she seemed much more optimistic and less stressed. She told him she was relieved to know what had been causing all those weird symptoms, but she admitted that she was even more relieved to know they weren't psychosomatic.

Since Kenzie was still feeling wobbly, she had leaned more and more on Jonah to get the harvest pageant on its feet. Jonah found himself grateful for the distraction. It forced him to focus on accomplishing tasks rather than thinking about the future. Working so closely with Kenzie and Pippa in the weeks before the pageant gave him time to observe and interact with them both. And he had to admit he liked what he saw. A lot.

The more he got to know Pippa, the prouder he was to be her father. When he'd apologized to her for his anger, she'd graciously accepted his apology and opened her heart to him as her real daddy.

They'd asked the kids to keep quiet about Mr. Raymond being Pippa's father, knowing it might raise questions they weren't prepared to answer. But even though they weren't officially siblings, Frankie and Pippa's bond kept growing stronger. Jonah was amazed how much his troubled boy blossomed in a short time. Habitual moodiness was replaced with frequent laughter and a silly streak Jonah had never seen before. It was clear Frankie already saw Kenzie as his mother and ran to her for cuddles and comfort almost as often as he ran to Jonah.

Jolie was still Jolie, and Jonah loved to see Kenzie scoop her up and cover her with kisses as if she were Kenzie's own baby. The hungry, lost look no longer appeared on her face when she held Jolie in her arms. Instead, she looked deeply content.

ON A GORGEOUS Sunday afternoon in late October, the Good Shepherd students clustered in the church vestibule to enter for the harvest pageant. All dressed up in their costumes and masks, they were more than ready to perform. The fourth and fifth graders looked adorable as the farmers and their families. The second and third graders wore angel costumes, and the first graders wore farm animal masks they'd created themselves.

Kenzie and Jonah beamed at the excited group. "Everyone take hands," Kenzie stage-whispered, knowing the pews were packed with excited parents and parishioners. The kids squirmed around to find hands to hold until they formed a ragged circle. "I'm going to say a quick prayer and I want you all to listen and pray along with me silently. Okay?"

When they all nodded, Kenzie cleared her throat and squeezed Jonah's hand.

"Dear Lord, please bless us as we perform our little pageant. Help us to keep You first in our hearts and give thanks for all Your blessings. Amen."

Most of the children mumbled "amen" after Kenzie finished, but one little voice shouted it out.

"A-men!"

When the other children giggled, Pippa shrugged her angel wings. "God made me loud," she said philosophically, "so I guess He wants me to shout."

"Okay, is everyone ready?" Farmer hats, tinsel halos and animal ears nodded. "Let's go! Farmers first."

The farmers walked solemnly up the aisle to the altar and recited their lines with innocent conviction. Then the white-robed angels filed in singing simple hymns of praise and encouraging the farmers.

Kenzie felt tears spring to her eyes as she listened to the childish voices singing. Her own little girl sang a bit more lustily than the others as she held the hands of the angels on either side of her. Kenzie felt Jonah's arm slip around her shoulders as he whispered, "That's our girl."

Finally the animals danced their way to the altar, evoking laughter and applause from the audience. Even shy Frankie sang out happily from behind his horse mask and gave a spontaneous whinny when he reached the altar.

As the lights came back on, Kenzie could hear happy chatter coming from the pews. Jonah put his arms around her and kissed the top of her head.

"I think God answered your prayer."

His arms stayed around her when she turned to look up at him. "I couldn't have done it without you."

Jonah's eyes crinkled as he smiled down at her. "Wow, whatever happened to Miss Independence?"

Feeling suddenly shy, Kenzie returned his smile. "I guess the teacher learned a few lessons herself."

He nodded, his face softening. "This one did as well."

For a moment they gazed into each other's eyes. Then Jonah bent down and she stood on her toes to meet his kiss halfway. While holding each other close Kenzie felt a deep, solid peace fill her heart and soul.

Her reverie was interrupted by someone tapping on her shoulder. She turned to see Enid staring at her, a look of displeasure stamped on her features. "Everyone wants you two to come take a bow, which you very much deserve. Then I think we need to have another talk."

Jonah grabbed Kenzie's hand and led her up the aisle to the altar, where the children burst into applause, then ran over to engulf their teachers with hugs. Parents and fellow teachers came up to the altar and mingled with them, thanking and congratulating everyone for their hard work. Many asked when the next pageant would be.

The school's first ever public performance was a big success.

Gradually the children and audience filtered out. Diane and Paul, who had watched the show with little Jolie, took Pippa and Frankie back to the farm, leaving Kenzie and Jonah alone with Enid Mullin.

"Let's sit down," the headmistress suggested, indicating the way to the front row of pews. She pulled the piano bench out so she could face the two teachers, her arms crossed. "I think you need to tell me what's going on here. Do you remember the talks we had not long ago, where each of you insisted that there was no way you'd get together again?"

Fighting down memories of being in trouble with her high school principal, Kenzie raised her head. "Jonah is Pippa's father."

Enid's large eyes grew even larger. She opened her mouth but no words came out.

"Jonah and Pippa only found out a little over a week ago." Kenzie's cheeks were burning, but she kept her gaze fixed on the headmistress. "And Frankie knows, but he and Pippa know not to tell the other kids for now."

"I see." Enid's voice was nearly a whisper. She unfolded her arms and coughed, her eyes switching back and forth between Kenzie and Jonah. "Well. Needless to say, I wasn't prepared for this, um, explanation." Her forehead furrowed and she tapped her foot, studying the burgundy carpet as she thought. Finally she looked up. "You're right to keep this quiet. I'm still getting over the shock of finding you two in an obviously nonplatonic embrace, but with this new information…" Enid sighed, shaking her head. "I can understand that there's a bond, and I hope it leads to happiness for both of you." She leaned toward Jonah and Kenzie, a humorous sparkle in her dark eyes. "And if there's a wedding, I hope you'll let my husband do the honors."

EPILOGUE

IN THE WEEKS that followed, Kenzie's health continued to improve in fits and starts. The good spells lasted longer and the bad spells became rarer as time passed. She was able to throw herself into preparation for the Christmas pageant, once again with Jonah's help.

This time the classes were divided into the people at the manger—the holy family, shepherds and wise men—angels and friendly beasts. They learned Christmas carols from other countries as well as the more popular ones for the audience sing-along.

The more time she and Jonah spent together, the more Kenzie found herself loving and trusting him. His generous heart and tenderness toward the children and herself felt like the best gift of all. Now that they'd forgiven each other for past misunderstandings, there was no longer a barrier between them. Kenzie had no doubt they would be together for a long time, and the knowledge made her wait patiently for the day it became official.

One Sunday a few days before Christmas, the Good Shepherd Church was packed not only with parents and teachers, but with people from the whole Chapelton community. After hearing everyone rave about the harvest pageant, they were eager to see the children's Christmas performance.

The audience's energy encouraged the children to put everything they had into the pageant. They recited their lines and sang their songs with unrestrained joy, and everyone rose and sang along with the more familiar carols.

The headmistress wiped more than one tear from her eyes as the pageant ended. She came over to the vestry where Jonah and Kenzie stood and gave them her biggest beaming smile. "You two go up there and take a bow. You deserve it." And Kenzie was pretty sure Enid winked at Jonah as she sent them down the aisle.

Holding hands, they bowed along with the children. Then to Kenzie's astonishment, Jonah got down on one knee and pulled a little velvet box from his pocket. The children around them and the audience in the pews gasped.

"I know what it is!" Frankie shouted as he ran to his father's side. "C'mon, Pippa!"

"Oh!" Pippa exclaimed, rushing to stand by her mother. "Mommy, you hafta say yes, okay? Please?"

The onlookers chuckled, then fell silent, seeming to hold their breath.

"Mackenzie Reid," Jonah said. "I should have asked you this eight years ago. I hope it's not too late."

Kenzie's eyes sparkled and her smile grew almost too big for her face. "It isn't."

Opening the box, Jonah held it up to her. "I'd like my family to marry your family. Will you marry us, Kenzie and Pippa?"

"Yes!" Pippa yelled at the top of her lungs.

Everyone burst out laughing, then stopped as Kenzie gazed lovingly at Jonah. "We will."

The sanctuary exploded with applause as Jonah rose to his feet, slipped the antique ring on Kenzie's finger and threw his arms around her.

"Are you happy?" Jonah whispered into Kenzie's ear.

"Are you kidding?" Kenzie pulled back to show him her glowing face. "I have the love of my life back, my little girl has her daddy, and we have the love of a beautiful family. I've never felt so happy in my entire life."

"Thank God," Jonah murmured, kissing her cheek.

"I do," Kenzie whispered. "With all my heart."

WESTERN

Rugged men looking for love...

Available Next Month

The Maverick Makes The Grade Stella Bagwell
The Heart Of A Rancher Trish Milburn

....

Nine Months To A Fortune Elizabeth Bevarly
Hill Country Hero Kit Hawthorne

....

LOVE INSPIRED

A Companion For His Son Lee Tobin McClain
Hidden Secrets Between Them Mindy Obenhaus

Available from Big W, Kmart and selected bookstores.
OR call 1300 659 500 (AU), 0800 265 546 (NZ) to order.

Visit **millsandboon.com.au**

BRAND NEW RELEASE

Don't miss the next instalment of the Powder River series by bestselling author B.J. Daniels! For lovers of sexy Western heroes, small-town settings and suspense with your romance.

RIVER JUSTICE

—R—

A POWDER RIVER NOVEL

PERFECT FOR FANS OF YELLOWSTONE!

Previous titles in the Powder River series

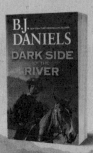

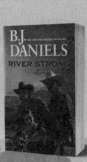

September 2023   January 2024   In-store and online August 2024

MILLS & BOON

millsandboon.com.au